D0173574

. . . and the killer
will push her to the brink.

"I didn't know the Richter girl was from Langley," **Kay said under her breath as they headed to the car.**

Finn remembered the morning the girl had been discovered, the two of them in Kay's bed, watching the early news on Channel 11. Lying next to him, Kay had made some comment about hoping there weren't others.

"Have you heard anything about the case lately?" Kay asked. Her gaze was hard when she met his over the roof of the Lumina, and a sharp breeze ruffled her hair as she watched a Beemer spin out of the high school's lot and onto Lawndale, its stereo cranked. Finn felt its bass vibrate in his feet.

"No," he said, "but I'm definitely interested in talking to Laubach. I hope to God this isn't related to his case."

"I hope not too. Otherwise we've got a goddamn serial killer on our hands."

BLUE VALOR

ILLONA HAUS

POCKET BOOKS
New York London Toronto Sydney

An *Original* Publication of POCKET BOOKS

 POCKET BOOKS, a division of Simon & Schuster, Inc.
1230 Avenue of the Americas, New York, NY 10020

This book is a work of fiction. Names, characters, places and incidents are products of the author's imagination or are used fictitiously. Any resemblance to actual events or locales or persons, living or dead, is entirely coincidental.

ISBN-13: 978-0-7434-5809-2
ISBN-10: 0-7434-5809-5

This Pocket Books paperback edition February 2006

10 9 8 7 6 5 4 3 2 1

POCKET and colophon are registered trademarks of Simon & Schuster, Inc.

Front cover design by Jae Song
Cover image © Baldomero Fernandez/Getty Images

Manufactured in the United States of America

For information regarding special discounts for bulk purchases, please contact Simon & Schuster Special Sales at 1-800-456-6798 or business@simonandschuster.com.

For Vickie Wash

Acknowledgments

My work cannot be done in a vacuum and in the course of researching and writing this book, I have relied on the expertise, wisdom, and experience of many. These are the major players to whom I am indebted:

Det. Sgt. (retired) Steve "Sparky" Lehmann,
BPD Homicide
Vickie L. Wash, Assistant State's Attorney (retired)
for Baltimore City
Mary G. Ripple, M.D., Deputy Chief Medical
Examiner, State of Maryland
Det. Robert F. Cherry, Jr., BPD Homicide
Det. Mike Hammel, BPD Homicide
Det. Sgt. Gary Childs, formerly BPD Homicide,
currently Baltimore County Homicide
Jon Goldey, CrimeScope, SPEX Forensics
Dr. George Berrigan, M.D.
Lianne Dingle, R.N.
Bob Cox, the ultimate Baltimore guide
Warren Smith of The Smith Family Lofts,
pigeon aficionado

Any mistakes are my own.

Also, much thanks goes to Chris Brett-Perring for his expertise and his brainstorming capabilities, and to my readers—Beatriz Briceno, Janet Dixon, Lucie Levasseur, and Jackie Gibbons—for their time and eye for detail.

And huge thanks to Annelise Robey of the Jane Rotrosen Agency for her infinite patience and constant encouragement.

In valor there is hope.
—Publius Cornelius Tacitus
(AD 55–117)

BLUE VALOR

1

Monday, April 17

"HE'S OUT HERE."

Kay Delaney eased the unmarked police car through the amber at Franklin. In the passenger seat, Bobby Curran balanced his double latte, saving his tailor-made suit as the Lumina's tires took a pothole.

"I tell you, Kay, no dealer's gonna be dogging the streets this early in the morning."

She ignored his comment. Kept scanning.

Two years as a deputized agent with the Redrum Unit—a special gang squad working with DEA—Bobby Curran knew a thing or two about the streets. But when it came to murders, Kay thought, the former Bostonian and the newest detective on her squad was a rookie.

"Trust me, he'll show," she said, turning onto Edmondson.

"Wasting a lot of time and gas for a dead drug dealer," Bobby added. "Texaco was just another slinger. If Dante Toomey hadn't put those .45 slugs in his brain, someone else would've. Welcome to the lifestyle of death."

Bobby had a point: What was another dead dealer in Baltimore City? With convictions in drug murders no better than a coin toss, with witnesses too afraid to talk or, more often, taking the law into their own hands, with the system clogged, the result for a killer like Dante was usually a walk. At best, a plea. Why not let one dealer finish off another?

But for Kay, this one was different. Texaco, the dead

dealer Bobby was referring to, had a kid brother. And she'd made that kid a promise.

Under a gunmetal sky, Baltimore's Harlem Park was a bleak stretch of despair, owned by dealers at night, and haunted by crack-addicted ghosts during the day. Last night's freak snowfall had blanketed the city with a pristine camouflage but now the streets were gray again.

Kay slowed the car, passing a couple homeboys, their hoods drawn up for warmth as they shivered next to a public bench. On the back of the bench, the rampant slogan "Baltimore: the city that reads"—a dying memory of the former mayor's Literacy Campaign—had been altered with spray paint to read "the city that bleeds."

She'd done patrol here in the Western a decade ago. Back when the neighborhood wasn't so bold. When a shield meant something.

"Look, I know Dante's crew," Bobby went on, licking foamed milk from his lip. "They don't crawl outta their cribs till noon."

"Dante's got murder warrants on his head. He's hardly keeping dealer's hours anymore."

Kay had driven these streets a dozen times in the past three weeks, usually at night, the streets ripe with drug activity. She'd cruise them as if she were working a grid on a crime scene, while teenage dealers scowled at the unmarked and gave the "five-oh" to their hand-to-hand men on the corners to signal police.

"Well, if Dante *is* still around, then that dumb-ass must be filling his prescriptions for Stupid Pills at the Eckerd," Bobby said.

Kay smiled. If nothing else, riding with Bobby Curran, babysitting the rookie through his first homicide, had replenished Kay's stock of one-liners.

"It's not about stupid, Bobby. It's nature. When a homeboy like Dante's feeling insecure, last place he's headed is out of town."

Just past Harlem Park Middle School three boys dragged their sneakers through the slush, fists jammed into their pockets. They knew she was police. In the rearview mirror, Kay saw one give her the finger.

"Dante needs to feel safe," she said to Bobby. "Needs the security of his own turf. He's here."

"Then let Fugitive flush him. 'Sides, the longer Dante Toomey's out here, the more chance someone else'll pop a bullet in him."

Kay steered north off Edmondson and spared Bobby a sideways glance.

"When exactly did you stop caring, Bobby?" she asked.

As he started to respond, Kay slowed the Lumina and pointed out the windshield. "Bingo." And the first shot of adrenaline licked through her.

Kay spotted him two hundred feet down the block, shuffling past crumbling stoops and boarded-up doors in his $200 Nikes, and wearing the same Jamaican Rasta hat their witness had described.

"That ain't Dante." Bobby tipped his disposable cup at her target.

"No, Detective Curran, *that's* Tyrel Squirl. And my daddy always says if you're aiming to catch the big fish, sometimes you gotta follow the little ones."

Kay tossed the police radio into Bobby's lap. "Call it in."

Then Tyrel Squirl turned. In the three seconds it took Dante Toomey's main runner to case the situation, Kay slammed the car into park in the middle of the street and was out the door.

"Hey, Squirl!"

Squirl ran. And so did Kay.

At five foot eleven, Tyrel Squirl covered more ground in

those flashy sneakers. Still, Kay gained on him, swallowing up the littered sidewalk behind him.

She heard Bobby behind her. But Kay's eyes locked on Squirl's back, his arms pumping in the oversize hoodie and those dreadlocks flapping wildly in the air behind him.

Her heart was beating fast, her senses jacked up. Twenty yards between them. Squirl's sneakers smacked through the icy puddles.

Nineteen yards. Eighteen. Then Squirl skidded. She hoped he'd trip. Instead, he veered left, headlong into the side alley.

By the time she reached the alley, Kay's hand was on the grip of her nine. Behind her Bobby dodged traffic.

She couldn't wait.

Drawing a breath, she ducked around the corner, her eyes adjusting to the dark.

And then, through her halo of breath vapor, Kay spotted the hat. The red-and-yellow Rasta bobbed at the end of the alley, and there was the clash of chain-link as Squirl scaled the fence.

"Son of a bitch!" She was running again, negotiating trash cans and greasy pools of refuse. Kay threw herself at the fence, and when she hit the top, she swung over too fast. She landed hard, almost winded herself as she slipped on soaked cardboard boxes.

At the end of the alley he cut right, bounding into the light. When she hit the street, Squirl was zigzagging through traffic.

So close now she could hear his breath, smell his sweat on his slipstream. When Squirl ducked into the next alley, Kay didn't enter as cautiously. And she regretted it the second she did.

Kay caught the flash of gold on Squirl's wide, black fist and ducked. No time to draw her gun. Instead, with one sharp kick to his knee, the sole of her shoe met delicate cartilage. She heard his cry and wished she'd aimed higher.

He staggered, swore, almost went down, as Kay snagged a fistful of his hoodie and tried to wrestle him to the ground. But in a heartbeat Squirl wriggled out of the oversize shirt and turned. Too fast. His hands on her. Grabbing.

Kay brought her elbow up in a hard, well-aimed swing. Felt bone and saw a stream of blood and spit fly from Squirl's mouth, spray red against the grime-slicked wall of the alley.

Rage flared in the runner's eyes. "Crazy-ass bitch!"

And then there was Bobby. "What did you call her, Squirl?"

When Bobby spun him around, he followed the question with a smooth upward arch of his knee.

Squirl buckled, then faltered, one hand skidding along the sidewalk. And just when Kay thought he was at last going down, Tyrel Squirl kicked back. Pain knifed up her leg and she had to catch herself on the alley wall. Then Squirl was crawling, scurrying to get his feet under him, crab-walking toward the street.

He was almost vertical again when Bobby nailed him from behind, this time keeping the runner down while Kay unclipped the cuffs from her belt.

"Son of a bitch, Squirl!" She worked the cuffs around his thick wrists while Bobby pinned him. "When are you idiots gonna learn that when you put up a fight, you only go to jail tired?"

Together, she and Bobby hauled Tyrel Squirl to his feet. Only then did Kay spot the stain splashed across Bobby's crisp linen shirt.

"Shit, Bobby. Sorry about your latte."

"Dumb-ass ruined my best shirt." He punctuated his anger by giving Squirl a shove.

The runner sucked silently at his split lip.

"All right, Squirl, how about you start by giving Detective Curran here an apology," Kay said, "and then you can tell us nice where your dawg Dante's laying his head these days, hmm?"

Squirl thrust his chin in the air, his mouth a tight, bloody line, when Kay's cell went off.

Cleaning her palm on her pant leg, Kay answered on the second ring. "Delaney."

"It's Finn. You busy?"

"Not at all."

"Good, cuz I need you on something."

"You catch a case?"

"You could say that."

"Where's the body?" Kay asked.

"Well, that's the freaky part: there isn't one."

2

THE FIRST THING Detective Danny Finnerty had noticed when responding to the crime scene in Roland Park a half hour ago was the crows. A turf war had broken out over the narrow strip of woods bordering the west edge of the grounds. The trees were black with the squabbling, quasi-reptilian birds, and the air filled with their shrieks as they circled and dove, oblivious to the police tape and crime scene below.

The gray mid-April sky pressed down on the sports field of Langley Country School, and the unseasonable dusting of snow wasn't melting fast. Finn warmed his hands in the pockets of his leather coat and watched the Mobile Crime Lab shoot the scene. What little there was.

"Watch those tracks there," he warned the tech. "We need those."

Other than their own, only one path in the snow ran east, from the school's cul-de-sac to the crime scene at the base of a silver-barked sycamore. The rest of the white expanse was unmarred except for a trail that branched west, left by the witness who'd made the early-morning discovery.

Officer Michelle Luttrell had done well in preserving the scene, and Finn would make sure to have a letter entered into Luttrell's personnel jacket by the end of the week, commending her professionalism on the scene.

Luttrell was young and blond, with a face that looked far too ingenuous for the job. She shivered slightly in her uniform jacket, made bulky from the Kevlar vest she wore underneath, and when she caught Finn's stare, she dropped her gaze.

"So you think that came from a person?" she asked, gesturing toward the tree.

"I don't know. ME's investigator should be able to tell us."

She nodded. "You need anything else, Detective?"

Finn glanced back at the school. Three patrol cars and the Crime Lab's van lined the narrow drive in front of the columned portico of the main entrance. He shoved a thumb in the direction of the Northern District uniforms lingering by their vehicles. "Yeah. You can keep those knuckleheads off the snow. I don't want my perp's prints messed up. And tell your witness I need to talk to him."

Luttrell headed back across the grounds, just as Kay pulled in. The young officer waved Kay's unmarked to the side.

When Kay rounded the hood of the car, she straightened her jacket over the holster strapped to her small waist. At five-four, she looked tiny next to the uniforms. She said something to them, and one of the officers let loose a deep laugh. Then Finn heard a "Yes, ma'am" and they parted for her.

Finn caught her smile. Over the past year he'd seen Kay's demons fade, but the memories lingered. There were still times, in the dead of night, when Finn held her sweat-slicked body until she found sleep again.

Some scars even time couldn't heal.

As he watched her cross the field, the rookie Bobby Curran in tow, Finn noticed her slight limp and the grime on her suit.

"What happened to you?" he asked.

"Just brought in Dante Toomey's main runner," Kay said.

"Tyrel Squirl? I'm impressed." He nodded at Bobby then and at the rookie's stained shirt. "And who d'you arrest this morning, Slick? Your coffee cup?"

He only imagined the look Bobby shot him from behind the Oakley wire-framed sunglasses.

Finn motioned toward the tree and as Kay fell in step beside him he lowered his voice. "I missed you this morning."

When he'd woken to the empty bed, Finn had wondered how Kay had managed to slip out before dawn. After a weeklong shift of midnights, they'd used their one day off yesterday to take the boat out onto the bay for the first sail of the season, not docking till well after dark.

"You get enough sleep?" he asked her.

"Sure. *I* don't need my beauty rest." She shot him a smile. "So, what have you got?"

"Whatever it is, it tops the scale of weird." He stopped them several feet from the base of the sycamore. "I haven't talked to the witness yet, but the responding officer says the guy saw someone dump this."

"Holy Christ," Finn heard Bobby behind him. "Is that . . . is that someone's heart?"

"Very good, Slick. You were one of those brainiacs in science class, weren't you?"

Kay squatted, visually examining the heart.

The fist-sized organ glistened dully. Smears of blood caked the exterior membrane and stained the snow around it, and where the aorta and arteries had been severed, the ragged edges appeared to be drying.

"What the hell?" Kay said under her breath, then scanned the open field, the school, and the tracks. When her gaze came back to the heart, she leaned in closer. "Look at the snow around it. It's melted."

"I know, like the heart was still warm when he dumped it," Finn finished for her. "Christ, Kay, you ever see shit like this before? Is it some kind of cult thing?"

She shook her head, seemed a little pale as she stood.

"Maybe it's from a transplant clinic or something," Bobby suggested. "Or from some Johns Hopkins cadaver."

"No," Kay said. "Look at the cuts. They're not surgical. This heart was butchered out of someone."

"Well, maybe it's not even human. Maybe it's some pig's heart from the school biology lab," Bobby said.

"It's not from a pig, Detectives." The witness that accompanied Officer Luttrell was a small man with nervous eyes spaced too close together and set too deep. He pushed a pair of glasses farther up his nose and shifted his weight from one foot to the other, his suede deck shoes soaked from snow.

"This is Jonathan Durso," Luttrell introduced.

"Dr. Durso. And *that* is not a pig's," he repeated, hugging

himself from the cold. "In a porcine heart the left atrial appendage is of comparable size to the right. You can see that's not the case with this one. Also, the shape is wrong. *That*, Detectives, is human."

"Officer Luttrell says you saw the person who dumped it?" Finn asked.

Durso shrugged. "Not well from the distance I was at." He pointed to the backyards of the neighboring houses. "And it was dark."

"What time?" Kay asked.

"A little after five."

"And what exactly did you see?"

"First just the flashlight's beam across the grounds. Then a man squatting at the base of the tree. I didn't know for sure it was a man until he stood and walked to the school."

"Did he have a vehicle?"

"Not that I could see from my kitchen window. But there may have been headlights."

"And what made you come and check it out?" Finn asked, sensing the doctor's impatience even before the man checked his Rolex.

"It wasn't until daybreak that I could see for certain something had been left. I became curious, Detective. My son attends Langley. Call me overprotective."

"Thank you, Doctor. We appreciate your time." Kay nodded toward the heart. "And your expertise. Officer Luttrell has your information?"

"Yes. Am I free to leave?"

"Absolutely." But Kay stopped him once more. "Of course, Doctor, you know we'd appreciate discretion in this matter."

A final nod, and Durso left them, making his way across the wet field to the back of his house.

"This is too freaky," Bobby said, still staring at the heart. "How do you work a homicide with no body?"

"You work with what you've got," Kay said, but Finn knew she was as spooked as the rest of them.

He watched as she waved a technician over.

"You have any dental stone?" she asked. "Can we cast those prints?"

The technician shook his head. "You won't get anything from those. There's not enough snow, and the ground isn't muddy enough. You got tire tracks though. Looks like a vehicle came up on the lawn. Could be your perp's."

"Good. Get on that before we lose it."

Finn could see the intensity brewing inside Kay.

"We need a cadaver dog out here," she said. "And a team from the Academy. We have to grid this entire area and sweep the woods."

"Man"—Bobby looked across the sprawl of Roland Park—"think there's more body parts?"

"I hope to hell not. But it's just as important to know what's *not* on a scene as what is. Bobby, I need you to organize those uniforms, and search around the school. Dumpsters, garbage cans, any nook and cranny. We can secure the fields, but"—she checked her watch—"in less than an hour we're going to be overrun by students."

Taking one last, uneasy look at the excised organ, Bobby headed across the field.

Finn scanned the area again and wondered what kinds of horrors might await them in the woods.

"What kind of person carves a heart out of a body, and then leaves it in the middle of a play field?" he asked.

Kay shook her head.

He hadn't really expected any answers. In a city where 90 percent of homicides were either gang- or drug-related, where it was Poopy shooting Stinky in a back alley over a $20 rock of crack, it was the weird cases that got to you. And Finn knew Kay wouldn't admit it, but she too was disturbed by the thought of a body, somewhere, cut open and minus its heart.

3

THE SCENE AT Roland Park had become a circus, replete with satellite vans and media. Students of the private school had started filtering in shortly after the ME's investigator had carted off the heart in a small plastic cooler. Shiny Land Rovers, Acuras, and Lexuses drew up to the cul-de-sac, spewing out more students, until the onslaught of gawking teenagers became a barely manageable flood.

When the bell rang at nine, the team worked in relative privacy again, with only the media as a presence beyond the police tape. Kay had tried to be patient, but when it came to Jane Gallagher, WBAL's chief investigative reporter, Kay had little control. It was almost three years ago when Joe Spencer, Kay's partner, had been shot and killed with her duty weapon, and Kay had been left for dead at the hands of Bernard Eales. Gallagher had been far from gracious toward Kay in her coverage of the tragedy.

The reporter's attempt at redemption came a year later when she covered Kay and Finn's capture of a serial killer responsible for the brutal deaths of six women, even attending the BPD annual awards where they both received Bronze Stars for their work on the case. But the bad blood ran too deep for clemency. So, this morning, Finn had done his best to steer Kay away from Jane.

By noon the ME's office had called, and Kay and Finn left the scene as a class of recruits from the Academy concluded a grid search and two K9 teams had cleared the woods. At first when the dogs had come up empty on the search, Kay had been relieved. It had been hard enough stomaching the excised heart; she hadn't wanted to stand over any more body parts.

But now, parked outside Maryland's Office of the Chief Medical Examiner at 111 Penn Street, Kay wished they *had* found more, because with nothing but the heart, there was little to go on. She reached for the fresh suit she'd taken from her 4Runner back at HQ and wondered what Eddie Jones, the assistant ME, could actually give them today.

"So do you and Slick have enough to hold Tyrel Squirl for a bit?" Finn asked.

"Not on our case," Kay said, shedding the jacket of her ruined suit and tossing it in the rear seat, "but Narcotics has got some warrants on him."

"Enough to negotiate with?"

"Won't know till we interview him this afternoon," she said, contorting within the tight confines of the car to change out of her shirt.

Finn had nudged the nose of the unmarked under the parking structure's overhang, granting Kay a degree of privacy. He kept an eye out, she noticed, but at the same time watched her. He didn't hide his appreciation, and Kay was flattered to see that after four years the sight of her body could still excite him.

"What we really need," she said, "is for Squirl to flip on Dante. Clear a few murders." Dante's name wasn't on just Texaco's murder. He was wanted for three other homicides. And all three had shaky evidence and mute witnesses. It would take some pretty slick talking to convince Tyrel Squirl to give up his homeboy.

"If you can't get him to flip," Finn said, "all you've got is the testimony of a little street thug."

Kay held up her hand to silence Finn. They'd been down that road before.

The "little street thug" was Antwon Washington, the brother of Jerome "Texaco" Washington. Texaco had been shot three times in the face with a .45 for cutting in on Dante's territory by selling ten pieces of crack from a Dumpster behind a Texaco station on Mosher.

And twelve-year-old Antwon was the only witness, the only person in *any* of the charges against Dante willing to testify, and the only sure card in the prosecution's hand. He was a streetwise kid with an IQ off the charts according to his teacher. But Antwon hung with the wrong crowd, asked too many questions, and Finn had wagered the kid's prying into his brother's murder would get him killed before the year was out. Kay had hoped to prove Finn wrong, to get Antwon off the corners, give the kid a chance at a real life.

But that didn't look too promising now. Antwon had disappeared from the foster home she'd arranged for him out in Dundalk, and was last seen cutting classes from Patapsco High three days ago. She knew Antwon was back on the streets and all weekend Kay had prayed he'd call.

It wasn't just about his testimony and that Dante Toomey could walk without it. Kay cared about Antwon. Too much.

"You hear from the kid yet?"

Kay shimmied into her slacks. "No." She worked her belt through the loop of her hip holster.

"I warned you not to get your hopes up, Kay. You can't save them all."

"No?" She arranged her jacket's collar and remembered the last witness she'd tried to help. She'd gotten the young girl off the streets, out of hooking, only to find her murdered before she could testify against Bernard Eales. "Well, I guess I'd like to save just one," she said.

"So why Antwon? Why *this* kid?"

But Kay shook her head. She couldn't put it into words, couldn't describe the connection she felt with the kid, or the strange sort of symmetry they shared: existing on opposite sides of the same world yet living parallel lives in their need for justice, for themselves and for others. She'd recognized it from the moment she'd met Antwon Washington, three weeks ago, behind the Boys Center on Braddish.

"You listen to Rondall and his boys, and you'll end up just like my brother. You want that, Midge? Huh?" Kay had overheard Antwon with another kid behind the Center. "You can't go mixin' with them guys and not git yourself killt, hear?"

She'd barely been able to make out Midge's response. "But they gonna look out for me, know what I'm sayin'? They stick together."

"Got that right. *They* stick together, Midge. You be nothin' to Rondall and his crew. You think they care if you dead or alive?"

The kid nicknamed Midge had mumbled something then, and Kay had rounded the corner enough to see Antwon lean into him. "You need to start listenin' to Ms. Latonya . . ."

Kay had eavesdropped on the rest of Antwon's diatribe to his younger counterpart about the wisdom of staying off the corners, staying in school, and when Midge had finally slouched away he looked as if he'd just taken a parental browbeating.

"I heard what you told your friend," Kay had said to Antwon after she'd introduced herself.

"Midge? Ain't no friend o' mine."

"No? Sounds like you're looking out for him."

"I don't look out for no one but me."

But Kay had seen through the bravado. "Good advice you gave him about school."

He'd shrugged off her attempt at praise.

"I talked to your teacher, Antwon. She says you haven't been in school since your brother was shot." Under his mop of short dreads she'd caught the mistrust in his brown eyes. She was just another cop to him. "Maybe you should take your own advice."

She'd been met with a sneer as he kicked at the dirt. "Can't," he'd said.

"Why's that?"

"It's too late for me." He'd left her then, but not before Kay had seen something in his hard look that she'd taken as hope, as the kid reaching out.

Now, three weeks later, with Antwon out on the streets again, Kay had started to wonder if she'd read the kid wrong from the start.

"Come on," she said to Finn, opening the car door. "Let's see what Jonesy's got on this heart."

But Finn caught her wrist. "Hey. I'm sorry the kid let you down."

She nodded. And when he drew her across the seat, she let his kiss linger for a bit, accepting the comfort he offered. But the only thing that could truly ease her anxiety would be her cell ringing and Antwon on the other end.

"We'll get a call in to the district," Finn said, touching her cheek. "Ask them to keep an eye out."

"Thanks." And this time when she opened the car door, Finn followed her.

Inside the sterile foyer of the OCME, they signed in and took the elevator to the basement. Autopsies in the city of Baltimore were generally performed in the mornings, with two medical examiners on the floor and several interns handling anywhere from a dozen to two dozen cases a day.

Through the cloying stench of formaldehyde, Kay led the way to the cutting room. After fifteen years on the force and countless autopsies, Kay had developed the ability to block out certain aspects of the job, but the smell of viscera and death had never settled with her.

She and Finn moved past stainless-steel tables, some empty and gleaming, others with late-morning cases still waiting for the path assistants to sew them up, their innards bundled neatly in red plastic bags and returned to the abdominal cavity.

They found Eddie Jones perched on a tall stool at the back counter, hunched over a clipboard. His lab coat was stained and his clogs were worn.

"Good afternoon, Detectives," he said without turning. "I'm missing a lunch date."

"We appreciate this, Jonesy." Kay softened the assistant ME with a smile she knew always worked on him.

A transplant from California, Jonesy was tall with beach-blond hair and a lean physique that went along with the surfboard she'd seen strapped to the roof of his Audi once. Last summer he'd asked her to join him one weekend in Ocean City. Promised he'd teach her how to surf. But Kay knew Jonesy's intentions went beyond catching a few waves off High Point. She'd told him she was seeing someone, and he'd guessed it was Finn. He'd been good about keeping the relationship quiet.

Jonesy came off the stool and reached for a large, sealed jar.

The heart swam in formalin, the severed edges floating raggedly in the clear fluid.

"So you're here about your girl?" he asked.

"It's female?" Finn leaned in for a better look. "How can you tell?"

"Well, we can't a hundred percent until you find us a body. But based on the weight and size, it's a good bet you're looking for a girl."

"Young?"

"Most likely. There's no coronary atherosclerosis, no presence of natural disease processes, or hypertensive changes that would indicate high blood pressure, so I'd say she's at least under forty. Probably younger. And by all appearances, healthy."

"Not too healthy now," Finn mumbled.

"Anything else you can give us?" Kay asked.

"Not much. There are several slashes into the heart's right ventricle, likely made as he was trying to carve it out of the thoracic cavity. And whatever he used wasn't sharp, at least not surgically sharp." Jonesy pointed to the cut vessels. "The edges of the cuts are relatively clean with only minor crushing of tissue. Still, there's nothing that gives a definitive impression of the tool he used."

"What about time of death?" she asked.

Jonesy shrugged. "Can't give you one. Not based on the heart alone. But if she'd been dead any longer than eight hours, you'd see lividity. The blood will settle and pool in organs, not just the skin. There's no lividity here." He returned the jar to the counter.

"I sent a section to Toxicology," he said, "and another is packed away in the freezer so when you do find me a body, we can run DNA. But you know the analysis takes weeks. Your best bet is to find me a body that's minus its heart, and I can match it up to the cuts."

"So that's it then?" Finn asked. "We're looking for a woman under the age of forty, murdered sometime last night. Nothing else?"

"Yeah, this is *CSI: Baltimore,*" Jonesy joked. "I'll plug a blood sample into my supercomputer upstairs and get you a full DNA profile along with your victim's name and astrological sign in three minutes flat. You got me a heart, Finn. Bring me the body." Jonesy slipped out of his lab coat. "Until then, there's not much else I can give you."

Scooping up his clipboard, he walked them out. "Without the body you've got nothing but a mystery," Jonesy said, punching the elevator button. "I see a lot of weird shit down here, including body parts. Just a couple months ago we had that human penis obviously lopped off at some funeral home. Still don't know which internment is missing his privates. But this"—Jonesy shook his head as the elevator doors opened—"this one's got spooky written all over it."

4

AT THREE THIRTY the halls of Langley Country School erupted into chaos. Finn had parked in the school's cul-de-sac, and when he and Kay had stepped through the main doors, the final bell had blasted.

Now the two-hundred-year-old corridors were awash with uniformed students, the air electric with the second-hand hiss from MP3 players and the competing melodies of cell phones. Lockers slammed and the din amped up as more students spilled from high-ceilinged, wood-paneled classrooms.

Langley was top class. A college-preparatory school with annual tuition over fifteen grand per student, it served the elite of Baltimore, boasting a wide curriculum and advanced annex programs, all with the Quaker stamp of approval. The kind of school Finn only dreamed of sending his daughter to. But on a cop's salary, with a mortgage on the house his ex-wife and daughter lived in, Finn could barely keep up with sixteen-year-old Maeve's private tennis lessons.

They found Langley's headmaster in her office. Jillian Somerville was a tiny woman with a man's confident stride and an air of authority Finn doubted many students challenged. She greeted them with a firm handshake and introduced the school's security supervisor, Gus Glazier. Somerville paced behind them as Glazier cued the surveillance tape.

"We've had these newer outdoor cameras two years now," he told them. "Quality's good, but the range is limited. I've already taken a look at the tape and there's not much."

With Kay seated next to him in front of the twenty-inch TV, Finn watched from the vantage point of the camera he'd spotted this morning, mounted high above the main entrance. The black-and-white footage covered the wide front steps and the top of the cul-de-sac, the nighttime scene washed in halogen floods. Snow slanted across the frame, caught in the cross glare of two floodlights and then in the low beams of a white panel van.

"Your perp pulls up here." Glazier pointed on the screen, and Finn imagined the security supervisor had once harbored fantasies of being a cop. "Stops just out of range of the camera. Another couple feet and you'd have had his tag number."

Finn leaned in, anticipating a glimpse of their suspect as he got out. But the driver circled behind the van and disappeared.

Glazier looped the tape back, played the driver's exit again, only this time he freeze-framed it. The figure exiting the van seemed suspended in the white blur of snow. A jittering ghost in the night.

"Nothing distinguishing," Glazier said. "Looks like work pants or jeans, some kind of a canvas field coat. Can't make out anything else."

"What about when he returns to the van?" Kay asked.

Glazier fast-forwarded the tape as the seconds ticked by in the corner of the display. "Right here."

From the left of the screen the driver entered the frame again, hurrying but not running. He passed in front of the van this time, his legs scissoring across the headlights. But the man's face was hidden, the beak of his ball cap pulled low.

And then he was gone. The van jostled, the door closed, a second passed, and then the grille and headlights backed out of the frame.

"He didn't use the turnabout?" Finn asked.

Glazier shook his head.

Kay gestured for the remote, looped the tape back. "There." She paused the tape. "See that? Just as he comes into frame, he pulls his cap down farther over his face. He *knew* the camera was there. Do the groundskeepers use white vans? Or maybe the janitorial staff?"

"No." Jillian Somerville's mouth was pinched with tension, and the two lines marking her brow furrowed deeper.

"What about park maintenance?"

"They use green pickups."

"We need the original of this tape," Kay stated. "Are there any others? Cameras at the side of the building that might have caught the van farther down the drive?"

"No. I've run them all," Glazier said.

"We'll need them anyway. What about this guy? Anything about him seem familiar?"

The security supervisor shook his head.

"Ms. Somerville?"

"No, I'm sorry." She lowered herself into the high-backed leather chair behind her desk. "What is this about, Detectives? There's rumor that it was a . . . a body part?"

"That's not information we can release right now," Kay said.

"Ms. Somerville," Finn said, "I have to ask, were all your students accounted for today?"

"Well, yes. You're not thinking—"

"We'll need that verified with attendance records. What about anything else going on in the school? Any suspensions? Threats? Vandalism? Anything stand out?"

"No. Only . . ." The headmaster turned her gaze out the tall windows. The snow had melted now and the grounds glistened green as clutches of students made their way along the paved paths that snaked parallel to the swatch of forest.

"Only what, Ms. Somerville?"

"Leslie Richter." She searched her desk for a moment before producing a four-by-six school photo. Against the backdrop of the school's stone facade, the girl smiled for the photographer: golden hair tossed over one shoulder, blue eyes riveted on the lens, and a smile wide enough to show off the kind of teeth only good money could buy.

"She was murdered two months ago."

Kay took the photo. "This is the girl from Clipper Mill Road?"

"I believe that's where they found her body, yes."

"I remember this," Kay said.

So did Finn. And unless there'd been progress they weren't aware of, the case was still sitting open under Reggie Laubach's name. Finn remembered the morning the girl had been discovered, he and Kay in bed, watching the early news on Channel 11. Lying next to him, Kay had made some comment about hoping there weren't others.

"Leslie was one of our top students." Somerville's voice was distant. "She was even enrolled in our annex program with the Peabody Conservatory for gifted musicians." When Somerville turned to Finn, there was a lost look on her face. "Help me understand, Detective, what kind of monster takes another life?"

Finn shook his head. There were no answers. And there were no monsters. Only human beings gone wrong. *Terribly* wrong in the case of a heart ripped out of a person and left in a school play field.

They left Somerville and Glazier in the headmaster's office and took the main corridor. A handful of students lingered at their lockers, a few more sat in the sun on the front steps. They watched as he and Kay passed, curious whispers rippling in their wake.

The team had released the scene since Kay and Finn had left for the ME's office, and now several students wandered within feet of where the heart had lain this morning. To their right, in a stone-paved plaza, a young girl danced for her friends to a tune off a boom box, no doubt mimicking some music video, her gyrations erotic and suggestive. She stopped suddenly when she caught Finn's stare. The girl smiled. Carefree. Not like Maeve.

The Maeve Finn knew today was a sullen sixteen-year-old staring mutely out the passenger-side window as he drove her to tennis lessons. Somewhere along the way, or along the divorce, Maeve seemed to have lost her enthusiasm for life, or at least, her enthusiasm for her father.

Finn made a mental note to call Maeve tonight. He couldn't remember the last time he'd spoken to his daughter.

"I didn't know the Richter girl was from Langley," Kay

said at the car. A breeze ruffled her hair as her gaze followed a Beemer that spun out of the lot, its stereo cranked. Finn felt its bass vibrate in his feet.

"Well, I'm definitely interested in talking to Laubach. I hope to God this isn't related to his case."

"I hope not too, Finn. Otherwise we've got a goddamn serial killer on our hands."

5

THE MARINA ON the north side of the Hanover Street Basin was home to a mishmash of forgotten speedboats, fiberglass shells, and gutted vessels in various stages of refurbishment. No fancy yachts or catamarans. The millionaire boats were all docked at Fells Point or the upscale Inner Harbor marinas.

Here, sandwiched between the looming Locke Insulator Plant and the bridge's concrete vaults, the view wasn't nearly as glamorous. Still, the locale offered a peace that was worth the limited vista.

Clutching the Leslie Richter case files under one arm, Kay used her hip to close the door of her 4Runner. She felt the dull pain from the bruise she knew was forming there after her run-in with Tyrel Squirl this morning. Her muscles were sore, and her knee stiff as she crossed the graveled lot to the docks.

The Blue Angel, Finn's forty-three-foot Slocum cutter, bobbed under a half-moon at the end of the east pier. The boat had been Finn's primary residence for the past six years since his marriage ended, and the marina's owner didn't charge Finn docking fees on account of his liking a cop on the premises. An arrangement that worked for

Kay as well. In spite of their feelings for each other, she and Finn still needed their own space from time to time.

Kay took to the planks. Riggings slapped dully along the masts, and water lapped against the hollow shells of boats. From the end of the pier she heard Finn's stereo, a saxophone lilting out across the black surface of the basin.

Finn was in the galley, putting away dishes from the dry rack, when she came down the companionway steps. He greeted her with a kiss. There was comfort in coming home to Finn, to someone who knew the job, knew its effects. The violence that touched them every day set them apart from the rest of society. There were things—such as a ripped-out human heart—that Kay could never fully share with anyone else.

"I gotta get out of this suit." She dropped the files on the galley table and headed to the aft cabin.

"How'd the interview go with Squirl?" Finn asked, standing in the doorway.

"Fine."

"And how was Slick?"

"All right," she lied. Truth was, Bobby had pushed too hard. *And* he'd let too much slip.

In the last precious minutes before Squirl had demanded his lawyer as a result of Bobby's badgering, the rookie had taken it upon himself to inform Dante's main runner that they had an eyewitness. Kay had been reluctant to play that detail so early, if at all. Because giving up that information had been the equivalent of giving up Antwon.

"Eyewitness?" Squirl had sucked at the cut along his bottom lip. *"You ain't got nobody seen nothin."*

"Sure do, Squirl. We got someone puts you standing right there alongside Dante when he buried those slugs in Texaco's brain.

And unless you give us Dante, you're both going down for the murder. What do you say to that?"

"I say you're a delusional motherfucker and you ain't got shit for a witness. And if anyone says they seen anything, they're lyin'."

Bobby had leaned in close then, his voice a whisper. *"Kid's not lying, Squirl. He puts you there."*

"Kid? What fucking kid?" But behind Squirl's squint realization had sparked. *"Wait, you talkin' 'bout Wattage?"*

"Who?"

"Antwon. Cuz that little retard weren't there."

"So you admit you were there."

Tyrel Squirl had demanded a lawyer then, but the damage was done. Even though Squirl could be held on narcotics charges, Kay knew word would filter back to the street, and Antwon would be a target.

"So Bobby gave up Antwon just like that?" Finn asked after she'd related the details of the interview. He was shaking his head.

"Bobby's priority isn't Antwon. He still thinks Antwon's safe in Dundalk."

"You haven't told him the kid bailed?"

"I want to give him a couple more days, Finn. Bobby finds out, he'll get an on-the-wing warrant for the kid from Vicki," she said, referring to Assistant State's Attorney Di Grazzio. "Antwon needs to come in without the color of the law."

Finn seemed to accept her reasoning, even if he didn't entirely agree.

He nodded at her outfit then—the oversize shirt she'd taken from his closet and a pair of his sweats with the cuffs rolled up. "You know," he said then, "you could bring some of your own clothes over."

"You don't like me wearing your shirt?"

"I love you in my shirt."

"So there's no problem then." She smiled and led him to the galley.

But Kay knew it bothered Finn that she had almost nothing of hers on his boat, especially when he'd filled an entire drawer at her apartment. Still, she *had* tried. During a session with her therapist last summer, Constance O'Donnell had challenged Kay on the issue of commitment, and Kay had finally stuffed a pair of shorts and a tee in one of Finn's drawers. But in spite of her good intentions, it had been little more than a gesture.

"So what did you find on the Richter girl?" Finn handed Kay a soda and joined her at the table.

"Laubach's off till Wednesday," she said about the lead detective on the case. "I pulled the files, but haven't had a chance to look at them yet."

Finn opened the closest folder. Together they flipped through the investigative documentation held together with red pressboard covers, the city's forty-second homicide of the year. Past the evidence reports, witness statements, and lab correspondence, Kay skipped to the crime-scene photos.

Leslie Richter had been found in a drainage ditch under a concrete overpass of the JFX—the Jones Falls Expressway, which ran south into the heart of the city—her nude body discarded amidst broken glass, winter-strewn trash, and a rusted shopping cart. According to Laubach's reports, she'd been found by a dog walker on a bright Monday morning in mid-February.

She hadn't been laid out long, and, if not by the dog walker, she could have easily been spotted by a passing motorist, her stark nudity glaring against the damp concrete and litter. In a couple of the five-by-seven shots, the Crime Lab's photographer had captured Reggie Laubach on the scene, his fat hands on his hips, his gut spilling over the belt of his creased suit pants. And in another shot Kay spotted the dog walker, a young wan-faced woman with a leashed collie at her side. Behind them, the Falls Road off-ramp arched north, and the tops of the bare trees of Druid Hill Park rose like boney fingers reaching for the sky.

In death, Leslie Richter's shining beauty and youth were gone. Her blond hair was matted, her slender limbs smeared with grime, her gold necklace tangled and one earring missing. She looked nothing like the girl in the photo that Langley's headmaster had shown them this afternoon.

"Well, this was definitely a dump site," Finn said. "No clothes. No personal belongings. He brought her here when he was done with her."

Kay flipped to the photos taken at the ME's office. "There're brush-burn injuries on her buttocks and the backs of her legs and heels," she pointed out.

"So he dragged her down there. Probably parked up on Clipper Mill Road. No primary crime scene?"

"No."

"Laubach got any trace evidence?"

Kay scanned the report. "Not much. Carpet fibers. Glass fragments. A couple hairs. Nothing under her nails."

"Any signs of rape?"

Kay found it on page two of the autopsy protocol. "No seminal fluid. No spermicide. But there was vaginal and cervical bruising."

"So he probably used an object. Any indication what?"

"No."

"Who was the ME?" Finn asked.

"Dixon."

"Stated cause of death?"

"Asphyxiation . . . 'presence of petechial hemorrhages evident in the lateral aspect of both lower eyelids on the inner conjunctival surface,' " Kay read Sarah Dixon's typed report, " 'as well as the upper eyelids bilaterally, consistent with suffocation.' "

"There're no ligature marks." Finn was still going through the photos of Richter.

"Duct tape." Kay found the reference in the report. "There was glue residue on her neck. And look." She slid the folder over. A close-up of Richter's neck showed a swath of erratic pink marks across her throat, like creases in the pale skin.

"What's that from?" Finn studied the photo. "A plastic bag?"

"That was Dixie's guess. The killer must have pulled it tight around her throat, then secured it with the tape." Kay tried not to think of the seventeen-year-old's last moments.

"And what's that?" Finn pointed to a purplish mark along the girl's cheek.

Kay searched for a close-up. "Is that writing?" But the letters were blurred and looked backward. "It's like some kind of residue," she said. "Like maybe a sales receipt from the bag he used to suffocate her. The moisture must have transferred the ink onto her skin." But deciphering the letters was impossible.

"What else?" Finn asked, and Kay read further.

"Urine tested positive for gamma hydroxybutyrate."

"GHB. Well, that would explain the lack of any signs of a struggle," Finn said. "Slipped her a little Georgia Home Boy, and she never knew what hit her."

"Not necessarily." Kay had the last of the ME's photos and had to double-check to be sure they hadn't been misfiled.

Kay pushed the folder toward him. "These were taken thirty-six hours after they brought her in."

"Holy shit. That *can't* be the same victim."

The bruises that riddled Richter's body in the later photos told a very different story. Often bruising and contusions didn't reveal themselves until the next day or even longer, the extravasation of blood from the torn and crushed vessels into the surrounding tissue requiring time to settle since the heart no longer pumped.

"Someone beat the shit out of this girl," Finn said.

"Only, he did it *after* she was dead."

"What do you mean?"

" 'The bruising is artefactual,' " she read. "Finn, these were inflicted postmortem."

"But you don't bruise after you're dead."

"Yeah, I've seen it. As long as there's fluid blood in the capillaries and veins, and if the blow is violent enough to crush the vessels, it will show as bruising. Even then a postmortem bruise is usually disproportionately small compared to the degree of force used." But the bruises on Richter's body weren't small. "These were severe blows."

In another photo, the path assistant had aimed the ME's camera at an abrasion on Richter's slender hip, the flesh over the ilium thin and the compression of tissue against bone more forcible. The mark looked like a boot heel.

"Grit found in this abrasion was consistent with the area," she told Finn. "Which means the postmortem attack occurred at the dump site." Kay remembered their serial case a year ago, how the killer had stomped in the skull of one of his dead victims during the disposal, directing his rage on to the body.

When Finn handed her a close-up of the girl's throat taken thirty-six hours later, Kay saw the faint bruising that settled there.

"Dixie says in her report that the killer throttled

Richter," he said. "Like the beating, *after* she was already dead.

"And look at this, Kay." Finn slid over the last photo. "That's the handprint they got off her throat."

Kay had to study the latent print for almost a minute, turning the photo several times, before she understood what she was looking at. The hand that had violently throttled Richter after death did not look human.

6

PAUL SIGMUND GRAVES lived on Blucher Street in his uncle's house.

He'd never actually met Uncle Roy on his mother's side, but he'd gotten to know the hateful bastard through his belongings and the squalor of the two-bedroom bungalow he'd inherited.

It had taken Graves weeks to dispose of the old man's legacy: bundles of Holocaust-denial literature from Ernst Zundel to shoddy, mimeographed pamphlets distributed by white-supremacist hate groups, Nazi regalia, and WWII memorabilia. All of it Graves had driven to the dump, loath to leave any of it at the curb. And through the entire process, Graves had felt no kinship with the man, had wondered how the same blood could course through his veins.

The old man had died a deservedly lonely death in the back bedroom, and Graves had kept the room closed up, a small part of him believing that evil lurked behind the paint-chipped door. Necessity, however, led people to undertake tasks they would otherwise not have dreamed possible. He'd already performed a few such tasks recently. Reclaiming the back room was only one of those.

He surveyed its dinginess now and tried not to think of the old man. As he angled the high-wattage work lamp and ferreted through his toolbox, Graves turned his attention to his divine mission.

His Angel.

He knew her name, but refused to use it. He hated the sound of it coming off the lips of the ogling boys at her school, or from her girlie friends who'd sunbathe in her backyard. From the first time he spied her through the slats of the fence, Graves had known she was special. He hadn't been ashamed of the erection he'd gotten watching her that afternoon, or the countless afternoons following. His adoration for her went beyond the physical, beyond the infatuation of the sex-driven adolescents whose hungry gazes followed her everywhere. They didn't know his Angel the way he did. They knew nothing of Destiny, of divine Providence, and were ignorant of the deeper connections possible between two people.

Connections that perhaps even his Angel was not yet aware of. But soon she would understand that their souls were entwined. And as Graves worked, he wondered if she knew the heart was for her, if she comprehended its symbolism.

Overhead, there was a rustling on the roof. Tiny nails scratching at the asphalt shingles.

Tick, tick, tick . . .

It was probably the cock, Graves thought. The pale-saddled Rafeno Pouter he'd named Freud. He'd spotted the homing pigeon circling yesterday, returning to the empty loft behind the house, searching for feed. Now the bird had taken to the roof, perhaps believing he could gain Graves's attention.

Tick. Tick.

He thought he'd miss the birds. But now, whenever he

passed the whitewashed cages in the backyard, the doors open, the roosts empty, Graves felt nothing. Gone was the nostalgia of having raised several generations in the loft, of watching them take to the sky, the air alive with their energy. No longer did he miss their calm cooing, or the feel of their warm bodies tucked between his palms.

He'd thought of his mother when he'd sold the birds, remembered her long-winded lessons on focus: by undertaking too many interests, one spread oneself too thin, and perfection became unattainable.

So when his new passion replaced his old, his mother's teachings had forced him to disperse the flock. He resented her for it. But then he resented the harridan for many things.

From below, Graves heard the furnace rumble, then felt the heat begin to pour into the room as the fan forced the stale air up through the vents. Within minutes sweat dampened his shirt.

Still, he wouldn't abandon his work to turn down the thermostat. Instead, Graves took up the power drill, secured the bit, and imagined his Angel's eyes.

7

Tuesday, April 18

WITHOUT A BODY there was no foundation. In any homicide investigation, the body was key. It was where all trails ended and without ends there was no tracking back to the beginning.

Like Jonesy had said, without a body, all you had was a mystery.

And that mystery had kept Kay awake all night. As the morning sun filtered into the cabin of *The Blue Angel*, Kay had stared at the teak ceiling, thinking about the heart, replaying the photos of Leslie Richter under the JFX, and wondering about the possible connection between the two.

By 9 a.m. she parked outside the OCME's. Fueled by two large coffees, Kay took the elevator to the third floor and followed the corridor of closed doors. She found Dr. Sarah Dixon in her office.

"Dixie" was an overachiever. Rumor had it she'd finished med school by the age of twenty-two and completed her forensic pathology fellowship at twenty-five. She'd moved to Baltimore from her hometown of Atlanta and still spoke with a soft drawl. She was a fine-boned woman with slim features, a small mouth marked by a sober sincerity and wide, deliberate eyes that were always framed by one of several pairs of funky glasses. Under the white lab coat Kay suspected Dixie concealed a true fashion sense.

"The Richter case? Sure, what did you want to know?" Dixie perched on her desk, amidst a flood of files. With her blond hair drawn back into a ponytail, she looked more like an intern than a seasoned ME.

"The handprint," Kay said.

"From the girl's throat? That's one for the books," Dixie said, her smile boasting her pride. "You just don't get that level of detail from cyanoacrylate fuming or a silver-transfer method. Often the prints blur or the ridge detail is ruined in transfer. With Richter, I used a newer technique, incorporating alpha-naphthoflavone with the traditional iodine fuming. Developed through Canada's RCMP. Because we get a clear image of the print visually, there's no need for transferring and the print doesn't get all messed up."

"So I wasn't seeing it wrong, then?" Kay asked. "The fingers were . . . they're fused or something?"

Dixie nodded. "Of course, from the print, it's difficult to

say whether the hand's deformity is a simple or complex syndactyly involving the fusion of soft tissue or actual bone. But in layman's terms, you're talking about a mitten hand."

"I don't suppose that kind of deformity tells you anything else about our suspect?"

"Syndactyly is the expression of a recessive gene, sometimes reflecting an underlying genetic anomaly generally thought to be associated with Poland or Apert's syndrome. But really, there are a half dozen different acrocephalosyndactyly syndromes that cause congenital hand anomalies like this."

"And would any of these syndromes indicate other kinds of deformities?"

"Poland syndrome, besides extremity deformities, affects the muscles of the chest wall. With Apert's you're looking at craniofacial deformities."

"So this could be someone with a deformed face?" Kay asked, not liking the image that was taking root in her mind.

"Not necessarily. Only five percent of congenital hand anomalies occur as part of a recognized syndrome. There's no determining the extent of deformities based on just one handprint. He could have syndactyly in one or both hands, maybe even his feet." Dixie pushed off her desk and retrieved her coffee from the top of a file cabinet. The mug bore a transferred photograph of Dixie standing next to her Harley Sportster parked on a beach.

"I'm surprised it hadn't been corrected," Dixie said over the lip of her cup.

"What do you mean?"

"Most of these kinds of congenital hand conditions are corrected by surgically separating the digits during childhood, while there's a greater potential for anatomic adaptation."

"So you're saying this guy's hand could have been fixed?"

Dixie shrugged. "I'm only speculating based on one print, but it doesn't appear to be an overly complicated deformity. I don't know what kind of parent doesn't have a procedure like that done. Hell of a way for a kid to grow up."

Kay thought about Antwon Washington then. In spite of the twelve-year-old's phenomenal IQ and his street smarts, he'd been nicknamed Wattage—for "low wattage," he'd admitted—because of a lazy eye. On the street, Kay had witnessed his quiet acceptance of the denigrating name, but she suspected that beneath Antwon's calm there brewed a bitter resentment.

Kay wondered if it was the same for Leslie Richter's killer.

"Did you guys ever find out anything about the dog hairs?" Dixie asked as she rinsed her mug in the small office sink.

"What dog hairs?" Kay didn't remember seeing any reference in the reports but she remembered the photo of the woman with her collie who'd found Richter's body.

"It was in the duct-tape residue on the girl's neck."

"Stuck in the glue?"

Dixie nodded. "When my interns and I found them, we figured they were likely from the primary scene. Or at least wherever the tape was applied."

"And they were definitely dog hairs?"

"That's what I heard," Dixie said. "I don't know what direction Detective Laubach went with them but I'd think those hairs should be pretty important. Last I heard, they were being sent up to Trace."

8

FROM THE ME'S OFFICE, Kay drove the short distance to Headquarters, the mammoth brick-and-concrete structure that dominated the corner of Fayette and President at the bottom of the JFX. She found a spot in the police garage and walked down through the airless heat to the unmarked door that served as the back entrance.

With renovations still under way on the lower floors, and only one functioning elevator, Kay opted for the stairs. She took her time, turning over the image of Leslie Richter's killer in her mind, the print of the gnarled hand, the bruising from the brutal postmortem attack on her body. Unlike Jillian Somerville, Kay didn't believe in monsters, but the image that was forming in her mind was unlike any she'd encountered in her almost eight years in Homicide.

"Where you off to?"

Sergeant Gunderson stood above her on the eighth-floor landing. He looked fresh and only slightly worn at the edges. The off-the-rack sports jacket didn't quite fit his shoulders, and an area over his right hip was frayed from years of covering his duty weapon.

When the former police commissioner had implemented a rotation program that required Homicide veterans to rotate back into uniform, a lot of the unit's best investigators opted for early retirement. Sarge had stuck out the backwards regime with style, as though knowing such insanity couldn't last. And now that the commissioner with his West Coast ideas had been replaced and the unit was finding its feet again, Kay guessed it was only a matter of time before Ed Gunderson finally retired to spend the rest of his days steering a golf cart along the greens of Wakefield Valley.

"I'm heading up to Trace," Kay answered him.

"Something come up on your heart case?"

"Not exactly."

Sarge chewed feverishly at a wad of Nicorette.

"How'd Bobby do with Squirl yesterday?" he asked.

Its being Bobby's first interview in homicide, Kay knew Sarge would be requesting an informal performance evaluation from her.

"Fine," she told him. Gunderson didn't need to know about Bobby's slipup to Squirl about Antwon. "We didn't get much out of him before he lawyered up, but Bobby did manage to get Squirl to put himself on the scene."

"Good." Gunderson nodded. "You know, Jane Gallagher's hounding me about that search team you had out at Langley."

"What did you tell her?" Kay tried to keep her voice even, but her sergeant knew there was no love lost between her and the WBAL reporter.

"Training exercises."

"Thanks."

"Can't keep the press at bay for long, though. We need to give them something before Jane starts making shit up."

"I know."

"Can I count on something for a press release this afternoon?"

Kay felt the pressure in her gut, but suspected the pressure from the brass on Sarge was greater. "I need another day, Sarge."

"Tomorrow then," he said finally, and Kay felt his disappointment when he brushed past her.

The echo of Gunderson's hard-soled oxfords filled the stairwell as Kay took the last couple flights up. The tenth floor of Headquarters was dedicated solely to the labs: Latent Prints, Drug Analysis, and Trace, and the rest of the Crime Lab Section. At the front counter of Trace, Kay asked for Manuel Costilla, the lab technician whose name appeared on the reports from the Richter case two months ago.

Costilla was young, with a lean, reedy frame, his words punctuated by quick hand movements. And behind his open lab coat, he sported a T-shirt with an eye-bending neon camouflage pattern.

"Richter," Kay said, as he ushered her behind the counter and into the lab. "The Clipper Mill Road girl?"

"Right. Detective Laubach's case."

"There were dog hairs recovered off the body."

"Yeah. Four of them. I'll show you mine if you show me yours."

Kay smiled at his awkward humor, then waited as he dug out the cardboard box.

"Not everything's been sent down to Evidence Control yet," he said. "I was hanging on to these in case I needed to do more with them."

The analyst rifled through the box and removed a small, clear baggie. "There's a couple in here. The other two I mounted on slides."

Kay held the bag to the light. The two hairs were no more than a half inch in length. They looked coarse and dark tan.

"Any way you can tell me if these could've come off the dog that found the body?"

Costilla's face seemed to light up. "What kind of dog was it?"

"A collie."

The analyst shook his head. "No way. These hairs aren't consistent with any breed of collie dog."

"You're saying that based on a visual exam?"

"No. Microscopic. And using an optical-based fiber diameter analyzer. OFDA is quick and easy. It gives you the diameter and curvature of the hair. And microscopically, you can assess morphology, pigment, and the stage of the hair cycle."

"You already looked at them then?"

"Sure. When I determined they were canine, I figured I'd take it to the next level. In case anyone was interested."

"The next level?"

Costilla smiled as he scuttled to one of the workstations, motioning for Kay to join him. "I did my grad work at Texas A&M," he said. "Around that time they'd started a study on the coat differences in dog breeds. Mostly to enable vets to diagnose skin and coat diseases, and to help breeders determine which dogs to use for breeding."

He slipped through a tray of slides, his movements animated now.

"Hair analysis has three aspects," he explained, "the microscopic features of the hair, analysis by OFDA, and, if possible, DNA. But since dog hair is usually shed, the follicles aren't as viable. Most don't have enough DNA to be definitive, and you have to resort to extracting mitochondrial DNA from the hair shaft. Still, using the techniques and data Texas A&M developed, you can tell a lot just through the hair analysis."

When he found the slide he was after, he snapped it onto the bed of a large scope. With a few clicks of a mouse, the image of the single hair appeared on the neighboring monitor, blurred and wide. He brought the field into focus, and Kay saw the brittle shingles along the strand.

"You're saying you can actually determine what breed of dog this came from?"

"I can't, but someone at TAMU certainly should. Their

study has come as close as distinguishing the coat differences between a standard and a miniature poodle. Of course, if your pooch here is just some Bawlmer Heinz 57, then the numbers will be all over the map."

"And did you explain any of this to Detective Laubach?"

Costilla shrugged, eyes still glued to the screen like a kid salivating over a jar of gum balls. "He never asked."

"So any guesses on what kind of dog this is?"

"I'm a scientist, Detective. I don't hazard guesses. But I can send the slides to TAMU and see what they say."

Kay patted the analyst on the shoulder then. "You do that for me today, Manuel, and I owe you. I *need* to know what kind of dog that came from."

And as Kay left Trace, she wondered how it was that Reggie Laubach hadn't wanted to know the same thing.

9

"YOU GOTTA UNDERSTAND, Leslie and I, we weren't friends."

"So you're not one of the girls she was meeting at the Barnes and Noble the night she was killed?" Kay asked, remembering the notation in Reggie Laubach's notes.

Amber Estcott shook her head. The Langley senior was a pretty girl with a perfect complexion, perfect teeth, and perfect hair. The kind of student Kay pegged immediately as a cheerleader, a class president, valedictorian, and prom queen. Kay had hated high school because of girls like Amber Estcott.

"Leslie wasn't part of your crowd?" Finn asked the girl.

"Leslie wasn't part of anyone's crowd."

Jillian Somerville had given Kay and Finn the school

counselor's office across the hall from Administration. The room was stuffy, and an aged AC unit sat idle in one of the tall Palladian windows. Dark wood paneling and heavy cherry furnishings dominated the office, and Kay had louvered the blinds to let in more light.

Afternoon sun slanted across the room and warmed the girl's features where she sat in one of the leather wing chairs. Like the dozen girls before her, Estcott's attention tended more toward Finn, clearly captivated by his charming smile and intriguing looks: his ebony hair drawn into a short ponytail, his olive skin and easy brown eyes, and those striking black-Irish features.

Finn hadn't put up a fight about working Laubach's case, especially when they had little else to go on with theirs.

After a fruitless morning down at Missing Persons, Finn had punched into the NCIC. The FBI's National Crime Information Center was a central repository and computerized index of criminal-justice information based in Clarksburg, West Virginia. If any investigator—federal, state, or local—recovered a body that was missing any part, including the heart down in the OCME's freezer, the details could be matched via the database. But the search, he told Kay, had come up empty.

So, this afternoon, Finn had accommodated a gut feeling of Kay's. A big one: connecting Leslie Richter's murder with the bodyless heart.

But now, a dozen interviews into the afternoon, Kay was beginning to wonder if she *was* wasting their time. She'd seen enough braces and pimples, jelly bracelets and piercings, to make up for all the Tyrel Squirls in her life.

"You're saying Leslie didn't have any friends?" Finn asked Estcott.

The girl gave a limp shrug. "She was more of a prep. I mean, her parents didn't let her go out. I kinda felt sorry for her, you know what I mean? Her parents always pushing her with her music."

Kay consulted the list Somerville had prepared for them. "That's right," she said. "You and Leslie were both in the annex program with the Peabody Institute. You didn't socialize with her through that?"

"No." Amber nudged a shock of chemically treated blond hair behind one ear. "Leslie was, well, I guess you'd say a little uptight. She was always pushing to keep things real, you know? Like, serious? I don't know if she knew *how* to just kick it with friends. I only ever saw her at one party."

"Did she have a boyfriend?" Finn asked.

Amber shrugged, and something in the way she averted her gaze briefly made Kay wonder if they were getting the whole story.

"Leslie wasn't the type to hook up."

"So you never saw her with anyone?" Kay asked. "No one outside of school maybe?"

Amber fidgeted in her chair, the leather squeaking against the back of the girl's bare thighs as her blue eyes flitted from Kay back to Finn. When she brought one slender hand up, she toyed with a piercing in her eyebrow. It looked fresh, still a little raw.

Finn drew himself to the edge of his seat. All afternoon, he'd managed a rapport with the students they'd interviewed. Kay guessed he saw something of his own daughter in each of them. "Come on, Amber," he said quietly, "help us out here. If there's anything you know . . ."

Amber hesitated. Then: "Okay, I did see her with one guy once. But I don't know his name. He picked Leslie up after school."

"When?"

"Back in February, I think," she said, as though figuring

dates in her head. "A couple weeks before they found her. You don't think it's related, do you?"

"Probably not," Finn said, calming the sudden alarm in Amber's face. "Did you get a look at this guy?"

"Only the car. He parked across the street. It was a black sports car. I'm not sure what kind, but it had a loud engine, like he'd souped it up. That's what they call it right? *Souped-up?*"

Finn nodded. "Anyone else see this guy?"

"I doubt it. It was after volleyball practice. There weren't many people around. And I don't even know if he wasn't, like, her cousin or something."

"Did you ask Leslie about this boy?"

"No, she was real private. Wouldn't have told me anyway."

"Anything else you can think of, Amber? Anything Leslie might have said about this boy? Anything odd about her behavior?"

When Amber shook her head, the lock of hair fell forward again. "No. Like I told that other detective, the fat one—"

"Detective Laubach?"

"Yeah. Like I told him, I've been racking my brain to remember anything, ever since they found her, and I just can't."

"That's all right, Amber." Finn took one of his cards out of his pocket and handed it to the girl. "But if you think of anything else, or hear anything, can you give me a call?"

"Sure," she said, with just a little too much eagerness. "Does this mean you're investigating Leslie's murder now?"

Finn passed a look to Kay. Then: "Detective Delaney and I are just doing some follow-up."

"Does it have anything to do with the cops being all over the school yesterday?"

"No. That was just a standard training drill," Kay said, and stood. "Thanks for your time, Amber."

When Amber stood, she accepted Kay's handshake, and when she shook Finn's, Kay noticed the girl's hand lingered in his a little longer. She righted a leather backpack over her shoulder and left the counselor's office, the din of the after-school corridors rushing in around her.

"What do you think?" Kay asked Finn as they headed out themselves.

"I think that we shouldn't be doing Laubach's work for him. Why the hell didn't he get that info about the kid in a black sports car?"

"Guess he just doesn't have a way with the girls like you do."

"Yeah, right." Finn held the front door for her.

As they walked to the car, Kay sensed the weight of Finn's thoughts, knew they weren't on the case. "You thinking of Maeve?"

Finn nodded. "You know, I talk better with those girls in there than I do my own daughter. How fucked is that?"

"Sounds pretty normal. I never talked to my dad much when I was sixteen. I wouldn't worry about it, Finn." But she knew he did. Since the loss of his son six years ago and the separation from his wife, Finn had become more and more detached from his only remaining child. In the four years she'd known Finn, Kay had never once met Maeve.

By the time they reached the Lumina, Kay's cell was ringing. She recognized Manuel Costilla's quick enthusiasm over the digital connection.

"Just got off the phone with TAMU," the senior analyst told her. "Based on the figures and the PowerPoint slides I sent them, you're almost definitely looking for a tan pit bull. Of course, you realize this kind of science won't stand up in court like DNA, but if you find a suspect and get his dog, we can use these hairs to match the mitochondrial haplotype of the dog. That would put your victim in your suspect's house, or at least in contact with him."

"Great. Now all we have to do is find a pit bull. Piece of cake," Kay said, feeling suddenly deflated. With pits and other muscle dogs like rotties and Presas the breeds of choice of drug dealers, they might as well be looking for the proverbial needle.

"You could try Animal Control," Costilla suggested. "Owners have to license their dogs."

But Kay doubted the man who'd taken Leslie Richter's life was the type to license his pet.

"And it gets better," Costilla said. "There's another case, came up three weeks ago. Dog hairs as well. I'm not the primary analyst on it, but I did take a peek."

"And?"

"And the hairs from the two cases . . . they match. This Richter girl, she's not your only victim."

10

Journal Entry #23
Dahmer used a drill.

Jeffrey Lionel Dahmer. Or maybe his middle name was Lloyd. I can't figure out which source is right. But they all say he first killed when he was only eighteen years old.

He didn't use the drill though. Not till later, when he got better at killing and getting away with it. He said he wanted to create his own zombie. A sex slave. So he drilled holes in his victims' skulls and poured hydrochloric acid into their brains. It didn't work though.

I also don't believe that he didn't kill anyone between his first murder of that hitchhiker till later when he was living with his grandma. I read he flunked out of college and enlisted in the army but then was discharged. While he was in the service, though, he was stationed in Düsseldorf. I KNOW Jeffrey Lloyd/Lionel Dahmer killed there too. During his time in Germany there was a bunch of unsolved murders. The victims were all young men.

Those were Dahmer's.

The German cops couldn't pin the murders on him, but I bet you anything he killed those boys. No way someone kills and then doesn't do it again for so long.

But then Dahmer was an idiot. Just like the rest of them. He got caught.

Some serial killers say they actually want to get captured. That's not true though. That's just their way of not looking so stupid for getting caught with a body in the trunk of their car when they get pulled over for a broken taillight or running a light. I'm sure if they had it their way, they'd keep right on killing.

I know I want to.

I can still see her eyes, all wide and panicked behind the plastic as she wheezed on the last bit of air and the plastic sucked in around her face. I didn't believe all those

things you read about killers getting off on
it. I didn't think I would, especially with
that first one.

But I did.

It's the kind of high you don't get from
anything else.

Yeah, I know Dahmer killed those German boys
too. I know because I know how that first one
excites you for the next. I know how that first
one makes you never want to stop.

11

"IT'S NOT A HOMICIDE," Kay had told Finn when
she'd finished on the phone with the Trace lab. "Rape Unit
got the investigation, but Homicide was called in."

"So she was bad."

Kay drove them to Mercy Medical Center downtown.

"I just want to see what kind of shape this girl's in," she
said, as they took the enclosed walkway from the lot to the
main lobby. "Besides, until a body turns up that matches
our heart, there's not much else we can do."

At the front desk they were directed to the Tower Building that housed the Critical Care areas. The elevator stank
of antiseptic and industrial cleaner, smells that conjured up
Finn's worst memories: first, losing his son, Toby, and then
nearly losing Kay after Eales had beaten her to within
inches of death.

At the eleventh-floor nurses' station, he and Kay in-
quired about Julia Harris. The girl had been at Mercy for
three weeks and had only six days ago been moved from
the ICU to Intermediate Care. When they found her pri-

vate room, Finn recognized Detective Greer exiting the room.

Maureen Greer had worked Rape twelve years. She'd acquired the nickname Bulldog partly because of her stocky build, but no doubt from the tenacity with which she tackled her cases. A tough-as-nails, no-bullshit cop, she had a barely controlled tolerance for the acts her suspects perpetrated on women. For Mo, the victims were all that mattered.

When Mo spotted them, her eyes lit up briefly. "Congratulations," she said to Kay. "I hear you got a decent sentence in the Eales case."

Finn watched Kay struggle with a smile. Bernard Eales's sentencing had concluded just last week. By all accounts, sixty years was respectable. But for Finn, the sentence of the man who'd almost killed Kay wasn't nearly enough for his liking.

Kay, on the other hand, had reacted quietly in the courtroom last week, and Finn had sensed regret from her, as though she'd almost wished they'd taken it easier on the big, sad fuck.

"So did you come to pick up your daughter?" Mo asked, turning to Finn.

"What do you mean?"

"Maeve, right? She was just here. She visits my vic." Mo shoved a thumb at the door behind her. "Harris and your daughter go to the same school. I thought you knew."

"No, we haven't looked at the file yet," Finn said, momentarily taken aback.

"Actually, we're here about Julia," Kay said.

"You taking over for Goran?" Mo asked, referring to the Homicide detective assigned to the case in the event Harris died.

"Not really."

"Too bad. I'm getting tired of his ugly mug. He's been circling this girl from day one like a goddamned vulture. Haven't seen him in a week so I figure he got bored waiting."

"How bad is she?" Kay asked.

"My opinion? She's a donor," Mo said. "But then I ain't the doc. The prognosis I'm hearing isn't good. Seems like no one wants to call it and unfortunately the family's not the type to go pulling any plugs."

As though to emphasize her point, Mo swung open the door of Harris's room.

The curtains were drawn, and in the cool duskiness of the room, monitors blipped and a ventilator swished rhythmically.

Julia Harris might have been pretty. Finn couldn't tell. Her features were lost to gauze strips and faded bruising. A cervical-spine collar housed her neck, and around it spilled a tangle of lines and IV drips. She was still intubated. Never a good sign, Finn thought. On one side of the bed a monitor pulsed out her heartbeat, while another gave readings on her blood gases and pressure. Finn's eyes fixed on the single line that ran from a screen to a bolt in the girl's head.

He was only vaguely aware of Mo at the foot of the bed, Kay beside her. Past the bolt in the girl's head, Finn stared at the single lock of red-blond hair that had escaped the careful bandaging.

"What's the damage?" he heard Kay ask.

"Depressed skull fracture." Mo lowered her voice as if the girl could hear. "She took a couple major blows to the head. Even lost a couple teeth. But the hardest blow actually forced the skull into the brain. According to the doc, it probably caused immediate loss of consciousness, then a coma-induced shock. She'd lost a fair amount of blood, so her pulse would have been barely palpable. Low vitals like that, I'm thinking her rapist dumped her, figuring her for dead.

"By the time I got called in, her brain had swelled and she had an intracerebral hemorrhage. They had to cut her open to decompress the pressure."

Finn noted the sign posted at the head of the girl's bed, informing the IMC nurses that she had no bone flap on the right side of her skull.

"So what about the rape."

"There was bleeding. Ruptured hymen. Vaginal tearing. SAFE was all over this one," Mo said, referring to the Sexual Assault Forensic Examination program Mercy was renowned for. "They ran a kit, but didn't get anything."

"Trace said they found a dog hair on her?"

"Yeah. Actually, that came up later. One of the nurses found it. She'd been cleaning the girl, and found the hair caught inside her bottom eyelid."

"Does the family have a dog?" Kay asked.

"No. I asked as soon as I found out about the hair."

"Lab says the hair from your girl matches one from the Clipper Mill Road homicide. Laubach's case from two months ago."

"You're kidding."

"And it's been typed to a pit bull."

"They can do that? Shit. That paints a pretty picture, doesn't it?" Mo said. "So how come you two are on this?"

"We're not," Finn said, at last taking his eyes off Julia Harris's battered face. "We're just connecting the dots. What can you tell us about her?"

"Julia's a good kid. Good student, good grades, good daughter. No one's got a bad thing to say about her. She was last seen down on Pratt Street. At a club called The Crypt."

"She's seventeen."

"Probably had fake ID. Most of them do these days."

"She have a boyfriend?" Finn asked.

Mo shook her head. "Not that I can get out of anyone."

"Where was she found?"

"Dumped down a slope off the 95, out by Morrell Park. If she hadn't been found so fast, she'd have been dead."

"And who found her?"

Mo shrugged. "Don't know. The 911 call came from a service-station phone booth a mile from the dump site. Of course, our Good Samaritan never left a name."

"You have a recording?" Kay asked.

"Sure, but unless we find a suspect, voice printing's useless. And honestly, from the sounds of the call, I'm not thinking it was her attacker. The caller sounded pretty shaken up."

Mo motioned to the door. "You headed to the office? You can listen to the tape. Go over the pics. If you think she looks bad now"—Mo shook her head—"you won't believe what someone did to this girl."

12

"YOU OKAY?" Kay studied Finn's profile as he steered west along the I-95.

She'd recognized his uneasiness the moment he'd stepped into Julia Harris's hospital room. His expression had darkened when he'd laid eyes on the battered teen, and then again as they'd studied the crime-scene photos back at Headquarters.

"I'm fine." A muscle flexed along Finn's jaw as he studied traffic.

The photos taken by Mercy's SAFE staff the night Harris was brought in were disturbing. Brutal close-ups of the girl's head injuries, the bloodied genitalia, and the abrasions sustained when she'd been dumped illustrated the violence that had nearly taken her life.

"So you think this guy cut her nails?" Finn asked.

Kay nodded.

Harris's fingernails had been freshly clipped. Too short for any young girl's tastes. And too short for any viable evidence to be found under them.

"Then this guy knows what he's doing. He's being careful," Finn suggested.

"Not careful enough if he's tossing out a live victim."

The muscle danced along Finn's jaw again. He changed lanes, following Mo Greer's unmarked as she navigated the early-evening traffic.

Kay fingered the audio cassette in her lap—a copy of the 911 call. They'd listened to it twice at the office, but Kay popped it into the car stereo now.

The male voice over the emergency line sounded thin, shaky. Kay had already memorized his few words: *". . . there's a girl down in the ditch. You better hurry."* Then he'd offered the closest exit number and hung up.

It was the background noise that Kay focused on this time: the sound of traffic on the interstate, tires swishing across the wet asphalt. And music.

Kay rewound the tape, listened for the music. There were no lyrics. Just electronics. Bizarre blips and synthetic whines propelled by a computer-generated beat.

"You think that music's from the caller's car?" she asked Finn.

"Who knows?"

Kay played it again. "What kind of music is that?"

"Dance or something. Like they play at those teen raves. Who the fuck knows?"

When the turn signal of Mo's car flashed, Finn followed her to the shoulder.

Dusk settled over the six lanes arching out of the city, and traffic had thinned marginally. Still, when Kay stepped out of the Lumina, the velocity of passing cars whipped at her suit.

Straddling the steel guardrail, they joined Mo at the brink of the ditch.

Mo pointed down the steep concrete embankment to the culvert that crossed under the interstate. "Medics found her there, ten feet from that plastic traffic barrel. Had a hell of a time getting down to her."

Shreds of yellow police tape still clung to a chain-link fence and several struggling saplings farther up the opposite slope. Kay recalled the photos and visualized Julia Harris's nude body in the cold culvert. Then she strode back to the guardrail, studying the angles, the depth of the ditch.

"No way in hell anyone saw her from the highway," Kay shouted over the southbound traffic. "How did he know she was there?"

"Maybe he saw her being dumped," Finn suggested.

"I considered that," Mo said. "The 911 call came in just after three a.m. Even then you've got some traffic along here. Her rapist wouldn't have been able to toss her without being seen. So that got me thinking."

Mo pointed to the opposite slope some thirty feet above them, where the concrete gave way to a tangle of brush and winter-dead grasses. "I drove around a bit. Found that spot up there. Come on, I'll show you."

They followed Mo's unmarked to the next exit and navigated through the quiet Morrell Park community. Leaving the cars, Mo led them to the rusted barrier at the end of a dead-end street, the last house sitting more than a hundred feet behind them.

Trash had tangled in the thick brush, and broken glass ground beneath Kay's duty shoes. She tried to imagine the man with the club hand turning down this forgotten strip of Baltimore.

"I came up here the morning after they found her," Mo said, negotiating the undergrowth.

Traffic hissed below them, and headlights flickered through the brush.

"Took me a while to coordinate the dump site and this street." Mo pushed branches aside, holding them for Kay and Finn as they followed. "There was snow back then, but I found a few marks that might have been drag marks. No useable prints though."

They stopped at the top of the grade, and Kay's eyes went to the spot where Julia Harris had lain.

"Was there any indication that someone had gone down there?"

Mo shook her head. "Like I said, with the fresh snow, I couldn't say for certain."

"Come on, there's no way someone just happened to see her down there. Not from here or from the highway," Finn said. "And if the guy did dump her from here, what are the chances a driver saw this girl go down the slope?"

"Not much," Mo said. "I've come back here a few times. Once it's dark up here, it's dark. Last streetlamp is a good fifty yards back."

"Well, this 911 caller had to have either seen her being dumped, or he's the dumper, right?" Finn asked.

Mo shrugged, and the seriousness in her expression left no doubt in Kay's mind that the woman had been over and over the possibilities in her head since the night Julia Harris was found.

"What's your theory, Mo?" Kay asked.

The Rape detective shoved her hands in her jacket

pockets and gazed into the dark culvert. "I've talked to every resident up here, figuring the caller was someone who'd maybe seen the guy come down this street. Nothing. Then I figured the caller could be someone who wasn't supposed to have been up here. You know, some loser screwing around on his wife, making out in a car, when he sees the girl get dumped. But not wanting to get caught with his pants down, he doesn't leave a name."

"And what about the service station where the 911 call originated?"

"It's just off the exit we took," Mo said.

"Did you get any surveillance tapes from the service station?"

"One camera. I've got the tape, but there's not much on it. The angle of the camera doesn't give any direct footage of our caller. But I've gone over the tape and coordinated the foot traffic with the vehicles that pulled in during that time frame."

"And?"

"And my best guess is the caller was driving a white van."

"A panel van?" Finn asked.

"Yeah, but don't get excited. We didn't get anything on it. No tag. Nothing. The camera only caught the corner of the roof as it passed under it. Why? You think there's a connection to your case?"

Kay nodded slowly, her eyes still on the piece of pavement where Julia Harris's body had come to rest. She thought of the tape again, the caller's words. "There is one other thing," Kay said eventually, as a transport truck roared past. "Whoever made that 911 call, he *knew* Harris was still alive."

"How's that?" Finn asked.

"He said 'there's a girl down there.' Most people would say 'a body.' This guy not only knew her gender, but I think he knew she was still alive. Like maybe he'd gone down and checked."

13

PAUL GRAVES had grown up believing in Fate. He hadn't been deaf to his mother's arguments that one created one's own future, but he knew better. He knew Fate was always there, like an entity on his shoulder. Sometimes tempting him. Other times taunting.

In his youth, Fate had never been a friend. From the very beginning She'd been cruel, giving him the gnarled Hand, the fingers fused together into an ineffectual monstrosity that Graves never considered a part of himself.

But Fate had a sense of humor too. After all, his conception had been the biggest flaw in his mother's otherwise perfect life. So from the moment Fate had torn him from his mother's womb, and the doctor had held him up, Paul Graves had been his mother's greatest imperfection.

Still, the woman had exacted her justice for the imperfection he represented. She'd refused to correct the Hand. Had told him it would make him stronger, that it defined him. But he understood the truth. Even as a child he knew the uncorrected Hand was his punishment for ruining her Elysian life.

Lately, though, Fate had begun to smile on him. Fate had introduced him to his Angel, with her porcelain skin and her pure features. And it was Fate that was bringing them together now.

At his computer, Graves tapped the keyboard, his right fingers hunting and pecking the keys, while the Hand thumped the space bar in a broken rhythm. He worked quietly for some time, in the bungalow belonging to his dead uncle, uninterrupted until the sudden whine of the fridge in the kitchen broke his concentration.

Graves's thoughts went to its contents, and to the memories of his task two nights ago.

All for his Angel.

Of course, he hadn't known *what* he was going to do when he'd followed the taillights out past the city limits. He'd only known that he needed to show his Angel, to demonstrate his ability to be hers. Even when he'd gone back to the van for the box cutter, the notion hadn't truly formed.

Only when he'd stood over the girl's body, with the snow falling around him and his flashlight's beam directed at her vacant gaze, had the idea at last settled in his mind. A calm, clear resolve had come over him then.

And as he kneeled, there'd been a fleeting apprehension. He'd been startled to discover she was still warm. Graves had touched the blade against the girl's chest, and the resolve waned. But then he imagined his Angel. His Angel did not tolerate weakness.

The blade slid smoothly, easier than he'd imagined, and in the shaft of light he watched the steam rise out of her. He was almost sick, but swallowed the frailty, and reached deeper inside himself to the anger. The same anger he'd spent years trying to tame, like a wild wolf.

But out there, in the dark snowy calm, with his Angel's eyes in his mind and the dead girl at his knees, Graves had let the wolf out.

14

THE CRYPT was a hole-in-the-wall club on Pratt in Little Italy, catering to Goth-fetish types and encouraging a dress code of latex and leather. It opened its doors to patrons eighteen and up even though the bar refused to serve those underage, and it boasted a members-only, after-hours club on Thursday and Friday nights from 1:30 a.m. till closing.

It was also the last place Julia Harris had been seen alive.

The club wasn't packed. Kay moved easily through the tight maze of tables and velvet-upholstered couches, and past a small dance floor with strobing lights and lasers. Industrial techno music belched across the dark interior, vibrating through her. At the end of the bar, three pale girls dressed in black and sipping bright red cocktails observed Kay's approach. Even in their fishnet stockings, black platform shoes, and micro-skirts, they didn't look twenty-one.

Tending bar, a young slab of a man straightened glasses. Fake candles flickered behind him, their artificial light dancing across the rows of bottles. His hair was dyed a striking blond, and on each wrist were heavily studded leather bracelets to match his wide dog collar. Kay wondered how much pain he'd gone through for the thick nose ring he sported.

"What can I get for you?" he asked Kay over the music.

"Just a few answers." Kay brushed back her jacket, and the kid's eyes went to the shield at her belt. "You Jason?"

The eyeliner he wore drew his smile to his eyes. "That's what my mother named me. People call me Memnoch."

Back at the office, after they'd viewed the grainy surveillance tape from the service station, Mo Greer had walked Kay and Finn through her investigation. Mo had been to The Crypt several times asking questions, convinced the girl had been abducted from the club.

"So what's this about?" Memnoch asked.

"Wondering if you've ever seen this girl?" Kay slid the school photo of Leslie Richter across the bar. Even though Harris had no affiliation with Langley school, the connection of the white van and the matching dog hairs was enough for Kay.

Memnoch shook his head.

"Look harder." Kay pushed the photo closer.

"I don't have to. She's not the type."

"Then imagine her in the whole getup." Kay nodded to the three girls at the end of the bar. "With the makeup and everything."

Again, the bartender shook his head. "Sorry, no. She's never been in here. Not on my watch."

"Anyone else I can ask?"

"Come back on a Friday or Saturday night maybe. Ask the bouncers or the other bartenders. But I've never seen that girl."

"What about her?" Kay took out the photo of Harris, borrowed from Mo's file.

"She's the one in the hospital, right? Already been a detective around asking about her. Did she die?"

Kay shook her head. She couldn't tell if the blankness in Memnoch's voice was from a lack of compassion or from the bizarre preoccupation with death that resonated through the place.

"Was she a regular here?" she asked.

"Nope. I only saw her that one time."

"But you remember her?"

"Yeah. She tried to get drinks for her and her friend, but I knew they were underage. The fake ID might get them in the door, but it doesn't fool me, you know? I think she ended up mooching off someone."

"You said she had a friend?"

"Yeah, came with another girl."

"Do you remember anything about the friend?"

"Nope. She was quiet."

"Has she been in since?"

"No."

"Did they leave together?" Kay asked.

"Couldn't tell you."

"So who was this girl mooching off of drinks, then?"

"Not sure. All I know is the last time I saw her she was headed to the back rooms and wasn't walking very straight." Memnoch poured a cocktail for another female patron in a black latex halter top and garters. "This other girl from the picture," he asked, "the blonde, what happened to her?"

"Nothing." Kay pocketed the photos, grateful the bartender hadn't recognized Leslie Richter from the news. "Thanks for your time."

She left the pulse of the techno grind behind her. Even at the police car, Kay's ears were still ringing.

In the peace of the Lumina she dialed Finn's cell number.

He answered on the second ring. "Where are you?"

"I'm just heading over to the Western. Figure I'll have a look around for Antwon. Where are you at?" But Kay already had her suspicions. After the visit to Mercy, Kay knew Finn needed to see his *own* daughter tonight.

"I'm at the house," he said. "Why? You need help with the kid?"

"No. I'm just going to drive around. You'll be home later?"

"Yeah. Don't stay out too late."

"I won't," she told him.

"Love you, babe."

"Me too." Kay tossed her cell into the passenger seat and pulled away from the curb. She headed west, crossing the downtown core to Harlem Park. She worked the side streets, steering through the bustle of drug activity, with her window down. The city washed over her: the boom of the bass from over-amped cars, the calls of dealers on the corner, and the five-oh shouts as she passed.

She drove for a half hour, parked for a while on Mosher, across from the Dumpster that had served as Antwon's brother's "shop," then drove to the alley where he'd been gunned down.

If Antwon *was* still alive, he'd be here. Keeping a low profile, but asking questions, nosing around, trying to find Dante. Determined to take care of his brother's murderer himself.

She'd been ready to head home when Kay saw movement in an alley off Calhoun. She didn't recognize Antwon immediately. At first it was just three boys having a dispute. She stopped the car and watched the beginnings of the scuffle. The smallest of the three wore a dark hoodie and jeans, and when his hood was yanked off in the fray, there were no short dreads like Antwon wore. Yet, something about the kid's stance, his demeanor, seemed familiar, and when he broke free from the two larger boys, Kay saw his face.

Antwon was running now, clearly aware he'd gotten himself in too deep. Stepping out of the car, Kay recognized the panic in his face. He hit the end of the alley and was about to veer left when he spotted her.

So did the boys. They skidded to a stop twenty feet from the mouth of the alley as Kay held up her shield in one hand and snagged Antwon by his hoodie with the other.

"There a problem here, boys?"

"You better arrest me," Antwon whispered just as the boys turned heel and ran.

And Kay knew, for Antwon's safety, she'd have to make it look good. When she shoved Antwon up against the car, the air rushed out of him.

"Who you running from, Wattage? You out here ripping

these boys off again?" she said loud enough for the corner
dealers to hear. "I'm getting tired of running your ass down
to Juvie all the time."

She snapped a set of cuffs on him, loose, and threw open
the back door of the Lumina. "Now get in the car."

15

FINN FLIPPED HIS cell open, snapped it shut. Open,
shut. Worrying the phone in his hands while he waited.
He'd have rather been with Kay right now, helping her find
Antwon. Not that he liked the kid. To him, Antwon Washington was just another punk, a prepubescent thug destined
to a life of jail or an early death on the streets. Still, Finn recognized what the kid meant to Kay.

And he admired her for that.

Kay was a fighter. It never ceased to amaze Finn that no
matter how much shit got thrown at her—in life, on the
job—the damage was only ever temporary. In the end, Finn
had seen how the Bernard Ealeses of the world fueled Kay
with an even fiercer level of determination. And while the
streets turned everyone else into burned-out cynics, they
seemed to give her hope.

From the day he'd met her, Finn recognized Kay as one
of those rare cops. One of those cops who stayed on the job
not for the paycheck, not for the tidy retirement package
after twenty years on, but because she believed, ultimately,
that she made a difference.

Antwon Washington was going to be her "difference."

Finn shifted on the top step and pocketed his cell,
checked his watch. Forty minutes now he'd been waiting
on his ex-wife's porch, and he'd wait all night if he had to.
He needed to see Maeve.

He flipped up the collar of his jacket against the chill in the night air. Nestled along the city limits, the 1920s community of Hunting Ridge seemed a world away from the city's hottest drug corners less than three miles north. With its rolling terrain and winding, three-lined streets the neighborhood had the feeling of a mountain retreat. The perfect setting to raise a family. When he and Angie bought the house fifteen years ago, Finn had never dreamed he'd live anywhere else.

Behind him, the windows were dark. Finn knew Angie kept the spare key wedged in a chink in the stonework in the back, but he wouldn't let himself in. It was Angie's house now. Had been for the past six years.

The light from the porch lamp flickered as large moths batted against the glass housing, and overhead a nighthawk screeched. At the bottom of the street, headlights panned off of Cooks Lane and an engine geared down as it took the hill. When the old Subaru pulled into the drive, Finn lifted his hand against the glare of the low beams.

Angie shut off the car, and he heard her pull the parking brake. He imagined her behind the dark windshield, in the driver's seat, planning her words.

The passenger side opened first, and Maeve folded herself out, her schoolbag slung over one shoulder and her tennis gear in hand. She took the flagstone walkway—the one he'd laid himself when Maeve was just learning to walk—and brushed past him.

"Hey, Dad."

"How are you, Maeve?"

But her key was in the door and she disappeared into the house without answering.

The staccato of Angie's heels against the drive broke the damp silence. With briefcase in hand, she stopped on the porch in front of him. The flickering light softened her expression even though she didn't smile. Angie was the opposite of Kay: tall, soft, demure. And to Finn, she'd never stopped looking beautiful.

Regret tightened his insides. Regret that he hadn't tried harder after Toby died, that he hadn't turned to his wife instead of the bottle.

"What's going on, Danny?" She brushed back her hair, long, red tresses.

"I just wanted to see Maeve."

Angie nodded at the open front door, a quick flash of a smile. "Well, you saw her." A stereo started up from inside. "You want to come in?"

"Sure."

The house felt good. Different smells, but still familiar. After he'd moved out, Angie had rearranged the furniture, but she hadn't done much since. As she turned on lights, Finn stood stiffly in the living room, his eyes scanning, realizing he had no idea if Angie was seeing someone. Maeve never discussed her mother's social life.

When Angie joined him, she looked exhausted. As the recently appointed director of research at the National Aquarium down at the Inner Harbor, Finn didn't doubt Angie's days were long.

She moved to the buffet cabinet. "You want a drink?" But the second she offered, Finn saw her mental stumble. "Sorry, habit."

"It's okay," he said.

An awkward silence. But then talking had never been their forte. Not in the later years anyway.

The music from Maeve's bedroom upstairs stopped. A three-second pause, then the growl of some rapper that made Finn think of the yos on their corners with their boom boxes.

"Since when does she listen to that shit?" he asked.

Angie closed her eyes, shook her head. Then: "Maeve, music!"

The stereo's volume muted as Maeve closed her door.

"So what's up?" Angie asked, pouring herself a Scotch.

"You know about Maeve's friend Julia Harris?"

"Of course."

"And you didn't think you should call me?"

"Why would I?"

"Maybe because a friend of our daughter's was brutally raped and beaten? Hits just a little close to home, doesn't it?"

Angie knocked back her drink and took off her jacket. "Julia Harris was picked up at a club downtown, obviously using fake ID. Don't you know your daughter better than that, Danny?"

"Do *you?*"

"Yes, I think so."

"Have you talked to her about it?"

"Of course."

"So how *is* she doing?"

Angie shrugged. "She's coping. I think visiting Julia at the hospital helps, but she doesn't talk about it much." She poured herself a second drink, then dropped to the couch. "The school set up a counselor for the students. Maeve's talked to her."

And then, as though sensing his doubt, she added, "She's all right, Danny. If you don't believe me, go and talk to her yourself."

Finn looked to the staircase that curved to the second floor and imagined Maeve behind her closed door, behind the impenetrable wall of music that lay beyond it. Would she even talk to him?

Whether deliberate or not, his daughter was a master at

making him feel inadequate, and facing that failure tonight was more than he could bear.

"Maybe this isn't the best time," he said, and moved to the foyer.

Angie was behind him. At the door she slipped her hand into his. It felt cool, soft. Familiar.

"She's fine, Danny. Really." She turned him to face her.

He nodded.

"It's . . . it's good to see you," she said then, her words sounding awkward, uncertain. And before he could step out the door, Angie wrapped her arms around him, brought her body close.

She felt good.

"I miss you, Danny." Her voice was barely a whisper in his ear, and as he held her in return, Finn was surprised at his body's response to his ex-wife's touch.

16

"DID I HURT YOU?"

Sitting in a back booth at Jimmy's, Antwon picked at his food. Pouting. Still, he looked older than his twelve years, the bob of dreadlocks gone. Kay didn't know if Antwon had shaved his head so he didn't stand out on the street, or if he was moving more toward the lifestyle formerly embraced by his dead brother.

She'd brought Antwon to the diner in Fells Point, catching his scowl in the rearview mirror as he'd slumped in the backseat. He'd uttered only a disgruntled "Thanks" when she'd pulled over several blocks later to remove his cuffs.

"Antwon, did I hurt you?" she asked again.

"Naw." A half shrug. He tapped a piece of toast against a

congealing egg. Around his wrist hung a heavy gold watch. He'd told Kay before it had been his brother's.

Kay reached across the table and grabbed his chin, turned his face to inspect a scrape on his cheek. The abrasion glared pink against his dark skin.

"That's not from me, is it?"

"Naw." He pulled away from her.

"You should get that cleaned."

"I'm aaiight."

"Those guys could have really messed you up."

"I was handlin' it." A sneer tugged at the corner of his mouth and he let out a short burst of air, brushing her off.

"You're not like them, Antwon. You can't take on those guys and expect—"

"I *said*, I was *handlin'* it."

"And how are you going to handle Dante and his crew?"

He gave her an apathetic shrug.

"You're going to get yourself killed, Antwon."

"Yeah? Well, I don't see *you* out there doin' nothin'." He flung the slice of toast down.

"You think I'm just sitting around with my thumb up my ass all day?"

"You catch my brother's killer yet?"

"Detective Curran and I are busting our humps on this case. In case you hadn't heard, we brought in Tyrel Squirl yesterday."

The cynicism left Antwon's face. But only his right eye fixed on her as the lazy one strayed to the side. "You got Squirl?"

Kay focused on his good eye. "Absolutely."

"He gonna flip on Dante?"

"We don't know yet. But even with him in custody, it's dangerous for you."

"How's that?"

"Squirl knows we've got an eyewitness, and he's guessed it's you. He could get word to Dante."

"I be fine," Antwon said, and Kay caught a glimmer of the twelve-year-old in him, the boy she'd met three weeks ago, the boy she'd thought was young enough, naive enough, to be saved. But twelve wasn't young by street standards, not when drive-by shootings could be executed from the seat of a BMX bike.

Still, Kay couldn't give up. The kid deserved a chance.

Antwon Washington—dumped by his crack-whore mother, raised by his grandma alongside seven other children, his only role model his brother, a dead corner dealer. A brilliant kid coming of age in a city where hope was hard to hold. Kay had wanted to give him that hope—hope that *she* needed as much as Antwon.

"I'm taking you back to Dundalk," she said, to the foster home she'd arranged through Vicki's contact with Child Protective Services.

"Fuck that shit."

"You can talk like that to your homeboys, but not me. Listen, you got a chance here, Antwon. You're a smart kid. You can *do* something with your life."

"Why you gotta rescue *me*, huh? You wanna rescue somethin', then go to the pound 'n' adopt a puppy."

It wasn't the first time Kay was surprised by Antwon's acute insight. "It's not about saving 'something.' It's about giving *you* a chance. A chance that the goddamned streets don't give you, okay?" Kay washed down her anger with the last of her iced tea.

When Antwon matched her stare, she thought he might

bolt. Instead, she watched a profound wisdom wash over his face.

"What'd you do so wrong that's got you feeling so guilty you gotta help someone like me anyhow?"

If you only knew.

"This isn't about me, Antwon." But it was. It was about Valerie Regester. And it was about Kay *needing* Antwon to make it.

She watched him toss back his Coke—a kid at a crossroads. Only a couple steps away from working the corners himself. And with Antwon's smarts, he'd be running his own crew in short time.

Or . . . she could get him out.

"You've got a choice to make, kid," she said, pulling a ten out of her wallet and tossing it onto the table. "You can keep on hanging with your bloods in the crib, selling dime bags to all the strung-out gutter junkies like your brother did, get yourself shot just like him. Or you can actually *do* something with your life. I'm here for you, Antwon. All you gotta do is ask."

"Why?" The mistrust in his voice made Kay wonder if anyone in Antwon's life had ever *not* had an ulterior motive.

"Because you're worth it," she told him.

When he stared at her, Kay thought she saw the first tentative glimmer of trust. Maybe even hope.

"No one's ever told you that before, have they?" she asked.

The shake of his head was barely noticeable, but it was there. He pushed his plate away then, and when he started to stand, Kay caught his wrist.

"I'm taking you to Dundalk."

"Not tonight y'ain't. Not till I find Dante. *Then* I'll go back. Swear." He crossed his heart and smiled, but a cold seriousness was behind it.

There was no point arguing, Kay knew. He'd only run again. But next time she would lose his trust.

"Where are you staying?" she asked.

"I got my bros."

"And what will you do if you find Dante?"

When he didn't immediately answer, Kay wondered if she'd get the truth.

"I'll call you," he said finally, and she wanted to believe him.

And as Kay slid a business card across the table along with a twenty, making Antwon promise to call, a sick feeling started to grow in her gut.

17

Wednesday, April 19

THE BODY HAD NO HEART. That's what the Cockeysville precinct in Baltimore County relayed from the field.

During the twenty-minute drive, Kay had had to refer to the map as Finn gunned the car along snaking county roads blanketed in morning fog. Hurtling north toward the Loch Raven Reservoir, Kay felt wired, despite the restless night she'd had.

After dropping off Antwon last night, Kay had gone home. Finn had barely stirred when she'd slid into her bed next to him. She'd wanted him. Wanted their sex, their connection, to feel alive in their passion.

But Kay had let him sleep. She'd listened to the rain, woke constantly, and by five thirty took a mug of coffee up to her roof. As the sky lightened over the harbor and Mr. Drummond's pigeons cooed in their hutches on the neighboring rooftop, Finn had joined her in the Adirondack chair. As he'd held her, Kay had wondered where Antwon was.

"Is that it?" Finn asked now, nodding past the windshield.

A traffic flare cut through the fog, and he slowed the Lumina as a county patrol emerged from the grayness.

Finn flashed his shield through the open window.

"Waitin' for you," the officer said, and pointed down the side road.

Less than a quarter mile in, Finn steered past several county units and parked.

Emergency response vehicles shared both shoulders, light bars and cherries strobing into the mist. Uniforms and plainclothes were little more than silhouettes in the swirling gray.

The air was stagnant, heavy to breathe, as Kay crossed the mud-slicked road. Through the trees and new growth, she could make out the yellow police tape bright against the rain-blackened trunks.

"We're looking for Sergeant Pitts," she said.

The nearest officer scanned the fog for a moment, then: "Sarge, City's here."

Sergeant Detective Blaine Pitts of County Homicide was a broad-shouldered man with the round face of a child. Wading through the blanket of last autumn's leaves, he followed a path others had carefully created to and from the scene.

He tapped his hat in greeting. "Heard about the heart you guys got down in the city," he said. "Not sure if this here's a match, but she's definitely minus a few parts."

Two grooves marked the narrow space between his heavy eyebrows, and he shook his head, clearly distressed. "It's a mess back in there. Perp just about field-dressed this girl. I tell you, you don't see stuff like this but maybe once in a career, you know? If this *is* your girl, you guys sure do get the weird ones. You thinking this here's a serial?" Pitts asked.

"How about we take a look first?" Kay nodded to the yellow tape, and Pitts led the way.

"Victim looks in her midtwenties," he explained as they fell in step behind him. "Our coroner's taken a quick look. Didn't want to poke around too much, but from what he could tell, it's only the heart missing. But I guess you won't know till you take her downtown and start counting the pieces."

In the dense air, beneath the scent of rotting leaves and rich earth, Kay thought she could smell death already. A fine mist of green shimmered in the undergrowth, buds, and new leaves. A hundred feet to the right of the crime scene, a woman gripped the reins of a tall bay horse, barely a hulking outline in the fog, then becoming clearer as they neared.

"She the one who found the body?" Kay asked, nodding as the rider struggled with the massive animal. It pawed the soft earth and danced around the small woman, its nostrils flaring as it fought the bit, reacting strongly to the presence of death.

Pitts nodded. "The stables up the road use the trails through here and down to the reservoir. She called us from her cell. Nice way to start the morning, huh?"

Pitts held up the police tape for Kay and Finn, the smell of decomposition stronger now. Kay's eyes went to the pale mound in the leaves.

"Looks like she's been out here a couple days," Pitts said. "Probably brought her in off the road and didn't even know the trail was here . . ."

Kay wasn't hearing Blaine Pitts. She wasn't hearing the horse turning up the earth with its hooves, or the buzzing of slow flies that hung in the damp air. She heard only her own heart as she stood over the ravaged remains. A shiver moved through her.

The girl had been opened wide. Whatever blood had spilled during the arduous task of removing her heart had been washed away by last night's rain. Water pooled in the exposed abdominal cavity, reflecting the gray sky and the branches above, masking the tangle of intestines nestled below the still surface.

Marbling had started to form along her pelvis, arms, and legs, the mottled, greenish purple color caused by the decomposition of blood in the vessels just beneath the skin. Kay moved closer. The body glittered with the metallic shimmer of blue blowflies, disturbed by her approach. Their eggs clung in clusters around the ragged opening that ran from the girl's navel up past her sternum, and early-stage maggots had begun working at the exposed flesh.

But the girl's face was untouched. Her features were only slightly bloated, and there were none of the telltale signs of gross insect activity. No larvae and no eggs where normally the highest concentration would be found around the facial orifices.

Kay squatted next to the girl. Imagined the killer in the same position, in the dead of night, the freak snowstorm they'd had, knife in hand while the beam of his flashlight caught the vapor of his breath.

"Her face was covered?" Kay asked, her gaze fixed on the girl's clouded eyes.

"Yeah. We got photos," Pitts said behind her. "He piled leaves over her face. Guess he couldn't stand looking at her while he gutted her."

"He felt remorse," Kay said, uncertain she'd actually spoken the words aloud until Finn moved in beside her.

"Just like why he called 911 for Julia Harris," he said.

"Bastard took her breasts too," Pitts said. "Probably trophies. Unless they're lying around somewhere like the heart was."

"We don't know whether this is a match yet," Finn said. But Kay knew.

The removal of the girl's breasts was relatively clean. They'd been sliced off, although not neatly. It had been work. Just like the removal of the heart.

In the ragged edges left by the blade Kay could see the killer's frustration. As though he'd had the plan before he realized the arduousness of going up and under the rib cage for the heart.

Kay wondered if the girl had still been warm as he'd slid his deformed hand inside her, groping around for the fist-sized organ.

"Come on"—Finn gave Kay a hand up—"we better get the team up here. I want her down to Jonesy as soon as possible. Find out who she is, and what *her* connection is to Langley."

18

AS THE SUN BURNED the last of the fog, the reality of the scene in Baltimore County became even more stark. For Finn, nine years on Homicide and several with Arson, where he'd witnessed tortured bodies burned beyond recognition, nothing had prepared him for the violence that had been rendered on the young woman near the reservoir.

For five hours Finn and Kay worked with the Mobile Crime Lab and the ME's investigator, while Blaine Pitts vacated his men. Countless times Finn stood over the mutilated body as though it could provide him answers. But all Finn saw was a madman's frenzy.

"He's not nuts," Kay argued.

"Come on, Kay, that's not sane. Look at what he did to this girl."

"He planned all of this, Finn. Orchestrated the disposal, knew what he was doing."

"Okay, so he's smart enough to dump her, but then he does this?" He waved a hand at the girl's body. "This guy's not wired right."

Finn thought of the textbooks lining the shelves in the spare bedroom Kay used as an office: sexual homicide, psychopathology, profiling. He'd leafed through some of them himself, but couldn't remember seeing anything like this. He shook his head and paced to the perimeter of the police tape.

"Is it just me, or is this guy getting sicker with each victim?" he asked.

Kay nodded. "He's definitely progressing." She shuffled through the leaves to join him. "Let's hope we get an ID from her prints, because with the early decomp there's no way we can use her face on the news."

Past Kay's shoulder, Finn watched Ray Molander, the ME's investigator, work.

"We should probably take some of these maggots," Molander told them. "Not sure if you want an entomologist to look at these."

The investigator manipulated a pair of forceps, collecting specimens off the girl's body and dropping them into a small jar of ethanol, while he placed several others in a live-specimen container.

"These should help us calculate a time frame," he added.

"Any thoughts?" Kay asked.

"I'm no bug expert," Molander said, holding one of the wriggling larvae in the air. "But these look like first crop."

"So how long do you figure she's been out here?"

"Couple days. Typically blowfly eggs hatch between one and three days, depending on the weather. Cooler temps cause lower levels of activity. We should get a few ground temperatures in case you do want an entomologist to give you a more accurate reading. You wanna help me roll her?"

Finn snapped on a fresh pair of gloves. The girl's skin was cold through the thin latex, the flesh dense and unyielding. With Kay taking the girl's shoulders, they rolled her slowly, some of the soupy water splashing out of the abdominal cavity.

It was Molander, squatting in the damp leaves, who noticed the marks first. "Sweet Jesus, what the hell's all that?"

Then Finn saw them.

Lividity had settled along the girl's back and buttocks, gravity having drawn the dead blood down, filling the lower capillaries and shading the skin a purplish hue. More striking than that, however, were the gashes and puncture wounds riddling the girl's back, hips, and thighs.

"These are bites," Kay said, prodding the closest injury, the flesh separating to reveal the depth of the puncture. "And these . . . Finn, my God, I think these are claw marks."

19

"THEY'RE NOT SCAVENGER BITES. These are predatory."

Jonesy's latex gloves were slick with body fluids as he leaned over the mangled remains of the Jane Doe from the reservoir.

With the aid of a path assistant, the ME half-rolled the body and propped her hip with a steel pan. The girl's organ block had already been removed, one solid mass of innards beginning at the tongue and ending with the pelvic organs. Lungs, liver, kidneys, stomach, intestines—everything but the already extirpated heart—had individually been weighed, dissected, sampled, and now lay across the stainless-steel work area by the back sinks.

"This isn't postmortem animal activity." Jonesy prodded the puncture wounds. "See here?"

Kay followed the path of his gloved finger.

"You've got visible bruising and hemorrhage within the wound track, indicating these were inflicted antemortem," he explained.

Kay's head throbbed and the glare of the fluorescent lamps overhead had started her eyes aching an hour ago.

There'd been no time for breakfast or lunch. She and Finn had left Loch Raven shortly after one when Jonesy had called to inform them he'd be working on the girl.

"This is the result of an attack," Jonesy went on. "Look at these patterned injuries. Claw marks. Punctures from the canines. And these oblique parallel scratches, those are from the teeth of the upper jaw. A compact jaw. And wide. This girl was mauled. Of course, that's not what killed her."

"So what did?" Finn asked.

"Lack of oxygen. She suffocated."

"Was there any glue residue on her neck?" Kay leaned in, studying the pale curve of the girl's nape.

"Not that we found."

"What about hairs?" Finn asked. "Did you find any dog hairs on her?"

The ME shook his head. "We hit her with the lasers for trace. Nothing resembling animal hairs."

"Can you do her again? If there's even a single dog hair on this girl, we need it." Finn looked washed-out, Kay noticed then, as he maintained a measured distance between himself and the exam table this afternoon.

"What about saliva?" Kay asked.

"You mean from the bite wounds?" Jonesy asked. "Sure, we can swab, check for amylase, then follow up with DNA testing. Doubtful you'll get anything from around the bites, but the canines went deep. The rain can't have washed it all away."

"And then you can compare that to the mitochondrial DNA from the dog hairs?"

"You mean from the Richter case?"

Kay nodded.

"You know how much time that'll take?"

"Run it anyway," Kay said.

Her gaze went from the evidence of the violent mauling to the heart found two mornings ago, sitting in its jar of formalin on the next table. Jonesy had already confirmed the match to the girl based on the severed edges.

Why? What did the heart mean to him?

There had to be a reason, a motivation that Kay was missing.

"What about the way he removed the heart?" she asked Jonesy. "Anything stand out?"

"Well, she was at least a couple hours dead before he started working on her. See here?" He indicated the path of the killer's blade. "See how the wound edges are more yellow in appearance? This area was bloodless when he cut into her, so lividity had already begun setting."

Jonesy went on. "He had a hell of a time removing it too. Looks like your genius tried to get into her from up here." He pointed to where the skin sank inward over the now-removed sternum. "Maybe he figured he'd cut through the cartilage on the anterior chest, next to the breastplate. But you can only get so high before you run into the collarbone. When that didn't work, he ran the blade straight down to her navel and went through the diaphragm. Not an easy job. That's probably why he cut her so wide, so he could get the blade up and under there."

"Any thoughts on the knife?"

"Not a knife. Something sharp. Thin blade but not long. If I had to guess, I'd say a box cutter."

The image of the killer at work rattled through Kay's brain. She took in the girl's lifeless face. The dirt and leaves had been washed away, and someone had closed her eyes. Her gray features sagged slightly, her scalp already sliced from her cranium to afford access to her brain.

She'd been a pretty girl.

"So was she raped?" Finn sounded edgy.

Kay caught Jonesy's partial nod when she looked up.

"She's got bruising," he said, "indicative of some kind of forcible intercourse, but no presence of spermatozoa."

"He used a condom then. You can analyze for traces for spermicide, right?"

"Presence of particulates, lubricants, and spermicides can indicate condom use and even narrow the field down to individual brands. I'd have to send samples to the FBI labs."

"What about drugs?" Kay asked. "Leslie Richter tested positive for GHB."

"We wouldn't normally look for GHB, but we can test the urine."

When Kay glanced across to Finn, he'd loosened his tie. Under the harsh glare of the cutting-room lights, she recognized his frustration.

"Give us *something*, Jonesy," he said, starting to pace the hard linoleum. "We don't even know who this girl is."

"We've got good prints. They've already been sent up. If this girl's got a record or is on file somewhere, you'll get a hit."

Kay's eyes went back to the bites. Over two dozen of

them, Jonesy had counted. And Kay tried not to imagine the girl's desperate battle for survival.

How did you die? What were your last moments?

Had the dog attacked her before her killer had? Or during? And as the image took hold in Kay's mind, the two of them—dog and killer—going at the girl, the ceiling seemed suddenly too low, the hiss of cold, filtered air through the vents too loud.

"What else can you tell me about these bites?" she asked.

Jonesy shook his head.

"Could they have been made by a pit bull?"

"Sorry. That's not my area. But . . ."

Kay followed his nod just as Dr. Sarah Dixon passed in the corridor.

". . . Dixie might know." Jonesy waved over the other ME. "What do you make of these?" he asked her.

Kay caught the scent of Dixie's perfume as she snapped on a fresh pair of gloves and leaned in to examine the bites. Something subtle, yet strikingly foreign in the basement of the OCME.

"Dog bites," she said matter-of-factly.

"Any idea *what* kind of dog?" Finn asked.

"I'm not board-certified in odontology."

"No," Jonesy said, "but you had that dog-mauling case just last week. What kind of dog was it that chewed up that kid?"

"A pit bull."

"And are these the same?"

Dixie nodded. "They're almost identical. The level of damage, the width of the jaw." She prodded the wounds. "Of course, that doesn't mean these were made by a pit."

"But it's more probably a pit?" Kay asked.

Dixie gave her a noncommittal shrug. "Can't make that call, Kay. You're going to need dental impressions and have a forensic anthropologist make that determination. And find the dog to compare these to. Sorry."

Dixie pulled off her gloves and stood back from the slab. Her gaze stopped on Kay. "Wait a second, I heard about your breed-typing of the dog hairs from the Richter and Harris cases. Are you thinking this girl's related?"

Kay nodded.

"Nice call," Dixie said, surveying the mauled remains one last time.

But Kay shook her head. "Not so nice when you consider that it looks like we've definitely got a serial killer on our hands."

20

FINN AND KAY'S CUBICLE at the back corner of the Homicide office smelled of Chinese takeout. Finn had run by the Bamboo Hut on their way back to Headquarters, and now their baffled workstation was strewn with paper boxes of half-eaten shrimp lo mein and moo shu pork.

From other cubicles across the newly renovated eighth floor, phones bleated and conversations were only marginally muted. For two years they'd endured construction dust and substandard ventilation, taking the stairs when the elevators were down to one car, and today, the maze of modular furnishings that they'd waited so long for offered less privacy than their previous sixth-floor digs.

Sitting behind their shared computer, Kay had barely touched her wonton soup. She was at the keyboard, all ten fingers flying as she filled in a VICAP submission on the Jane Doe. The fifteen-page crime-analysis forms detailing MO, body condition, and a victim's profile would be submitted to the FBI's Violent Criminal Apprehension Program in Quantico, the national clearinghouse for unsolved violent crimes. There, a series of computers and analysts could run comparisons against investigations from other jurisdictions, and contact detectives from across the country with supposedly similar cases. Nothing more than a national dating service for detectives, Finn had always thought. In his experience, there were rarely enough commonalities between the crimes.

"All right, brief me." Vicki DiGrazzio crossed her arms and leaned against one of the tall one-way panes that overlooked the city. "What are the similarities you've got in the three cases?" Her candy-apple dress and matching pumps looked out of place in the gray tones of the steel-cased workstations. But behind the blond-bombshell image and those wide blue eyes lay the genius of the state's attorney's top prosecutor for the Homicide Division.

Ed Gunderson had joined them as well, advising them of the County's official decision to hand over the Jane Doe. Bobby sat next to the big man.

"Okay." Kay wheeled her chair away from the computer. "First there's Leslie Richter, murdered and dumped off the JFX in February. Then three weeks ago, Julia Harris is raped, beaten, and left for dead in a culvert in Morrell Park. And now this Jane Doe. Physical similarities: they were all young, all pretty, and all three were raped. The killer left minimal trace evidence: their nails were clipped, clothes disposed of. Both Richter and the Jane Doe were suffocated. And then we've got the dog hairs."

"On all three?" Gunderson asked.

"Only on Richter and Harris. But the hairs are a match, typed to a pit bull. And the bites on the Jane Doe could very well have been inflicted by the same kind of dog."

"Well, that part's a bit shaky," Vicki stopped her. "But on the rest, if you're after probable cause once you have a suspect, I think you've got something."

Vicki turned to Gunderson. "So what about a task force?"

He shook his head. "Too soon. Besides, we go task force now, and the media'll be crawling all over this. We'll get Laubach and Whitey on board with the Ricther case. And Mo Greer. Compare notes. You too, Bobby. Soon as you're done with the paperwork on Tyrel Squirl, I want you on this. But I'm not calling it a task force."

"And how *do* you intend to handle the media?" Vicki asked.

"I don't want the evisceration or the removal of the heart going to the press," Kay stated.

Gunderson nodded in agreement. "And the dog bites?"

"I say we keep back as much as possible," Finn said. "The less this guy hears about himself in the news, the less likely he's gonna feel he's gotta prove something."

"Unless it's the attention he wants," Bobby suggested over the rim of his take-out cappuccino. "He might act again just to get some coverage."

Kay shook her head. "I don't think his goal is attention. He didn't leave any of these victims specifically to be found. And given the work he performed on our Jane Doe and the thing with the heart, I think he's got a plan."

Her gaze panned the spread of crime-scene photos across her desk. "No, it's not attention this guy wants," she said again. "I agree we keep back what we can, especially the heart. And the hand deformity. But we should leak the dog bites."

"Why? So he can get rid of his mutt?" Finn asked.

"Even if he does, it can't ruin our case. Doesn't matter how well he cleans up, there'll still be dog hairs in his place once we find him, and those we'll be able to match to Richter and Harris. But leaking the dog mauling might get us a lead. This girl"—Kay pointed to the photo of the Jane Doe's riddled back—"she didn't die without screaming. A lot. Put that together with a guy owning a big dog or a pit bull, and you might hook a tip from a nosy neighbor or a passerby."

"Kay's right," Vicki said, taking up her briefcase. "Let's go with it. But keep the heart and mutilation as our hold-back."

Vicki started to leave, but turned to Kay one last time. "By the way, Tyrel Squirl is starting to talk," she told her. "I guess a night at the Pen was enough to convince him to at least try to lighten the sentence he's looking at. He called for Grady in Narcotics."

"No one told me."

"You were out on the Jane Doe. I did the interview with Bobby. I wanted to hear for myself what Squirl had to say about the shooting before I started offering any deals."

"And?"

"Sounds like, with the right deal, he might give up Dante. But I need Antwon again."

"Why?"

"Something's not jibing between the two stories." Vicki shouldered her briefcase. "One of them isn't telling the whole truth. So we need to iron out some inconsistencies. When can you get the kid down here?"

Finn barely saw Kay's panic before she concealed it. No doubt she still hadn't informed Vicki that the kid was AWOL.

"Give me a couple days," Kay said. "I'll make the arrangements."

Vicki nodded. "And let me know when you have a name on this Jane Doe," she said before leaving, Gunderson and Bobby behind her.

Finn swiveled his chair back to his desk and started to clear away the containers of cold food. "So I guess all we gotta do is find a guy with a deformed hand and a pit bull," he said to Kay. "How hard can that be?"

Kay ignored his sarcasm, flipping pages in the Richter case file. In one hand she held a magnifying glass.

"Do you have the Yellow Book over there?" she asked eventually.

"What are you after?" Finn handed her the book.

"I don't know yet."

He watched as she opened the volume and riffled through the listings. "Music stores?" he asked. "You looking for a new hobby?"

"No. But maybe our killer has one." Her finger skimmed over the dozens of stores and instrument-dealer listings.

"How do you figure?"

Kay handed him the magnifying glass and the Richter file. Using the end of a pen she pointed at the upper corner of the ink transfer on the girl's cheek. "What does that look like to you?"

Finn angled the magnifying glass. The printing was blurred, the letters not only backward but completely indecipherable. "I can't make any of it out."

"This part here. Reverse it. What do you have?"

"It looks like . . . one of those squiggly music things."

"A treble clef," Kay said, and Finn remembered Kay's mother's dust-covered piano and the violin case at her father's house back in Jonesport from their visit to Maine last fall, both instruments reverently untouched since her mother's passing over twenty years ago.

"So our guy's a musician?"

"What else have we got to go on?" Kay asked, ripping out the page of listings.

"You want to case these places out? See if any of them

remembers a customer with a fucked-up hand? Not a lot of time before closing," Finn said. "I can take Slick. I know you've got that appointment."

Kay checked her watch, realizing she might have forgotten the session with her shrink if not for Finn. "Sure." She handed him the page. "And start with the stores down around Little Italy and Pratt Street."

"Why there?"

"That's where the club is. The Crypt. Where Julia Harris was likely abducted."

Finn nodded. He'd learned not to question Kay's hunches.

"Hey, Slick," he shouted across the partitions to Bobby. "Straighten your tie. You're coming with me."

"Hey, what's this I hear about yous two taking over my Richter case?" Reggie Laubach, wearing one of his bargain basement polyester suits, parked himself against the corner partition, the baffle swaying.

"We're not stealing your case, Reggie," Finn said, handing him the case file from Kay's desk. "We got a Jane Doe this morning. Might be connected. We're just going over the details."

Laubach took the file with a snort, then wiped a hand over his sparse, gelled-back hair. Finn could see Kay biting her tongue. Reggie Laubach was a lazy ass and a drunk who should have been rotated out of Homicide long before some of the veterans.

"Gunderson wants us to compare notes," Kay said. "You available tomorrow?"

Laubach shook his head. "I'm nights this week."

"So, what are you saying? It'll cut into your beauty rest?"

Laubach didn't laugh. "I'm sayin', if Gunderson signs the overtime, fine. Otherwise, I'm not dragging my ass in here for day work then have to stay all night too."

"Course not," Kay said, reaching for her jacket.

"And what the hell's that supposed to mean?" Two small gobs of spit flew from his meaty lips and landed on Kay's desk.

Kay ignored the question. "Tell me, Reggie, what did you make of the dog hairs found on the Richter girl?"

"Dog hairs?" His beefy shoulders came up into an exaggerated shrug. "They came from the lady's dog that found the body."

"And what kind of dog was that?"

"I don't know. A fucking dog."

"Well, was it little? Big? Short-haired? Long? Do you have any idea?"

Laubach's eyes narrowed. "I'll have to check my notes."

"Jesus." Kay shook her head. "A young girl was violated, murdered, and dumped in a drainage ditch, and you gotta check your notes?"

"It was a fucking dog, Delaney. Christ." He was about to push away from the partition.

"The dog was a collie, Reggie. A standard. Long, fine hair."

"So?"

"So, the hairs found on Leslie Richter were short and coarse. Like a pit bull. But I bet you didn't even bother looking at the hairs, huh? Or asking the lab if they could give you a breed type?" Kay took a step forward, closing the gap between them. "Did it occur to you to even *ask,* given that the hairs were embedded in the duct tape at the back of the victim's neck? Did you think to question how they got there when the girl was found faceup?"

Sensing things could get even uglier, Finn nudged her. "Kay, we gotta roll."

But she ignored him. So did Laubach.

"You want the fucking case, Delaney?" Laubach shoved the case file at Kay. "Here."

She accepted the binder, her eyes never leaving Laubach's as she tucked it under her arm.

"You're the one with the goddamn horseshoe up your ass, anyway," he added. "So go ahead, *you* clear it." He nodded to the wall-mounted white board at the far side of Homicide, the ongoing list of cases, organized by squads and individual detectives, the names of the victims in red or black depending on their status. Except for Texaco Washington, all the names under Kay's were in the black; all her cases closed with arrests. "I got enough red under my name."

"And it's no wonder," Kay said, as she brushed past him to leave.

"What the fuck's that mean?" Laubach called after her.

"Why don't you get your head out of your ass, Reggie, and do a little investigating once in a while?" she shouted over her shoulder. "Those names in black have nothing to do with luck."

"Yeah? Well, fuck you, Delaney!" the man's voice boomed across the floor.

"Nice, Reg. Real nice," Finn muttered as he left the cubicle. "Come on, Slick, we're rolling."

At the door Finn caught up with Kay. "Sure do have a way of making friends," he said to her, but she didn't turn to see his grin.

"Sorry, Finn, but I'm not here to make friends." She yanked open the steel fire door and started for the stairs. "I'm here for the victims. For Leslie Richter and Julia Harris. And for whoever that girl is down there in Jonesy's freezer."

21

"SO NO MORE nightmares about Eales?"

"Not for months."

"How *are* you sleeping?"

"Fine."

Constance O'Donnell shifted in her chair, crossing her long legs and arranging her Chanel jacket. From her slender fingers the Mont Blanc pen was poised over the blank page of her notebook.

"Any stress? Anxiety?"

"Not really." But Kay was lying. There was Antwon, and now Vicki wanting the kid in for a second statement.

"You know," Constance said, "you could switch your sessions to every two weeks."

For almost three years now, Kay had been coming to see the police-appointed therapist. At first it had been a departmental requirement. Losing her partner, *and* nearly her own life, Kay had known the standard policy of two visits would be long extended. For several months, still bruised and battered, she'd had to sit with the therapist weekly, watch her document pages of notes on Kay's mental state while she waited for the green light to be let back out on the streets.

But when Constance had finally signed the forms, Kay had surprised her by asking to stay on. Kay paid for the sessions herself now, so there'd be no record of it through her departmental insurance. These sessions were for her. This was her place and time every week to decompress, to let go of everything—the fear, the guilt, the anger.

Of course, in the beginning, Kay hadn't liked Constance. She'd hated the drive up to Towson, the hours wasted on the leather couch. And she'd hated the obsessive perfection of the shrink's office.

Now Kay took comfort in the order of Constance's therapy room: the neat lines of texts in the bookcases, the strategically angled furnishings, each throw pillow fluffed and purposefully placed. In the early months, Kay would crush the pillows under one elbow. Now, she made certain to straighten the pillows after each session, respecting the calm order of the room that she had come to feel a partial claim to.

"No. I'm fine coming every week," she told the therapist, as though she were doing Constance a favor by showing up each week.

Constance nodded. Pen still poised. Thirty minutes into the fifty-minute hour, and the therapist had still found nothing to document. It wasn't the first time Kay had imagined going for coffee with the therapist instead of a formal session. Coffee would be cheaper.

"And how are things with Finn?"

"The same." Kay didn't doubt that Constance sensed the tension behind her quick smile.

This morning when her pager had gone off, she'd had to reach over Finn for the phone. And when the detective had finished giving her the information about the Jane Doe, he'd asked her if Finn was with her. *"I'm not getting a response from his pager."*

"I'll swing by and pick him up," Kay had lied, before hanging up.

She and Finn had strived to keep their relationship quiet. And even though Kay worried others might know, she'd never truly suspected anyone did.

"I think the guys on the unit have figured it out," she told Constance. "Me and Finn."

"And that bothers you?"

"Of course it does. We keep our relationship out of the office, so it's no one's business."

"If it bothers you, what about a transfer?"

Kay shook her head. "Homicide's what I do. It's what I'm good at."

"And Finn?"

"I wouldn't want any other partner. We know how each other works. And I trust him."

Still, the notion of a transfer wasn't a new one. Finn had suggested it himself more than once, offering not just to go to another squad, but a completely different unit. Each time, Kay had shut the conversation down.

"So has Finn ever brought up the subject of marriage again?" Constance asked.

"No. I think he knows I'll say no." Just as she had last fall when he'd blindsided her with the proposal.

"And why no?"

Kay shrugged. "I wish I knew. Maybe it has to do with losing Spencer. Maybe it's because, with the job, I've just never seen my life that way."

"What way?"

"Settled. Structured. Normal."

"Happy?"

"I am happy." But Kay realized she didn't sound convincing. "I'm happy the way things *are.*"

Still, how often had she wished she *could* embrace a more structured life? How often had she thought that "normal" would be easier? Fact was, she'd never been one of those girls dreaming of "the day," collecting bridal magazines in a hope chest. And at thirty-seven, Kay wasn't about to start.

Constance shifted in her chair. "So is it the commitment you're afraid of?"

"I don't think so."

"Your parents had a good marriage?"

Kay nodded. "As short as it was." Two weeks after their fifteenth wedding anniversary, her mother's depleted body had lost its battle with cancer. "I don't know how happy my mother truly was, giving up her dreams to be with my father, to raise me."

"By dreams, you mean her music?"

"Yeah." She still gave lessons, but even as a kid Kay had sensed it was never truly enough.

"And you think you'd have to do the same if you married?"

"Maybe."

"What dreams won't you be able to fulfill if you committed to Finn?"

Kay didn't have an answer.

"*Do* you have dreams?"

"I'm not sure."

"You talked before about taking the sergeant's exam. Any decisions on that?"

Kay shook her head. "It'd be nice to prove myself, I guess. But it's the streets that I want. It's the streets where you make a difference, you know? Not pushing papers and signing overtime slips for your squad."

"And what about personal dreams?"

"Like what?"

"I don't know, children?"

Kay's laugh came before she could stop it. "No. It's not my thing."

"Why's that?"

"Well, I know Finn would like it, but kids . . . I wouldn't be very good at it."

"Why do you think that?"

Kay shrugged. "I'm just better off doing what I'm doing, working for the victims. Someone has to speak for them."

And someone needed to speak for the Jane Doe from Baltimore County.

"I need your input on something," Kay said, reaching for her soft leather briefcase.

"A case?"

Kay nodded and drew out this morning's photos of the Jane Doe. Photos of Leslie Richter and Julia Harris. Sixteen months ago, Constance had helped Kay understand the motive behind six brutal murders, helped Kay get inside the head of the man whose sick obsession had almost cost her her own life.

The bottom two rows of the bookcases behind Constance housed an extensive collection of texts covering psychopathology, sexual deviance, and serial killings. "An extracurricular interest," Constance had called it when Kay had first sought her advice. Today, no explanations were needed. They both understood that if Kay moved on any advice Constance gave her, she'd do so with the full awareness that it could be challenged down the road by a defense attorney.

Kay mumbled an apology now as she laid out the photos from the reservoir. Constance flinched.

"Just when you think you've seen everything," Kay said, "something like this comes along."

"Wow." Constance's voice sounded thin. "These are worse than the last case."

She was silent for a long time then, listening as Kay filled her in on the cases, on the evidence, the dog hairs, the deformed hand, until finally she sat back from the squalor of photos. "There's a lot about this that is highly organized," Constance stated.

"But look at what he did to her." Kay pushed the picture of the Jane Doe to the top of the pile. "This points to a psychosis, doesn't it? He depersonalized her, covered her face, removed her breasts. Those are usually signs of a disorganized offender, aren't they?"

Constance nodded thoughtfully, her mind processing the images before her. Then she shook her head. "You're right. But he's still organized in the disposal of the bodies, in keeping the trace evidence to a minimum. He removes the body from the primary crime scene, likely his home, to minimize detection, to separate himself from the crime. That in itself shows us he's *aware* of the criminality of his act.

"And the removal of the heart," Constance went on, "there was an element of planning there. Disorganized offenders don't generally carry out such complex tasks. He was systematic in the job even though it wasn't neat. And then you've got the abductions. As far as you've been able to tell, no one saw him, correct?"

Kay nodded, remembering Memnoch at The Crypt.

"So he's socially adept," Constance said. "He plans. He's careful. Efficient in both the abductions and the killings." She pointed to the photo of Julia Harris, taken when she was brought in to Mercy. "As far as you know, he snatched this girl from the club without force, without anyone noticing. So he's got the verbal and social skills required to charm his victims. If he's psychotic, he couldn't have coerced them, and there *would* be witnesses."

"What about the breasts?" Kay asked Constance. "He removed them as trophies, right?"

"Quite likely. They're more representative of the woman, of the 'body,' than the heart is."

Kay imagined the breasts. Did he have them in a jar in his home? In his refrigerator? A freezer?

"Or it could be your perp doesn't like women," Constance suggested. "He chooses them because he can overpower them, but then removes their breasts to defeminize them. There can be lots of reasons."

"And the heart? Is he toying with us?"

Constance shook her head. "Could be. Or there could be other motives. The heart could be symbolic. The school field could mean something to him. He could have a connection to the school, or he might live in the area. Maybe he enjoys watching his ability to outmaneuver police, and left the heart there knowing he'd be able to watch the investigation unfold in his own backyard. You could speculate forever, Kay."

Kay glanced at the clock, the timer about to go off. She started to gather the photos, stopping when she picked up the shot of postmortem bruising on Leslie Richter's body.

"But what makes someone do this?" she asked. "He beat the shit out of her, throttled her *after* she was dead. And then this girl in the woods. It's like he goes off on them once they're dead. Like something triggers this eruption of violence."

Constance clicked her pen, processing.

"It's almost like we're looking at two different personalities," Kay went on. "One, organized and careful, and the other, deranged. This couldn't be a split-personality thing or some other kind of psychological disorder, could it?"

"Possibly. He could be working through different phases of his character. It's hard to tell from just photos," Constance said as Kay slid them back into her briefcase.

"But remember, Kay, the most answers almost always come from the first victim. It's the first victim who usually has direct connections to the killer. That's where you need to go. That's where you'll find direction."

22

Journal Entry #38

I don't know what Gary Leon Ridgway was talking about when he told investigators he wished he'd had a bottomless mine shaft to drop all his victims into. Disposing of the bodies, he said, was a burden. "Took time away from the killin'."

Still, he had a good thing going, that Ridgway. Twenty-one years, over forty women, police never knew he was the Green River killer. He was doing something right. None of this bullshit about wanting to be caught.

I also like how Ridgway would take the jewelry of his victims and leave it in the women's washroom at his work. Then watch his coworkers walk around wearing the stuff from his victims. That must have been cool.

What I can't relate to, though, is the mineshaft idea.

When I think about that drive up to the reservoir, I can still remember my heart racing. And then the forest. So quiet you could hear the snow fall. And the low beams cutting through the trees . . . there was just something so peaceful about it all. Like that warm feeling after sex, when your body goes all slack. That's what it was like standing there in the middle of the forest, looking down at her in the snow and the leaves.

Probably should have dumped her in the

reservoir though. I didn't think they'd find her so fast. Would have been better to weight her down and toss her off the dam. But you have to do more than weight a body down. That's where killers go wrong. They figure a couple cement blocks will hold a body under, but it takes more than that. All those gases. You gotta make sure the body doesn't bloat. So you have to slice it open so it won't.

If it doesn't bloat, it can't float.

The Green River killer didn't know that. When he used the river, he just tossed them in, and I think a couple times he tried to bury them under rocks in the riverbed. But some fisherman would always find them bobbing down-stream.

Not that it really matters that they found her at the reservoir. They're not making any connections anyway. Nothing in the paper. No details. Only that the case has gone to the City.

Just takes one call from a phone booth to the Homicide Unit to find out who the lead investigator is: Detective Kay Delaney.

And you can find anyone on the internet these days by typing a name into a search engine. Kay Delaney gets you quite a few hits.

Two medals of honor. And for what? Getting her partner killed? Almost getting herself killed. Twice.

The City's finest.

I can't believe she hasn't made any connections yet. Maybe she needs a little help.

23

MEMORIES OF THE GIRL IN the woods this morning led Kay to Rocky's Iron Pit, her gym on Pratt. She spent forty minutes on the corner treadmill and an hour doing weights in an effort to rid herself of the images. Even driving home, Kay struggled to purge the thoughts from her mind, with little success.

When she walked through the door of her apartment, Finn was on the couch, already showered and wearing jeans and a tee. He looked good.

"I started without you," he said, waving a hand at the take-out containers from the Greek deli down on Cross Street.

When Kay kissed him, he tasted of lamb and garlic.

She found reassurance in his presence, comfort in being with someone who knew and saw what she did. It was Finn who'd stood beside her at the reservoir this morning and at the ME's office later. It was Finn who understood, as no one else could and probably better than even she did, how important it was to shed the horrors of their every day.

"Who's winning?" she asked, nodding to the TV where the Orioles and the Red Sox sat at the bottom of the seventh.

"No one. They're tied."

"I need a shower." She dropped her gym bag in the foyer and made her way to the bathroom. She pulled her sweatshirt over her head. "How'd you and Bobby do with the music stores?"

Finn followed her. "Nothing so far. We'll hit more tomorrow."

"And did you behave with young Bobby?" She shot him a smile as she started the shower.

"Of course. Slick's a good kid. Little cocky, but he'll come down a notch soon enough. I set him up with Missing Persons, see if we find anyone resembling our Jane Doe."

"Anything from her prints?"

"Not yet."

Kay stepped into the shower. Needles of hot water bit into her skin as she slid the stall door shut.

"Damn," she heard him say from the door. "I wish I'd waited."

"So do I." But after everything she'd seen today, Kay knew she had neither the mental nor the physical energy for anything more than Finn's comfort tonight.

She closed her eyes, willing the tension to ease, the images of the day to wash off her skin and down the drain.

"How was your appointment with the shrink?" Finn normally didn't ask about Kay's sessions, respecting that they were for her. But no doubt he'd figured Kay would use the session today to bounce ideas off Constance.

Through the pebbled glass stall door, Kay saw Finn's blurred silhouette leaning against the doorjamb. She lathered shampoo into her hair and filled Finn in on her theories until the broadcast cheers from Camden Yards drew Finn back to the ball game.

Ten minutes later, wearing her terry robe, Kay joined him in the living room. Finn teetered on the edge of the couch, glued to the game. Bases loaded, and Riley kicking dirt from the pitcher's mound. It wasn't looking good for the O's.

On the coffee table, between the containers of cooling takeout, sat her copy of the *Sun*. Finn had folded it to the brief coverage of the Jane Doe. Kay wondered if the killer had read it, if he was disappointed by the meager information or if he even cared about the media.

Next to the paper lay a real-estate publication, a couple of the pages dog-eared.

The TV volume exploded with cheers as Riley struck out the Red Sox batter, and Finn turned it down. When he reached for her hand, she let him draw her onto the couch next to him.

"You doing okay?" Finn asked.

Kay nodded. Silent. Accepting his comfort.

"Do you want me to leave?"

"No. It's just the case."

"Someone'll know this guy, Kay. This one's a no-brainer."

"And how many more girls do we let him kill before then?"

"Messed-up hand like his, it won't take long to find him. Trust me, someone'll know who this mope is."

But Kay *knew* it wasn't going to be that easy.

She wanted a drink but didn't keep booze in the house anymore. Drinking and being a homicide cop went hand in hand. A lot of the guys drank. It was a coping mechanism, a way to dampen the effects of the job. And for Finn, it had also dampened the pain of losing his son.

But for three years now Finn had been sober, and Kay supported that.

She pointed to the realty magazine. "What's that?"

"Just looking." Finn reached for it, fanned the pages, and pointed to one quarter-page ad.

Kay let her eyes take in the quaint Cape Cod–style house and scanned the details of the two-bedroom "handyman's special" down in Essex.

"It's on the river," Finn said. "I talked to the Realtor this afternoon, and he can show it to us tomorrow."

"Us?"

Finn took a breath. "Kay, face it, this place is too small. The boat's even smaller. I hate feeling like I'm always underfoot, you know?"

"A house for us?"

"Come on, Kay. I'm only asking that you look at the place."

"We haven't even really talked about living together."

"Well, I'm talking about it now. You're saying you're happy with this constant back-and-forth? The way things are?"

"As a matter of fact, yes." Kay stood from the couch, suddenly feeling trapped.

"Well, I'm not." Impatience clipped his words. Then, no doubt seeing her surprise, he added, "Christ, it's just a house, Kay."

When he stood, he towered over her. "How long should I wait, Kay, huh?"

She held up her hands. "Finn, I'm exhausted. Can't we talk about this tomorrow?"

"No. We're talking about it now. How long? I waited after Eales beat you down, after Spencer was killed. A whole year. I gave you the time you needed, sat on the sidelines watching you nearly self-destruct. How much longer do you need? How much longer do I wait? Just tell me, Kay, so I can mark it on the calendar."

She didn't know what to say, not when her impulse was to run, not when she couldn't explain.

"You don't get it, do you, Kay?"

"Finn—"

"I want more than this." And when he brushed past her, she could feel the anger radiating off him.

She followed.

At the foyer, he snatched his jacket from the hook.

"Finn, wait." She grabbed his arm, but he pulled away, shrugging the jacket onto his shoulders. "Don't leave. Please."

"Just tell me. Tell me when you think you'll be ready."

"I'm just not . . . I'm not ready for a house."

He shook his head, and there was a kind of surrender in his eyes. "You just don't get it. This has absolutely nothing to do with real estate, Kay."

When he turned out the door, Kay knew there was no stopping him. And like a climber looking up, powerless, at the slow fraying of a guideline, Kay felt the beginning of the unraveling.

24

Thursday, April 20

HER NAME WAS Nina Simone Gatsby.

Latents called after lunch with a hit on the Jane Doe's prints. One arrest for solicitation and another for possession had planted the twenty-four-year-old in the system.

Finn had chosen to hit the streets with Bobby this morning, understandably preferring the rookie's company over Kay's after last night's argument. Kay had called them with Gatsby's address, and an hour later, Finn and Bobby returned from the basement apartment Gatsby shared with a roommate; Nina hadn't been home since late Saturday afternoon, when she'd left for work.

Through phone calls to Gatsby's family in Richmond, Kay learned she'd come to Baltimore when she was eighteen. She'd worked other jobs for short periods, serving coffee at The Daily Grind down in Fells Point, waitressing at a Chinese place on Broadway, and most recently a stint at The Condor Club on East Baltimore Street.

The Condor Club was just one of several strip joints along The Block: the red-light district of Baltimore City, a garish, neon-lit artery lined with porno, pawnshops, and strip clubs serving up a steady supply of gyrating genitalia and watery drinks. Three blocks of human desecration and squalor running between Holliday Street and the Jones Falls, populated by prostitutes, johns, junkies, exotic dancers, and cheap-thrill seekers.

And, ironically, the entire mess lay within a stone's throw of Police Headquarters.

Kay and Finn had walked the two blocks to The Condor Club, nestled between a tattoo parlor and a fifth-rate movie house on the north side of Baltimore Street, its windows boasting sun-bleached posters of scantily clad women. The lunchtime clientele had started to trickle in, a half dozen men spacing themselves at the chest-high stage, waiting at the railing that would separate them from the dancers.

The man behind the bar was a graffitied wall of flesh, all muscle and clearly a collector of frequent-flier points at the tattoo joint next door.

"No violations here," he said, and Kay realized she and Finn had immediately been made as cops.

"We're not here about any codes." Finn pulled up a stool, drew out the mug shot of Nina Gatsby, and slid it across the bar. "Know her?"

"That's Nina. What's she gone and done now?"

"She's 'gone and done' got herself murdered," Finn said.

"No shit?" If the man felt anything over the girl's death, his wide, pocked face with its once-broken nose showed no reaction as he continued to dry glasses behind the bar.

"We need to talk to the owner," Kay said.

"So talk. You wanna know when I seen Nina last?"

"That'd be a start," Finn said, pocketing the photo.

"Saturday night."

"With all the girls you got here, you don't want to check the schedule to be sure?"

"Don't need to. I know cuz I don't usually let her work Saturday nights."

"What exactly did Nina do here?" Kay asked.

The owner nodded to the semicircular stage backed with mirrors and lights. Four smaller stages skirted it, each occupied by a vacant pole that Kay imagined saw a lot of thighs on a Saturday night.

"How long had she been dancing for you?"

"Ten months, give or take." The owner inspected a glass in the dim light. "She wasn't very good though. I had her on afternoons mostly. Lunch crowd don't care so much. But she wanted bigger tips, so I'd let her do the odd night. Brought her on late, when everyone's wasted enough not to notice her tits were too small and she didn't give enough crotch, know what I mean?" The man winked at Finn.

"No, actually I don't," Finn answered.

"How late did she work Saturday night?" Kay asked.

"Till closing." When he looked past Kay's shoulder, his eyes narrowed. "Candy! You're fucking late again," he shouted across the bar.

Kay turned in time to see the girl, her T-shirt rumpled, her hair hanging in limp tresses around her thin face.

"Sorry, Tank."

"One more time and you're fucking fired."

The girl disappeared through a door at the side of the stage.

"Did Nina leave with anyone Saturday night?" Kay asked Tank as he took up another glass.

"Yeah. Some guy."

"Anything you can tell us about him?"

"Just that he ain't a regular."

"Must get crowded in here. How do you remember him in particular?"

"He stood out."

"How's that?"

"He was a pretty boy."

"Go on," Kay prompted.

Tank licked his lips. "College. Preppy. Dark hair, bit of a ponytail. Like yours," he said, pointing to Finn.

"Did you see his hands?" Finn asked him.

"Huh? His hands? Can't say as I noticed."

"Did he buy drinks?"

"Sure."

"At the bar?"

"Yeah."

"So he handed you money?"

"Look, Detective, if you just ask me what it is you're after we can stop doing the two-step here."

"Did the guy have a deformed hand?"

Tank seemed to take a mental stumble. "Not that I noticed. But I wasn't at the bar the whole time." He checked his watch. "Gimme a minute."

When he came out from behind the bar, Tank seemed even bigger. He marched through the maze of tables to the side door at the back of the stage, and within seconds Kay heard muffled yelling. No doubt Candy was at the brunt of it.

"If that was our boy who picked up Gatsby Saturday night," Kay said to Finn, "then he kept her twenty-four hours before killing her."

"Didn't do that with the other two. So what are you thinking? This guy's fantasy's changing?"

Kay shook her head. "Or he's working toward something else. Either way, he's getting bolder."

There was more shouting backstage, and then the music started, the grinding pulse vibrating across the dingy bar.

"Why am I not seeing the connection between these victims?" Kay said, raising her voice no louder than necessary. "Two schoolgirls, and the third a stripper. Gatsby's picked up here, Harris is most likely picked up at an underage club in Little Italy, and Richter . . . who knows where he grabbed her? What's the link?"

"Maybe there isn't one. Maybe they're random."

Kay shook her head. *"The most answers almost always come from the first victim,"* Constance had reminded her yesterday. *"It's the first victim who usually has direct connections to the killer."*

"Gatsby was random," Kay theorized then. "Richter wasn't. He's hitting farther from home, targeting girls from different socioeconomic statuses. This guy, Finn, he knows what he's doing."

Finn nodded across the bar, and Kay turned in time to see Tank returning. Behind him, Candy and another girl slunk out onto the stage, each taking one of the two front poles. In their thongs and scanty bras pushing up their silicone, the girls' smiles looked painful as they began gyrating.

"So this guy with Nina," Finn asked as the owner stepped behind the bar again, "was he here alone?"

Tank nodded, took up his towel, and wiped more glasses. "Far as I could tell. Sat on his own for a couple hours, just him and his drink, checkin' out the girls. He was on his cell phone a few times. When Nina got off the floor, they got friendly, then left together."

"Did Nina act like she knew him?"

"Don't think so."

"So he paid for her?"

Tank gave Finn a look. "Like I said, got no violations here. My girls are dancers. That's it. You want a piece of ass, you go out to the street."

"Right." Kay failed at concealing her sarcasm. "So Nina walks him to his car out of the goodness of her heart."

"What the girls do after hours ain't my business."

"Would you recognize this guy?" Finn asked.

"Sure."

Kay slid her card across the bar. "Then you'll give us a call if he comes in again, right?"

He picked up the card in one meaty hand. "You think he's the son of a bitch killed Nina?"

"Let's just say he's a person of interest in the investigation," Kay said.

Tank tucked the card under the bar. "Yeah. I'll call."

Leaving the murky bar behind them, Kay had to squint when they stepped out onto Baltimore Street.

"So where to now?" Finn asked. "You want to see how Slick's making out with those music stores?" Kay hated that Finn's voice sounded so neutral.

When Finn checked his watch, she wondered if he'd canceled the appointment with the Realtor in Essex.

Last night, after he'd left her apartment, Kay wanted to go after him. But she hadn't known what to say. So, she'd turned to what she was best at. In her home office, she'd sorted through the photocopied reports from the Richter case. The dead needed to take priority.

Seeing Finn in the light of day now, Kay truly wished she'd handled last night differently.

"I want more than this," Finn had said. *"I need more."*

And he was right. This had nothing to do with real estate.

For the past two years, Finn *had* been patient. Eales was behind her. So were Joe Spencer and Valerie Regester.

And even though she would carry the guilt of those deaths forever, Kay had begun to forgive herself, as much as she could. She was moving on, feeling stronger.

Maybe Finn knew more than she did. Maybe it was time for more.

And Kay wondered if there was still a chance for them to look at the property in Essex together.

"Kay?" Finn touched her shoulder. "Where to?"

She scanned The Block. Down near Gay Street a pimp was giving one of his girls a hard time. A black Lincoln with tinted windows lurched roughly to the opposite curb and let out another hooker. She stumbled to the sidewalk, righting a bra strap and belting out a curse as the big car sped away.

"To the beginning," Kay answered. "We need to go back to his first kill. To Leslie Richter and his connection to her."

25

HE WAITED FOR HIS ANGEL.

Skimming the net across the pool's still surface, Paul Graves lifted blackened leaves and winter debris from the murky water. After each sweep, he flicked out the net into the wheelbarrow he'd parked just off the Saltillo-tile deck, his movements systematic.

The smell of decaying leaves rose with each tap of the net. The musty odor roused the memories. The girl in the woods. The winter-rotted leaves turning under his boots.

He'd read once that smell was the strongest human sense linked to memory. "Odor memory" they called it. Olfaction, he'd read, was the sensory modality physically closest to the limbic system, the primitive part of the brain that controls memory, emotions, and behavior. As a result, odor-evoked memories were unusually emotionally potent.

When he inhaled the scent of the leaves now, his heart raced and his gut tightened. He tried to push the memories away.

Past the eight-foot wooden fence he looked at his Angel's house, up to where the second-floor blinds were half-louvered. His Angel's bedroom.

A pair of pigeons wheeled in the air over her house, then landed on the roof, cooing softly. The male was a big gray slatey ducking and bobbing his head, strutting along the peak of the shingled roof in boastful courtship of the female. She looked like a washed-out Staf Van Reet, but was clearly a mutt. Still, he took it as a sign. He watched the pair and contemplated the fact that pigeons mated for life.

He thought of the room at his uncle's house. It was ready.

When the birds took to the air again, Graves turned to the buckets of chemicals. Using a test strip he monitored the pH and alkalinity of the pool and set to work preparing the liquid shock and an algaecide, then switched on the pump.

Fifteen minutes later, as the debris stirred and the smell of chlorine filled the air, a dark shadow churned in the murkiness of the deep end. Graves squinted against the sun's glare on the pool's surface and extended the telescopic pole.

Clouds of debris parted in the wake of the net as Graves sifted it along the bottom until finally feeling the weight of the object. The pole bowed as he guided the object along the side of the pool, up the slow grade of the bottom. In the three-foot depth of the shallow end he knew what it was.

A drowned rabbit, its body rigid and waterlogged. Graves shortened the pole, doubling its strength, and fished the dead animal from the cold water, flipping it into the wheelbarrow.

For several long minutes, he stood over the small carcass, staring into one wide, clouded eye. He wasn't sure what compelled him, but he stroked its wet fur and stiff ears for a moment before covering its death grimace with a handful of soaked leaves.

He looked again to his Angel's house. Hoped to see her. He thought of the room. Imagined her in it. And Graves knew it couldn't be much longer.

26

THE HALLS OF LANGLEY were about to erupt.

Finn checked his watch as Jillian Somerville led them down the corridors of lockers to the music room.

"You can't know how much I wish I could help," Somerville said over the staccato of her heels on the polished floors. "But I just don't know anyone with the kind of handicap you're describing."

They'd sat in the headmaster's office for twenty minutes as she went through personnel files—faculty, custodial, grounds, cafeteria—hoping to jog her memory on any employee, past or present, who might have had a club hand. The name Nina Gatsby had also drawn a blank.

"I'll consult with the staff," she added.

Kay had said little in the meeting and even less during the drive up to Langley. Finn had seen her gaze stray to the real-estate brochures he'd tossed on the dash yesterday, and he wished he'd thrown them out. He'd pushed too hard last night. Knew better than to corner Kay like that.

He should have learned that lesson after the rejection he'd received when he'd asked her to marry him last fall.

He'd done it when Kay had taken him out East to meet her father.

He and Kay's dad had hit it off, taking the boat out early each morning and hauling up the catch. But Kay had seemed uncomfortable from the moment Finn had stepped onto the front porch of the clapboard house overlooking the harbor of Chandler Bay and shaken Frank Delaney's net-calloused hand.

At first Finn had thought Kay's unease was from being home: she seemed out of her element in the small fishing village, away from the streets, without her gun at her hip. But by the end of the visit, Finn knew the real reason. It was his growing relationship with her father that unsettled Kay, as though she worried they'd become too close.

Replaying that week, Finn was sorry he'd asked Frank Delaney for his daughter's hand first, wished he'd kept it between him and Kay.

"You shouldn't have asked him," she'd said on the drive back to Baltimore, the ring Finn had bought before the trip sitting on the center console, still in its case. "You'll just get his hopes up."

What Finn remembered most about the eleven-hour drive home was the silence. Even when Kay had relinquished the wheel and curled up in the passenger seat, he'd doubted she was sleeping. When he finally pulled to the curb outside her apartment that night, she'd kissed him and apologized, mumbling that it was too much, too soon. It was only when she'd gotten out of the car that Finn spoke. "You know," he'd said, "your father wasn't the only one getting his hopes up."

And the next day, back at work, Kay had been business as usual. As though Finn's proposal had never happened.

"Mr. Bruger's classroom is just up here to the left," Jillian

Somerville said as she guided them. "He has no students in the last period."

The classroom smelled old to Finn, of tarnished brass and old wood. In a broad shaft of sun from the tall, west-facing windows, a baby grand piano sat under a thin veneer of dust. Behind it, a tight bank of computers and electronic keyboards dominated the side wall.

Mr. Bruger sat at his desk at the front of the classroom. He had birdlike features, and Finn thought of the crows three mornings ago when the heart had been discovered.

Somerville made introductions. "Mr. Bruger is one of the founders of the annex program we have with the Peabody Conservatory," she explained. "He knew Leslie quite well."

"She was taking a special class at Peabody," Bruger explained, once Somerville left them. "Digital music technology. We can offer only a taste of it here."

Finn saw the shift in Kay's eyes, knew she was thinking of the electronic music on the 911 tape.

"She also received some exposure playing with Peabody's junior orchestra. A student like Leslie . . . it's what makes teaching worth it. That one in a million."

From the corridor, the final bell buzzed and Finn heard the halls begin to fill.

"Did Leslie have any friends at Peabody? Any Hopkins students she may have hung out with?" Kay asked.

Bruger shook his head. "Not that she spoke of."

"She would have told you if she had?"

"I'd like to think so, yes."

Just then the music-room door swung open.

"Sorry, Mr. Bruger." Amber Estcott stopped in the doorway, her blond hair flung over one slender shoulder. The uniform skirt seemed even shorter today than it had when he and Kay had interviewed her two days ago.

"Hi, Detectives." Amber squared her backpack on her shoulders. "I didn't mean to interrupt, Mr. Bruger, I just came for my assignment."

Bruger nodded, and the girl crossed the room to a printer. She sorted through the papers before extracting several sheets. When she turned again, her eyes were on Finn.

"Nice to see you again, Detectives." She started for the door.

Finn stopped her. "It's Amber, right?"

The girl nodded.

"Can we have a word with you?"

"Sure." Her smile was not as quick and easy today. "I have volleyball practice though."

"We'll walk with you," Finn offered.

The halls were bedlam. Students tangled in the corridors, shouting and jeering, locker doors slamming. Kay had to fall in step behind them as they elbowed their way through the wave of bodies.

Finn lowered his voice. "We're just wondering, Amber, since you go to Peabody, if you know of any friends Leslie might have had there?"

Amber shook her head as she walked. "I doubt it. Like I said before, Leslie pretty much kept to herself. Even at Peabody. She'd just go to class, then catch a cab home. At least, whenever I saw her."

"Were you in any of her Peabody classes?"

"Just the one. My digital and electronic music class." Amber steered them to the right, into a quieter corridor, past a science classroom, the smell of formaldehyde and the humid odor of dead specimens wafting out the open door.

"We're curious about this guy you saw in the sports car, picking up Leslie," Finn said. "You have no idea who he is?"

"No. But . . ." The girl stopped in the hall and turned to face him. She chewed one corner of her lip. Uncertain. "I think I saw him again."

"Recently?" Kay asked.

She nodded. "Yesterday."

"Where?"

"Here."

"Was he picking someone up?"

"I don't think so. It was after practice. The same car parked across the street. I wasn't really sure it was him at first, until he drove away."

"So did you get a look at him this time?"

"Sorta. He was just sitting there, the engine running. I tried to get a look at him, but I didn't wanna get too close, you know?"

She hesitated again, and Finn couldn't be sure if she was trying to remember or if she was debating how much to share.

"Come on, Amber," he urged. "It could be important."

"Okay, well, all I saw was that he was dark, you know?"

"You mean black?"

"No, dark, like maybe Hispanic or Italian. And he had black hair."

"Short? Long?"

"Long, I guess. But not ratty or anything."

Finn thought of the owner back at The Condor Club, and his description of the guy who'd picked up Nina Gatsby Saturday night. "Amber, was his hair tied back, in a ponytail? Like mine maybe?"

"No." She shook her head and turned to keep walking. "I'm really sorry. I did try to get a look at him. I guess I should have gotten his license plate number huh?"

"It would help. If you see him again," Finn said.

Amber stopped at a set of doors and opened one. There was the sound of sneakers squeaking against the maple flooring of the gymnasium. "I really gotta go," she said. "Coach gets all in your face if you're late."

Finn held the door for her, but it was Kay who stopped Amber this time.

"One more question," Kay said. "You haven't seen anybody around or know somebody who's got a club hand, do you?"

"A what?"

"A deformed hand," Finn clarified as confusion settled across the girl's perfect features.

She shook her head. "No. Why? Does the guy who killed Leslie have a deformed hand?"

"It's just someone we need to talk to," Kay said. "Thanks for your time, Amber."

The girl looked unsettled when she finally turned into the gym and disappeared around the collapsible stands.

"What's on your mind, Kay?" Finn asked as the gymnasium door swung closed. He could almost see the thought process unfolding behind her eyes as they headed out.

"What if the connection is Peabody?" she asked.

"I'm listening."

"You've got the electronic-music class Richter was taking there. And then the music on the 911 tape. The receipt in the bag used to kill her."

"You think her killer knew her through the class?"

Kay nodded slowly. "It's definitely worth a trip to the Peabody."

In the main corridor, the din of students rose. Kay was smoothing her jacket over her gun's holster as she rounded the corner, one step ahead of Finn, when a student broadsided her. Kay caught herself on Finn.

Behind the mop of thick, curly hair, the kid looked like a senior. The Ravens starter jacket—two sizes too large—sagged off his thin frame, as he staggered several steps backward, staring at Kay as he did. Finn caught the flash of dark eyes.

"Hey, buddy, an apology, maybe?" Finn called out.

But the kid turned with a sneer. Finn heard him mumble "Five-oh" to a friend before he was swallowed up by the chaos of students.

"Guess they're not that far from the streets after all," Finn said to Kay. "You okay?"

"Yeah. Let's just get out of here."

It wasn't until they reached the Lumina that Kay turned to Finn again. "You know, if the connection *is* Peabody, if that's where our killer is, then we've got a shitload of faculty and staff to interview."

But an even darker thought moved through Finn now. *"And* students, Kay."

27

THE PEABODY SAT in the heart of Baltimore's historic and cultural district of Mount Vernon Place, ten blocks up from the Inner Harbor. The Institute's main building dominated the southeast corner overlooking four garden squares and the Washington Monument tower. The neighborhood boasted cafés and galleries, restaurants, and an eclectic mix of brownstones. Tires thumped as cars took the cobblestoned roundabout circling the white-marble memorial to the first president.

Kay and Finn had spent three hours within the halls of Peabody, tracking down the preparatory dean, the registrar, and finally two of Leslie Richter's instructors. All their interviews confirmed Amber Estcott's description of Leslie's minimal interaction with the Peabody students. A quiet girl whose focus had been devoted solidly to her music, priming herself for an entrance scholarship to Peabody or any top-level music institution she might have chosen.

They'd also asked about anyone with a deformed hand, but no one could recall there ever being a student with the disfigurement they described. Nor had Nina Gatsby appeared to have had any affiliation with the Institute.

On the main steps, Kay's cell phone went off.

"Delaney."

"Kay, it's Bobby." She could tell he wasn't happy. "Listen, this music-store thing, it's a wild-fucking-goose chase. No one knows what the hell I'm talking about . . . some freak with a fucked-up hand."

"You hit all the stores?"

"Yeah."

The digital connection crackled briefly and Kay guessed Bobby was driving. "So I'm over here on the west side. Been asking a few of the corner boys about Dante. No one's seen him. But I thought you should know"—more crackling—"been talk on the street of seeing your boy around these parts."

Kay felt the tension take over.

"Or did you already know Wattage ditched Dundalk?" Bobby asked.

She hesitated. "Yeah."

"And you didn't think I should know? How long's he been AWOL?"

"I'll bring Antwon in."

"Would that be before or *after* Dante whacks him? He's *my* witness, Kay. *My* homicide, remember? You might think we do things different with the Feebs over in Redrum, but we tend to prefer our witnesses *alive.*"

"Bobby, I said I'll bring him in."

"Not if I see the kid first. And I won't be near as gentle as you." A last burst of crackling and Bobby ended the call.

"Slick find out about Antwon?" Finn asked.

"Fuck." Kay snapped her cell phone shut.

"You wanna go look for the kid?" Finn asked, taking the steps down to Mount Vernon Place.

Kay shook her head. "Gatsby's the priority right now." Besides, after seeing how close she'd come to losing the kid by pushing him the other night, Kay had already decided she needed to let Antwon call on his own.

"Maybe we need to talk to the nighttime staff at The Condor Club and see if any of them remembers more about this guy Gatsby left with," Finn said as she followed him to where they parked on Charles. "What time did the owner say he saw her leave?"

Kay stopped, withdrew her police notebook from her jacket pocket, its card-stock cover scraping against something. Handing Finn the spiral-bound notebook, Kay fished into her pocket.

"What is it?" Finn asked, no doubt seeing her confusion.

Between her fingers the small metal object felt foreign. She let it roll into her palm and then Kay recognized the teardrop earring. She turned the gold piece over, the diamond glinting. The post was bent, and the butterfly holder was missing.

Finn took the piece and inspected it.

Kay's pulse quickened as she looked back up the street at the Peabody. "This is Leslie Richter's earring."

"Are you sure?"

"I recognize it from the photos. And they found only one on her. Finn, someone put this in my pocket."

Staring at the gold earring, Kay's mind stumbled back over the past few hours.

"And the only person who could have done that, the only person who could have had this, is her killer, right?" she added.

Her mind raced. She barely heard Finn mutter, "Christ, Kay. That means . . ."

She nodded.

He'd kept the piece of jewelry. Carried it with him.

A chill swept over her as she imagined the earring in his hand, clenched tight. He'd come within a breath of her, maybe even touched her. The Condor Club. Langley. The Peabody.

And Kay wondered if Leslie Richter's killer had smiled when he'd slipped it into her pocket.

28

WHEN THE ELEVATOR DOORS had opened on the eleventh floor of the Mercy Medical Center's Tower Building twenty minutes ago, Kay had had to force back the memories. The smells and sounds took her back to a time she'd rather forget, lying in a hospital bed for almost two weeks after Eales had beaten her to within inches of death.

She remembered Finn sitting at her bedside, there when she woke, there as the drugs kicked in and she faded again. She remembered the day he'd told her about Eales's surrender, and the recovery of her duty weapon. The gun that had killed Spence. And she remembered finally asking Finn to stop coming, her shame too great to face anyone.

She remembered Gunderson too, standing at the foot of the bed, refusing to accept her shield. *"You get your ass outta here, Delaney, and back on the streets, you hear me?"* he'd growled at her, tossing her badge wallet onto her sheets. *"I'm not losing two good cops to that son of a bitch."*

Now, as Kay sat by Julia Harris's bed, she tried not to imagine herself in that bed. A victim of violence just like Harris. Only, Harris wasn't here because of her own cocky bravado.

The girl's hand was warm beneath hers. And as Kay watched the cascade of vitals blip across the monitors and listened to the low hiss of the ventilator, she prayed. Her faith had dimmed the day her mother died—Kay only thirteen years old and already a fierce defiance of God—but today she prayed anyway. She wanted Harris to survive. It wasn't just so the girl might tell them something about her attacker. There was more to it than that, for Kay.

The good guys need to win once in a while.

Kay's other hand went to her jacket pocket. She tumbled Richter's earring through her fingers and thought of the man who'd killed her, who'd raped and beaten Harris, and who had boldly brushed up against Kay today. He knew who she was, had to be following the media coverage. Imagining the sick thrill he must have felt when slipping the earring into her pocket raised a new anger within her.

Kay started when the door opened. The room's hush was suddenly broken by the paging system and phones from the nurses' station.

"Oh. Sorry." The girl in the doorway pulled up short, her eyes flitting from Kay to Harris and back again, then dropping to the floor as she started to retreat from the room.

"Wait." Kay stood. "You're Maeve, aren't you?"

Kay almost didn't recognize her, but on second glance the resemblance to her father was uncanny. Her hair—as black as Finn's—had been chopped into a ragged, haphazard cut that looked slept in. Still she was a striking girl. Her complexion was fair, not Finn's black-Irish olive, in spite of the hours Kay knew Maeve put in on the tennis courts each week. But her tight mouth, the defiant tilt of her chin, and the narrowing of those dark eyes revealed the seriousness Kay knew Maeve inherited from her dad.

"I recognize you from the photos. On your dad's desk. I work with your dad. We're . . . we're partners."

As the door closed behind her, Maeve slouched under the weight of her sports bag slung over one shoulder. A wariness crept into her eyes when she accepted Kay's handshake across Harris's supine body.

Maeve's hand was slim and cool in hers, and Kay found it suddenly odd that this was the first time she'd met Finn's daughter.

Seeing her now, in the flesh, Kay realized that all of that could be about to change. And in that brief moment, with Maeve's hand lingering in hers, Kay could almost envision a life with Finn, the house in Essex, and maybe even his daughter becoming a greater part of their life.

"I'm Detective Delaney. Kay," she said as Maeve withdrew her hand.

"I know."

Animosity bristled in the teen's attitude, and Kay suspected Maeve already knew of Kay's relationship with her father.

"Your father speaks very highly of you. And your tennis career," Kay ventured.

One corner of Maeve's mouth turned down. A tic from Finn.

"So you're a friend of Julia's?" Kay asked.

"Yeah." The girl's eyes softened by a degree as she looked to her friend.

"I'm sorry about what happened to your friend," Kay offered.

Maeve nodded. And when her gaze returned, the wariness was back. "Look, I can come back—"

"No." Kay circled the bed, feeling suddenly as if she were the one intruding. "You stay. I was about to leave anyway."

But Maeve stopped her at the door. "Detective Delaney?" She fidgeted with the strap of her sports bag and chewed at a nail. "Why are you here?"

Kay looked to Harris, the bandages, the wires running to the machines. "Your father and I are trying to find the man who did this."

Maeve nodded. Pensive.

"Do you know anything that could help us, Maeve?"

"Nope."

"You go to the same school, right?"

"Yeah."

"Do you know if Julia had a boyfriend?"

Maeve dropped her bag and jammed her hands into the front pockets of her low-riding, black jeans. Kay caught the glimpse of the navel ring just below her short T-shirt and wondered if Finn knew about it.

"No, she didn't," Maeve answered.

"I talked to the bartender at The Crypt," Kay said, "the club where Julia was seen last. Did you know she was going?"

Maeve shook her head, stared at her sneakers.

"I was told she was there with someone. She didn't tell you about going there with a friend?"

"No."

"Did she go to The Crypt a lot?"

"No idea."

"All right." Kay gave her a smile, but Maeve wasn't looking. "Well, thanks. It was nice meeting you, Maeve." When Kay reached out to touch the girl's arm, she finally looked up. "I'm really sorry."

"Uh-huh."

She left Maeve then, but when the door swung shut behind her, Kay paused at the small window and watched Finn's daughter sit next to Julia on the narrow bed.

Clearly, as she took her friend's hand, Maeve didn't know she was being watched. Or she didn't care.

Still, Kay didn't move from the door. She watched as Maeve brushed her friend's cheek with her fingertips, caressing her. There was a rare tenderness about the touch, not something Kay would have expected from a girl. And then, when Maeve leaned in and pressed a kiss to the girl's lips, Kay felt like a voyeur.

29

"BUT YOU'RE NOT calling this a task force?" Reggie Laubach filled one of the extra chairs Gunderson had dragged into his office.

The eight of them crammed into the sergeant's office, reviewing the cases behind closed doors. Gunderson, Vicki, Kay, Finn, Bobby, Mo Greer, Laubach, and Stuart White. Whitey, Laubach's partner on the Richter case, was a tall, reedy black cop, who—like Laubach—seemed to be skating through the last of his career to retirement. Kay suspected that, left in the hands of Laubach and Whitey, Leslie Richter's murder might never have stood the chance of being closed.

"So what about overtime, then?" Laubach asked, scraping the dirt from under his nails.

Gunderson ignored Laubach's last question. "I'm only asking that you all collaborate. Obviously we have connections here. But if we call this a task force," he said, leaning back and lacing his fingers behind his head, "we're going to get too much attention from the media. We wanna keep this at a simmer. What about the dog angle?"

"We let Palmer from the *Sun* play that detail," Finn said, referring to the brief mention in today's paper of the pitbull mauling on their latest victim. "No phone calls on it yet."

"Maybe we need to run it bigger," Gunderson suggested. "Run it through Jane."

"And still keep the whole thing at a simmer?" Bobby asked.

Kay went over the dates in her head: Richter in February, Harris five weeks later, and Nina Gatsby not even three weeks after her. "Maybe we *shouldn't* be simmering this."

"What do you mean?" Vicki asked. "Give him the attention he wants?"

"No. I still don't think this is about attention."

"Then what about the earring he slipped into your pocket?"

"It's not the media's attention he's after. It's ours. He's playing with us," Kay said.

"He's playing with *you*," Finn corrected, and Kay heard the protectiveness in his voice.

"He's telling us that he knows," she said. "Telling *me* that he knows who I am, but I don't know who he is."

"So what are you proposing, Kay?" Gunderson asked.

"He's toying with us, so I say we toy back. I think we should talk to this guy. Through the press. He's obviously following the story enough to know that Finn and I are investigating Nina Gatsby's murder. By planting Richter's earring in my pocket, he's either showing off, or he's assuming we already know the connection between these murders."

"You realize, this could be someone you've already talked to, Kay," Vicki said. "You've been asking a lot of questions about all three girls. It's from your questioning that he could know you've made the connection."

Kay had already considered that possibility and cringed at the thought that she could actually have spoken with the man responsible for the three murders, could have looked him square in the eye and hadn't recognized the cold madness lurking beneath.

"So if you're going to toy with this guy, what is it you want to give to the media?" Gunderson asked her.

On the drive from Mercy back to Headquarters, Kay had already felt the plan begin to root, and now, in her sergeant's stuffy office, it blossomed.

"Julia Harris is a live victim," she explained. "Obviously we keep her name out of this for now. But I think it's time we publicly link Richter and Gatsby. At this point, we've got nothing to lose."

"Nothing, 'cept we'll be under a fucking microscope once they know we got a serial killer cutting up women," Laubach said.

"What else?" Gunderson asked.

Kay dropped off the corner of the table and paced the short length of the office. "If these three are his only murders . . . attempted murders," she corrected, "then he's escalating. The times between these attacks are decreasing. He could already be targeting his next victim. What we need is more time."

"What we *need* is to get this guy riled up. Flush him out by telling the media he's an impotent fuckup," Laubach suggested, relying on the tired, textbook stereotypes.

Kay was already shaking her head. "And get another girl killed? No. What we need to do is make him back off, not act out. Buy us some time."

"And how do we do that?" Finn asked.

"We tell the media that we *have* a suspect, that he's wanted for questioning. Let this guy think we know who he is. If he believes we're onto him, he's going to get nervous. Lay low."

"Unless he's already got his next girl," said Laubach.

The fat-ass had a point, Kay thought, but she hoped he was wrong. Was counting on it.

She caught Vicki's nod then. "I think you're onto something, Kay."

"We need to bring up the Peabody connection. The music is the key," Kay explained. "We've got the sales receipt, the music on the 911 tape, and Richter's ties to the Conservatory. If we play the Peabody card right, it'll add more weight to this whole strategy."

"*If* he's from Peabody," Gunderson said. "It's a hunch."

Kay met her sergeant's eyes then. "When you run out of cold, hard evidence," she said, "it's the hunches you've gotta play."

Gunderson's chair snapped back into position, and he reached for the phone. "All right. I'll set it up with Jane."

"Wait." Kay stopped him. "I think it needs to be me. It's *me* he's playing with, *my* face he's looking for."

"Okay."

"And I'm not giving Gallagher anything," she added.

"Who else're you gonna trust with this?" Finn asked.

"I'll go to Channel Thirteen."

"Silver?" Gunderson asked, referring to Jane Gallagher's direct rival.

Kay nodded and was immediately grateful that Gunderson didn't put up a fight.

"All right," he said, standing at last. "It's your call, Kay. Get a hold of Silver and play this through him. Get it on the air tonight. And nothing else goes to the press unless it's through Kay, got it?" he said to the rest of them as they filed out.

Outside the sergeant's office, Vicki stopped her. "Kay, I know you're tied up with this, but I need Antwon in here."

Past Vicki's shoulder Kay caught Bobby's stare. Wondered how long he'd bite his tongue for her.

"You want me to send Bobby down to get him from Dundalk?" Vicki asked.

"No." Kay's eyes never left Bobby's. "I'll make the time."

Back at their cubicle, Finn was already pulling Rick Silver's number off the Rolodex. When he handed the card to her, it was clear he'd overheard. "After Silver, do you want me to help you look for the kid?"

Kay appreciated the offer, but shook her head. "Actually, I think you need to see your daughter."

Confusion crossed his face.

"I saw her today, Finn. At the hospital." Kay's eyes went to the photo tacked to the fabric of Finn's partition. Taken courtside, the photo captured the sixteen-year-old smashing a ball with a racquet that looked far too big for her slender hands. The chopped hair was tucked under a white cap, and her face was as pale and serious as Kay had seen earlier in the dim light of the hospital room.

"Did you introduce yourself?" Finn asked.

"I didn't need to."

More silence.

"You should talk to her," she said again.

"About us?"

"About Harris."

He seemed disappointed.

"I think . . ." Kay thought of the kiss she'd witnessed. "I think there's more behind Maeve going to the hospital every day."

"What do you mean?"

She guessed Finn had no idea, but it wasn't her place to tell him about his daughter's sexuality. After all, it could be the very reason Maeve had been pushing her father away the past couple of years.

"Just talk to your daughter, Finn."

30

FINN PARKED BEHIND Angie's Subaru, the Aquarium's "Have you hugged a dolphin today?" bumper sticker glaring in the low beams.

He could see Maeve's lights on the second floor. Downstairs, he caught the movement of the living-room curtains, knew Angie had seen him pull in. Through the open window of the Lumina the earthy smells from Leakin Park brought with them a familiarity. And regret.

His gaze fell to the realty brochures on the dash of the car.

He'd left Kay at Headquarters, negotiating with Rick Silver over the phone. He thought of the awkward smile she'd flashed him when he'd left. He thought of the confusion on her face last night, the near panic, when he'd mentioned the property in Essex. And he thought of Frank Delaney back in Jonesport.

"Be nice to know a good boy like you was lookin' out after my daughter," Delaney had said when Finn had made his intentions known to the old man. And then later, on the salt-encrusted fishing boat: *"Her mother woulda liked you, Danny Finnerty."*

Finn snatched up the realty brochures and left the car. At the end of the driveway, he shoved the publications into the trash can, before heading to the house.

"You okay?" Angie asked when she greeted him at the door.

"Yeah. Why?"

"You look . . . tired." She settled a hand on his arm.

"I'm fine." He nodded up the stairs. "Does she know I'm coming?"

"I told her. You know how she hates surprises." Angie smiled and Finn knew she was remembering seven-year-old Maeve's tears at the first, and only, surprise birthday party they'd ever thrown for their daughter.

He found Maeve in her room, flopped across her bed with a calculus text. She still wore her tennis shorts and the faded Wimbledon sweatshirt Angie had bought her two summers ago. Along the angles of the east-facing dormer a poster of Venus Williams faced an even larger one of Amelie Mauresmo. And beneath it, a racquet signed by the tennis star.

Maeve snapped the headphones from her ears. "Hey, Dad."

Finn paced the small room, wondering how he could be more intimidated by his own daughter than the street thugs he dealt with daily.

"Heard you were at the hospital today," he said.

Maeve focused on the open text. "Did your girlfriend tell you?" Her tone was harsh.

Finn didn't know what surprised him more: the contempt in his daughter's voice or that she knew about his relationship with Kay.

"How—"

"God, Dad, it's no secret. Even Mom knows." Maeve was silent as she watched him for a response, then her voice softened. "Gotta hand it to you though, she's really pretty."

Sitting on the edge of the bed, Finn snapped her textbook shut.

"Well, my pretty girlfriend said I should talk to you."

"About what?" Maeve rolled over and drew her legs under her, sitting cross-legged in the middle of the bed. For a second he imagined her five years old, sitting the same way, only with stuffed animals surrounding her instead of tennis paraphernalia, wide-eyed and in love with a father who could do no wrong.

"I thought you could tell me," he said. "Kay said I should ask you about your visits to the hospital."

There was a change in her eyes that Finn couldn't put his finger on.

"Is there something you should be telling me, Maeve?"

"About what?"

"Julia Harris."

"She's a friend," Maeve said, rolling her eyes, and Finn wondered if she knew how much he hated that. She pushed herself off the bed, and flopped into her desk chair. "What do you want, Dad?"

He circled to the other side of the bed, positioning himself closer to her. "If you're such good friends, then maybe you can tell me what she was doing at a club like The Crypt."

Maeve shrugged.

"Did she go clubbing a lot?" he asked.

"I don't know."

And then Finn saw the defensiveness come up. He'd have to tread lightly.

"She'd need fake ID to get into The Crypt," he said. "Any idea how she would have gotten that?"

Maeve shook her head.

"Do many of the kids at your school have fake ID?"

She shrugged. "I guess so."

"They get it through a student there, don't they?"

Maeve shrugged again, chewed at a fingernail.

"Do you have one?"

"Everyone's got one, Dad."

"I'll take that as a yes?"

Maeve stood suddenly, as though needing to put space between them, and moved to the dormer window. Her nod was barely perceptible. In the dark pane, Finn watched her reflection. Couldn't remember his daughter ever looking so sad.

He joined her, placed one hand on her slim shoulder, and felt her tension. "Talk to me, Maeve. I promise you're not in trouble."

She chewed on her lip.

"Have you ever been to any of those clubs?"

Another nod.

And then Finn knew. "You were with Julia that night, weren't you?"

When her gaze caught his in the window's reflection, Finn thought she was going to cry.

She turned. "That was the first and only time, Dad. I swear. I've never done anything like that before."

"And Julia?"

"It was her first time too. Other kids go to The Crypt all the time. We just wanted to see what it was about."

"Did you drink?"

"One beer. I didn't even finish it."

"And Julia?"

"She only had one too. But she wasn't feeling so good, so I said we should go home."

"But you didn't?"

Maeve shook her head. She sat on the dormer's window seat, staring at her hands trembling in her lap. "This guy wanted me to dance. I didn't want to, but Julia made me. She said she wanted me to have fun. And when I finished . . . she was gone."

"Did you see her leave?"

"I didn't see anything, Dad. The dance floor was so packed."

"And you didn't ask anyone?"

"Course I did. The bartender said he saw her go to the bathrooms. I checked, but she wasn't there. And when I got back to the bar, some girl told me Julia had left. Said she asked her to tell me she'd cab it home."

"And is that something Julia would have done? Just leave you there?"

"I don't know. Like I said, we never did anything like that before. But when I got home, and she didn't answer her cell, and then she wasn't in class the next morning . . . that's when I knew something was wrong."

Tears streaked Maeve's cheeks now, and Finn sensed her relief at having finally told someone. When she reached under the cushion of the window seat, hands shaking, she withdrew the fake ID she'd used. Gave it to him.

"I should ask who sold this to you," Finn said. "But I'm going to trust you won't be getting a replacement."

Maeve nodded. "You won't tell Mom, will you?"

"She needs to know."

Maeve nodded again, and the tears flowed. "I shouldn't have left the club. I should have stayed. I should have called the cops. I should have called *you.*" She struggled to breathe through her sobbing. "Julia would never have just left me there, Dad. I *know* she wouldn't. But that night . . . I was just so mad at her for leaving me. But I should have called someone. I just want Julia to be okay. Dad. It's my fault . . ."

"It's not." He guided her into his arms, and Finn felt the shudders rack her body. He stroked her hair and waited for her crying to ease.

And for the first time in years Finn felt the beginnings of the wall between them start to crumble.

When he left Maeve's room ten minutes later, he heard her stereo come on. Angie was waiting for him at the end of the hall, sitting on the top step.

"We need to talk," he said.

"I know." And she slid her hand into his as they took the stairs.

"DANTE AIN'T GONE NOWHERE. I seen him just last night."

"Did he see you?" Kay asked.

Antwon had called Kay's cell phone shortly after her interview with Rick Silver. She'd waited on Mosher while the kid slunk out of the side alley, scanned the street, and climbed in. Kay had backed her 4Runner onto Moore then, parking under a broken streetlamp.

"Antwon, did Dante see *you?*" she asked him again.

"Naw."

"Look, you need to let me take you back. Dante's probably gotten word from Squirl. He could know you're a witness. It's not safe."

"I told you, he didn't see me. Also told you I ain't going back till we get Dante. 'Sides, I got my boys."

At the mouth of the alley across Mosher, Kay saw movement: Antwon's homeys keeping a lookout. She wondered if they were already a working crew, if Antwon had established himself as their boss, if they were selling drugs, jockeying for turf.

Antwon slumped in the passenger seat, his hoodie drawn up over his shorn head. Only a couple blocks south Kay could just make out the glow of the red Texaco sign, the lot that Antwon's brother had been dealing out of before Dante had executed him. Kay tried not to imagine that night three weeks ago: Antwon watching the .45 jammed into his brother's face, the crack of the shot, his brother's

head snapping back from the pressure of the projectile ex-
ploding from the muzzle as half his skull blew out the back
under a rain of blood and brain matter.

Far more than anyone should ever have to witness in a
lifetime, much less a twelve-year-old child.

"Assistant State's Attorney DiGrazzio needs a statement
from you," Kay said.

"Already gave it."

"She needs it again. Your story isn't jibing with Squirl's."

"So I gotta come in cuz that shit-for-brains is lyin'?
Nuh-uh." His left eye wandered, and she knew he wasn't
looking at her.

"If you don't come in, she'll put a warrant out for you.
She still thinks you're down in Dundalk."

"Y'ain't told her?"

"No."

"Huh." He turned away, but Kay sensed he'd found new
respect for her for not giving him up to Vicki.

"Listen, Antwon, you're pushing some serious buttons
out here."

"Good." He stared solidly out the windshield. In time,
his lazy eye began to waver again.

"And what will you do if you find Dante?" she asked.
"Have you thought about that?"

"Every day for the past three weeks."

"He's going to kill you just like your brother. You want
that?"

Silence.

"Goddammit, Antwon, would you listen to me?"

She'd startled him. He shot her a quick glance, but
couldn't hold it. "What the fuck you want from me,
huh?"

"You know what I want, Antwon. I want you off these
goddamn streets. I want you to let me do my job. I'll get

Dante, I promise. He's going to jail. Probably get the death sentence."

"Dante's already got hisself a death sentence."

Kay recognized that single-minded focus. The obsession. It had consumed her as well, sixteen months ago, standing over the murdered and charred remains of her witness and friend Valerie Regester. Kay was well acquainted with the blinding drive of revenge.

When she reached across the center console, Antwon wasn't expecting her move. He flinched as she yanked the front of his hoodie up, and he muttered something indiscernible when her hand closed around the polymer grip of the semiautomatic tucked into the waistband of his jeans.

The Bersa .380 gleamed dully in the pale light, its compact weight heavy in her hand. The gun had paid its dues on the street; the satin nickel finish was marred and scuffed.

"So *you're* gonna shoot Dante?"

He gave her one of his apathetic shrugs.

"You go waving this around and it's going to be *your* murder scene I walk onto next, *not* Dante's." She dropped the magazine from the Bersa's grip and locked back the slide, ejecting the chambered round. "Jesus Christ, Antwon. You're a kid!"

"Yeah? Well, least I got the courage to do something about Dante."

"Courage?" She held up the empty semiautomatic. "You think it takes courage to put a bullet in someone?"

Another shrug.

"This *isn't* about courage," she said.

"Yeah. It is. And if all men were just, we wouldn't need no valor."

"What?"

"It's a saying. You know? From history. It goes, 'If all men were just, there would be no need of valor.' "

Kay thought she should recognize the quote, but didn't.

"Some guy Agesilaus said it," Antwon explained. "He was the King of Sparta way back in ancient history. I read about him."

It shouldn't have surprised Kay. *"Antwon's something of a closet scholar,"* his teacher had told her when Kay had gone to Harlem Park Middle School looking for him. *"Signs books out of the library. History mostly. The child's a ravenous reader. Reads anything he can get his hands on."*

"They called him the lame king," Antwon went on, "cuz he had one leg shorter than the other. But even bein' a crip, he was still this kick-ass warrior. And he got respect, you know?"

Kay wondered if Antwon was just throwing the quote at her, or if he actually viewed the historical figure as an influence.

She slid the gun and its magazine under her seat, wondering if he'd have another jammed into his baggy jeans before the night was out.

"Not like this, Antwon. Besides, the valor is in letting the system take care of Dante." But even as she spoke the words, Kay felt her own broken faith in the justice system, which so often failed, especially in cases like Dante Toomey.

When Kay looked at Antwon now, his face half-obscured by shadow, she realized the kid had no intention of calling her when he found Dante.

There was only one thing to do.

Reaching across his lap, Kay popped the glove box. Antwon stiffened when he spotted the cuffs.

"If you won't let me take you to the foster home, then I'm running you into Juvie."

But Antwon had the door open and the dome light of the 4Runner blazed.

Kay felt exposed. She snatched his wrist, surprised at

how small it felt under the heavy cotton fleece. A child's wrist. With her other hand she yanked the door shut. The light went off.

"*I'll* get Dante, you got that?" she said to him. "*Me.* Not you."

Kay felt his anger fill the interior of the SUV.

"You don't get it, do you?" he asked. "If anyone's gonna find Dante it's *me!*"

"And how do you figure that?"

"Cuz *I* know Dante. I know these streets, these corners. I know where Dante's from. Where he goes. What he's thinking." Antwon's dark eyes shifted onto hers, and Kay saw his unwavering determination. "*I* can find him cuz I'm inside his brain."

Kay was shaking her head even before he finished.

"Think about it," he said.

But she was. And she knew the kid had a point. He *did* stand a far better chance of locating Dante than the Fugitive Squad, no matter how many informants they paid.

"You know I'm right, Ms. Kay."

"Fugitive *will* find him, Antwon."

"And how many other brothers he gonna shoot in the meantime?"

Kay looked at the cuffs in her lap, then back to Antwon, the kid's future in her hands.

She hated that he was right.

"All right, Antwon." She took a deep breath, looked him square in the eye. "Time to deal."

He turned in his seat, interest piqued, feeling her compliancy.

"There's only *one* way this is going to play out," she told him. "You and me. A pact."

Antwon nodded. Intent.

"If I let you out of this car tonight, you're giving me your word, as a man, that when you find Dante, you're going to call me. I don't care when, I don't care how, but you're gonna call me. And we'll get Dante. You and me."

His nod was slow coming, but it was there. And with it, a quiver of gratitude touched the corners of his mouth.

"I need your word," she said.

"You got it."

"On your brother's grave, Antwon." And when Kay made a fist and held it out to him, he tapped it with his own, sealing the pact.

"Cool," he said, and the earnestness in his voice reassured Kay.

When his gaze turned out the windshield, she followed it. His homeboys. One of them gave a hand signal from the shadows. She didn't recognize it, but Antwon leaned forward and searched the street.

His hand went for the door handle again. "I gotta go. Doesn't look good me sittin' in your ride like this."

But Kay grabbed him one last time. Gentler. "You've got till Monday morning, Antwon."

"Wadda you mean?"

"Detective Curran's already got a hard-on for bringing you in. You've got till the end of the weekend. I can't hold him off any longer."

He took a moment, weighing his options. Then: "Aaiight."

And he was out the door.

He tugged his hoodie farther down over his forehead, burying his hands in the front uni-pocket as he slouched past the grille of the 4Runner. When he reached the side alley, he turned. With both hands raised, he made matching guns with his fists, cocked them sideways at her before slipping into the shadows with his boys.

Kay's stomach churned as she saw the last flash of the kid's white sneakers.

Starting up the 4Runner, she steered east, cruising slowly with the night air washing over her. She tried to shift her thoughts from Antwon to the case, to the man *she* was hunting.

Like Antwon understood Dante, she needed to understand the man who'd slaughtered Nina Gatsby. Like Antwon with Dante, she needed to be inside his head.

Killers weren't born. They were made, she believed. Nurtured. The way the streets and drug culture had nurtured Dante. And Antwon.

Kay thought about the killer's club hand. A disfigurement like that—especially one that could have been corrected—surely played a role in his nurturing. Much as Antwon's lazy eye had earned him the nickname Wattage, demoralizing him before he'd ever developed the ability to defend himself.

Thirty-six hours ago she'd stood in a swirl of fog over the eviscerated remains of Nina Gatsby. It was hard to imagine any human doing what had been done to the twenty-four-year-old. But if there was one thought Kay needed to embrace the most, it was that Nina Gatsby's killer *was* human. She couldn't allow herself to view him as a monster because if she did, she would never be able to know him. If she did, she'd be blind to the reality of his existence.

And Nina Gatsby's killer was real. Very real.

She needed to know him like Antwon knew Dante. She needed to know where Nina Gatsby's killer came from, how he thought, what motivated him. Without that knowledge, only luck would catch him, and Kay knew they'd need far more than luck.

Two blocks from home, Kay's cell went off. She grappled

for it off her belt. Was surprised to hear Bobby's voice, even more surprised by the gravity in his voice: "Did you catch the news? Rick Silver fucked up."

32

IN THE LIGHT OF the portable work lamp, Paul Graves surveyed his accomplishment.

All memory of his uncle had been erased from the room at the end of the hall. The closet emptied, the old stained mattress and the veneer dressers long since picked up at the curb. In their place: his Angel's bed.

The four-poster had cost more than he'd planned on spending, but when he'd seen the Victorian replica in the dusty warehouse down on North Howard Street, with its sturdy mahogany frame and its carved headboard, he knew it had to be hers. Even with the broken poster and two missing finials, he'd known nothing else would suffice.

Graves felt a twist in his groin as he envisioned his Angel on the bed.

Soon.

He lay on the bed now. Naked. Spread-eagled across the quilted comforter. From below, the rumble of the furnace pulsed and hot air tumbled into the room. He felt its circulation brush across his goose-pimpled skin. Just beneath the stale air, Graves could smell the sweet mustiness of the bed's old wood.

Above him, the popcorn stucco speckled with shadow in the glare of the upturned work lamp. In all his weeks of work, he hadn't considered the ceiling before, and now he eyed the large stain. Dark rings of fifty-year-old filth had spread out at countless intervals, in different patterns. A leak in the roof. A ring for each major storm.

Graves tried to ignore the flaw in the otherwise perfect room.

With his good hand, he fingered the cool percale of the empty pillowcase, brought it to his face and inhaled the traces of her perfume. Patchouli and bergamot. He moved the pillowcase down along his body, the fine fabric sliding like satin across his chest and abdomen.

He massaged his groin with it, but he was already hard, his erection prominent, his scrotum tightening. His cock quivered in the cocoon of the soft fabric, its shaft contracting and palpitating under the expert pressure of his hand.

Graves imagined the eyes of his Angel. Imagined her smile turned onto him.

Soon. She would be here. On this very bed.

He would touch her body. Feel her breath against his cheek. Feel her fingers caress his own skin.

His hand worked more feverishly.

But the stain across the ceiling . . . A mar in the fantasy.

Graves closed his eyes, tried to give himself over to the climax. But the stain . . .

His grasp tightened around his erection, his rhythm increasingly desperate.

The stain . . .

He tried to imagine his Angel, but couldn't. All there was, was the blemish across the stucco. The ragged rings formed a shape. And as Graves's hand pumped harder, the shape took form. He recognized the outline of the face, the severe slash of a mouth. Shadows in the irregular stucco took on the contour of eyes and the pocked features.

And then, his erection wilting, Graves recognized the face. He knew it from the photos his mother had kept around the house. The austere features of his uncle Roy were unmistakable. And they stared down at him now with reproach and censure.

Graves lunged off the bed. The rage boiled inside him. Roared in his ears.

No. The room had to be perfect, the image of his uncle's face blotted out.

Barefoot, Graves stormed down the corridor, his cock flaccid by the time he reached the living room. He hoped the aerosol can of white paint in the garage hadn't gone dead.

But he didn't make it to the garage. In the middle of the living room, Graves stopped. The Channel 13 reporter stood outside Police Headquarters with the detective, the lobby doors and glass facade illuminated in the dusk over downtown. The segment had been filmed earlier, Graves realized, but not in time for the six-o'clock news.

". . . we're not dismissing the possibility of a connection between the murder of Leslie Richter two months ago and that of Nina Gatsby." Detective Kay Delaney's name appeared in the caption across the bottom of the screen. "We have nothing definitive at this time."

"Nina Gatsby's remains were discovered early yesterday morning . . ." The reporter's voice-over accompanied footage shot in the county yesterday. Squad cars and the ME's van sitting on the shoulder of the side road off Warren. There too Graves spotted Delaney at the hood of a silver, unmarked police car.

Graves watched, a voyeur of his own handiwork.

His erection, the stained stucco, his uncle's face . . . all were forgotten as he watched the scene again. He'd seen it yesterday in the news as well. And when the girl's body was carried out of the tangle of underbrush, Graves imagined her pillaged remains under the white plastic body bag.

They'd match it to the heart.

And as Graves watched the reporter's face fill the screen one last time, he felt the slow strangle of fear. It snatched at his throat and settled in his groin.

Wind buffeted the reporter's mike. "Police are releasing no further information, but report that they do have a suspect currently being questioned . . ."

The hot prickle of panic started at Graves's shoulders. It worked up his scalp as if his hair were on fire. The reporter's words were drowned by the ringing in his ears. He heard the words "Peabody Institute," "students," and "serial."

And then, as Graves stood naked, washed by the flickering glow of the television, he knew it was time for his Angel's deliverance.

33

Friday, April 21

"ADMIT IT, Delaney, you dropped the fucking ball."

"Jesus, Reggie, why can't you just shut up for once?" Mo Greer's words were clipped. "Rick Silver dropped the fucking ball."

"Yeah, well, she shouldn't have gone to that dipshit in the first place."

Kay hated to agree with Laubach, but all night and morning she'd kicked herself for using the Channel 13 reporter. Sure, it had been an innocent slip—saying they had a suspect *in* questioning instead of *wanted for* questioning— but Kay was left wondering if Jane Gallagher would have made such an error.

"Nobody should have gotten that story wrong. It was a no-brainer," Greer said.

From his desk, Gunderson cleared his throat. "Drop the blaming game, hear? We got a killer I want in custody before the fucking media gives him a name." Gunderson dragged his gaze across all four of them: Mo, Laubach, Bobby, and Kay. Whitey had called in sick, and Finn hadn't yet shown this morning.

After Bobby explained Silver's blunder last night, Kay had tried to reach Finn on his cell. When he hadn't answered, she'd gone to Mercy Medical to sit with Julia Harris again, and eventually to the marina. Waiting for Finn on his boat, she'd reviewed the Gatsby file and listened to the 911 tape over and over, then paced the galley for an hour, and went to bed.

She hadn't slept well in Finn's bed, waking alone from dreams of the man who'd slipped Leslie Richter's earring into her pocket. By 5 a.m. Kay had given up on sleep. She'd driven home, showered and dressed, and come into the office. She had reached Rick Silver at the station by 6, warned him not to run the story again. The reporter offered to do damage control, but Kay wanted him muted until she'd regrouped with the others.

Gunderson went on, "Even if our guy did catch Silver's segment last night, it doesn't mean he's going to do anything because of it. He might lay low anyway and see what happens with this alleged suspect we have."

But Kay couldn't escape the fear that another girl might die because the killer believed police were barking up the wrong tree.

"So what have we got so far on this mope?" Gunderson asked. "Where are we at with the dog bites?"

"Eddie Jones has a forensic odontologist on board," Kay said. "But we need an actual dog for a dental cast before we can run any kind of comparison."

"What about DNA from the hairs?" Mo asked.

"A comparison'll be run with the saliva in the bite wounds, but it'll take time. And again, until we get a dog . . ."

"And what's going on with the Peabody?" Gunderson asked.

Kay nodded to Bobby and Mo. "We're going to start interviewing faculty and staff, as well as students. And we need to go back to Langley," she explained, "make sure we've covered all the bases there. Maybe do a second canvass of the neighborhood."

Finn stepped through the open door. He looked worn.

"Sorry. Didn't know there was a meeting," he said, pulling up a chair.

As he sat, Kay sensed his eyes on her. She refused to meet them.

"What else?" Gunderson asked.

Bobby shifted in his chair, smoothing down his tie. "Well, I caught a couple shows at The Condor Club last night," he said. "Asked a few questions."

"And?"

"And I got a witness. Girl named Sapphire. One of the dancers. She's coming in later today to make a statement."

"What's she got?"

"She's got Nina Gatsby getting into a dark green Neon Saturday night after her shift."

"Is the lead legit?" Gunderson asked.

Bobby nodded. "She was out back having a smoke. Saw Gatsby come around the side with some guy. Description she gives matches the one from the bartender," he said to Kay.

"Anything else about the guy? Or the car?"

Bobby sipped from his extralarge latte, taking his time. Kay sensed his smugness. And finally he said, "Only that the guy had a driver."

"A driver?"

Bobby nodded. "The girl says the car was already running. Gatsby and the guy got in the back."

"She get a look at the driver?" Finn asked.

Bobby shook his head.

Kay stood, needing to move as the reality snaked through her. "There's *two* of them."

"A team? Come on, how likely is that?" Laubach asked.

"But we don't even know if Gatsby didn't maybe go off with these two guys in the Neon and then meet up with our club-handed perp *later,*" Bobby said.

"No. The team theory makes sense." Kay felt charged. The room wasn't big enough. "It could explain the two profiles. Organized versus disorganized. I thought, based on how he goes off on the girls once they're dead, that maybe this guy had a split-personality disorder or was enacting two separate fantasies. But maybe it's two different people."

Kay could picture the bar, could see the man the owner had described picking up Nina Gatsby. He didn't have a club hand.

"Either that or this guy in the bar, the pretty boy who picked up Gatsby, he could just be the snatcher for our perp with the hand. Grabs up these girls for him. He might have nothing to do with the killings or the disposal, and for all we know, our perp doesn't even use the same guy with each victim."

The man with the fused hand . . . Kay had spent her morning trying to understand him. After calling Rick Silver, Kay had settled behind her computer. She'd Googled *Apert's* and *Poland's syndrome,* and several other terms Dixie had given her during her visit with the assistant ME three days ago. Kay had browsed countless medical articles and viewed dozens of photographs of congenital hand deformities, finding numerous examples that could have matched the print left on Leslie Richter's throat.

It would make sense that he'd need someone else to pick up the girls, to coax them into his vehicle. Even Dixie hadn't been able to say for sure whether his deformity was restricted to one hand, both, or included other extremities, the chest, or even his face.

"All right, then, let's see what we can get on this green Neon," Gunderson said. "And get out to the Peabody. Langley. See if anyone can make some connections for us." He gestured to the door, dismissing them.

Kay fell in step behind Finn until Bobby stopped her.

"Something you need to know," he told Kay, his voice low. "I put some feelers out, some old CIs I still have from Redrum."

Kay hadn't met any of Bobby's confidential informants from his days with the gang unit, but word was that Redrum CIs delivered only the real goods.

"One of them tells me your kid Antwon's got a bull's-eye on his back."

"Dante?"

Bobby nodded. "And Dante's whole crew. Guess Squirl leaked that the kid needs taking care of."

Kay tamped down on the anger that rippled through her as she realized Antwon must already have known last night that he was a target. The kid's whole life was the streets; he had feelers everywhere. He *had* to have known Dante was after him.

In a heartbeat Kay remembered the feel of Antwon's knuckles against her own, their pact, swearing on his brother's grave. But he'd known.

"Son of a bitch."

"Just thought you'd wanna know," Bobby said, and Kay

hated the I-told-you-so in the rookie's voice before he walked away.

At her desk, Kay pocketed her notebook and took her gun from the locked drawer. She tried to ignore the tension that filled the cubicle as she sensed Finn's eyes on her.

"You up to hitting the streets?" she asked him, holstering the Glock.

When she looked over, Finn gave her a silent nod.

In the elevator he was silent as well. She wanted to ask him where he'd been last night, but intuition gave her a pretty good idea, and she didn't really want to hear it.

By the time the car jostled to a stop and the doors opened on the garage level, Kay's frustration had peaked. She barged past several uniforms waiting for the elevator, and Finn had to jog to keep up as she headed to the parking garage.

The smell of old grease, cigarette smoke, and exhaust fumes hit her when she crossed the main ramp that spilled out onto Frederick Street. From somewhere in the structure above them, a car's steering squealed as its driver jacked the wheel too far, no doubt in order to claim one of the last tight parking spaces.

"Where the hell's our car?" Kay started up the oil-stained ramp, unable to restrain the anger now. Anger at Antwon. At Finn. But mostly at herself.

Finn caught up with her halfway to the next level. He snatched her shoulder and spun her around. "Hang on. What's going on?"

"Nothing."

"Kay."

"It's nothing, Finn."

"Bullshit."

"Fine, then. Where were you last night?"

"I was at Angie's. I went to talk to Maeve. Like you told me I should."

"And?" In Kay's mind, the image of Maeve kissing Julia Harris flashed. She wondered how Maeve had explained it to her father.

But what Finn told her next, Kay had not been expecting.

"She was with her. Maeve was with Harris at The Crypt the night she was abducted."

"Wait a second, Finn. She's got to come in. She needs to make a statement."

"She didn't see anything, Kay. Doesn't know anything."

"I don't care. She's a goddamn witness."

Finn shook his head. "I'm not going to put her through that. This is killing her. She feels responsible."

"Responsible? Responsible would be coming in and making a statement."

"She didn't see anything," he said, his words clipped.

"Then she can come in and make a statement to that effect. Bobby can interview her. Keep it neutral."

"Kay—"

"Finn, it's procedure."

Down the line of cars she spotted the white Lumina. She circled to the driver's side and unlocked it.

"Wait a second, Kay. Stop." Over the roof of the unmarked, his eyes looked darker than usual. "Listen, if you're pissed off, take it out on me, *not* my daughter."

"I'm not taking anything out on anyone."

"What's this really about?"

"It's about procedure, Finn."

"Like hell! If all you cared about was procedure, then Antwon Washington wouldn't still be out there on the goddamn streets with Dante Toomey after him."

"All right. Then what else I'm supposed to be pissed at? That you didn't come home last night? That you stayed at your ex-wife's?"

Finn looked suddenly deflated and Kay knew she'd guessed right.

"It's not what you think."

"And how is it you know what I'm thinking, Finn?" When Kay threw open the door of the Lumina, her face felt hot. "Now, you can come or not, but I'm going to get your daughter. Right now."

34

THEY PULLED MAEVE out of her third-period biology class and brought her downtown for Bobby to interview. She seemed to warm to the smooth-talking Bostonian, even cracked a smile for him. Still, the only thing Bobby had gotten out of her was the name of the kid selling fake IDs at her high school.

They drove Maeve to Mercy after that to see Julia. She assured them she had no afternoon classes, but Finn suspected she was lying. In the rearview mirror, he'd snatched glimpses of Maeve's dour expression in the backseat of the unmarked. And when he dropped her at the hospital doors, she mumbled a good-bye and didn't look back.

They fought traffic all the way up to Roland Park, and even as they pushed their way through the crowded halls of Langley, Finn couldn't shed the image of Maeve's eyes, the sense of guilt he'd seen in them, the grief and anguish.

They found Mr. Bruger in the faculty lounge as promised. From HQ Kay had made arrangements with the music teacher to reinterview his Peabody students. When

Bruger spotted Finn and Kay, he scooped up his container of carrot sticks and celery. His eyes shifted quickly, never quite meeting Finn's.

"I've asked the students to meet you in the music room," he said.

They followed Bruger through throngs of students, and at the music-room door, Finn stopped him.

"I'm after a student we ran into yesterday. Tall, lanky kid. Rude little bastard. Wore an oversized Ravens starter jacket. You know who that could be?"

Bruger blinked rapidly, then nodded. "I believe that would be our young Mr. Resnick."

"Any chance we can talk to him too?"

"I'll try to locate him."

When Bruger ushered them into the room, three of the six teens sat straighter. The other three slumped in the hard wooden chairs, their gazes apathetic. None of them resembled the man seen picking up Gatsby at The Condor Club. Only two had dark hair, and neither long enough for a ponytail. Nor did any of them appear as though he could actually weasel his way into a strip joint like The Condor, no matter how good the fake ID.

For the next hour and a half, Finn and Kay spoke with the six boys separately, using one of the small practice rooms down the hall. It was cramped and stuffy, and by the final interview Finn was feeling claustrophobic.

Dismissing the last boy, they found Jillian Somerville waiting for them with Bruger in the music room.

"I'm afraid Adrian Resnick went home for the day," she told them, handing Finn an index card. "But this is his address." In neat block letters, the school's headmaster had written out the Cross Keys address. "I don't know how you think he might be tied up in all of this. From my understanding, he never associated with Leslie."

"It's probably nothing," Finn told the headmaster. And a long shot. Adrian Resnick didn't even come close to the description the owner of The Condor Club had given them. Still, *someone* had slipped Leslie Richter's earring into Kay's pocket yesterday.

"So those six boys are the only students enrolled in the Peabody annex program?" Kay asked. "No girls?"

Bruger nodded. "Only Leslie Richter, and, of course, Amber Estcott, whom you've spoken with."

"And where is Amber today?" Kay asked.

"She has riding lessons Friday afternoons," Jillian Somerville offered. "She leaves before last period. Did you want to set something up with her for Monday?"

But Kay ignored the question. "Where does she ride?"

"Pardon me?"

"Where's the stables?"

Somerville seemed taken aback by Kay's sudden intensity. "I'm . . . I'm not entirely certain. I know it's up in the county somewhere."

Finn envisioned Nina Gatsby's body, laid out in the woods in Baltimore County.

"That's why Amber needs the last period off, so she can get up there in time for her lessons. I can give you her parents' number, if you like."

They followed Somerville to her office for the phone number, then took the main corridor to the front doors. Kay paused briefly at the bottom of the wide steps to look out at the lush green field.

The crows were at it again. Wheeling and plummeting through the air, relentless over the strip of woods to the west.

"If the connection *is* Peabody," Kay said, her gaze fixed on the spot where Nina Gatsby's heart had lain in the snow only four days ago, "what about Amber Estcott?"

"What about her?"

"What if she's a target? He left the heart here for a reason. Maybe he was staking territory somehow, laying claim to his next victim."

"If that's the case, he could be targeting anyone at the school, Kay."

She shook her head. "It's the music, Finn. That's the connection. We need to talk to Estcott. Make sure she's safe."

The school parking lot was almost empty now. Gone were the Beemers and the Audis and the sporty little numbers that parents used to buy their overprivileged children's affections.

Finn thought of Angie, of the wonderful job she'd done in raising Maeve. Their daughter never demanded, never expected. Tennis lessons were all she asked for. And even though he rarely received it, he knew Maeve's affection could never be bought through material things as, he imagined, was the case with many of Langley's students.

Last night, after leaving Maeve's bedroom, he'd sat downstairs with Angie, talking. About Maeve, about Julia Harris, about the job. In twelve years of marriage Finn had rarely confided in Angie about his work, believing that not sharing it could somehow stop the violence he saw every day from ever touching her or their children.

And as Angie listened on the sofa last night, Finn realized just how wrong he'd been by never letting her in. He'd always been jealous of the bond Angie shared with Maeve, but now he knew: in the loneliness of their marriage, the kids were all she had.

He understood now what it must have been like for his ex-wife. Understood how his silence had damaged their marriage. He understood because—for the past couple of years—Kay had done the same to him. Even though they had the job in common, Kay had only ever let Finn in so far, only rarely allowing him to witness her vulnerability. There were depths to Kay Finn still wanted to know, but he was beginning to believe no one could ever truly comprehend.

So last night, he and Angie had talked. They'd talked about Toby, about missing him, about what he might be doing today if he were alive. They talked about the accident on that rain-slicked interstate. Finn had broken down last night when he'd described being wedged behind the wheel of the Sentra, his ribs broken, his collarbone crushed, the diesel fumes from the tanker filling the mangled interior while he waited almost an hour for the Fire Department to cut through the Nissan's frame.

Angie had held him as he described his inability to reach Toby, how—for every second of that entire hour—he'd stared at Toby's small, bloodied body pinned under a swath of twisted metal. An hour that became an eternity, not knowing whether his son was unconscious or dead.

She didn't blame him, Angie admitted sometime after midnight. She'd never blamed Finn for the accident. But she'd hated him for not sharing their grief, hated him for turning to the bottle instead of her.

And in spite of the years of silence, and drinking, last night Finn felt the bond he'd shared with Angie. Toby's loss was part of that bond; Maeve an even bigger piece. It was the kind of bond Finn knew he'd never share with Kay no matter how much he loved her.

Last night, realizing how close they'd come to maybe losing Maeve as well, had been frightening. Galvanizing. And this time Finn hadn't been afraid to voice that fear.

They'd held each other then and must have fallen asleep on the couch. Finn had woken alone under a blanket and with a stiff neck. He'd left before Maeve woke.

Now, in Langley's parking lot, he watched Kay unlock

the car and wondered if she could ever understand the ties that bound him to Angie.

"We need to talk to Amber's parents," Kay said.

When Kay's cell phone trilled at her hip, she took the call. She said little more than two affirmatives, and when she snapped the phone shut, there was a level of despair in her eyes that Finn had never seen before.

"What is it?"

"That was Mo, calling from Mercy. Julia Harris just died."

35

ON THE DRIVE to Mercy, Kay had offered only mono-syllabic responses to Finn's questions, concentrating on traf-fic, biting back her sadness and patent defeat. Stepping off the elevator on the eleventh floor, she didn't sign in at the nurses' station, just headed straight to Julia Harris's room.

Mo Greer was waiting for them. The Rape detective sat on the wide window ledge, dusk settling over the city be-hind her. Kay couldn't remember if she'd ever seen Mo quite so defeated.

"Un-fucking-believable." Mo shook her head. She nod-ded at the empty bed. "A goddamn waste."

"What happened?" Kay could barely form the words. She felt winded, hollow, and her legs were shaky as she stared at the nest of rumpled sheets where Julia Harris had lain unconscious for three weeks.

Just last night, Kay had sat next to the girl's bed for over an hour, studying her slack expression, her youthful fea-tures, imagining the light behind the girl's eyes and the smile that would one day grace her lips again. Kay had prayed last night, holding Harris's hand in hers, watching the colored waveforms float across the monitors and listening to the machines that forced her to breathe.

The room was silent now. The machines still.

"They pronounced her at five. Took her out just a while ago," Mo said. "Not sure yet what happened. Doc said it could have been another intracranial bleed, or an embolism. Won't know till an autopsy." Mo was riled. She moved from the windowsill and paced. "I tell ya, it's a real fucking shame her parents refused to sign the donor paperwork. At least *something* positive could have come out of her death, you know? This way, the girl died for nothing."

Behind Kay, Finn cleared his throat. "My daughter, Mo. Did you see Maeve?"

Mo nodded, the hostility in her expression softening to concern. "She was here, Finn."

"So she knows?"

"She was *here*. When it happened. All the machines going haywire, nurses rushing in. Maeve was here."

"Christ."

Kay turned to him then. Wished there were some way she could ease the distress she saw in his face, but she felt helpless. "Finn, you need to go to her."

He nodded. His eyes still on the empty sheets.

"I offered to drive her home," Mo said, "but she refused. Said she'd take a cab."

"Finn." Kay touched his arm.

Still, his gaze went unbroken. He looked lost, and Kay imagined he was seeing his own daughter where Julia Harris had been.

"Finn, you have to talk to her. Now."

He didn't argue.

He said little as they walked to the car, even less while Kay drove them to Hunting Ridge.

"It could have been her," he said when Kay finally

steered the Lumina into his ex-wife's drive. "The son of a bitch could have picked up Maeve that night instead. He probably spiked Julia's drink. How easily could Maeve have picked up that beer instead of Julia?"

"But she didn't, Finn." Kay squeezed his hand. "Maeve's alive."

He opened the car door. "Do you want to come in?"

"Better I wait here." Past the hood of the unmarked, the stone house looked picture-perfect, everything Kay had imagined it would be when Finn had talked about it in the past. The landscaping, the walk, the inviting warmth of the light from the windows.

"Take your time," she added.

And as she watched Finn go, Kay doubted Maeve had told him of her true relationship with Harris, doubted she'd told him she was gay. Kay wondered if Maeve would tonight, or if the teen would continue to hide it from her father.

From the dark interior of the car Kay watched uncomfortably as Finn accepted his ex-wife's hug at the door, then stepped inside. She settled back into the seat and thought about Julia Harris.

She had wanted to know the girl. To congratulate her on surviving.

She'd wanted to see the smile on the girl's parched lips when she woke to find Maeve next to her.

Kay had counted on Julia making it, however unreasonable that fantasy might have been.

And now, as Kay imagined the dead girl's smile, as she remembered Richter's from the photograph, and envisioned Gatsby's pretty face buried under a pile of last year's leaves, Kay felt a twist deep inside of her. A change.

It was more personal now than ever.

And when she finally found the man with the club hand

who'd beaten Julia Harris to death, the man with the pit bull that had torn into Nina Gatsby, Kay prayed Finn was there to stop her from murdering the son of a bitch.

36

MAEVE HAD INHERITED his stoicism.

When Finn walked into her bedroom, her eyes were red and swollen, and her stubborn refusal to cry forced her mouth into a tight line.

Seeing the devastation in her eyes cut deep. Finn hadn't stayed long, unable to bear the feeling of helplessness at his inability to console, to comfort.

Kay started the car as he'd said good-night to Angie on the front porch, and they drove north to Guilford. They discussed how to speak with Amber Estcott's parents without tripping panic buttons, especially when the notion of Amber Estcott being targeted was only a hunch. Still, it was a hunch neither of them was willing to ignore.

In scale, Guilford was several notches up from Hunting Ridge. Manicured boulevards with old-fashioned street-lamps snaked through the almost hundred-year-old neighborhood. Gracious homes sat back from the street, some behind wrought-iron fences and elaborate landscaping, their grand exteriors flooded by spotlights. One of Baltimore's first planned communities, Guilford was a heritage neighborhood where most of the homes had been occupied by three generations, and where residents subsidized a private security force.

It was rare to see police presence within the boundaries, so the District cruiser and the unmarked parked in the cul-de-sac at the Estcott address sparked immediate unease.

Kay left the Lumina at the curb. "This is Braddock's car,"

she said, pointing to the plastic Jesus glued on the dash of the silver Cavalier as they passed it.

Adam Braddock was a zealous born-again who'd pissed off more than a few of his fellow detectives on the Violent Crimes Unit with his ecclesiastical pontificating since his overnight salvation.

Kay took the steps to the porticoed entranceway two at a time. A District uniform answered the door, and Kay flashed her shield. "What's going on?" she asked.

The officer nodded past the foyer to a lavish sitting room where Braddock paced the plush, cream-colored area rug in his hard-soled brogues.

"We don't know anything for sure, right now, ma'am," Braddock said.

"I'm going up there. See for myself."

"That's not a good idea, ma'am. It's a crime scene, and it needs to be processed. We don't even know for certain the girl was snatched."

"The *girl*, Detective, is my daughter. And her name is Amber." On the edge of an overstuffed leather sofa, Mrs. Estcott wrung her hands. Fine-boned, blond, and fair-skinned, she clearly possessed the dominant genetics. She looked as if she could pass as Amber Estcott's older sister. Her mouth was a pale slash across her face, her eyes angry as she stared down Braddock.

Behind Mrs. Estcott, her husband stood at the back of the sofa, one hand on her shoulder. Finn recognized the austere but handsome features, as well as the signature charcoal gray tailored suit.

Mark Estcott was one of Baltimore's most-sought-after criminal defense attorneys. His success came primarily from defending drug cases, and rumors had Estcott in the back pocket of several of the city's biggest dealers. Still, the lawyer had managed to gain a reputation for fairness, even with the cops whose arrests didn't lead to convictions because of Estcott's finesse in the courtroom. When it came to putting cops on the stand, Estcott never harassed, never patronized, and only rarely harangued.

Finn hadn't known Estcott had a daughter, hadn't made the connection with the name earlier. And neither had Kay, obviously.

"Mark?" There was surprise in her voice.

When Estcott turned, his expression sank. "Kay." He shook his head. "Tell me you're not here because . . . Tell me you were just in the neighborhood."

"What is it, Mark?" his wife asked, frantic. "What's happened?"

"Barb, this is Detective Delaney; her partner, Danny Finnerty."

Finn accepted the woman's handshake, but the firm pressure of the woman's grip went instantly limp when Estcott added, "They're from Homicide."

"Oh my God, oh my God," Barb Estcott began chanting, her body rocking at the edge of the sofa.

"Give it to me straight, Kay," Estcott said.

"I don't know anything, Mark. Seriously. We came here to talk about your daughter, in connection to Langley. I didn't even know you were Amber's father."

"What's going on?" Finn asked Braddock then.

The Violent Crimes detective chewed at the inside of his cheek for a second. "They found the girl's . . . *Amber's* car abandoned up in Baltimore County. We got the call to come over and speak with Mr. Estcott."

"Where exactly in the county?"

"Not sure," Braddock said.

"She was at riding lessons," Mrs. Estcott answered. "When she didn't come home on time, I knew something was wrong."

"Where does Amber ride, Mark?" Kay asked.

"Windybrook Stables. Just off Warren Road."

"Up by the reservoir?" Finn asked, remembering the rider and the spooked horse at the scene of Gatsby's body.

"Yeah. Why?" Mark Estcott asked, a tremor in his voice. "Kay, what the hell is going on?"

37

IT FELT LIKE RAIN. The air was heavy with a dampness that rolled in from the Loch Raven reservoir, bringing with it the dense smell of rotting leaves and damp stone.

Amber Estcott's electric-blue Miata had been deserted on the shoulder of a side road, barely a mile off Warren, the main artery that stretched north through the parkland.

County cars blocked the side road, revolving light-bars flickering through the night and washing the dark tree trunks with rhythmic splashes of blue.

Kay had barely tucked the Lumina in behind one of the radio cars when Sergeant Blaine Pitts crossed over to them. In the flood of headlamps his shadow loomed across the scene.

"You think this is related to that girl we found down the road?" Pitts asked. A half mile back, Kay knew the police tape from Gatsby's dump site would still be laced through the trees.

"Could be," she said.

"If this *is* a city boy you're after," Pitts said, "then he's certainly expanded his hunting ground."

Finn shook his head. "We think he may have targeted this girl. Followed her up here."

Pitts removed his uniform hat, wiped his brow with the back of one forearm, then nodded to the Miata.

"We don't know for sure she's been grabbed, but it's lookin' that way." He led them to the shoulder, thirty feet from the nose of the small sports car. "Ground's good and soft here. Got some boot prints. Small ones. Larger ones too."

Pitts panned his flashlight across the surface. Kay flicked on her own police-issue Mag-Lite and passed the bright beam over the prints in the sandy mud. The smaller ones looked like the low-tread soles of riding boots and several of them were obliterated by larger ones. A man's work boot.

Kay envisioned the scene unfolding. Estcott pulling over. *Why?*

You must have talked to him. Did you leave your car? Did he seem in trouble? Kay thought of Ted Bundy, luring his victims with his arm in a fake cast. *Or did you know him?*

"We've got scuff marks over here," Pitts was saying, leading them in the direction of the sports car.

Again more prints along the shoulder. Then the signs of a struggle. Heels had dug in, gouging the sandy surface. And finally drag marks.

"We found some tire tracks along the shoulder." Pitts nodded to where the Crime Lab had a halogen lamp set up and a technician mixed dental stone in a small bucket. "Good impressions. We're getting a cast. So you said on the phone the girl was up at the riding stables here?"

"Yeah. Windybrook."

"That's a couple miles up."

"Her parents called the stables and were told she'd left at six thirty." Kay checked her watch. "Makes this scene almost four hours old."

"Would have been dusk then," Finn pointed out.

Kay nodded to the compact car. Another Crime Lab tech worked on the Miata, a Mag-Lite clenched between his teeth while he worked a fingerprinting brush across the hood. Magnetic dust plumed in the beam of the flashlight. "Anything wrong with the car?" Kay asked.

"Not that we can tell. We'll tow it in. Take a better look. But I figured we should print the exterior while we can. Rain could hit before we get the thing to Cockeysville."

"Anything to indicate why she pulled over?"

Pitts nodded. "Got a skid down here." He walked them another hundred feet to where an officer photographed the asphalt.

It was a braking skid, the beginning of the pattern lighter, then getting darker as the vehicle had come to a hard stop.

"We'll need to match the tire print with the Miata," Kay said, examining the remnants of rubber left on the roadway.

"We'll get confirmation, but I've been on enough traffic incidents to tell you, you probably got a match," Pitts said.

The girl had locked the Miata's tires. *Why?*

Kay stood and crossed to the right-hand shoulder farther back. The sandy surface was smooth here. And then, Kay saw the prints.

"Got the same work-boot prints here," she pointed out to Finn. "Coming from the ditch."

Shadows danced as Kay panned the Mag's beam through the first edges of brush, the muddy ditch, and thick leaves. *You waited for her here, sitting in the long grass and scrub. You set it up so she* had *to stop.*

Kay couldn't imagine a girl like Amber pulling over for just anyone. Not without using her cell phone. Had she known him? Had he used a decoy of some kind?

Kay headed back to the Miata, Finn and Pitts behind her.

Circling the sports car, she scanned the grille and fenders

until, in the angled beam of her Mag, she saw the shallow dent on the car's polished hood.

"She hit something," Kay said, squatting before the front bumper, indicating the dent before aiming the flashlight to the license plate, one corner of its frame wrenched away from the bumper. Kay spotted some fabric snagged on one of the plastic bolts.

"We'll need this." She pointed out the threads to Pitts. "He set this up, Finn," she said as the county detective went to retrieve a Lab technician. "He had to know she wouldn't just stop, so he needed to give her a good reason."

"How?"

"Maybe he put himself into the middle of the road. Stepped out of the ditch and she didn't see him until the last second, hit the brakes, but she still struck him."

Kay envisioned the scenario. He couldn't know if the Miata's brakes would stop the small car in time, but he'd risked it anyway.

Kay crossed the strip of asphalt back to where Amber had locked her wheels. There was no sign of blood. No serious injury. But it had probably scared the shit out of the girl. She would have gotten out, checked on the man lying in the road. And that's when he grabbed her.

"So he shoves her in his van," Finn said, following Kay back again to the Miata. "Then moves her car off the road."

Snapping on a latex glove, Kay opened the driver's side of the small car. The interior smelled of perfume and leather. "The seat's been put back," she pointed out for Finn. "He was in this car."

The lab technician straightened up from his work then on the Miata's hood. "I got something here, Detectives," he said. "Not sure how good it is. The print looks kind of messed up, but it's solid."

Kay was aware of Finn beside her. She was aware of the wind in the new leaves somewhere in the darkness overhead, of the sound of water spilling along the reservoir, and she was aware of her heart hammering in her chest.

"It's him," she said finally, staring at the familiar handprint in silver magna-powder across the shiny hood of Amber Estcott's car. "The son of a bitch has her."

38

THE ROLL-CALL ROOM of the Northwestern District smelled of coffee and shoe polish, men's cologne and floor wax. From the side of the room, Finn watched as Lieutenant Carter relinquished the podium to Kay so she could brief the uniforms on the abduction of Amber Estcott.

Almost two hours ago they'd convened in Ed Gunderson's office back at Headquarters with Mo, Bobby, Laubach, and Whitey. They'd argued about how much to give the media. Too many details could spook Estcott's abductor, Kay had suggested, and force his hand into getting rid of her. But not enough coverage would limit the chances of someone identifying her captor.

Gunderson had fielded Jane Gallagher's interview, pleading to the public for information.

"We're looking for someone who drives a white panel van. He might own a dog. Possibly a pit bull. This individual is only a person of interest in the case, not a suspect," Gunderson had said into Jane's microphone in the lobby of Headquarters.

"Foul play hasn't been ruled out, but at this point in time we also haven't determined whether this was an actual abduction. Clearly," he'd said, wrapping up the interview, *"if anyone has any information on the whereabouts of Amber Estcott, it's imperative they contact police."*

They'd debated whether to even call it an abduction. If Estcott's abductor could be convinced that they believed the girl may simply have disappeared on her own, then they might manage to buy themselves a little more time.

Now, as Kay addressed the Northwestern night shift, Finn hoped the media coverage would have the desired effect. Kay had decided they should split up and communicate with the district offices in person. Make an impact.

"If this is the same guy," she said to the roll call, "we don't have much time. We believe he kept his last victim twenty-four hours. The two previous victims weren't kept at all. So we're hoping he's attempting to harbor his victims now. Still, we may only have a day or two."

As Kay passed out photocopies of Estcott's school photo, Finn noticed the tremble in her hands. She was exhausted, looked drawn under the flickering glare of the fluorescent lights. Julia Harris's death had hit her hard. Perhaps harder than him. Finn knew the level of faith Kay had placed in the girl's recovery. And now that faith was shattered.

"County is searching the immediate area," she said, "but because his first two victims were dumped in the city, we believe our suspect lives here. We have confirmation of a match between the tire tracks left at the abduction scene tonight and ones from the white panel van used in connection with the last victim's murder. So we need you checking every white van."

A quiet ripple of murmurs moved through the room. "You have any idea how many white panel vans are driving around this city right now?" an officer in the front row heckled.

"Not that many driven by a guy with a deformed hand who owns a tan pit bull. A girl's life is at stake," Kay said, taking the podium again. "I don't care if you have to pull over every van you see tonight. And tomorrow night. And the next. Until we find this girl."

Kay still seemed shaken when they left through the back door and crossed the side lot to the car. "Who the fuck is this guy?" she said, turning the key in the ignition and adjusting the rearview.

"We'll find him, Kay."

"Yeah. Before or after he kills Amber Estcott?"

"We're doing everything we can." But Finn shared her frustration.

Unlike other cases, this one hit home now more than ever, because they actually knew the victim.

"We need to do more." Kay steered the unmarked car from the lot too sharply and the rear wheel took the curb.

"Kay, you need to go home."

"How can you even think about going home when she's out there? When he's got her?"

"There's nothing else you can do tonight. You need sleep."

"I don't need sleep, Finn," Kay said, running the yellow light at Wabash. "I need to find this girl."

39

"WE'RE DOING everything we can," Kay said, wishing her voice didn't sound so empty. Hopeless.

"I know. We saw the news." Mark Estcott was still wearing his suit. It hung, slightly creased, off his tall frame, and the silk tie was loose around his opened collar.

The attorney whom she'd seen dominate a courtroom by simply standing from the defense table and buttoning down his Armani looked suddenly small in the doorway of his daughter's room.

"We've briefed the districts. We have an AMBER Alert running. We'll find her, Mark," she said, trying to find conviction in her own words.

"Be honest, Kay, do you think she's dead?"

"You can't think that, Mark."

"One of Homicide's best detectives is standing in my daughter's bedroom at eleven o'clock at night. It's hard not to think that."

"We don't know—"

"Listen, Kay, placate my wife all you want, but don't bullshit *me*. Is this the same guy?"

Kay nodded cautiously.

She hadn't told the Estcotts much when she'd arrived on their doorstep a short time ago. After dropping Finn at Headquarters for his car, she'd driven to Guilford. She'd known it was late, but she also knew that Mark and Barbara Estcott would not be sleeping. Not tonight. Probably not tomorrow night or any other unless Amber came home.

Now Kay filled Mark in, holding back nothing: the dent in the hood of his daughter's Miata, the matching tire tracks, and the handprint.

When she'd finished, Mark nodded into his daughter's room. "So you think this could be someone Amber knows?"

"I'm not sure. But I believe he targeted her. Knew her schedule. Knew she'd be up in the county."

Kay scanned the girl's room. It was huge. Easily four or five times bigger than the one she'd had growing up. Spanning the entire southeast side of the house, the bedroom was decorated in seventies-groove-meets-society-designer. Acid-pink walls, white shag carpeting, and the furniture all smooth, clean lines. Concert posters had been professionally laminated and hung, not taped like Kay's teenhood posters. Sum 41, alexisonfire, Primus, Tugnut. On the opposite wall, shadow-box frames held ribbons from horse shows and photos of Amber in full riding regalia standing at the head of a large bay horse.

In the nook under a front dormer window, two beanbag chairs were pulled up around a low table. On it, an Apple laptop sat open, but not on. Another computer dominated the long table that butted up against the southeast window, overlooking the neighbor's backyard through a bank of diamond-shape-paned windows.

Kay crossed to the desk and reached for the blue iMac. "May I?" she asked Mark, her finger on the power button.

"Go ahead." He joined her at the desk and wheeled back the white plastic steno chair, positioning himself at the keyboard as the system booted up. "She's got pass codes," he explained, "but Amber's always shared them."

As they waited, Kay surveyed the teen's neat desk. A biology text, and American history, spiral notebooks, and a literature paper on *Macbeth* with a bold, red *A* emblazoned on the cover. A mug from Disney World held colored highlighters and glittery gel pens, beside it a blue iPod, and CDs.

Kay's eyes fell to a brass picture frame next to the monitor. She leaned in and studied the photo of a young girl holding a baby. The colors had faded, and the focus wasn't sharp, but she thought she recognized the girl.

"That's Amber," Mark said. "She was six there."

"And the baby?"

"Nathaniel. Amber's brother."

Kay straightened. "I didn't realize she has a brother."

"She doesn't. He passed away shortly after that photo was taken. A crib death."

A short burst of electronic music snapped across the computer's speakers as the system's programs launched.

"Is that Amber's music?" Kay asked.

"I think so."

"She's pretty serious about her music?"

"It's important to her, but she really wants to study law." There was pride in Mark Estcott's tone, the kind Kay had only ever imagined hearing in her own father's voice. "She's always been interested in what I do, but she's adamant she'll never defend criminals. She wants to work for the State's Attorney's Office. Amber always looks for the good in people, you know?"

Mark Estcott commandeered the mouse. With several clicks he logged on to his daughter's computer. When an error message flashed across the screen, he tried again.

Estcott made a third attempt. When it failed as well, he consulted a Post-it on the side of the monitor. In neat penmanship, Amber had recorded several passwords for different applications and websites. Estcott shook his head. "This doesn't make sense. She changed her pass code."

"Did she always let you know it?"

"Yes. I use her computer sometimes. Mostly the internet."

Estcott tried the pass code yet again, like a man repeatedly pressing an elevator button to hurry along a car that won't come.

"We might need to get a computer expert in here to hack in," she said. "Same with the laptop. Either that or we'll take them downtown. Listen, Mark, have there been any strange occurrences in Amber's life recently?"

Estcott looked blank, clearly more mystified by the altered pass codes.

"Did Amber ever say anything about feeling as though she was being followed maybe? Watched?"

"The only thing odd was that we thought someone might have been in the house," Mark said, standing from his daughter's desk.

"When?"

"Four, maybe five weeks ago. We came home and found the back door unlocked. Barbara thought she'd forgotten to lock it. But there were a couple shoe prints through the kitchen. Water and salt stains on the tile."

"Did you report it?"

"No. Nothing was taken. And honestly, at the time, I figured Amber had a friend over, you know?"

"Like a boyfriend?"

Arms folded tightly across his chest, Mark Estcott shook his head with a father's blind denial. "No. She doesn't have a boyfriend."

He nodded back toward the hall then. "I'm going to check on Barbara. Shout if you need anything."

"I will."

When he left the room, exhaustion bowed his shoulders inward.

"Mark?"

He stopped halfway down the carpeted corridor.

"I'm going to get this guy."

"I don't care about the guy, Kay. I want Amber. I want her back. Safe. Can you promise me that?"

Kay was sure Mark Estcott caught her slow nod before he took the wide, curved staircase, his eyes cast downward, his gait slow and heavy.

Alone in the room, Kay breathed in the scents that were Amber Estcott. Something spicy, almost oriental. Patchouli, Kay guessed.

The earthy perfume was stronger in the closet, lingering on the girl's neatly hung clothes—designer labels, some with the price tags still attached. The closet organizer brimmed with sweaters and school uniforms, and racks of shoes overflowed: high-end runners and riding boots to cheap, plastic flip-flops. Kay cast her eye over the tailored show jackets and hunt coats, deerskin-patched jodhpurs and riding breeches. Her fingertips brushed the soft velvet of one of several helmets that lined the shelf. Kay's own memories of riding filtered back—the secondhand gear, the ill-fitting clothes, and finally the canceled lessons when the money ran out. Kay wondered if Amber was even aware of the great privileges she had in life.

Kay needed to be cautious of her own prejudices, she realized as she closed the closet door. Couldn't let them get in the way. She couldn't allow her past resentments of the more privileged girls she'd grown up with prevent her from knowing Amber.

And she needed to know Amber. To know her would be to understand the killer. He'd chosen Amber for a reason, and if Kay could figure out why, then she'd be that much closer to him.

Kay scanned the desk again and tried to like Amber. Because liking the girl would make Kay care, and she needed to care.

Kay searched for something that could connect her with the girl. She found it in the framed photo of young Amber Estcott with her baby brother. Amber was an only child. Just like Kay. And both had lost a brother they'd never truly known.

Kay was eleven when her brother had arrived stillborn and they'd found her mother's cancer. She remembered her mother's devastation, the resonance of her father's deep silence, and finally the unbearable depression that hung over the house. She wondered if Amber too often thought of the brother she'd almost had, if the girl felt the emptiness as Kay did.

Stay strong, Amber.

Past the photo and the sun-bleached knickknacks crowding the windowsill, Kay looked into the neighbor's backyard. Underwater lights illuminated the large, kidney-shaped pool, and low landscaping lamps circled the elaborate deck. She imagined Amber taking in the same calming view each night. Imagined her sitting at her desk.

Kay laid one hand over the computer's mouse, as though she could feel the girl through the things she touched daily.

She thought of Julia Harris. The girl was gone. But there was still time for Amber.

I'm coming for you, Amber. Just stay strong.

40

HER THROAT BURNED, and a gag reflex made her cough. When she did, her head felt as if it would split and she wanted to throw up.

Amber Estcott's consciousness slid back by degrees, shades of gray and indistinct forms swimming behind her eyelids. She heard her own breathing, the air filling, then leaving her lungs. Her heart felt like a small animal moving about in her rib cage, like a bird beating its tiny wings as it struggled to find a way out.

When she opened her eyes, her focus was slow as she absorbed her surroundings, taking in the dim room. A small night-light cast a dull yellow glow across the bare walls. To her right was a window, heavy drapes blocking any light. Or maybe it was still night.

The room smelled musty, like the antique shops her mother dragged her to. Old wood and mothballs. The four-poster bed was massive, and the three and a half posts rising above her were intricately carved, the footboard spindles elaborate.

When Amber Estcott attempted to rub her eyes, the first wave of panic ratcheted through her numb body. Ropes bit into her wrists, and pins and needles coursed down her arms. A whimper slipped from her parched lips as she tugged at the bonds, trying not to let the panic take over.

She took in several shallow breaths and worked at remembering.

She remembered putting Leon into his stall, saying good-bye to Shirley, then leaving Windybrook. It was getting dark as she'd headed to Warren Road, and she'd been listening to DJ Tiësto on the stereo. Too loud. The bass throbbing as the small sports car hugged the curves. And when she'd reached across to skip tracks on the CD, she'd spotted the white van at the side of the road, its four-ways flashing. She'd slowed. Curious. And in the last split second she saw the man step out onto the road.

She remembered the locking of the Miata's brakes, thinking she should turn the wheel, but couldn't. Thinking that the car should stop in time, but it hadn't. There'd been the gut-wrenching lurch and the sickening thud as the man folded against the hood, then disappeared below the headlights.

Her hands shook when she'd fumbled with the door handle, and her legs were jelly as she circled to the front, to where the man lay on the dark asphalt, clutching his arms around his stomach.

"Oh, God. Oh, God. Tell me you're okay. I didn't see you. Please tell me you're okay."

He moaned, tried to push himself up.

And the rest happened too fast. She'd reached down, offering him one trembling hand, but instead, he'd snatched her ankle. She'd felt the strength in his wide hand as it clamped around the shank of her riding boot. There was no time to catch her balance.

The landing winded her, and her skull hit the pavement. She'd seen stars briefly, thought she'd pass out. He'd come at her then, scrabbling across the asphalt.

And then she recognized him.

She gasped. Was about to say something, but there was a burning in her throat as he'd covered her face.

Finally, there were only his eyes. She remembered thinking it was joy she saw in his face before she passed out.

Amber drew in a deep breath. The air was hot against her raw throat. She tried not to cry.

What was he going to do with her?

Amber tugged at the bonds again, feeling them tighten around her wrists, and feeling for the first time the knots at her ankles. She craned her head, tried to look down along her body.

She wore a silky nightgown. White and smooth against her skin. Flowing across her breasts and flat stomach, buoyed slightly by her pubic hair. No bra. No panties.

He'd undressed her. All of her.

A thin cry slipped from her lips. Weak and pathetic.

She tore at the bonds again, pulling and twisting until she thought she might be bleeding. And with each effort the mewling sounds rose—as if they weren't hers—until it was screams she heard.

Her screams. Rising in pitch.

She didn't hear his approach. And when the door swung open suddenly, her final scream locked in her throat. His silhouette seemed enormous in the doorway. Backlit. She squinted against the glare. Couldn't see his face, but she knew it was him.

Then there was his voice. Soft, calm.

"Shh. There's no one to hear you." And she thought he smiled. "It's just you and me now, Angel."

41

Saturday, April 22

SHE'D WOKEN WITH dread clawing in her belly and the sour taste of panic in her mouth. An uneasiness she knew could be pacified by only one outcome: Amber Estcott's survival.

Kay hadn't slept more than an hour at a time, watching the steady red glow of the digital alarm clock. Mentally she'd reviewed the cases. Leslie Richter: sexually violated, suffocated, found in a drainage ditch off the JFX where she'd been brutally beaten postmortem. Julia Harris: picked up at The Crypt nightclub where she'd gone with Finn's daughter, raped, suffocated, bludgeoned, and dumped down a slope, barely alive. And then Nina Gatsby: kept for twenty-four hours, drugged, violated, beaten, and mauled by a dog, before her body was driven to the county, where her killer hacked her open to remove her heart as a morbid offering to his next victim.

What was the commonality? What was she missing?

The disposals were all over the map. So were the abductions. Geographic profiling was useless. Victimology seemed pointless as there were only fleeting connections among the girls. Nothing concrete.

By 7 a.m. Kay had showered and dressed, stopped by the Dunkin' Donuts on Light Street, and driven to the marina. Finn's car wasn't in the lot. Clearly, he hadn't been home, and that bothered her.

Last night, seeing the warmth of Finn's house, the tenderness of his ex-wife at the door, had affected Kay. She'd thought of her last session with Constance, how she'd told the therapist that she'd never embraced that sense of normalcy. But seeing it there before her, last night—the life Finn had shared with Angie—Kay was surprised that she almost envied it now. That she *did* want it.

From the marina Kay had headed north, out to the county, and tried to shed her personal anger as she drove. She'd stopped in at Windybrook and spoken with the stables' owner. Shirley Davitt had been understandably upset over her student's disappearance, desperate to help but unable to offer any leads. She'd seen no suspicious white vans or strangers in the stables' vicinity. Amber had concluded her Friday lesson with no incident and seemed normal when she headed home. Kay had thanked Davitt and left Windybrook, but not before Davitt extended her an open invitation to ride sometime.

From the stables, Kay had gone to the abduction scene. For an hour she'd studied the scene as the morning sun tinged the sky, going over the same details from last night: the skid, the tire marks in the soft shoulder, the boot impressions. With the dampness of the forest around her, Kay tried to imagine Amber Estcott's abductor. Tried to get in his head as she paced that ribbon of blacktop.

She'd walked the scene countless times, looking for anything they might have missed last night, until finally her obsessiveness paid off. It was in the brush, only a few feet off the roadway, that Kay had found the pendant, the gold glinting from the fall-dried weeds and fresh green shoots.

Now Kay handed the necklace to Constance O'Donnell.

"This is a Mensa pendant," Constance said, turning the piece over within the evidence bag Kay had deposited it in back at the scene. "It's their international logo." The therapist rubbed her thumb across the stylized *M* topped by a globe.

"Mensa? As in the geniuses?"

Constance shrugged. "Sort of. High IQs. The international society registers people who have scored in the top two percentiles of the general population on an IQ test. That's not to say it's an indication of utilized genius. Their membership is a broad range, everything from scientists and engineers to barbers and taxi drivers."

"And now we can add serial killer to the list."

"You're sure this belongs to the killer?"

Kay nodded. She'd already called Mark Estcott this morning, described the chain to him.

"It's not Amber's. And it hadn't been sitting out there very long." The chain had been broken, one of the links wrenched open. "I think he lost it in the struggle, possibly getting her into his van." Kay had already imagined his frustration, exhausted, possibly injured from his collision with the sports car, and unable to find the chain he'd lost in the dusk, if he'd even been aware of its loss at the time.

Constance nodded thoughtfully, staring at the pendant in the evidence bag.

Kay had called her therapist from the road, intending to convince her to meet at the Towson office to get her take on Amber's abductor. The therapist had instead given Kay directions to her home, a ranch-style house on an acre of land in Harford County, and Kay wondered how her visit to Constance's home would change their relationship.

For almost two hours now, Constance and Kay had sat in the therapist's private study and gone over the case, the reports and crime-scene photos spread across a glass coffee table. Still, Kay wasn't grasping the psyche of the man who must have thrown himself in front of Amber's Miata last night.

"He's not stupid," Constance said about the act. "So far he's been very deliberate in his disposal of the bodies, as well as the abductions. If your theory is right, for him to risk what he did to get Amber to stop . . . I don't see it as reckless as much as desperate. It was planned. He knew what he was doing, but his desperation certainly seems to have overridden his usual caution. Something made this particular abduction more vital than the others."

And Kay couldn't escape the feeling that it could have been Silver's fucked-up news report that had spurred the killer into such a bold move.

"Or," Constance added, "this girl is more important to him, so he was willing to take greater risk to get her."

"Do you think it's possible Amber was his primary target all along?"

"It's a good possibility. The abduction *is* very different. Plus you've got the heart, left almost as an offering. Perhaps to her," Constance said, echoing the feeling that had started to come over Kay back at the abduction site.

Kay took the pendant from Constance. "So this guy's some fucking genius?"

"Well, if you're assuming the pendant is his, and not a keepsake from a parent or other relative. If it *is* his, it could have been a gift, or he could have purchased it for himself."

"Egotistical?" Kay suggested.

"Could be. Or it could be that, in light of his other inadequacies, like the deformed hand, he places a high value on his 'genius.'"

"You'd think he'd play with us more, then."

"He somehow got Leslie Richter's earring into your pocket," Constance reminded her. "That could be viewed as a gesture of his own perceived superiority."

A clock from deeper inside the house chimed, then started the series of bongs signifying eleven. If it was Kay's clock, she decided then, after suffering the chimes of nine and ten, and every quarter hour in between, it would have long-since succumbed to a violent death.

"Who the fuck is this guy?" she asked, sitting back from the table. "I need to know him, Constance."

"You know I'm not trained in this stuff. What about taking it to the FBI? Have them put together a profile?"

"We don't have time." Besides, Kay had little faith in FBI profilers. Only once in her career had she called in the Feebs on a serial case: Randal Hinch, a pedophile who'd left his young victims strangled in abandoned schools. It had been one of the earlier cases she'd worked with Spencer, and she'd pushed for a profiler. The three suits had arrived from Quantico requesting a full day of briefing, and in the end, all Kay and Spence had gotten from the exercise was some hard-shelled crabs on the FBI's tab and a profile vague enough to fit any suspect. Kay had learned then that it was intuition and sheer doggedness that closed cases.

"You helped me before," she reminded Constance. "Help me get inside this guy's head, or I'm going to lose this girl too."

Kay rifled through the photos again. "It's like there are two different people at work here. One is calm and calculating, abducting without struggle or witnesses. He disposes of the body with the same care. And then"—she pulled out the photo of Gatsby's eviscerated remains—"then he just loses it. Not just on her, but Harris and Richter as well. He beat these girls. Almost like he was in a frenzy. What's that about?"

Constance shrugged. Contemplated. "Resentment. Rage, perhaps."

"Rage at what?"

"That, you may never know, even once you *do* catch him. It could be rage at a life of ridicule. Rage at some inadequacy beyond that of his deformity, beyond anything we could begin to guess at. Rage at his mother. A girlfriend. A wife. At women in general."

Kay looked at the images of the girls' faces before they were murdered. "Rage that they weren't Amber Estcott?" she asked quietly.

Constance seemed to ponder the possibility, then nodded. "I suppose so. It would certainly fit if Amber has always been his main target."

And it was then that Kay began to pray their theory was right. Because if it was, if Amber *was* his primary goal, then it could give the girl more time. It could be the one thing that saved her life.

42

"I WOULD HAVE come with you." From the passenger seat, Finn watched the stately homes of Guilford slip past them as Kay drove.

When she'd walked into the office a half hour ago, she'd filled him in on her morning: her visit to the stables, to the scene of Estcott's abduction, and finally her talk with Constance. All of it delivered with a detachment that Finn tried not to take personally.

"I stopped by the boat," she said. "You weren't there."

"Sorry." But he didn't offer an explanation.

Finn watched a muscle work along Kay's jaw and suspected that she'd guessed he'd stayed the night at Angie's again.

After Kay had dropped him at Headquarters late last night, he'd called his ex-wife, asked how Maeve was doing, then turned the car around and drove to Hunting Ridge instead of the boat.

Maeve had been in bed by the time he got there. He'd looked in on her anyway, watched her sleep.

And then there'd been Ang.

He hadn't intended to stay the night or to allow his feelings to cloud the real reason for his visit. And he certainly hadn't intended to sleep with Angie. Or maybe he had.

Across the police car's stale interior he stared at Kay: her face all harsh lines and angles.

"What?" she asked him suddenly, clearly sensing his stare even though her eyes never left the traffic ahead of them.

"Nothing." He turned away.

When Kay steered onto Norwood, they could already spot the TV satellite trucks outside the Estcott house.

"Fucking vultures," Kay mumbled as they parked behind Braddock's car.

She'd wanted to join the canvass she'd told Finn back at the office, wanted to check out the neighbors. Finn followed her up the drive, past rows of boxwood hedges and azalea bushes. On the wide front porch, Mark Estcott addressed a neighborhood group. They carried staple guns and fistfuls of flyers. Next to Estcott, Adam Braddock seemed to be vying for a possible photo op.

"You want to talk to Mark?" Finn asked.

Kay shook her head. She lifted a hand to acknowledge the defense attorney, then started around the east side of the garage.

"Amber's abductor knew her schedule," Kay explained to Finn once they were away from the crowd. "So he had to be watching her."

She pointed up to the bank of windows. "That's Amber's bedroom." Then she gestured to the adjacent house. It sat closer to the street than the Estcott residence, so Amber's bedroom windows directly overlooked the fenced backyard. The underside of the new leaves on the trees backing the yard were speckled with light: the sun reflecting off the surface of a pool, Finn guessed.

He followed Kay to the house. At the front porch, Kay

rang the bell. Beyond the double doors Finn heard the ostentatious chimes.

But there was no answer.

Kay rang again, only this time the chime was drowned out by the low throttle of a car's engine behind them.

Finn watched as the black Mustang with its professionally detailed racing flames and logo careened past the satellite trucks and lurched into the short drive.

"What did Amber say about the guy she'd seen pick up Leslie Richter? Drove a black sports car?" Kay asked as the Mustang's bass reverberated.

Finn nodded. Together they took the walkway down to the drive, the engine and the music dying before they reached the bottom.

The kid who extracted himself from the driver's seat was lanky and greasy-looking, as though he'd spent the night on someone's couch after a bender. He wore a black leather jacket that matched his studded Western boots, and Finn didn't want to know what the stains across the formerly white T-shirt were.

"You live here, Cowboy?" Finn asked as the driver threw shut the car door.

The kid started at Finn's voice and flipped back the long, unwashed strands of hair from his face. "What's it to you?"

Finn flashed his shield. "Let me ask again, do you live here?"

"Yeah. Why? Something happen?"

"What's your name?"

"Well, it ain't Cowboy."

The kid started to push past them, but Finn snagged his arm, felt the flex of sinewy muscle beneath the fine leather. "You might want to reconsider the attitude there, Cowboy, or we're going to have to talk to your mommy and daddy. Now what's your name?"

The name slipped through the kid's sneer. "Edward Bahn."

"Well, Teddy, maybe you could answer a few questions for us."

"'Bout what?"

"Amber Estcott."

"What about her?"

"You watch the news, Edward?" Kay asked.

"Not lately."

"Amber's missing."

"Well I don't know anything about it."

"Any idea who might want to harm her?"

"I'm sure a few guys out there'd like to teach her a lesson."

"And what's that supposed to mean?" Finn asked.

"Amber's a slut. Always has been. Coming over here to skinny-dip, flirting with just about anything with a dick."

"So you're saying *you'd* want to teach her a lesson?"

The first flicker of nervousness tightened Edward Bahn's face.

"Does the name Leslie Richter mean anything to you?" Kay asked, showing him the school photo from her police notebook.

"Nuh-uh."

When he looked away, she moved the photo more firmly into his line of vision. "You don't recognize her?"

"Naw."

"You go to Langley Country School?" she asked.

"No. I went to Gilman."

"So you'd have no reason to drive to Langley? Hang out there? Pick someone up in your Mustang?"

"No. Do I need to be calling my parents' lawyer or something?"

"Only if you got something to hide, Teddy. How old are you?"

"Twenty."

"And still living with the folks. How's that working for you?"

Another sneer. "I'm just gonna go inside now and call my dad's lawyer, Detective, if you don't mind."

"Absolutely not, Edward." Kay stepped aside to let the kid pass, and as he did she handed him her card. "You'll call us if you think of anything, right?"

His only response was a snort before he worked his key in the door.

"It's not him," Kay said when the kid disappeared inside. She led the way back toward the Estcott residence. "He might fit the description Amber gave us, but you'd think she'd recognize her own neighbor."

43

IT WAS MORNING, but there was no sunshine in his Angel's room. No way to discern day or night.

Sensory deprivation. Paul Graves had studied the theory. Removing light and sound, and any sense of time. He'd read all about it in his mother's textbooks when he was a kid. Read about the Patty Hearst case. He hoped he wouldn't have to subject his Angel to the horrors supposedly inflicted on Hearst to bring her around to her captors' way of thinking.

He listened for her breathing now, his back pressed against the wall, his own breaths shallow and controlled. Five minutes ago, when he'd slipped into her room, she hadn't moved. He'd closed the door silently, holding the knob so the latch wouldn't catch, then stood, unmoving, waiting. Sensing her.

When he breathed through his mouth, he could almost taste her on his tongue.

He wondered if she knew he was with her, if she was listening, feeling, as he was. Through the darkness, he could almost imagine her eyes reaching out for him.

Graves brought his hand up to the switch plate on the wall behind him, but didn't turn on the light. He felt the protest of his muscles, the ache from last night's face-off with the Miata. In the shower this morning, he'd seen the bruise starting on his thigh and hip, saw the purpling along his shoulder from where he'd rolled off the small car's hood and hit the asphalt.

He'd lost his pendant too. He hadn't noticed until his shower. He imagined it somewhere along that stretch of road, wondered if he should go look for it.

It had been a stupid maneuver, really. But he hadn't known of any other way to ensure his Angel would stop for him along that stretch of road.

Graves fingered the switch that worked the electrical socket across the room, as though daring it to flip and set off the halogen work lamp he'd plugged into it. When the switch finally jumped under the pressure of his hand and the room flooded with light, he wasn't surprised that his eyes had indeed found his Angel's through the dark. What *did* surprise him was that she'd found his.

She squinted against the sudden glare, and as Graves stared at her, he tasted his first quiver of hope: hope that she might feel the same connection he did.

It had been a long night. From behind the closed door, Graves had endured her screams. First, thin, tremulous cries leading to wails and finally whole strings of shouted profanities. Not until after three a.m. did she stop, her sudden silence alarming him.

He'd listened through her door for a long time before finally opening it, and in the dim glow of the nightlight he saw the streaks across her face from her crying.

"I need to pee," she'd said to him, her bravado suddenly gone, her voice dry in her throat.

As planned, he'd blindfolded her then, keeping her at a disadvantage. Leaving her hands tied, he led her down the hall to the bathroom. She'd stiffened when he hiked up her nightie and lowered her to the toilet seat. For a long time she just sat there, and when she attempted to remove the blindfold, he scolded her. She jumped, obviously thinking he'd left her.

It took her forever to pee after that. He'd helped her wash before leading her back to the bedroom. At the doorway her bare feet must have felt the change from the parquet flooring to the bedroom's carpeting, and she'd tried to fight him. Blindly, she'd swung back with her tied wrists and caught his shoulder in the same soft depression that the Miata had. He'd cursed and shoved her hard, resolving to tie her hands behind her next time.

In the struggle she'd torn the blindfold off and in her eyes he saw hate, behind the fear, determination. He'd overpowered her quickly then, throwing her back onto the bed and binding her again.

Once done, he suffered more verbal attack. He'd tried to pretend that the insults weren't spewing from his Angel's lips. Instead, he'd taken himself back to a time of childhood taunts and when he'd begun to grow the thick skin. Like rings on a tree, Graves often imagined one could count the abuse, each blow adding another protective layer until the shield had become impenetrable. But his Angel's hostility cut through.

She'd still been screaming when he'd finally turned to leave, and Graves had kicked the night-light on his way out, smashing it and leaving her in complete darkness. She'd screamed even more after that.

This morning, though, she seemed calmer. Spent.

Cautiously, Graves lowered himself to the side of the bed next to her. She turned her face away.

The illumination of the work lamp raked the far wall and the corner of the ceiling, washing a cold light across her skin. When he touched her arm, she flinched.

"What do you want from me?"

The flatness of her tone made Graves withdraw.

"It's going to be all right, Angel. You'll see."

"Is it money you want? Cuz my father will pay you." Her voice cracked, and he didn't doubt her throat was raw from screaming.

"I don't need money."

"What then? What the fuck do you want?" She turned suddenly, and the defiance in her eyes startled him.

"I have everything I want now."

He watched her lips tighten into an angry line as she comprehended the meaning of his answer. *"Fuck* you."

He tried to touch her again. Only this time she twisted away.

"You'll understand soon enough," he said.

He lowered his face close to hers. He could smell her shampoo, and just beneath her spicy perfume there was the hint of sweat.

When he lowered his mouth to her bare shoulder and pressed his lips to the hollow beneath her collarbone, his Angel bucked away from him. "I'll die before I let you touch me, you *fucking* freak!"

"Let's hope that won't be necessary," he said, standing at last.

There was a flicker of fear behind her eyes, and then the profanities started again.

Graves turned from the bed. *George W. Bush. William J. Clinton. George H. W. Bush. Ronald Reagan. Jimmy Carter.*

"The presidents, Sigmund," his mother would always instruct him whenever the wolf threatened to come out. *"Recite them. And don't even look at me until you're finished."*

Gerald Ford. Richard Nixon. Lyndon Johnson.

Graves crossed the room, turned off the light. Closed the door behind him.

John F. Kennedy. Dwight Eisenhower.

He'd made it to President James Buchanan by the time he reached the living room. There, he lowered himself onto the sofa and turned up the volume on *The Price Is Right.* And as another contestant made the mad dash to the stage, the cheers of the audience melded with his Angel's screams.

44

"WE'RE CLOSE TO the twenty-four-hour mark." Bobby Curran straddled one of the chairs in the Homicide boardroom. The kid looked crisp in spite of the long hours.

"What does that mean?" Reggie Laubach asked him, digging into a bag of salt-and-vinegar Utz's.

The boardroom was stuffy and even Kay was becoming irritable from the heat. A headache had started behind her eyes shortly after they'd convened in the boardroom at Gunderson's request, spreading notes and reports across the long, mahogany tables and organizing crime-scene photos on the whiteboards.

"In any sexual-abduction case the first twenty-four hours are the most critical," Bobby explained, his eyes quick and alert. "After that, the victim becomes dehumanized for the kidnapper and he'll be far more likely to kill his victim."

Laubach crumpled the foil bag into one meaty fist and tossed it at the trash can. He missed. "Girl's probably already dead anyway," he said.

"Not necessarily." Kay removed her jacket and retrieved Laubach's Utz bag. Her aim was accurate. "I think he wants her alive."

"How do you figure that?" Bobby asked.

Kay thought about the killer who'd now taken up permanent residence in her head.

"It's his experience with his victims that's important," she explained. "Especially while they're still alive. In fact, I think he's angry when they're dead. He beat Richter's body postmortem. He beat Harris too, probably thinking she was already dead. He mutilated Gatsby."

"So you figure he'll keep her longer?" Finn asked.

"We can only hope. But I *do* think that Amber Estcott means more to this guy than his other victims."

"How's that?"

Kay made her way to the whiteboard. "He took drastic measures to get Amber." She pointed to the map where a marker indicated the abduction site. "He risked life and limb to stop her, if we're to assume he put *himself* in front of that car. Plus you've got him leaving the heart."

"And?" Finn asked.

"And, put those together and the twenty-four-hour theory doesn't hold as much weight here. I also think Amber's conduct in this situation is critical," Kay said. "If she can play along a little with whatever fantasy he's got going, I think he's likely to keep her alive longer."

"So where do we go from here?" Bobby asked, enthusiastic. Because the serial case was ramping up, Bobby seemed to have let go of the issue of Antwon having gone MIA.

Gunderson stood from the table. His tie hung loose and he looked weary. Kay wondered how much heat he was taking from the brass on the case.

"The AMBER Alert Plan has been activated since ten last night." Gunderson checked his watch. "We've got another seven hours before it self-cancels."

Another grunt from Laubach. Kay predicted his remark before he opened his fat mouth. "How ironical is that, huh? Same name and all."

Kay wasn't the only one who ignored him.

"We've got Missing Persons handling the calls coming in," Gunderson went on. "Sifting the legits from the cranks. In the meantime, we're keeping the particulars quiet. I don't want to downplay this to the media, but we don't wanna spook this guy either and force his hand. If Kay's right and this girl means something to him, we need to get a victimology worked up on Estcott, nail down the players in her world. Who knows her? Who hates her? Who might have been watching her?"

He turned to Kay. "What have you got on this neighbor?"

"Edward Turner Bahn," she said. "Not much of a suspect. We have a vague description that could match him and his car at Langley picking up Richter back in February. Amber said she'd seen the same guy around the school again just recently, but you'd think she'd recognize her own neighbor."

"Got anything on him?" Gunderson asked.

Kay pulled out the printout of Bahn's record. "He was brought in once, a year ago, on possession charges. His daddy's Cameron Bahn."

"The circuit-court judge?"

Kay nodded. "Charges were dropped."

"What about prints?"

"Still on file," Finn offered. "But we've got nothing to compare them to at this point. The only prints we got off any of the victims were off Richter, and Latents tells me they're off the deformed hand. Same with Estcott's car."

"Do we bring this Bahn kid in?" Gunderson asked.

"We're having him tailed," Finn said, "in case he is connected somehow."

"All right," Gunderson said at last. "So we work with what we've got. See what comes in through the tip lines. In the meantime, start Estcott's victimology, compare it to the other girls, find the link. Any additional manpower we need, we've got it. You get this guy narrowed down to an area, we can have uniforms banging on doors."

Gunderson dismissed them and Kay gathered her files. At her desk there were a half dozen phone messages. Nothing from Antwon. And at the bottom of the stack, a message for Finn. From Angie.

Kay handed it to him as he came into their cubicle, then worked at ignoring the conversation he shared with his ex-wife, his back to Kay, his voice lowered.

She'd figured he'd spent the night with Angie, but hadn't known for certain until he'd driven to Guilford with her. In Finn's awkward silence, Kay had known. And that knowing left her with a profound feeling of emptiness, greater than she'd ever experienced.

"Delaney! Line three." The shout came from one of the farther cubicles.

Kay punched the line. The sound of Antwon's voice caught her off guard, but it was his words that alarmed her.

"I got him," he repeated when she thought she hadn't heard right. "I know where Dante been layin' his head."

"An address, Antwon. Give me an address and I can get a team over there."

"No! I ain't gonna have a buncha cop cars swarming

down on the place. Dante ain't gettin' outta this one. Not this time."

"We made a pact."

"Yeah. I promised I'd call you, and I'm calling."

"I know what you're doing, Antwon. I know you know Dante's got you marked."

Silence.

"You *can't* use yourself as bait."

"Ain't what I'm doing."

"They're going to fucking kill you, Antwon!"

Over the line something brushed loudly across the mouthpiece, and for a moment Kay thought the kid was going to hang up.

"Antwon?"

"What?"

"Listen to me." She softened her voice. "Let *me* go with you. No other cops, okay? You and me. We'll bring Dante in together."

More silence. Antwon weighing his options.

"Aaiight," he said at last, and relief swept through her. "I got him stayin' down on the eleven hunert block of Carey. I'm gonna be there in fifteen minutes."

Barely enough time for her to get there. And Kay realized he didn't intend for her to actually make it.

"But only you," Antwon added. "No five-oh and all them cars. If you're there, you're there."

The line went dead and Kay was already reaching for her gun. When she clipped the subcompact Glock 17 into her holster, Finn was on his feet.

"I'm going with you," he said, clearly having overheard the call.

Kay's hands were shaking as she fumbled for her keys. She looked at Finn, thought of Antwon, her mind racing. *"Only you."*

But there was no time to waste thinking, planning, arguing.

"Okay." She had no idea what else to do. All she knew was that she had to move.

And then: "Hope you two aren't going anywhere. I might have something." Daryl Macy from Missing Persons cleared the corner of their cubicle. "Got a kid downstairs, came in a half hour ago. Says he's Estcott's boyfriend."

"Shit," Kay muttered under her breath.

"I think you'll both wanna talk to this guy," Macy said. "He's barely two degrees shy of hinky, if you know what I mean."

Kay met Finn's stare. "Son of a bitch."

"I need you on this," Finn said.

"I know." Kay looked at her watch. Calculating. "I gotta make some calls first." And as she picked up the phone to call the district, she imagined Antwon already heading down Mosher toward Carey Street. Toward Dante Toomey.

45

THE KID Daryl Macy had in the Missing Persons interview room was twitchy.

Finn had left Kay upstairs on the phone while he followed Macy down to the sixth floor. When he'd looked through the one-way window, the kid was pacing the back wall. He wore a black Moby-concert T-shirt over faded jeans, and an army fatigue jacket hung over the back of one of the Steelcase chairs.

"Name's Ruben Ramirez," Macy told him. "And he hasn't sat still since he came in. Just a little too jumpy for my taste."

Ramirez had a limp handshake and his palm was

clammy when Macy introduced him to Finn. Finn bought the kid a soda and took him upstairs. In the elevator, he tried to catch the kid's eyes, but they were quick, almost feral, as he cased his surroundings. And when Finn ushered him down the hall from the elevators, past the "Homicide" plaque on the door, Ramirez had hesitated.

Kay joined them in Interview Two, setting two of the case files into the middle of the table.

"Everyone we've talked to tells us Amber doesn't have a boyfriend," Kay said after Ramirez explained his connection.

"She's not supposed to date. So we keep a low profile. Especially around campus."

"Campus?"

"I'm a sophomore at Peabody."

From the corner of his eye, Finn saw Kay sit straighter in her chair. Across from her, Ramirez flipped back his hair with long, tapered fingers, then tumbled a quarter between and over his fingers. A pianist's hands, Finn thought. Under the harsh fluorescents, his dark hair looked oily. It was poker-straight and shoulder-length. Certainly long enough to put into a ponytail, Finn noted.

The kid's eyes darted from the closed door to Kay and finally to the cuffs bolted to the table.

"So that's how you met Amber then? At Peabody?" Kay asked.

The kid had a bad case of disco leg, his knee bouncing almost uncontrollably as he looked across the table at Kay.

"Yeah. In digital music class."

"And what about Leslie Richter?" Finn asked.

"Who?"

Finn circled the table, opened the top file, and drew out the photo of Richter. "Leslie Richter," he repeated, biting down on his impatience, wondering if Ramirez was just that good at playing stupid. "She was in your class too."

"Oh, yeah." He planted one finger onto the five-by-seven school photo. "I remember her. Just never knew who she was. She's the one who was murdered, isn't she? I heard about it around campus. Wait a second." The quarter dropped from his hand. "Why am I here?"

The kid looked suddenly like a cornered weasel. His small black eyes darting, his face pinched, and his muscles bunched, ready to bolt. And he would, if they didn't go easy on him.

"I don't know, Ruben, you came to us." Kay sounded irritated.

Finn gave her a warning glance. But she wasn't looking. She was watching Ramirez as he retrieved his quarter and started the incessant tumbling of the coin between his fingers once again.

"I came to talk to Missing Persons. To find out more about Amber. To see if I could help somehow. Why am I up *here?* In Homicide?"

"Why the hell do you think?" Kay's tone was sharp, accusatory.

Her rhythm was off, her connection to Finn compromised, he thought, no doubt because their relationship was off.

Ramirez's eyes flitted from hers to Finn's. "You think Amber's already dead, don't you? Either that or you've found her body and you're not telling me cuz I'm not family."

Kay stood then and circled the table, stopping beside Ramirez. When she leaned into the kid's personal space, one hand planted on the table, the other along the back of his chair, Ramirez tried to lean away. But escape was impossible.

"Tell me something, Ruben, what's got you so damn nervous?"

"I'm not."

"No?" Kay closed her hand over Ramirez's, and the quarter clattered to the table, spinning noisily against its top.

"Hey, I came here to help," Ramirez whined.

It was Kay's turn to pick up the quarter, and Finn was surprised when she mimicked Ramirez, the coin flipping skillfully through her slender fingers, back and forth.

"Why are you treating me like I'm a suspect all of a sudden?"

"Tell us why we shouldn't, Ruben," Kay said. "After all, we got a slimeball matching your—"

"Detective Delaney," Finn interrupted her. "I think we should get Mr. Ramirez's alibi for last night, don't you?" He didn't want Kay playing their only solid card: their eyewitness putting someone fitting Ramirez's description at The Condor Club. Not yet.

"That way," Finn added, "we can clear up this whole issue once and for all, no?"

Finn was relieved to see Kay back off the kid, but she refused to meet his eyes.

Ramirez stood then, desperate to put distance between him and Kay. His black-and-white Converse high-tops squeaked against the polished linoleum as he started pacing again.

"If you wanna know where I was last night, I was home in my apartment, alone, trying to reach Amber on her cell. All night."

"You got anyone who can corroborate that?" Kay asked.

"Of course not. I said I was alone. Maybe you should check her phone records. And mine."

"And when did you actually see Amber last?" Finn asked.

Ramirez seemed to take a mental stumble, trying to calculate the days perhaps. "Thursday night."

"Where?"

"At my apartment." The kid's gaze dropped to Richter's photo and his eyes narrowed. "Hang on. You guys think this is connected to that dead girl?"

"We're not saying that, Rube."

Ramirez's olive complexion had blanched, and when he spoke again, his voice had suddenly gone shaky. "I'm free to leave, aren't I?"

For the first time, Finn suspected the kid might actually be legit, his twitchiness due to lack of sleep and worry.

"Of course you are," Finn told him. "But if there's anything you can tell us that might help . . ."

Ramirez shook his head again. "No. I don't know anything. I . . . I need to go."

Finn fished a card out of his pocket and handed it to Ramirez. "You'll call us if you think of anything, right, Ruben?"

"Uh-huh."

"And if you hear from Amber . . ."

But Ramirez was out the door. Finn waved to Bobby across the floor of Homicide. "Detective Curran will show you out," he told Ramirez, and they watched the music student follow Bobby, disappearing around the corner to the elevators.

"So you wanna tell me what that was all about?" Finn asked Kay, following her back to their cubicle.

"The kid's not right," she said.

"I don't care. What we needed was to be able to hold him for a bit, give us the chance to check his background. Hell, maybe even find out if the mope drives a green Neon. Did you happen to consider *that* before you decided to go all bad-cop on him?"

"I get it, Finn. We don't trust the kid. Fine, we'll put a tail on him. I'll make the arrangements."

Kay still wouldn't meet his stare. He watched as she clipped her holster to her belt, slammed her desk drawer shut, and started for the elevators.

"Kay, hold up." He had to jog to catch up to her, and she'd almost reached the elevators before he grabbed her.

When she spun around, Finn couldn't tell if it was him she was angry with for last night or if her agitation was more linked to Antwon.

"I gotta know," he asked as the elevator doors shuddered open. "What exactly is your priority here? Amber or Antwon?"

"Both," she said, and pushed past him to step into the empty car. "I want to find them both."

46

THE MEYERHOFF SYMPHONY HALL rose as a glowing glass-and-brick landmark at the corner of Cathedral and Preston streets. Kay had parked down in Mount Vernon, and she and Vicki had walked to the Hall.

She'd tried to cancel her monthly symphony date tonight, but for three years now Vicki had shared her season subscriptions with Kay and had never given in when Kay would try to prioritize her work over the outing. Generally, Kay would be grateful for the diversion. In the elegant, wood-appointed hall, decked out in heels and a dress, and rubbing elbows with Baltimore's elite, Kay was able to allow the worries and demands of the job to dissolve. When the lights dimmed and the music washed over her, she could at last let go of the reality of her work, the caseload, the unserved warrants, and allow herself to be consumed by the sheer power of the music.

Yet there was no losing herself in the music this evening, no letting go of thoughts of Antwon and Amber, and Vicki had clearly sensed it. She'd noted Kay's tension during the intermission and suggested they go for coffee instead of re-taking their seats.

They'd walked to Donna's, a café in the heart of Mount Vernon, and over lattes Vicki had once again brought up Antwon. Earlier, during their drive to the symphony, Kay had finally confessed to Vicki that Antwon had ditched the foster home. Vicki hadn't been impressed and vowed to have an on-the-wing warrant issued first thing Monday morning.

And after today, Kay guessed that a warrant was the only way they'd get Antwon in now. She'd ruined any chance of convincing the kid to come in on his own.

After the interview with Ruben Ramirez, Kay had raced to west Baltimore. When she'd turned onto Carey Street, she'd immediately spotted the cluster of radio cars at the address Antwon had given her. The row house had been rammed open by the Western District uniforms, the door splintered and broken under the feet of the tactical team she'd ordered when she'd known she couldn't get there herself.

There'd been no sense taking her Kevlar vest from the trunk. She'd been too late. And so had the tactical team.

"Got nothin'," the sergeant of the team informed her when she'd joined them on the sidewalk. "Place has been boarded up awhile."

"Any sign someone's been squatting?"

"Sure." The sergeant nodded to the second floor. "Front

room there. And it looks like we just missed him. Had a blunt still burning in an ashtray."

Kay had been about to enter the house herself when her cell phone had gone off.

It was Antwon.

"You lied to me," he said, and Kay turned several times in the street, looking for him, certain he was watching her from a pay phone.

"I had to call the team, Antwon. I couldn't get here in time."

"I coulda had him."

"Where are you?" She'd scanned the street, the side alley, the opposite corner. Nothing. "Antwon. You there?"

"Dante was mine," he said at last, anger in his voice.

"Where are you, Antwon?"

"I *told* you no five-oh. And you called 'em anyway. You fucked up my chance."

"Good."

He'd hung up before she could soften her response. The trust had been broken. Kay had felt it slip away for good as she stood in the middle of Carey and took one last, desperate search of the street. She'd lost him.

Across from her now, Vicki dragged her spoon through some spilled sugar. "So what have you got on this Ramirez kid?" she asked.

Kay stirred the last of the cinnamon-sprinkled foam into her latte. "Not much."

"Is he really Estcott's boyfriend?"

"Looks that way. I talked to Mark already. He's never heard of the kid, but he dug out Amber's cell phone records. She called Ramirez's number a lot over the past six months."

"And what's Finn think of the kid? Any vibes?"

Kay licked foamed milk off her spoon and tossed back the remainder of her latte. "Kid's definitely hiding something, but Finn thinks Ramirez is straight-up in his concern for Amber. You should have seen his face when he realized we were linking her disappearance to the other girls. He's scared, Vicki. Scared for *her.*"

Kay waved down their waitress for the bill. "Still, we put an unmarked on his apartment building."

"And this other kid? Estcott's neighbor?"

"We're tailing him too. But even if one of these kids was involved by picking up victims for this guy with the deformed hand, I don't think either of them is part of Amber's disappearance. If this ever was a team, Vicki, I'm convinced this guy's working solo now."

"What makes you think that?"

"There's just a completely different feel to this one. To Amber's abduction. She means more to him." The feeling that had started in Constance's home office this morning had only grown throughout the day.

When their waitress swung by with the bill, Kay lowered her voice. "Bottom line is, Amber Estcott could die, if she's not already dead. And it'll be because I couldn't figure this sick fuck out soon enough."

"Kay, this isn't on you alone. The entire department's working this one. You know, it's not your job to save the whole world."

And Kay knew she was referring to Spencer, Valerie, and now Antwon.

Vicki reached for her jacket as Kay picked up the tab. "If you're so determined to save someone, Kay, how about saving yourself first?"

Kay wasn't in the mood to hear it. She led the way to the door, but Vicki was relentless. Stride for stride, she matched

Kay's brisk gait, past the light-flooded Washington Monument and the illuminated columns of the Peabody. Kay imagined Amber Estcott on those wide marble steps.

"How about letting yourself actually *have* a life?" Vicki went on. "Live for *you* instead of the job. Tell me something, when was the last time you had a vacation?"

Kay stopped for the pedestrian light and tried to restrain a laugh. "I'm not sure who's the kettle and who's the pot in this scenario."

"Touché."

A warm breeze rolled down Cathedral Street then, carrying bits of trash and paper in its wake, and the glass-concrete paving stones of the Mount Vernon roundabout glittered in the headlamps of passing cars.

"So you wanna tell me what's going on with you and Finn?" Vicki asked, and Kay wished she hadn't parked so far north of the café.

Vicki had always known of Kay's relationship with Finn, from the start and all along their rocky road. After their year apart, Vicki had picked up on the renewed intimacy between Kay and Finn when the Eales investigation had brought them back together. So it shouldn't have surprised Kay today when Vicki sensed the tension between her and Finn.

Kay had avoided Finn most of the rest of the day, knowing she needed to apologize. She should have handled the questioning of Ramirez better, should have followed Finn's cues in the interview room instead of letting her frustration and disappointment with herself affect their teamwork.

She *did* owe him an apology, and the opportunity to explain himself.

But hearing the truth wasn't going to be easy.

Admitting it was even more difficult.

"It's over," Kay said now just as a Central District unit

blew past them, its siren blurting once, drowning her out. When she repeated herself, she was startled at the sadness and resignation in her voice.

"Just like that?" Vicki asked.

"No, not just like that. It's been a long time coming." And Kay considered—not for the first time—how ironic it was that she felt Finn leaving her just as she'd begun to arrive at the idea of a deeper commitment.

"His decision or yours?"

"In the end, does it really matter?"

Vicki said nothing for a half block, giving Kay the silence to fill.

"I can't give him enough," Kay said at last. The admission stung.

"And how do you figure that?"

She was tempted to tell Vicki about the house down in Essex, but it hurt too much.

"I'm only calling it as I see it, Vick. Finn needs more out of a relationship. Deserves more. And I'm just . . . I'm not there yet."

"I don't think you give yourself nearly enough credit."

Kay shrugged, hoping Vicki couldn't see how she struggled not to cry.

Reaching the 4Runner, Kay fished the keys from her pocket, and as she unlocked the passenger side for Vicki, a gust blew back the edge of her jacket. Kay felt naked in the short black dress. Exposed, like her emotions to Vicki. Vulnerable.

"Anyway," Kay added, "I think Finn's back together with Angie."

"And just like that you're going to let him walk away?"

"It's not my choice. Besides, they had children together."

"So?"

"So, they share things that I can't even come close to offering. Children, Vicki . . . that's a bond I can never compete with."

And as Kay climbed into the driver's seat of the SUV, she found it curious, and perhaps a little sad, how easily she could compartmentalize her emotions and the hurt, how her thoughts, tonight, were less with Finn and more with Amber Estcott.

47

Journal Entry #46
Ted Bundy. Now there's a guy who wasn't out to get caught. He escaped twice: the first time through a courthouse window, and then out a hole he'd cut in the ceiling of his cell with a hacksaw blade. What I'd like to know is where he got that blade.

Either way, he wasn't one of those whiners who says, after the fact, that they wanted to get caught.

Then again, for all his bragging about his high IQ and his time as a law student, he was an idiot for getting caught with a busted-out taillight.

It's all about the details. If you've covered the details, it's so simple to not get caught. Bundy was arrogant. He was cocky. Figured he was superior to everyone else so he didn't have to consider the details. I won't let MY superiority trip me up, though, get ME caught. No matter how good I get at this, I won't get complacent.

Paul Graves sat back from his computer, the letters across the screen blurring, his eyes tired.

She was quiet again.

He logged out of the server, closed the modem connection, and turned off his computer. Following the short corridor to his Angel's room, he unlatched the lock and opened the door slowly.

The room smelled of urine, the odor stronger as he approached the side of her bed.

His Angel refused to acknowledge him, staring at the window as though some indication of the time of day might slip through the heavy drapes.

The light from the work lamp paled her skin, made her look fragile. Like a porcelain doll. But her mascara had run, and her tears had left small black flakes in their path. She was beautiful.

"You need to eat," he told her. He'd been surprised she'd taken in anything. When he'd come in earlier, he'd managed to entice her with one triangle of toast, the butter congealing as he'd waited for her to finally surrender to her hunger.

But she hadn't spoken to him the last two times he'd come into her room. Not until he moved to the door to leave would she begin screaming at him, her eyes wild and desperate the second before he flipped the light.

In all his fantasies, Graves had never expected the foul mouth on his Angel.

"Just a little more," he coaxed with the cold toast, immediately regretting the supplication in his tone. He could never give her the upper hand. Should never let her realize the power she had over him.

He was tired. Keeping her deprived of sleep meant he got little himself. At first he'd go in a half hour after the screaming stopped, knowing she'd be on the edge of sleep.

But she screamed less now and Graves knew she was managing to find rest in between his visits.

He lifted the toast to her lips again, willing her to take a bite. She turned her head, her chin tilting up. Defiant.

Graves tossed the dried bread onto the plate.

"We should get you cleaned up." He wondered if she'd urinated on purpose. "You've made quite a mess." He worried that she might defecate at some point too. He wasn't sure he could deal with that. He'd have to go out today, buy a plastic sheet, then flip the mattress.

When he caressed her bare arm with the Hand, his Angel cringed.

"Don't touch me with that, you fucking freak."

He stopped, letting the Hand linger against her hot skin for a moment before lifting it to the light. He turned it several times, allowing her to see it: the twisted digits, the webbed tissue between them gnarled and pink as though it had been scarred from burning.

"It revolts me too," he told her finally. "Should I turn out the light so you don't have to look at it?"

She didn't respond, but he could tell she watched from the corner of her eye. Fascinated and repulsed at the same time.

"I've considered cutting it off, you know," he said. "They'd give me a prosthetic then."

She said nothing.

"I saw a man on TV once. His feet were paralyzed, from some accident. He could walk fine, but he couldn't run. And he wanted to run. He knew he'd be able to run with prosthetics, especially those new hydraulic ones. Only problem was his insurance wouldn't pay for them because it wasn't like he couldn't walk at all. So you know what he did?"

His Angel didn't acknowledge him, but he knew she was listening.

"He developed a website. Then he constructed a guillotine in order to chop off his feet. And he planned to do this live, broadcast it over the internet, and charge people twenty dollars to watch it. Then he would use the money to buy the prosthetics, and he'd be able to run again. I don't know if he ever went through with it though.

"I could do something like that. For you I would."

He could see she didn't believe him.

"You know that girl in the woods?" he asked then. "Up by the reservoir?"

She turned to him at last, her eyes flashing. Fear.

"I did that for you."

"Did what?" A crumb hung on the corner of her mouth, and when he attempted to brush it off, she jerked away.

"I cut her heart out."

Confusion tightened her face. "What?" The word strangled in her throat.

"I cut her heart out, and left it for you. That morning when all the police were at the school. You didn't even know, did you?"

Her complexion washed a shade paler.

"It wasn't easy either, but I needed to do it. So you'd know."

"You sick freak!" She pulled at her bonds, her movements increasingly desperate. Twisting and bucking. Her wrists began to redden under the pressure, and her hands turned purple.

"I just wish you'd seen it," he said.

He waited. And eventually she stopped struggling, her energy depleted, her breathing rapid, and her eyes wide. The temporal artery had risen along her temple, snaking back toward her hairline. He watched it pulse, blue under her white skin.

"What the fuck do you want from me?" Her voice was thin.

"I think you know."

This time when he touched her, he used his good hand. This time he didn't care that she cringed. The sheer fabric of her nightie caught on his calloused hand as he cupped one small breast in his palm, kneaded it gently, felt her about to fight. But she didn't.

Was she finally feeling what he felt?

He eased his fingers around the soft flesh of her other breast, suppressed the groan he felt originate in his groin. When he brought his gaze up to her face, her eyes were closed, her jaw clenched.

It was definitely going to take time.

With one last lingering caress, Graves removed his hand. His Angel's eyes opened. Cool. Blue. Mesmerizing.

From under the bed, he slid out a box. Saw the flicker of panic in her eyes when he placed it on the bed beside him.

"It's all right," he tried to soothe her. He opened the box, felt the softness of cashmere against his fingertips as he took out the dainty sweater. He guessed it barely covered her midriff. He held it out for her to see, as a girlfriend might in a clothing store at the mall.

"Where did you get my clothes? You stole my clothes?"

"You need to wear something." He removed another article from the box.

"You broke into my house and . . . What else did you steal, you pervert?!"

"I'll have to help you dress. Get you washed up."

"You were in my room." A new hostility sharpened her voice now.

"Or you can stay in your soiled nightie," he suggested, believing the threat would bring her to reason.

He was wrong.

"What else did you steal? Tell me!"

George Washington. John Adams. Thomas Jefferson. He'd work his way forward this time.

Graves stood from the bed. Looked down at his Angel.

"Tell me what else you stole!"

James Madison. James Monroe.

Her screams were merely white noise now. He had to block them out. Had to believe in the process. Believe in his Angel.

John Adams. Andrew Jackson. Martin Van Buren.

Believe in Fate.

48

Sunday, April 23

"AT THIS HOUR the AMBER Alert has been lifted per state protocol, but police are still searching for seventeen-year-old Amber Estcott, her abandoned car found Friday night here, just south of the Loch Raven Reservoir in Baltimore County." Jane Gallagher looked hollow-eyed in the glare of the camera's light, her dark hair lashing at her pale features.

The footage had been shot last night. No later than ten, Kay guessed. In time for the feed to be edited back at the station and run on the eleven-o'clock news. And then again this morning.

"We got a leak," Mo Greer had said in her voice mail to Kay last night. The Rape detective had left the message shortly after the first airing, but Kay had missed the segment, and it had been too late to call Mo back.

After dropping Vicki off last night, Kay had spent several hours going over the case files at Headquarters, sitting in the dry heat of the boardroom, staring at photos of the victims and the crime scenes, willing each to whisper the answers she hadn't yet found. The answers she needed to save Amber's life.

When the answers didn't come, Kay had driven to west Baltimore.

She never did find Antwon, although she cornered a couple of his homeboys. She knew they lied when they told her they didn't know where Antwon was, but she sent a message with them anyway: that there'd be a warrant out for Antwon and he should call.

". . . only a quarter mile west along this strip of asphalt, the body of Nina Gatsby, a Baltimore resident, was found last week," Jane went on, wind buffeting her mike.

Standing now in the middle of her bedroom, the remote in one limp hand, Kay fought another wave of nausea. She'd already thrown up her morning coffee a half hour ago. Exhaustion and stress.

". . . not the only connection. A police source also confirms a suspected link between the disappearance of Amber Estcott and the murder of fellow student Leslie Richter two months ago, *and* to Julia Harris, who succumbed to her injuries Friday afternoon at Mercy Medical. Police aren't saying *how* the three homicides are related or how Amber Estcott's abduction is connected . . ."

"Son of a bitch." And as Kay considered the members of the task force, she had a pretty good idea whom Jane would have been most able to manipulate information out of.

Kay clicked off the TV and tossed the remote onto her bed when she heard the knock at her door. Peering through the peephole, she saw Bobby. He shifted his weight from one foot to the next on her top-floor landing, about to knock again when Kay switched back the dead bolt.

"What the *fuck* were you thinking?"

Bobby didn't even flinch at her question, but the guilt on his face assured her she'd guessed right.

"You caught the news, then?" he asked.

She didn't invite him in, but instead turned back into her living room.

Bobby followed.

"Let me explain, Kay." His suit looked fresh, as did his shirt. But clearly there'd been less thought put into the co-ordination of Bobby's tie, and his hair was light on the gel this morning. Kay wondered how much sleep he'd gotten after realizing his screwup.

"So which head were you thinking with last night?" she asked.

"It wasn't like that."

"Right. And how drunk were you?"

"I wasn't."

"How many?"

He shook his head. "Four. Maybe five beers. But I wasn't drunk."

"And how many of those beers did Jane Gallagher buy for you?"

Bobby shrugged.

"Did she approach you?"

"Actually, no."

"And exactly where did this intimate little exchange take place?" But Kay wasn't sure she wanted to know.

"At The Sidebar." The bar, two blocks from the Clarence E. Mitchell Courthouse, was popular with cops and court-house regulars, journalists included. "I was there after shift. She came in. We got to talking. That's it. Fuck, Kay, it was off-the-record."

"For Christ's sake, Bobby. You were talking to Jane Fuck-ing Gallagher. What part did you really believe she would leave off-the-record?"

"It wasn't like that," he said again. "I *didn't* tell her we had a connection between the cases. I swear. She figured that herself."

"You told her who was working the investigation, didn't you?"

He nodded.

"Me and Finn. Laubach and Whitey. Mo."

Another nod.

"And what more do you think she needs to put the pieces together? Christ, Bobby!"

"I'm sorry."

"Sorry isn't going to save Amber Estcott's life."

If the man with the deformed hand knew they were connecting Amber's abduction with the murders, it could accelerate his plan, forcing him to get rid of her sooner.

"I'm getting dressed," she told him finally. "We have to see what kind of damage control needs to be run."

She turned then, but Bobby stopped her before she hit the hallway.

"There's something else, Kay."

He must have seen the anger flash behind her eyes because he added, "No. Something good. It's about Estcott's boyfriend."

"What about him?"

"I learned what kind of car he drives."

"He doesn't own a car."

"No, but that doesn't mean he doesn't drive one."

She hated the self-righteous smirk on Bobby's face, hated that it could take root so quickly in spite of the shame he should be feeling over the blunder with Jane.

"What are you talking about, Bobby?"

From the breast pocket of his suit jacket, Bobby withdrew a piece of paper. He unfolded the document and handed it to her.

A photocopied traffic report.

"Ramirez got a speeding ticket," he told her even as she read the details. "The car was registered to a Mrs. Jacinta Ramirez. The spic's mother. And"—Bobby moved beside Kay to point out the vehicle description—"it's the same kinda car used to pick up Gatsby. A dark green Neon."

49

"JANE WOULD HAVE connected the dots anyway, Sarge," Kay said.

Between her apartment and Gunderson's office, Kay had cooled down. With a girl's life at stake they couldn't start turning on each other now. If anyone was to blame for the leak, it was Jane Gallagher, with her ruthless, underhanded tactics.

"The only thing that *should* be surprising is that Jane didn't stoop to sleeping with that fat-ass Laubach for the information," Kay added.

Gunderson couldn't restrain his smile.

"Knowing Jane," she went on, "it was only a matter of time before she put two and two together: Finn and I on the Gatsby murder and now working the Estcott case. It was just a matter of time before she drew the conclusion anyway. I don't think you should come down on Bobby.

"Besides, it *was* Bobby who found out about Ramirez's mother's green Neon, Bobby who got the dancer who witnessed Gatsby getting into a Neon the night she disappeared."

"So you're thinking this Ramirez is our guy then?"

The idea hadn't settled with her yet. Kay shook her head. "His description *does* match the one given by The Condor Club's owner, meaning Ramirez could have been a broker, picking up Gatsby for the killer. The thing is, I just don't see a kid like Ramirez out there in the woods eviscerating that girl, you know? And his feelings for Estcott . . . there's something genuine there."

"And the other girls? Could Ramirez have been the broker for all of them?"

"I don't know."

"What if our perp knew Estcott was Ramirez's girlfriend?" Gunderson offered. "Targeted her because Ramirez couldn't get him another girl in time, so he took the kid's girlfriend instead?"

"It doesn't really fit. If Ramirez *does* have a relationship with the killer, knows who he is, then he would have given him to us. He wouldn't want Amber in danger."

"Damn it." Gunderson stood and his chair hit the back wall. "We're running out of time, if we haven't already. You got everyone in the boardroom?"

Kay nodded.

"Let's put some heads together. See if Missing Persons has come up with any leads. We gotta save this girl."

In the boardroom, Laubach had already staked out his territory next to a box of Krispy Kremes. Kay was surprised to see him hunched over the Leslie Richter file. He brushed crumbs off the pages when he looked up.

"Anything from Missing Persons?" she asked.

Both Whitey and Laubach shook their heads.

Kay joined Bobby at the whiteboards. His gaze didn't come off the photos of the girls as she stood beside him.

"You're covered," she whispered.

"Thanks. I owe you."

"No, you don't. Just stay away from Jane."

He nodded silently.

Kay's eyes met Amber's, frozen in celluloid, captured by a school photographer. She tried to see past the girl's perfect complexion, past the makeup and the expensive haircut.

She thought of Amber's bedroom, the photo of her dead brother. And then Kay thought of Amber in the clutches of the man who had brutally murdered three girls.

Thirty-nine hours he'd had her now. Longer than he'd kept Gatsby. How much longer would he keep her? And what was he doing to her?

"Hate to break up the party . . ." Finn walked into the boardroom. "Just got a call from the district. Apparently our boy's on the move."

"Which one?" Kay asked.

"Ramirez. Left his apartment fifteen minutes ago."

"Tail still on him?"

Finn nodded.

"Where's he headed?"

"The lobby. He's at the front desk right now. And he's asking for you and me."

50

ON THE POLICE RADIO, Kay contacted the district officer who'd followed Ruben Ramirez, instructing him to block the green Neon parked down on Gay Street while she called Vicki for a search-and-seizure warrant. She put Bobby in charge of the search and met Finn at the elevators just as he stepped off with Estcott's boyfriend.

Ramirez appeared even more beaten down with worry this morning, his features pinched, his complexion anemic. On a good day, with the thin, manicured sideburns and the kind of grooming Ramirez clearly embraced, Kay guessed he was probably a handsome kid. A bad boy. The kind of dark rebel girls like Amber fell hard for.

Today though was *not* a good day. He'd changed his T-shirt, but wore the same frayed jeans and rumpled army fatigue jacket. He hadn't shaved since Friday, Kay guessed, nor did it seem as though he'd washed his hair.

"What's up, Rube?" Finn asked, pulling out a chair for the kid in Interview One.

Ramirez acted even more agitated today. Drumming his fingers against his pant leg, he crossed the narrow room. He left his jacket on this time, ignoring the heat. On the faded canvas of the right shoulder someone had scrawled the oxymoron "Anarchy Rules" with black permanent marker.

"You have anything for us on Amber?" Kay asked.

The kid perched on the edge of the chair and shook his head. "I was hoping you'd have something new to tell me."

Kay laid down the case files and sat. "Nothing new, Ruben."

"You've got to find her," Ramirez said, and Kay thought the kid might cry. His eyes were glassy and his whites were red. When he ran his fingers through his greasy hair, his hands shook.

In less than twenty-four hours Ruben Ramirez had come completely unraveled.

"I saw the news. That reporter says you're linking Amber's disappearance to those other girls."

"The reporter simply jumped to some conclusions," Kay said.

"But she's right, isn't she? I saw the files you had out yesterday. You're trying to link Amber's kidnapping with those other girls. That's why I'm here. To tell you you're wasting time. It's *not* the same guy."

"Why don't you let us decide that, huh, Rube?" Finn stopped pacing the side of the interview room and sat on the table next to the kid.

Ramirez scratched at his scalp. "You got it all wrong, I'm telling you. It's not the same guy. Something's happened to Amber and you're wasting your time. Wasting *her* time."

"You on something, Rube?" Finn asked then.

"What?" the kid's voice squeaked.

"Are. You. On. Drugs?"

"I'm not fucking on anything. Damn it! I'm freakin' out about Amber and you dicks are walking around with your heads up each other's asses."

"Calm down, Rube," Finn warned.

"Don't tell me to fucking calm down. You—"

"Ruben." Kay waited until the kid's focus came back to her. "Ruben, what is it you're not telling us?"

"It's not him."

"Not who? We can't help you until you tell us what you know."

"It's not him. You just gotta believe me. You need to find her. Someone else has Amber, and you're wasting time trying to connect her to those other girls." He gestured to the files next to Kay. "Don't you get it? You're running out of time."

Behind those brown eyes, Kay recognized his desperation. Could see his love for the girl, and the panic that bubbled up as she and Finn let silence fill the room.

"Damn it! Are you just going to sit there?" Ramirez slammed his fists onto the table and bolted up from his chair to rise over her. "Why aren't you fucking doing—"

But Ramirez's words caught in his throat. Finn had him by the shoulders and hauled him back onto his chair.

"Easy there, Rube. I wouldn't want to have to arrest you for threatening an officer."

"Go ahead! Arrest me. Don't you get it? I don't care!"

"What are you saying, Ruben?" Kay asked, keeping her voice level.

"All I care about is Amber. It doesn't matter if you send me to prison. Give me the death sentence. I don't care! I just want Amber to be all right."

His eyes were wild now, his hands clenched into tight fists.

"Ruben, talk to me." Kay softened her voice.

His body rocked now on the edge of the hard chair. An inner struggle that boiled closer and closer to the surface.

"If you have something that can help us . . ."

Kay saw the glisten of tears in the kid's eyes, saw his body go slack, resigning at last.

"I'll confess, okay? I'll confess. For Christ's sake, you just gotta find Amber."

"What are you confessing to, Ruben?"

He reached across the table and laid one trembling hand on the case files, as though he were placing it on a Bible. In the simple gesture, Kay recognized that the inner battle was over. Ruben Ramirez had surrendered.

"Leslie Richter," he said, his voice flat now. "Julia Harris. That dancer from the club. *I* killed them."

51

FINN DIDN'T QUITE believe the kid. It was too easy. Suspects didn't just walk in off the street and confess.

Ruben Ramirez had waived his right to a lawyer. "We don't have time for that shit," he'd said. "A lawyer's only gonna advise me to shut up, and I'm not going to do that. There's no time."

They'd left Ramirez locked in Interview One while Kay retrieved a tape recorder and Finn fetched a couple sodas. They hadn't left him long, afraid the kid might change his mind. And when they started the official statement, Ramirez sipped his Coke and chose his words carefully. Too carefully. Finn knew they weren't getting the whole truth.

"How did you pick up Leslie Richter?" Finn asked.

"That was easy. We were in the same music class. I told her I had a piece I was working on, something I wanted her to listen to."

"And just like that, she comes up to your apartment?"

Ramirez nodded.

"A real Romeo, huh? Did you have sex with her?" Finn asked.

"Not exactly."

"What does that mean?"

"I played with her." His voice was flat, emotionless. "But Harris I had sex with."

Julia Harris. At The Crypt with Maeve. Finn liked to believe Maeve would never have left the club with a guy like Ramirez. But then, they'd found GHB in Richter's system and he'd most likely used it on Julia too. How easily could Maeve have gotten the spiked drink?

"I used a condom though," Ramirez went on. "So I know you won't find any traces of DNA."

Finn tried to unclench his jaw. "And Nina Gatsby?"

"The dancer? Yeah, I used a condom with her too."

"And then what?"

"What do you mean 'then what'? I dumped them."

Finn paced some more. "Why should we believe you, Rube, huh?"

"Why the hell would I *lie* about something like this?"

"You have no idea the kinds of nutbars we get coming in here aiming for their fifteen minutes."

"Ruben." Kay's voice was softer. More patient. "Tell us how you killed them."

The kid fidgeted on the hard chair, eyed the cuffs on the table, then scratched furiously at his scalp. Finn wondered if he felt the room closing in on him. Four cinder-block walls painted vomit green, tightening around him, squeezing the last of the hot air out of the room.

Sweat beaded across Ramirez's brow and temples, glistened along his nose. He rocked slightly now, staring someplace past Kay's shoulder, to the far wall.

"Ruben," Kay whispered. "We want to believe you. Why wouldn't we? We could clear our murders. More importantly, if someone else has Amber, then you're absolutely right, we *need* to shift the focus of our investigation. But unless you give us details that can corroborate your claim—"

"Fine." Ramirez took in a deep breath and held it. Finn saw the shift in his expression then. Subtle, but there. Where only a moment ago he'd been frantic and animated, now he seemed almost dispassionate.

"With Leslie, I used some GHB I got off a guy on campus. She was unconscious for a while, on the living room floor. When she started to come around, I put a bag over her head. It took her a while to die. And when she was dead, I dumped her under Falls Road. Same story with the other girl, from The Crypt, only I didn't get the chance to bag her. She came to and started screaming. I couldn't afford the neighbors hearing, so I whacked her."

"With what?"

"I don't remember."

"You don't remember?" Finn asked. "You fucking bashed her head in so hard you knocked a couple of her teeth out. And you don't remember?"

"A bottle. I think it was a wine bottle. I had to whack her a few times before she went down, and then I drove her out to Morrell Park. Tossed her into that culvert."

Ruben Ramirez's emotionless voice hung in the silence of the small room. His words chilling in their matter-of-factness.

"And you thought she was dead?" Kay asked.

"Of course I did."

"When did you discover she wasn't?"

"The next morning. When I heard the news."

"So it wasn't you who called 911?"

"Why the hell would I do that? Someone must have seen me."

"And what about the dancer, Ruben? How did you kill her?"

"Same way. I drugged her. Then put a bag over her head and I dumped her out in the county."

"Why there?"

"Because I didn't want a repeat of Harris. Figured I'd take her someplace remote."

"And once you got there," Finn interrupted, "you figured you'd carve her up a bit, is that it?"

"What?"

"Come on, Rube, your story's so good up till now. Lacking in a few details, but not bad. Give us the whole thing though. Tell us how you carved her up and maybe we'll believe the rest of your story."

Ramirez looked as though Finn had just spoken in a foreign language. When his eyes shot to Kay, she gave the kid an expectant shrug. Ramirez scratched at his scalp again, harder this time. When he brought his hand back down to the table, Finn noticed traces of blood under the short nails.

"I don't know what you're talking about."

"You're disappointing me, Rube."

"I don't know what you want."

"We want the fucking truth!" When Finn slammed his open palms against the table, Ramirez jumped, his body ratcheting back into the chair at last.

"I'm giving you the truth!"

"There's nothing you've given us that you couldn't have lifted from the fucking news."

"And why the *hell* would I do that?"

"You tell me."

"All I want is for you to find Amber, okay? The more time you waste on these other girls, the farther you are from finding Amber. You need to find her, because I don't know *who* the fuck's got her."

The knee started bouncing again, and Finn's impatience had worn thin.

"And what does Amber think about you killing these girls, Rube?"

"She doesn't know."

"Was she going to be next?"

"No. I love Amber. Listen, what's it going to take for you guys to believe me?"

Kay leaned forward, closing the gap between her and Ramirez. "While Detective Finnerty was escorting you up from the lobby, I ordered a warrant on your mother's car, the green Neon you parked down on Gay Street."

"Yeah?"

"If we find one hair, one fiber, blood, *any* trace of Nina Gatsby or either of those other two girls in that car, you know what that means?"

"Yeah. It means you'll believe me. But we don't have time for that!"

"Then give us more details," Finn said.

"Look, you find Amber and I'll tell you whatever you want. Every last gory fucking detail, okay?"

Ramirez was shaking his head, chewing the inside of his cheek. His eyes welled up. "You've *got* to find her. You've got to find her." He didn't stop until Kay took his wrist in her hand.

"Ruben." She waited for his eyes to meet hers. "Do you have a pet?"

"A pet?"

Kay nodded.

Ramirez seemed confused by the question. And then,

for the first time, Finn saw the quiver of a smile touch the kid's mouth.

"That's it, isn't it? That's the proof you need. Ellie," he said quietly.

"Who's Ellie?"

"My pit bull."

52

KAY WAS RIDING on pure adrenaline.

Four district cars were waiting for them at Ramirez's building in Butchers Hill. The three-story walk-up of disintegrating brick was an eyesore set in amongst the grander, restored post–Civil War row homes that dominated the neighborhood named in the 1800s for its population of butchers and poultry preparers.

Ramirez's ground-floor apartment took up the north corner of the building. Two windows faced the street, and a double slider opened onto to a low balcony in the back. Kay had circled the building, casing the entrance and exit, the alley. Ramirez's windows were heavily draped, and the slider was blocked with a bar to prevent break-in.

"Watch your step," Kay warned the two uniforms who positioned themselves at the back slider. It was clear Ramirez had trained his dog to jump the balcony railing to relieve itself on a patch of crumbling asphalt.

"Easy to remove the bodies," she pointed out to Finn as they scanned the maze of wooden fire escapes and tiny balconies that surrounded Ramirez's back patio. "Lots of privacy."

Kay thought about Ramirez back at HQ. They'd held him on involuntary detention, and when they'd left him in a holding cell, he'd once again begged them to find Amber.

On the drive to east Baltimore, Kay had wondered more about the romance between Ramirez and Amber. She wished she'd asked Ramirez if it was sexual. She'd simply assumed it had been, but what if his sexual violation of the girls was motivated by a lack of sex with his girlfriend? What if the fury vented in the postmortem attacks on Richter and Gatsby were *because* the girls weren't Amber?

Unless, of course, Ramirez *didn't* have anything to do with the after-death brutalities. In the interview, Kay believed the kid's confusion when Finn had brought up the evisceration of Gatsby. It was the one aspect of Ramirez's confession that left Kay uneasy, made her more certain than ever that more than one person had been involved with the girls' murders.

"Detectives." A uniform came around the side of the building. He stopped short when his duty boot came down on one of the fresher dog turds. He swore. "Animal Control's here," he said, scraping the sole against the concrete.

"Thanks. And put on your vest," Kay told the officer as she and Finn circled to the front.

The superintendent waited for them in the entryway. A half dozen mailboxes lined the wall in the stairwell, some of the brass doors were hanging askew, and flyers had banked up in one corner. Kay felt her sweat dampen her shirt under the Kevlar vest.

The super was an ox, filling the entryway with his girth and his body odor. In his fat hands he held the consent-to-search form signed by Ramirez. It would suffice for now, get them into the apartment in case Kay's read on Ramirez was wrong and he actually had Amber locked in his apartment. But a search-and-seizure warrant would hold more weight, so while the team had assembled, Kay had typed the warrant and left Mo Greer to search for a judge willing to sign on a Sunday.

"You have the key?" Kay asked the super.

He nodded.

They followed him down the narrow hallway to Ramirez's door, his keys jangling at one blubbery hip. Kay felt her heart race. The corridor was dim, and the carpeting—an eye-bending 1960s pattern in orange and red—was worn and stained. The place smelled of mold, bacon grease, and cat piss. A deep, rhythmic bass pulsed louder as they neared the end of the corridor. Electronic music.

The super stopped at apartment A, and Kay gestured for him to step away from door. She nodded at the four uniforms, directing two of them to the opposite side of the doorframe.

"We don't know that there isn't anyone in the apartment," she said, her voice low.

"You mean the music?" the super asked. "That shit's always on. Don't matter if he's home or not."

"Still, we could have someone inside," she told the uniforms. "Could be a victim. Could be a suspect. We *do* know there's probably a dog inside. A pit bull. And from what I know I wouldn't exactly call her friendly." Kay looked to the two Baltimore City Animal Control officers, then turned back to the door.

Kay's firm knock elicited one muffled gruff, then sniffing at the threshold.

There was a pause in the music, and for three seconds Kay imagined someone *was* inside. Ramirez's accomplice? But the music started up again, the same grinding bass that brought to mind The Crypt on Pratt Street. Kay knocked again. The only answer was the dog's snuffling. Then another low gruff.

Her third knock started the dog barking. There was a scuffle from inside the apartment. The dog pawing at the door.

"How do you wanna do this?" Finn asked her.

"I can unlock it for yous," the super said, "but I ain't opening it."

Kay gestured for the key, waited for him to sort through the ring with his sausage fingers and hand her the right one. It slid into the lock easily, the dead bolt clearing the jamb with a thud.

The dog stopped barking, and Kay visualized it on the other side, wagging its tail, expecting Ramirez. When the door didn't open, the barking started up again.

"You can go," Kay told the super, returning his keys and waiting for him to shuffle off down the corridor with a few backward glances.

The dog's barking rose in volume.

Kay looked to the BCAC officers. "I'm not sending you guys in until we clear the place. You wanna show me how to use one of those?" She gestured to their control sticks.

"I can get her for you." Mike Venable was a fresh-faced rookie who looked far too young for the uniform. He had introduced himself upon their arrival with a seriousness that didn't quite match his youth. "I've got a pit at home. And a rottie," he said.

"Can you work a stick?"

"Show me," he said to the BCAC officers as they gave him one of the aluminum poles with a padded loop at one end.

When he had it ready, Kay ushered him to the hinge side of the doorframe and started for the knob.

"Wait." Finn stopped her. From around his neck he removed his ID lanyard and hooked it over the doorknob.

"Better to use this. Don't want the dog going for your wrist."

"Good." She looked to Venable. "You ready?"

Venable nodded.

Kay turned the knob, cleared the latch.

Venable gave the door a nudge with the end of the stick. The dog quieted.

And as Kay fed the lanyard inch by inch, allowing the door to open inward, Venable eased the pole through the widening gap. Just below the electronic cadence of the stereo, she could hear the dog breathing. Then a soft whine. Saw its muzzle for a second as Venable twitched the pole.

And then: "I got her."

Kay saw the stick jerk hard in Venable's hands a couple times. "Are you sure?" she asked.

"Yeah, yeah. I got her."

Kay released the door then, backing away. She found reassurance with her hand on her Glock's grip.

The dog Venable had snared in the loop was pure, rippling muscle. Its tan hide appeared darker in the shadow of the apartment, and its square head looked enormous at the end of the control stick.

"Hound of the fucking Baskervilles," Finn whispered from behind her.

"No, no. She's fine. Come on, girl," Venable coaxed, giving the pole a few gentle pops. "What's her name?"

"Ellie," Kay said, her eyes not leaving the dog. Not trusting.

"Come on, Ellie. Atta girl." Venable made clucking noises in the side of his cheek, and Kay thought she saw the dog's ratlike tail wag stiffly. "She's all right. That's a good girl."

The dog didn't resist the control stick, inching to the

door, muscular legs shifting rigidly beneath its barreled chest. The heavy jaw hung open, panting, and the dog's eyes moved from one officer to the next. Kay didn't like its eyes. Pale yellow and predatory.

It balked suddenly, its cropped ears cocked, its tail stopping.

Venable encouraged her. "Come on, Ellie. There's a good dog." He slapped his uniformed thigh and Kay was about to say something about Venable's one-handed grip on the control stick.

But she was too late.

The dog erupted. In a flex of sheer muscle that reminded Kay of documentaries of sharks thrashing in the water, tearing at their prey, the pit bull arched at the end of the stick. It came off its front feet for one instant and had the pole in its jaws the next. One violent twist, the dog's weight behind it, and Kay saw the control stick tear from Venable's hand. She froze as the dog's expressionless eyes met hers. Blinked once. The exchange unfolding in slow motion. And in those two seconds Kay remembered Nina Gatsby's mauled body.

Kay took a step back, and her nine cleared leather.

The aluminum pole hung useless from the snare around the dog's neck, dragging when it took a quiet step forward. In her peripheral Kay saw Venable stoop down, reach for the stick, drawing the dog's focus away from Kay.

There was no sign. No growl. Not even a quiver of muscle. And the dog was airborne.

Venable muttered, "Jesus," just before the dog hit him, the force and weight of the animal almost taking the rookie off his feet. He reeled back, one arm pinwheeling behind him until he hit the corridor wall.

And then Venable was screaming.

The rookie's hand and wrist were lost in the pit bull's wide, scissoring jaws, his body jerking in response to each savage shake of the dog's thick head and neck.

Kay was aware of Finn grabbing the stick, dragging the dog backward, but Venable came with it. Screaming.

Blood splashed the rookie's uniform, his polished duty boots, and spilled onto the carpeting.

There was no time for thought. Only instinct and raw reaction. Kay's index finger moved from the Glock's guard to the gentle sweep of the trigger. The site lined. The air filling her lungs and then its slow release as she drew back on the five and a half pounds of trigger pull. The ear-shattering blast. The flash and the thin plume of gas and gunpowder. The sulfur odor of burned cordite. And the dense smell of fresh blood.

53

THE HOUSE WAS QUIET. Too quiet. Amber wondered if she was alone.

It was at least a half hour since she'd heard him last. Or maybe it had been ten minutes. Or two hours. There was no way to know. Hours and minutes meant nothing when time was measured by the breaths she took.

She'd already decided that at least one day had passed. It felt like three. And she'd concluded that the window behind the heavy drapes to her right was fake. Either that or it was boarded up. When he turned the lamp off, the only light was the narrow slit under the door—a dim, yellow glow that she stared at for hours.

She'd taken to keeping track of the sounds in the house. Trying to figure out a rhythm. His routine. His habits. She'd hear him move from room to room. Several times she heard power tools and hammering, the high-pitched whine of a saw screeching through what felt like the dead of night.

He liked game shows. If she screamed enough, he'd crank up the volume. *Wheel of Fortune. The Price Is Right.*

Jeopardy! was his favorite. She'd hear him blurt out the answers before the buzzer.

Once or twice she'd heard the squelch of an old dial-up modem.

Now she heard nothing but the hiss of air coming through the vents. Something scratching on the roof. A bird, probably, like the pair of pigeons that used the roof over her bedroom.

She wasn't sure what was real anymore, and what was a dream. At first she figured he was drugging her, but she suspected now it had more to do with not sleeping. He never let her sleep. And when she did, it was light. Especially after the last time she'd woken to find him standing next to her bed. The first couple times she'd been freaked out. But the last time had truly terrified her.

She'd opened her eyes, unsure of what had woken her. And there he was. Stark fucking naked. His body paperwhite. Almost hairless. He'd had a hard-on, half-mast, and he stood there, eyes closed, his hand rubbing his groin.

When he'd opened his eyes and seen her, he'd stopped. Shocked. Embarrassed, maybe. And he'd just stood there, his hand frozen, his erection fading.

It had taken all her willpower not to scream, to fight back the panic. Instead, she held his stare, said nothing, and peed.

She'd read somewhere once that a rapist would often stop if the victim urinated. It took a lot for her to do it, but she wasn't going to let the one-handed pervert rape her.

The bed was wet and cold now. Her skin was raw, and

she felt chilled in spite of the hot air that constantly pumped up through the floor vents. She wondered if peeing had been such a good idea after all.

Still, it had worked. When he'd seen what she'd done, his hand had dropped to his side—as limp as his dick. He'd looked from the spreading wet spot back up to her face and wordlessly left the room. She knew he was angry because he'd forgotten to turn off the light. It was on now, the glare of the work lamp washing across the stucco ceiling, flooding away the shadows. And she stared at the image of Ruben.

Immediately above her, a water stain had created rust-colored blotches in the old plaster. She saw Ruben's face in the stain. Looking down on her. Watching over her.

The stain had become her refuge. Staring at it, her thoughts could escape this place and the man with the hand.

The hand grossed her out. It felt like a lizard crawling across her skin when he touched her. Still, she worked at controlling her reaction to it. To him.

If nothing else, the last visit he'd made to her bedside—with his hard-on—convinced Amber that he wanted sex. *Not* to rape her. If he'd wanted to rape her, he would have done it already.

If it was just a body he wanted, she would have woken to find him on top of her. Or worse, he would have killed her already.

No. He wanted real sex. Not just a body. He wanted her to touch him as much as he wanted to touch her. He wanted her to be *his*.

And it was then, as she looked up at Ruben's face, that Amber knew what she had to do. She swallowed back the bitter taste of bile as she imagined it, tried not to cry as the lump formed in her throat. She had to be strong. Ruben would want her to be.

54

THEY'D HAD TO dislodge the dog's jaws from Mike Venable's wrecked arm. The rookie's wrist was a mess of mangled flesh, exposed bone and tendons. Venable had passed out briefly, twice, before EMS carted him off to Johns Hopkins. Kay had instructed Animal Control to retain the dead pit bull for evidence, and as they bagged it, she muttered, "Fucking dog. Fucking dog," several times under her breath. She'd spoken little after that.

"You had no choice, Kay," Finn had told her. "Dog had the kid's shooting arm. If the wrist isn't totally fucked, Venable owes you his career."

His words had seemed of little comfort. After shooting the animal she'd looked queasy. Finn had wanted to suggest she sit out the search on Ramirez's apartment, but knew she'd never agree.

To the monotonous squawk of Ramirez's electronic music vibrating over the half dozen speakers, the uniforms had cleared the one-bedroom apartment. There'd been no sign of Amber Estcott.

Finn finally killed the stereo, his ears still ringing from the discharge of Kay's gun. Preserving the scene, they'd waited outside. Got some fresh air. And by the time the Mobile Crime Lab arrived, Kay had started to regain some of her color.

For over two hours now they'd sifted through Ramirez's apartment.

The kid was a slob, either that or his life had literally disintegrated in the past forty-three hours that Estcott had been missing. Dishes sat unwashed in the sink and the dog had gotten into the trash. Shreds of plastic food wrappers and a couple of destroyed take-out containers were strewn across the old linoleum and the parquet of the living room.

The furniture was a combination of Salvation Army and low-end Ikea. A futon sofa. Scarred, veneer coffee table and side tables. A fake, acrylic Persian throw rug.

The bedroom furnishings were sparse. Another futon sat unmade on a low frame. Milk crates turned on their sides acted as shelving. Cheap dressers with the drawers half-open, and the closet awash with clothes and more Converse sneakers.

Having seen the Estcott home, Finn had difficulty imagining Amber Estcott being comfortable in the dingy student digs. He guessed a big draw for the girl was the wall of electronic equipment in the living room: computers, sound boards, speakers. Two office chairs sat behind the long desk of equipment, and Finn imagined Ramirez and Estcott composing together.

Finn watched Kay now. Her expression intense. She'd taken off her Kevlar and her shirt was damp, clinging to her toned body.

Finn wondered how long they could maintain the personal distance and still function as the finely synchronized partners that made them such a formidable team.

With gloved hands she poked through the clutter across Ramirez's desk, pushing aside papers and unmarked discs. At the stereo she hit the eject button and removed the CD that had been blasting earlier. She shook her head when she held up the disc.

"What is it?" he asked.

"Death Requiem," she said, turning it to show him the handwritten label. "How much you wanna bet it's *his* masterpiece?"

She bagged the disc. Then scanned the shelves.

"It doesn't fit," she said at last.

"What doesn't?"

"Whoever got rid of the girls' bodies knew what they were doing. But Ramirez doesn't have any books here on forensics or procedures. Nothing. Not even his computer." She waved her hand at the monitor. "I've been through his browser and there's nothing to indicate that he frequents the kinds of sites that would educate him. He doesn't even own a TV, so it's not like he's been watching crime documentaries on A&E or even fucking *CSI.*"

"So he had help," Finn said. "Someone who knows what they're doing. The guy with the deformed hand and the white van."

"There's also no porn. No fetishes. Nothing to indicate any kind of preoccupation with sex and death. Not a single deviance. From everything here, this kid's only obsession is his music."

"No trophies either," Finn pointed out. He'd already gone through the contents of Ramirez's fridge, sifting through containers of rotting takeout and unmarked packages of indistinguishable meat from the freezer. He'd taken a couple as evidence, uncertain of their origin, but even through the freezer burn he guessed they were chicken breasts. Not Nina Gatsby's.

"They don't all fit into neat little profiles, Kay."

"You guys okay with me killing the lights now?" Nadine Silvestri from the Mobile Crime Lab was a sleek, leggy woman who seemed more designed for a fashion runway than the grime and gore of a crime scene.

"Go ahead," Kay told her, switching off the two desk lamps.

Silvestri nudged a pair of yellow-tinted wraparound goggles over her own glasses and shouldered the portable CrimeScope. With the main living area dimmed, Silvestri started to work the high-intensity forensic light across the parquet flooring.

She didn't have far to look.

"You've got blood here," she said, squatting near the couch. "Lots of it. Your boy cleaned up but not well enough. Looks like it was a bloodbath."

"Where?" Finn asked.

Silvestri handed Finn the viewing goggles.

"What am I looking for?" he asked.

"Anything black." She aimed the violet beam of the CrimeScope, and through the goggles Finn could see the dark staining in the grooves and joints in the parquet. Spread out over half the room. Wherever Silvestri aimed the CrimeScope more black appeared.

"Bio stains like urine and saliva, semen and sweat, all react to ultraviolet by fluorescing," she explained. "Blood is the only bodily fluid that absorbs the wavelengths, so it shows up black."

"Could it be anything else?" Finn asked, handing back the goggles.

"Not likely." Silvestri was already taking out a Hemastix strip from her kit. Working a dampened swab into one of the crevices, she applied it to the strip, and together they watched the tip turn from bright yellow to green.

"You got blood," she said. "I'll start taking samples."

"Julia Harris," Kay whispered behind him.

"If this is from your victim, we'll put her here," Silvestri said. "There's lots to sample. And it's all good."

"How about the drain traps?" Kay asked.

"Got them already. Some nice samples of hair, even a few fingernail clippings. I tell you, any amateur could have processed this scene." Silvestri flashed a winning smile. "Don't know why you guys called in the best."

But Kay didn't smile. Even in the dim light of the room Finn could see she seemed unsettled.

"What is it, Kay?"

She shook her head. "This kid isn't the brains," she said finally. "He's obviously part of this, but the guy with the deformed hand, he's the one with the agenda, the one who knows what he's doing."

She nodded at the interior of the apartment. "Brains knew Ramirez would fuck up at some point. That's why there's no outward evidence of anyone else here. Nothing to point us beyond Ramirez."

Nadine Silvestri gestured back in the direction of the bedroom where Finn had last seen her partner working a magna brush under a plume of carbon powder. "Marty's got loads of prints. You'll have lots to compare to your guy. Submit the rest through Morpho," she said, referring to the newer automated fingerprint identification system the Department now utilized.

"Well, with this blood, we got the leverage we need for Ramirez," Finn said. "Kid definitely knows more than he's spilling. We'll get Vicki to offer him a deal. A life sentence versus the death penalty could be all we need to convince Ramirez to flip on this club-handed scumbag." And as much as it made Finn sick to imagine Ramirez *not* getting the death sentence, it would be a small price to pay if they could get Amber Estcott back. Alive.

"Jesus." Mo Greer stood in the doorway of the apartment, surveying the blood in the corridor. "Is that all from the dog?" she asked.

"And Venable," Finn said as she crossed the threshold and joined them.

"Glad I missed that," Mo said, and nodded to where Silvestri swabbed the floor. "You guys getting much?"

"Lots," Kay said. "Nothing that helps us find Amber though. Where's Bobby at with the warrant on the Neon?"

"Car's headed to the Impound. Lots of hairs and fibers throughout the interior."

"Any blood?"

"Enough. He must have wrapped 'em really well."

Finn wondered how the white van figured into Ramirez's orchestration of the disposals.

"We got Ramirez processed," Mo said. "Kept him at HQ though. Figured you two'll want to talk to him before he goes to Central Booking. I tell you, I'd like a crack at the bastard myself."

As Kay filled Mo in on the physical evidence from the apartment, Finn crossed to where Silvestri worked the floor by the futon couch, photographing and swabbing.

He pointed to the tinted goggles the crime-scene technician had set aside. "Do you mind?"

Silvestri handed them over along with the CrimeScope, showing him how to best angle the light source. Working it across the flooring, Finn saw again where blood had seeped into the cracks and grooves of the worn parquet, out of reach of Ramirez's mop. He wondered if the kid had planned on doing a proper job later, or if he thought what he'd done was enough. Kay was right: the kid wasn't the brains.

"Everything we've gotten needs analysis. Comparison," Finn heard Kay tell Mo. "We've got nothing that immediately puts any of the girls here."

Finn aimed the light source beyond where Nadine Silvestri worked, past the faux Persian rug, and knelt to examine the underside of the futon couch. More dark specks indicating blood, smaller flecks of other biological evidence, hair, fibers. But Finn stopped when the violet beam fluoresced something larger. It glowed pale yellow and he recognized it even before he reached under the futon to pick it up in his latex-gloved fingers. Touching it made his stomach turn.

". . . no trophies, no personal belongings from the girls," Kay was telling Mo. "It would be nice to put at least one of the victims here without having to wait on the lab. Have something to take back to Ramirez."

"How about this?" Finn asked, holding up his find.

"What is it?" Kay held out her hand and Finn settled it into her gloved palm.

"A tooth."

55

"THAT'S JULIA HARRIS'S, isn't it?" Finn tossed the evidence bag onto the table in front of Ramirez.

Through dozens of interviews together, Finn's patience in the "box" had almost always outlasted Kay's. Today, though, in the tight quarters of Interview Two he seemed almost out of control. Kay knew it was because of Maeve. She wondered how many times Finn had imagined his daughter playing the role of Julia Harris in the violent scene that had taken place in Ramirez's apartment.

Down in Booking, Ruben Ramirez had been relieved of his clothing, the jacket, jeans, T-shirt, and sneakers taken as potential evidence. They'd given him a one-piece Tyvek protective suit, the white polypropylene billowing around his rangy frame now as he leaned forward to examine the contents of the plastic evidence bag.

"What is it?" Ramirez asked, clearly loath to touch the bag.

Finn pushed it closer to the kid. "It's a tooth, Rube. You can't tell?"

"Jesus." The kid shot back, away from Julia Harris's cuspid, and his Adam's apple quivered several times as he swallowed hard.

"Is it Harris's?" Finn asked again.

"How the hell should I know?"

"It came from your apartment. You must have busted it out when you smashed in her face, huh?"

Behind Ramirez now, Finn leaned over his shoulder, bringing his face close to the kid's. Ramirez angled away.

"We got you, Rube," Finn whispered. "Got enough evidence from your apartment to stick a needle in your arm."

"Fine."

"I want the other guy too though. The guy who helped you."

"Nobody helped me."

"Then how come we got a witness at The Condor Club says otherwise?"

Ramirez shot him a look.

"That's right," Finn went on. "An eyewitness has you getting into your mother's Neon with Nina Gatsby and someone else behind the wheel. You wanna tell us about that?"

Ramirez shook his head.

"Who helped you?"

"No one. That . . . that night at the strip club, I was with a friend. He's got nothing to do with this."

"Then he won't mind talking to us. What's his name?"

Again, Ramirez shook his head.

"Was it Eddie?" Kay asked.

"Who?"

"Edward Bahn. Amber's neighbor."

"I don't even know the guy."

"Who helped you, Rube?" Finn pushed.

"No one!"

"You expect us to believe you carried those girls outta your place by yourself? And Gatsby . . . how did you get her all the way into the woods without help, huh?"

"I dragged her."

Kay felt Finn's hostility fill the interview room.

"Who the fuck helped you, Rube?" he asked.

"I already told you. No one."

"Bullshit! We *know* you didn't do these murders alone."

"I *did*."

"Who's the guy with the deformed hand?"

"The what?"

"Your friend with the fucked-up hand, Rube. Who the hell is he?"

Ramirez shot forward in his chair again, bringing himself closer to Kay, trying to distance himself from Finn.

"Come on, Ruben," she coaxed. "Help us out here. Help yourself."

"I don't know what you're talking about. I killed those girls. Me! No one else. You need to find Amber."

When he sat back again, the movement forced air up and out of the Tyvek suit. Kay smelled the kid's sweat.

"That's it. I'm not answering any more questions until you find her. And if you're going to badger me like this, then maybe I should get a lawyer in here."

Finn was about to erupt, but Kay met his eyes, silenced him with a look before he could start.

"Are you *asking* for a lawyer, Ruben?" she asked.

"I already told you, find Amber and I'll answer anything you want. We don't need to involve any lawyers."

Kay nodded. From inside the top folder of files she'd brought, Kay removed the other evidence bag. She slid it across the table. "Do you recognize that?"

Again Ramirez wouldn't touch it, worried the bag might contain another body part. When he'd assured himself it didn't, he pulled the bag closer: the necklace she'd found up in the county. He fingered the Mensa medallion through the plastic.

"I've never seen this before," he said.

"You're positive?"

"Yes."

She wasn't sure what it was about the kid, but Kay believed him then.

"What's it got to do with anything?" he asked. "Does it belong to the guy who took Amber?"

Kay didn't respond, only tucked the evidence bag back into the top folder.

"We had a little trouble getting into your apartment," she told him, uncertain how he'd take the news.

"What do you mean?"

"Your dog. Ellie?"

"Yeah?"

"She's dead."

Instantly, he wilted, his face going slack. "Aw, fuck. You killed my dog?" he said finally. "You shot her?"

Kay nodded.

"Why would you shoot Ellie?"

"She attacked one of our officers, Ruben."

"Aw, fuck. Fuck. That's just not right."

"We had no choice. At this point we don't even know if the officer will be able to resume duty."

She wasn't certain Ramirez even heard her now. She reached across the table, settled her hand on his arm, feeling the flex of muscle beneath the Tyvek suit.

"I'm sorry," she said after the silence stretched out too long.

"Probably just as well. No one would have looked after Ellie."

"Ruben." Kay waited for him to look at her. "I want to save Amber as much as you do. But you need to help us. You need to help yourself."

She waited for him to look at her.

"I talked to the State's Attorney's Office," she said. "There's a good chance they can offer a life sentence instead of the death penalty if you cooperate." The thought made her ill. "A deal could—"

"But I *am* cooperating. I came here. Confessed to the murders. What else can I do?"

"Tell me who helped you, Ruben."

"No one fucking helped me!"

"I understand you're maybe wanting to protect someone, Ruben, but has it crossed your mind that whoever did these murders with you, helped you dispose of them . . . did you ever stop to think that he might be the one who has Amber now?"

"No. You've got it wrong."

"How wrong?"

"All wrong. I killed those girls. *I* picked them up. I murdered them. And *I* dumped their bodies. Amber being taken has nothing to do with any of it. I swear. *Nothing."* When Kay looked at his hands, they were tight fists on the table.

"Ruben, Amber's life is at stake."

"You don't think I know that? Christ! What is fucking wrong with you people? Why can't you just get out there and find her?"

Finn circled the table, stopping at the stacked case files.

He didn't look at Ramirez. "So, you're saying it was all you, huh?"

"Yes!"

Finn pulled out the Gatsby file, flipping through the photos. "So it was you who ripped this girl's heart out then, right?"

"What?"

"After your dog went nuts on her, after you drove her up to the county and dragged her into the woods, you carved her up. Cut her wide open and stuck your hand up inside of her and pulled out her heart, is that what you're telling us? Then you cut her breasts off. What did you do with her tits, huh, Rube?"

"I don't know what the fuck you're talking about."

Finn slapped down a long shot of Gatsby's body in the woods, police personnel surrounding her ravaged body. The details weren't the best, but it was clear she'd been cut.

"I didn't do anything to her. Maybe it was wild animals."

Finn found a close-up: the rainwater pooled over her gray innards, her breasts carved off. He shoved the photo at the kid. "Animals didn't fucking do that!"

There was only a flicker of a warning, one that Kay caught but Finn was too slow to recognize. Kay stood from the table only a fraction of a second before Ramirez threw up. It spewed across the table, the photo, and spilled onto the floor.

The stench of hot bile made Kay's own stomach curl.

"Son of a bitch." Finn backed away, leaving Gatsby's photo in the center of it. "All right, Rube. You just got the room to yourself."

"We'll send someone in to help you get cleaned up," Kay said, scooping up the case files and following Finn out the door.

As they passed the first set of detectives' cubicles, Finn asked Bobby to escort Ramirez downstairs and get the cleaning staff to come in.

"What the fuck was that about?" Finn asked Kay when they reached their own cubicle. "How come the kid throws up seeing his own handiwork?"

"Maybe because it's not his own. That's not the kind of reaction you can fake."

"So what are you thinking?"

"Maybe it wasn't Ramirez who carved up Nina Gatsby."

"Okay, so it's the other guy. Ramirez's buddy goes back and does it after they've dumped her."

Kay nodded as she dropped into her chair. Exhaustion rippled through her. She looked to the photo of Amber Estcott, propped up on her desk. Prayed the girl was still alive.

"And if it wasn't Ramirez who cut out Gatsby's heart," Kay said, "then maybe it wasn't him who beat Richter postmortem or called 911 after dumping Harris. This other guy could have gone down into that culvert and realized she was still alive."

"And what, had a sudden bout of remorse?"

"It wouldn't have anything to do with remorse if the guy didn't have anything to do with the murders."

"What?"

Kay envisioned the bodies of Gatsby and Richter. The after-death attacks were brutal. There was real anger there. Rage. And Kay just didn't see Ramirez in that role.

"Maybe it's someone else entirely," she said. "Whoever did these postmortem acts, maybe he's got nothing to do with the murders, or Ramirez. Maybe it's someone Ramirez doesn't even know."

Finn was shaking his head.

Kay went on, "Look, we've got the van at both places. We've got the handprint. I really think that if Ramirez knew this guy with the deformed hand, he'd give him to us."

"Unless he's covering for him."

It was Kay's turn to shake her head. "No. There's nothing and no one in this world Ramirez cares about more than Amber. Even his own life means nothing in comparison."

Kay drew out the crime-scene photos of Gatsby and Richter. Saw the fury in each postmortem blow, in each slice of the blade.

"What if Ramirez didn't have help, Finn?" She pointed at the photos. "What if this is someone else? Someone who maybe doesn't even *have* a connection to Ramirez?"

"And what? This other guy just stumbled onto the kid's victims?"

"Maybe he's been following him. Who knows? Obviously Ramirez doesn't. And obviously trying to find Amber *through* Ramirez is a dead end."

56

ELIMINATE WHAT CANNOT BE ATTAINED. That was the only way to escape a sense of failure. His mother had taught him that without intention. When Paul Graves, at age nine, had failed miserably at the cello, balancing the bow in his club hand, his heart not in it, his mother had simply stopped taking him to lessons and sold the instrument. When his coach had benched him more than he'd let ten-year-old Paul onto the field, his mother had thrown his soccer uniform and cleats into the trash, and when the league card came in the mail the following season, she'd torn it up, muttering how she'd wasted her money.

Same with chess . . . it didn't matter that he'd moved through the ranks and placed second at the U.S. Amateur

Championship Midwest. When he lost to a boy two years younger, the first thing his mother had done when they'd returned home from the tournament was gather the board, the pieces, his books and ribbons, and thrown it all out for the trash the next morning. Every last stitch of evidence that would remind her of his failure was gone. Erased.

Graves sat in his van now, parked in the short drive, and wondered if he'd have to erase his Angel.

He wasn't sure how long he'd sat there, the engine idling, the garage door open, staring at the split-level bungalow. From the drive, and from the street, the house looked normal. Looked lived in. He'd hung drapes in the bay window, and a silk philodendron sat on the sill. The only other window on the front of the house was his Angel's. On that, he'd installed blinds inside the casing, so that the heavy plywood could not be seen.

His eyes fixed on his Angel's window now, as though he could see past the blinds, the plywood, and the heavy drapes. See his Angel in her bed. He'd left her for a good part of the afternoon and evening, unable to withstand her hostility any longer. Unable to face the very real threat of failure.

He wondered if she was sleeping. If she'd heard the garage door.

Beyond the gaping door, the garage was dark. He'd switched off the van's headlights, and with only the thin illumination of the streetlamp behind him, the contents of the garage were nothing but distorted shapes and shadows. Still, his gaze searched the murkiness, as though he could see the rolled-up tarp hanging along the west wall.

He could wrap her in the old tarp. He'd already wondered if he could carry her through the living room and the kitchen, or if he'd have to drag her the whole way to the garage.

The thought of killing her made him sick. He wasn't sure he could stomach it, but he was running out of options. His Angel might never be capable of loving him.

He'd already imagined putting her in the Patapsco, weighting her down. He'd imagined watching his Angel sink into her watery grave. But he suspected he wouldn't be able to do it. He knew he'd have to cut her open, make sure she didn't bloat. And he just couldn't imagine taking a knife to her beautiful porcelain skin.

Maybe he'd take her up to the county, find a place in the woods where no one could find her. He could use his uncle's scattergun.

The old Ithaca Auto & Burglar 20-gauge was almost an antique, but it worked. He'd found it in the house months ago, along with the original paperwork. His grandfather had bought it over seventy years ago for $40.55 before the newly enacted National Firearms Act had ended Ithaca's production of its version of a sawed-off because its short barrel didn't meet federal mandates.

It was an odd-looking weapon. Graves had been fascinated with the find, cleaning up the old piece, oiling the blue steel and polishing the walnut stock. With only four and a half thousand of the shotgun-pistols ever produced, the piece was worth well over a grand to collectors. But Graves had kept it. A keepsake from a grandfather he'd never known.

Yes, he could drive Amber up to the county and shoot her there. Cleaner that way. Less chance of someone finding her. The only risk was his own weakness. Leaving her in the county, Graves knew he'd be drawn to her. Again and again. He knew he'd have to fight the compulsion to return, knew he wouldn't be able to leave her. Not entirely.

But at least he'd be rid of her. And then he'd have to get

rid of the bed, her clothes, every last piece and fiber. Erase her. Erase his failure.

Erase it all.

57

HE CALLED HIMSELF MEMNOCH, like the character from the Anne Rice vampire novels. Finn recognized it from the books in Maeve's room.

The bartender at The Crypt with his spiked hair and studded dog collar had an attitude Finn would have liked to slap off his stupid face. For barely two seconds he studied the photo array Finn and Kay had prepared, then planted one heavily ringed finger onto Ramirez's face.

"You're sure?" Kay asked, her voice raised to compete with the techno music that vibrated through the club.

Finn scanned the bar. Nine o'clock on a Sunday night and the place was packed. Latex and black leather. Girls in fishnet stockings and skimpy skirts. Boys with eye makeup and black lipstick. Goths and freaks. Finn wondered how many of them were sexual predators like Ramirez.

"Of course I'm sure," Memnoch shouted across the bar. "His name's Ruben, right? Like the sandwich."

Kay nodded. "So he's a regular then?"

Memnoch shrugged. "I guess."

"Does he come in alone?"

"Not always. He has a girlfriend, I think."

Finn withdrew the school photo of Amber Estcott from his jacket pocket and slapped it onto the bar. "Her?"

"Yeah. She's been here a couple times. With him."

"She's underage," Finn said, accusation in his voice, but Memnoch merely shrugged. "You know her name?"

"'Fraid I never caught it."

Finn tucked the photo away and withdrew one of Julia Harris. "Any idea if this Ruben dude was here the night this girl was?"

The kid looked at Harris's photo. "That's the girl in the hospital, right? How's she doing?"

"She died."

"Whoa."

Finn didn't know what to make of the kid's reaction. "Was Ruben here the night she disappeared?"

Memnoch squinted, as though sorting back through his memory, then nodded. "Yeah. Yeah, I'm pretty sure he was."

"And you remember this how?" Kay asked.

"Cuz I hadn't seen him in a while. And he was weird."

"How so?"

"Just different. Twitchy, I guess. Didn't stay too long. Come to think of it, now that I see his picture, he mighta bought that girl a drink. The dead one, I mean."

"Was his girlfriend with him that night?"

Memnoch thought for a moment. "Honestly, I couldn't tell you." He excused himself to serve a couple of brightly colored drinks and two Natty Bos to a patron at the bar.

Finn watched the vampiric-looking youth balance the four drinks and weave his way through the crowded tables to where his friends waited for him. Finn couldn't imagine Maeve in a place like this.

"You ever seen Ruben in here with anyone else?" Kay asked the bartender when he returned. "A guy maybe?"

Memnoch nodded. "Yeah, a couple times. But not in a while."

"You know who his friend is?" Finn asked.

"Naw. Another student probably."

"He have a club hand?"

"A what?"

"A deformed hand."

The kid shook his head. "Not that I remember seeing. But it's not the brightest place, and it does get kinda busy." He nodded toward the opposite side of the bar where another patron awaited service and was about to excuse himself when Finn reached out and caught his arm.

"One more thing." Finn fished out his wallet, flipped past his ID to the photo of Maeve. He held it up to the bartender's face. "You ever see this girl?"

Memnoch's eyes narrowed as he studied the picture. "Yeah, she was with that other girl."

"The dead one," Finn finished for him. "Yeah. Well, take a good look at her. You ever see her in here again, you're not serving her drinks, you hear?"

"Sure. No problem." But the kid refused to meet Finn's eyes and was already moving away.

"I'm only asking once, shithead," Finn stopped him. "I hear about you serving her anything more than a soda and I'll have this whole place shut down, you got me?"

This time when Memnoch nodded, Finn felt satisfied he'd made his point. He closed his wallet and pocketed it, then turned from the bar.

Out on the street Finn could still feel the music from the club in his bones. It faded as they walked down Pratt to the car. He thought of Maeve at home. He thought of Amber Estcott, somewhere. Wondered if she was still alive. And he thought of Mark and Barbara Estcott, and the nightmare they were living.

"Where do we go from here?" he asked Kay.

Kay was silent as he unlocked the police car and tucked in behind the wheel. They'd already talked to Tank at The Condor Club tonight; in spite of his former confidence, the bartender hadn't ID'd Ramirez from the photo array.

"You want to head back to the office?" Finn asked.

Kay shook her head.

"What about Antwon?" He knew she had to be worried about the kid.

"No. I need sleep. Even just a few hours."

"I'll take you home." Finn started up the Lumina and pulled into traffic.

They said nothing to each other as he steered west. In the passing lights of the city, Kay looked wrecked. He doubted she'd slept the past two nights since Estcott's abduction, probably blaming herself for not having predicted the killer's move sooner.

When Finn pulled to the curb outside Kay's apartment, she didn't invite him up, but then he didn't turn off the car either.

Finn caught her arm before she could get out. "Kay, we need to talk."

He watched her stare out the windshield up Hamburg to where the hill dropped off to the Key Highway and the harbor. But Finn's mind was back in Maine, in Frank Delaney's parlor six months ago.

"Gotta hand it to you, you got guts, boy. You'll be damn lucky to ever get that girl nailed down," Frank Delaney had said when Finn had asked him for his daughter's hand. *"Kay . . . her spirit just never seems to settle, you know? Always looking for something she can't find, moving from one place to the next. That's how I know how much this job of hers means to her, because of her staying in Baltimore as long as she has."*

And Finn hadn't realized just how right the old man had been.

"I really need to explain," Finn said now, no longer able to tolerate the silence.

"No. You don't." She closed her eyes briefly, and when she turned to him at last, he saw her sadness.

"It's all right, Finn. There's nothing to explain. Whatever you decide, I'm fine with it. Really. I understand."

She settled her hand on his leg then and leaned across the center console, pressed a quick kiss to his cheek.

"I'll see you in the morning," she said.

And as he watched her cross the street and disappear into the converted row house, Finn wondered how Kay *could* understand, if she'd ever truly known how much he loved her. And he wondered how—after almost four years—it could end so quietly.

58

AMBER ESTCOTT lay in the woods. Dried leaves danced around her, some caught in her blond hair, others banked against her nude body. She'd been laid out in a manner that looked deliberate, exposed and shameless, white as the bare-bone branches rattled above her.

Tree trunks were gray forms in the fog, and there was the sound of running water from the reservoir. Kay's breath vapor hung on the cold air as she crossed the clearing to the girl.

A Mensa pendant had been placed around her neck, the medallion nestled between where her breasts should have been.

They'd been sliced off.

There were bugs on Amber's face. Spiders, Kay thought at first, around her mouth. But as Kay moved closer, she could see she'd been wrong. It was yarn. Heavy, black carpeting yarn. The pale skin around the girl's mouth puckered at each tight stitch, drawing the bloodless lips firmly closed.

What had he done to her?

Kay stood over the girl. Besides the cruelty inflicted on her mouth, she looked at peace, asleep, her eyes closed. Even in death, the girl was prom-queen pretty.

Kay wondered how horribly the girl had suffered. Wondered at the life taken too early, at the dreams never met. Her father had said she'd wanted to be a state's attorney. Kay wondered how many convictions Amber Estcott could have won in her lifetime, how many killers she could have put away.

She was about to kneel, bring herself closer to the girl's wasted beauty, when she stopped short. Nothing more than a flicker, she was sure. An eyelid twitching. Or had it been her imagination?

Kay looked closer. Studying the girl's face. Her heart in her throat. And when Amber's eyes flew open, Kay staggered back.

Terror filled the pale blue eyes, and a thin mewling sound started deep in her throat. The stitches over the girl's lips strained as she tried to open her mouth. Her cries rose to a keening pitch, and Amber's head swayed. Panic blossomed, and her movements intensified. Her head thrashing in the leaves. Violent. Frantic. Until, finally, her lips tore free of the heavy stitches and a scream erupted from her black mouth.

"We need medics! She's alive!"

It was Kay's own voice that jolted her from the nightmare. Taking several long breaths, she tried to shed the horrifying images even as the cordless phone pealed shrilly from the coffee table.

Kay dragged the phone to her ear and sat up. "Delaney."

"It's Bobby."

She was disoriented, grappled to gain her bearings as she heard the warble of the Homicide phones bleating behind Bobby over the line.

"What's going on?" she asked.

"Just got a call from Central Booking."

Antwon. "Is he safe?"

"Who?"

"Antwon."

"No. Who the hell knows where that little punk's got to. No, this is about Ramirez. Looks like an evening at the Pen made him rethink things. He says he's ready to talk."

"What do you mean?"

"Says he knows who you were asking about. But he's only talking to you. You want this to wait till morning?"

Kay thought of Amber. "No." She cleared the sleep from her throat, checked her watch: 11:25. She hadn't been asleep more than an hour.

After Finn had dropped her off, she'd come up to the empty silence of her apartment and for the first time let the tears flow. It was an hour later that she'd given herself a firm mental shake and shifted her focus instead to the case files.

"No," she said again. "Call the Pen and tell them we'll be there in twenty minutes."

"All right."

"Wait. Make it thirty."

When Kay hung up, she searched for the stereo's remote. Over the speakers Ramirez's *Requiem* pulsed quietly. She'd brought the CD home, listened to the trancelike composition as she'd gone through the files. Now the music wove into an eerie opus of mysterious bass rumbles supporting a higher melody of chanting and electronic cries.

Or were they screams? Kay couldn't tell. The idea that Ramirez could have recorded the vocalizations of his victims and laced them into his composition disturbed Kay.

She wondered if he'd composed the death mass for his victims. If he'd played it while he killed them. Or if he'd played it after, reliving his violence through each haunting note.

Kay shut the stereo off. Finn. Her hand hovered over the

phone's number pad, uncertain how hard it would be to hear his voice now that it was officially over.

He answered on the fifth ring, his voice filled with sleep. Kay heard a cough in the background, imagined Angie in bed next to him.

"It's going to take me a bit to get down there," Finn said after she'd explained the situation.

"I know. I told Bobby a half hour. I'll see you there."

59

"**HOW CAN I** *show* you what I feel?" Amber's attempt at seduction fell flat as she heard her voice waver. She tugged gently at her bonds, met his stare.

She'd rehearsed her plan in her mind dozens of time, in dozens of ways. But until he'd walked into her room a short time ago, she hadn't actually believed she could go through with it. Now, she knew she had to.

He seemed different this time. His eyes frightened her. They were blank. No emotion. Not like in his last visits where she knew he'd wanted her.

"Look, all I'm saying is I can try, you know?"

He just stared.

"I mean, I can tell you care . . . like, you love me. No one's really loved me before."

"What about your boyfriend?"

Amber swallowed against the sudden tightness in her throat. Looked to the stain on the ceiling. She couldn't let herself cry. "It's different with him," she said, worried she didn't sound convincing. "We just hang out, that's all. More like friends."

He looked suspicious.

"But I can't do anything if I'm tied up like this, you know what I mean?"

His gaze traveled down her body, barely covered with the short nightie, and she held back a shudder as though his lizard-hand had made the journey instead of his eyes.

"You've peed all over yourself," he said, his voice flat, his tone different somehow.

"I'm sorry. Maybe . . . maybe you could let me take a shower, you know? Clean up a little?"

"The bed's ruined."

"We could . . . use yours, right?"

He said nothing. And Amber wished he'd call her his Angel again; she needed him to still care about her, still want her.

"Look, I'm sorry about all those things I said. I was scared. I didn't mean to hurt your feelings. Really." She pulled against the restraints again. "Let me make it up to you, please? I swear I can make it up to you."

He stared at her longer. Unmoving. His khakis were creased, and there were white blotches where she imagined pool chemicals had bleached the tan cotton.

He hadn't shaved, she noticed then, and he looked tired. His eyes looked dark, empty. If she was free right now, she imagined leaping at him and scratching those eyes out, ripping them from their sockets, making him scream blindly as she made a dash for the door.

But she couldn't get ahead of herself.

"Let me make it up to you," she said again, trying not to beg. She attempted a smile.

"Fine," he said coldly. From his back pocket he pulled out the blindfold. "But if you try anything, you won't live to regret it, got it?"

Amber nodded, her pulse quickening.

As he secured the kerchief, she held back a cry. She hated

the blindfold, but needed to cooperate. She hadn't yet figured out why he used it. Maybe it was something simple: to keep her at a disadvantage by not seeing her surroundings. But Amber had imagined worse possibilities, all kinds of horrors in the rest of the house that maybe he didn't want her to see. Or, almost worse than that, there could be someone else in the house he didn't want her to know about, to identify later. She hadn't heard any sounds of another person in the house, but if there *was* . . .

Amber swallowed her fear. No. There was only him. She had to stay positive. She had to believe that if . . . *when* she got past him, she'd be home free.

He untied the bonds and she brought her knees up to ease the pain that had settled in her back. Her thighs were raw from her pee, but she pressed them together, uncertain where his gaze was.

He held the bonds when he helped her from the bed. "Behave now," he whispered in her ear, and drew her close.

She had to be strong.

For Ruben.

With his body tight against hers, he shuffled behind her, guiding her out of the room. The air in the rest of the house was stale too. Dry and dusty, but cooler than her room.

In the bathroom, he propped her against the vanity. She heard the shower start. Water hitting the acrylic liner of the tub. The slide of the enclosure's door. Still, he wouldn't remove the blindfold. He moved around her. She could smell him close.

"I'll be back in a few minutes," he said, and Amber flinched when she realized just how close he was. He slid his hands around her waist, and she could feel his belt buckle through the thin nightie as he untied her bonds, then yanked the blindfold off.

The brightness of the vanity lights made her squint. But

he didn't look at her. He turned even before her eyes had adjusted and was gone. From the other side of the door she heard the metallic rasp of a bolt sliding home, locking her inside. Over the pounding water, she imagined him on the other side, listening to her as she listened for him.

She took in the barrenness of the small bathroom, and a sob caught in her throat. She crossed the room, and her hand shook when she pressed it against the dry, rough surface of the plywood that covered the single window. Screw heads gleamed every couple inches around the entire frame, sunk deep into the heavy wood.

Still, she looked for something, anything she could use as a weapon. The towel racks had been removed, holes left from the screws, and years of paint and wallpaper marking where the brackets had been. No plunger. No toilet brush. Amber opened the cupboards under the sink. Empty.

And, short of breaking the mirror or the glass enclosure of the tub—which he would hear anyway—there was nothing that could serve as a weapon. Even the lid of the toilet tank had been removed as though he'd already thought of this.

Amber turned in the tight room, finally stopping at her reflection in the vanity mirror. This time she was unable to hold back her whimper.

Her face was chalk white and her hair was greasy. Dark circles haunted her eyes. Her makeup had run off a long time ago, and her lips were red and cracked.

But she refused to cry. She thought of Ruben. She thought of her parents. And as she did, Amber steeled herself.

There'd be only one chance.

If her plan didn't work . . . she knew he'd kill her.

60

KAY WAITED FOR FINN in the lobby of the Central Booking and Intake Facility on East Madison Street. When he came through the front doors, he looked pissed.

After signing in, Kay and Finn followed a guard through the maze of blue-gray corridors and gates of the CBIF.

The memories flooded back.

She flinched at the shrill blast of the release buzzer and hoped Finn didn't notice as she fell in step behind him through another series of heavy steel gates, each one sliding roughly open, then clashing home into its frame behind her.

Past a final sliding grill, they took a sharp right and the corridor narrowed. The guard stopped at a twelve-by-sixteen-foot iron cage: two sides barred, the other two walls painted cinder block. In the center: a metal table and three steel-cased chairs.

She'd been here before. Only this time it was Ruben Ramirez who occupied the farthest chair, not Eales, not the man who had beaten her to within inches of death.

Kay tried to shake away the memories. Focus on Ramirez.

The kid had been issued a yellow CBIF jumpsuit. And he'd shaved. The narrow sideburns were gone and his hair was tied back. He slouched over the table, his wrists shackled and his tapered fingers knitted together, the knuckles white.

"This better be good, Rube," Finn said, going through the cell door first. "Worth dragging me out of a warm bed."

He looked over at Kay quickly and she pretended not to have heard the comment.

Ramirez nodded, chewing feverishly on the inside of his cheek. "I know who you're after."

"You're going to give us your partner then?" Finn pulled out one of the chairs, brought one foot up on the seat, and leaned across the table.

"I told you, I don't have a partner."

"So why the fuck are we here? If you want a deal, you actually need something to deal with, or don't you get that concept?"

"I don't care about a goddamned deal, or don't you get *that* concept, Detective?" Ramirez's eyes went to Kay. "I only care about Amber."

"Talk to me, Ruben," Kay said.

"You said something about a guy with a deformed hand."

She nodded.

"Is that who you think's got her?" Ramirez asked.

"We're asking the questions, Rube," Finn said. "Why don't you tell us what you know first?"

Ramirez kept his focus on Kay. "I know who that is," he told her. "With the hand. It's the pool guy."

"What pool guy?" Kay asked.

"From Amber's neighbor's house."

"You've seen this guy?"

"No. I've never been to Amber's."

"Then how do you know about this pool guy?"

"Because she told me about him once. Told me he had this deformed hand. She said he'd watch her through the fence, stare at her bedroom windows. Amber said he creeped her out."

61

AMBER SUPPRESSED A SHUDDER as he sat next to her. The mattress sagged under his weight, drawing her close to him. She sat straighter, countering the pull to maintain the narrow space between them. But it hardly mattered. He was so close she could feel his breath tickle her bare arm.

She'd showered quickly, barely lathering the generic-brand shampoo through her hair. The washcloth had been rough against her raw thighs, and the soap stung her chafed wrists and ankles. She'd only just finished drying herself when he'd come back.

No warning. He'd unlocked the door and swung it open, standing well back in the hallway as though expecting an attack. Clutching the bath towel around herself, she'd stared at him through the steam that billowed out and swallowed her terror.

She guessed he was naked under the short, kimono-style robe.

Following his order, she'd turned her back to him so he could tie the blindfold. Then back down the hall, to the bedroom. She'd heard him close the door behind them.

She looked at the closed door now, calculating how many precious seconds it would take to get past him, to the door. And she tried to imagine the lock on the other side. She'd heard its rasp whenever he left her. A bolt of some kind or a padlock.

She'd get through the door, then lock the son of a bitch inside, listen to *him* scream instead.

While she'd been in the shower, he'd changed the sheets. She wondered if he'd flipped the mattress as well.

When his hand settled on her thigh, Amber tried not to cringe.

"I don't even know your name." She tried to smile. Tried hard to sound sexy.

"Is it important to you?"

"Yeah, actually." But in her nervousness her answer sounded more like a question.

"It's Paul." His palm felt like sandpaper across her thigh.

Amber clenched her jaw.

So far he'd kept the lizard-hand behind him, as though knowing it repulsed her.

"Maybe I'd better tie you again." He started to reach for the ropes.

"No!"

She'd made him jump, and she quickly caught his hand, ignoring the towel loosening around her chest.

"No." Softer this time, and she brought his hand back to her leg. "If you tie me, then I can't touch you." She rubbed the back of his hand with her thumb. The skin was dry and hot.

He stared at her for a long time, not trusting her. She needed his trust.

"All right," he said at last, fingering the trim on her towel.

His voice changed. Lower, with a hum to his words. "I've waited a long time for you, Angel."

It was working.

"I know."

His gaze came up, and Amber thought she saw hope flare in his eyes once again.

She thought about telling him she'd waited too. But doubted he'd fall for it.

"I guessed you did," she said instead. "I mean, I figured you liked me."

"And what would you have done if you'd known?" His voice sounded childlike all of a sudden. Eager.

"I don't know. I'm just sorry I didn't realize sooner." She attempted another smile.

When he slid his hand under the edge of the towel, she tried not to stiffen. But she couldn't help it.

His hand stopped.

"It's okay," she said. "I'm just . . . a little shy, you know?"

"You shouldn't be." When he removed his hand, her relief was short-lived.

He reached for the top of the towel, where it had already loosened around her chest. Her breath locked in her throat as the towel came free.

"You're beautiful," he mumbled. "But you know that, don't you?"

"No."

She didn't understand the smile that struggled at the corners of his mouth.

With his eyes still on hers, his fingers slithered past her collarbone to her chest. Slow, deliberate. And when he cupped one breast in his palm, Amber fought the urge to go for his eyes. But timing was everything. She needed to wait. Needed to target where she could hurt him most.

And for the first time, Amber wondered if she should let him fuck her. Let him exhaust himself. She'd stand a better chance that way.

But the idea terrified her.

Between his thumb and forefinger he rolled her nipple. She could see the caution in his eyes. But he wanted her. And she had counted on that.

Leaning in, he brought his mouth to her breast. The unshaved stubble of his chin bit into her skin and Amber tried not to pull away.

Eyes clamped shut, she tried to block what was happening. But when he shifted on the bed, bringing himself even closer, she stiffened.

He started to back away and Amber brought one hand up. She wove her fingers through his hair. It was short and coarse. Felt weird. Not at all like Ruben's. She encouraged him with fake whimpers even as the tears came to her eyes.

Only one chance.

For Ruben. For her parents.

When she opened her eyes again, Amber focused on the bedroom door. Five strides. Six at most. She imagined the daylight beyond it. And freedom.

Amber swallowed hard, tasted bile.

She could do this.

She slid her hand down, to his shoulder, his chest, and lower still. Only the thin fabric of his robe separated her from him. His moan almost caused her to stop. But she couldn't afford to.

His mouth moved to her other breast and he started to draw himself on top of her. Amber angled back, just enough. Her hand moving even farther down. She felt the flex of muscle along his abdomen, his thigh. Her wrist brushed his erection, and she stifled another cry. Hoped he thought it was pleasure.

It had to be all the way. No hesitation. No half-ass attempt. One chance was all she had.

And when she felt the heat of his lizard–hand crawl up her thigh, Amber drew in a breath, held it, and struck.

His scream—at first muffled by her breast—echoed through the room, its power so startling that she almost let go.

But she didn't.

His crotch was hot, his dick already partly swollen. She'd wanted to grab his balls, but she had hold of his erection as well. Her fist full. Still, there was no letting go.

No second chance.

She squeezed.

And he screamed.

It felt like two soft golf balls in her hand, and she hoped her nails were cutting into the hot skin of his scrotum.

More screaming.

Don't let go. Don't dare let go.

She clamped harder, the muscle in her forearm locking, and she imagined twisting his privates right off.

When she tried, his scream mutated into an all-out shriek. She dared to look into his face, saw the rage and blind fury in his eyes.

Don't let go.

Run!

Don't let go.

Then his hands were on her, desperate to tear her hand away, clamping onto her bare shoulders.

Dragging them both off the bed, he tried to thrust her away from him. Her balance faltered. Still, she would not let go. And he came down with her, their combined weight increasing the force of their descent. Nothing to break the fall except the leg of the four-poster bed.

The hard, knurled wood bit into her skull. She saw stars briefly, colors and lights swirling.

And as Amber Estcott blacked out, her final gaze fixing on the shaft of light from under the bedroom door, clarity came to her in a cold rush: she had just guaranteed her own death.

THEY GOT THE BAHNS out of bed.

The windows of the Estcotts' neighbor's house were

dark when Kay and Finn pulled into the drive. Lights came on in response to the musical chime of the doorbell. First upstairs, then down. And finally the porch light. A thick-bodied moth beat itself against the glass casing as Mr. Bahn opened the door. The man wore a set of silk pajamas and a robe. Kay hadn't thought men actually slept in full pajamas.

"I'm sorry about the hour, Mr. Bahn," she said after introductions. "There *is* some urgency."

"It's . . . it's fine." He squinted, and Kay guessed he normally wore glasses. "Is this about that Estcott girl?" He said it as if Amber had a reputation.

Kay nodded. "Do you have someone who maintains your pool, Mr. Bahn?"

He seemed confused by the question. "Yes. Paul. Why?"

Mrs. Bahn appeared in the doorway behind her husband, clutching her robe to her chest.

"It's urgent we speak with him," Finn said. "We need contact information, the company he's with, whatever you have."

"Sure. But . . . I think we've only got his cell number. He's independent." Bahn nodded for his wife to fetch Paul's business card, still clearly perplexed.

"Does he drive a white van?" Finn asked.

"Yes."

"Mr. Bahn, does Paul have any handicaps?"

"You're referring to his hand?"

"Yes."

"Sure, but that hardly affects his work. He's cleaned our pool for years now. I wouldn't hire anyone else."

"I noticed your pool's already been opened," Kay said. "So Paul's been around this season?" Kay had already imagined him in the Bahns' backyard. Watching Amber. Planning.

"Of course." Bahn looked suddenly worried. "You're not thinking he has anything to do with—"

Mrs. Bahn returned before either of them had to answer his question. She handed Kay the plain business card.

Paul Graves.

She fingered the card as though secrets were locked between the embossed letters. "No address?"

"No. Like I said, only his cell number."

"Where do you send his checks?"

"We pay him when he's here."

Kay handed the card over to Finn, saw his disappointment at the lack of information on it.

"What about supplies?" Kay asked. "Does Mr. Graves keep supplies here?"

"I believe so. In the pool shed."

"We'll need to see those."

"Sure."

Bahn brushed past them and led Kay and Finn around the side of the house, his leather slippers clearing a path through the dew. To Kay's left, Amber's bedroom windows were dark, but the rest of the house was lit. She guessed the Estcotts weren't sleeping much these days.

Bahn opened the side gate and led them around back. The night smelled of mowed grass and chlorine, and the kidney-shaped pool glowed turquoise, its surface dead calm. Past low landscaping lamps and across the tiled deck, Bahn directed them to a small shed. Inside, he flipped a light switch.

"He usually leaves his chemicals over here," Bahn said, pushing aside a floating lounger.

The labeled boxes and buckets had been neatly stacked in the corner. Kay took out her notepad and a pen as she moved past Bahn. A pool-supplies-company logo marked each box, and Kay made note of the Belair Road address.

When Bahn spoke again, deep concern was in his voice. "You don't think Paul knows something about that girl's disappearance, do you?"

Kay looked to Amber's dark window once more. "That's what we're hoping."

63

KAY SLIPPED THE Kevlar vest over her head for the second time in less than twenty-four hours. She righted the lightweight body armor over her shoulders, adjusted its straps, and tossed her suit jacket into the car. Goose pimples raised along her bare arms as the damp night air hit her skin.

Two Quick Response Team vans were parked fifty feet down from Paul Graves's south Baltimore address, and a couple radio cars hunkered at the curbs of the narrow street. Two more were positioned at either end of the alley that ran behind the darkened block of row houses in case Graves tried to run.

The night was still. Somewhere out on the harbor a boat's horn sounded low, and from the roof there was the rustle and soft cooing of pigeons. Kay looked up to see a half dozen small, dark forms huddled together on the asphalt shingles.

Just under two hours ago, Kay had accessed the Motor Vehical Administration database. There were seven Paul Graveses in the state of Maryland, three in Baltimore. And only one of those had registered a white Chevy panel van. Paul Graves was thirty-one, five foot eight, 145 pounds, with brown hair and hazel eyes.

When his MVA photo had popped up on the screen,

Kay had been startled at how ordinary Amber's abductor looked. An awkward half-smile for the MVA worker who'd snapped his picture. A calm in his eyes. He wasn't an unattractive man, Kay had decided. Clean-shaven. Well-kempt. The gold chain around his neck looked like the one she'd found at the abduction site, but if it held the Mensa pendant, it sat under the crisp, buttoned shirt.

Kay imagined him inside the squat Formstone house now. Tried to imagine Amber in there with him.

"You ready to do this?" Finn circled the car to join her.

She checked her Glock and stared at the dark windows. Curtains and blinds drawn. A plant on the sill of the living room window. A sun-faded sticker of Elmo on the steel bottom-panel of the painted screen door, left there, Kay imagined, by one of the neighborhood preschoolers.

"What's wrong?" Finn asked.

She shook her head, staring at the sticker. "Something doesn't feel right."

"We're set to go, Detectives." Sergeant Krieger of the QRT nodded at his men. All, including Krieger, were geared and ready: black body armor, tactical helmets, assault vests, and full equipment belts. Silent shadows in the dark street. Two of the shadows waited at the bottom of Graves's stoop, one of them balancing a steel entry ram.

The team had been briefed for the raid at the district office on the other side of the Middle Branch, and the train of vehicles had slipped through the early-morning hours across the near-empty Hanover Street bridge, back into south Baltimore. A convoy of testosterone.

Four a.m. and Kay was running on nothing but stale office coffee, chewing gum, and adrenaline. Looking at the dark windows again, she nodded. "Okay, let's do this."

They needed the element of surprise, could leave no opportunity for Graves to turn this into a hostage situation.

At the same time, they were going in blind with no idea what lay beyond the locked door, what defenses Graves might have in place.

Krieger mumbled into his radio, communicating with his men at the back, and finally gestured to the two lead members at the stoop.

They gained entry with one well-aimed swing of the ram. The resounding crack would have woken anyone inside. Wood splintered and the door flew back on its hinges. The QRT members moved fast. A rush of black through the ruined door. Krieger behind them. Weapons up, gun-mounted tactical laser illuminators sweeping the darkness ahead of them.

As Kay took the stoop, her Glock's muzzle down but ready, she could hear the team's heavy SWAT boots pounding the wood flooring. One "Clear!" Then another. Finn was tight behind her. Bobby out on the street, keeping an eye on the front windows.

The foyer was narrow, the air dense, musty.

It smelled all wrong.

Felt wrong.

The living room had been cleared. Kay swept the beam of her Mag-Lite across the well-used furnishings. A hurried scan, nothing more. Stay with the team. *Find Amber.*

In the kitchen. Only meager light from the back alley. Unwashed dishes. Open bags of potato chips, Chee•tos. Cereal boxes. Newspapers. An antique curio cabinet with bills and change stacked on top. At its base, a half-filled cat-food bowl on the floor.

It didn't fit.

Stay with the team. Boots thundered on the stairs. Then the team's voices. And finally a target.

"Don't move! Hands where I can see them!"

Kay was behind Krieger, mounting the tight stairwell.

Lights swaying. Footsteps echoing. More shouting. A door bursting open.

"Where's Paul Graves?" one of the members shouted. "Paul Graves!"

Something tumbled down the stairs in the wake of Krieger's boots. At first Kay thought it was the cat. Then realized her mistake even as Krieger said, "Fuck." And Kay heard a child's cry the same moment the shaft of her flashlight hit the stuffed animal rolling on past her.

All wrong.

At the top landing, Krieger stopped. Kay went around him. To her left two of the team members stood in a small bedroom, now flooded in light. A child's room. Mobiles swinging. More stuffed animals. Colored alphabets and zoo animals on the walls.

A doe-eyed woman in an oversize T-shirt and pajama pants clutched an infant to her chest, while a toddler—maybe three years old—clung to her leg. The child wailed, drowning out her mother's garbled hysteria.

"Jesus." Kay pushed past the QRT members. "Out! We got it." She holstered her Glock. "Go on."

She was aware of the members filing out, maneuvering their gear down the tight corridor and stairwell.

Kay kneeled in front of the child. "It's okay, honey. It's all right." She reached out to rub the girl's arm and the crying eased. Glassy eyes blinked as tears soaked her red face.

"It's just a bad dream, sweetie, okay?"

And when the girl took a tentative step forward, Kay opened her arms to the child, felt the tiny, hot hands wrap around her neck. "It's just a bad dream," she said again, rubbing the small back.

Krieger's whisper came from behind her then, laden with censure: "Looks like you got the wrong fucking address, Detective."

64

Monday, April 24

IT WASN'T THE wrong address. Finn and Kay had checked it three times.

From his position in the bedroom doorway, Finn had watched Kay pick up the crying child—arms wrapped tightly around Kay's neck, small legs around her waist, while Kay stroked the girl's hair. As the QRT members moved out, Kay had laid the girl into her bed and sat with her for a few minutes. Finn hadn't been able to make out Kay's consoling words to the child, but by the time Kay joined him and the mother in the corridor, the girl was quiet.

Cindy Epp, the tenant at Graves's former residence, had been renting the row house for just under a year, she'd told Kay and Finn. Since she had no forwarding address for Graves, she directed them to the landlord. But the owner of the south-Baltimore address had no current information on Graves either.

He *did,* however, provide them with Graves's old tenant application form, from which Finn and Kay acquired the name of Paul Graves's mother. Dr. Elizabeth Graves lived and practiced in Minneapolis. But at 8 a.m., with everyone assembled in the boardroom, it was decided that Dr. Graves would not be contacted. Kay warned them that the woman might tip off her son, and Gunderson had agreed. Still, it had been a tough call, knowing the woman could possibly lead them to Graves's current residence.

Instead, they focused on what they had: Graves's cell number. By 9 a.m., an emergency court order had been faxed to Graves's cell subscriber, and the Technical Assistance Response Unit had set up to monitor the location of the phone when activated for incoming and outgoing calls by tracking the cell sites Graves's phone hit off of. The location could be narrowed down to as little as a one-mile radius. But even by noon Graves hadn't used his cell once.

Finn and Kay had gone back to The Condor Club and The Crypt, but no one recognized Paul Graves's photo.

Mo and Bobby had spent the morning locating Edward Bahn and brought him in. Kay and Finn had worked the kid in the box for two hours, but could find no association between Amber Estcott's neighbor and Ramirez, and his alibi for the night of Estcott's abduction had been solid.

Kay and Finn had stopped for takeout and eaten on their way to the pool supply place out on Belair Road. There, the manager had given them what little information he had on Paul Graves—a suite number and address that turned out to be a rented box at a Mail Boxes Etc. in a shopping center in northeast Baltimore.

As they pulled into the strip mall off Moravia Road, Kay didn't look so good.

"We're going to get this girl," Finn tried to reassure her.

"It's been another entire day."

"I know." Finn reached across the center console and took her hand. He was surprised she didn't pull away.

"What's the connection between Ramirez and Graves?" she asked eventually.

"If Graves has been watching her, maybe he got jealous of Ramirez. Maybe he started following him."

"Even if he did, why would he throttle Richter postmortem? Why cut out Gatsby's heart? What's his purpose behind messing with Ramirez's victims?"

"Maybe he's perceiving some kind of competition between him and Ramirez? Showing him up?"

Kay shook her head, still uneasy. Finally she nodded at the store. "Come on. Let's talk to these people before they close."

The girl at the Mail Boxes Etc. counter looked put out that any customer should walk in two minutes before closing. Her scowl changed to interest when Finn showed her his badge, then slid Graves's photo across the counter.

"Yeah, he's got a box here. I don't see him much. He picks up mostly after hours." The girl pointed to the side door that opened to the vestibule of postboxes. "Customers can access their boxes twenty-four/seven. What's this about? Is he wanted or something?"

"Something," Kay said. She'd been studying the different-sized postboxes, then turned to the girl. "Does this guy ever receive parcels? Packages that don't fit into his box?"

"Sure. Not often, but he had one a while ago. I remember 'cause he was ticked off that he had to come in during regular hours to pick it up."

"No other way for him to get it?"

"Well, sure, we coulda left a key in his box for one of the larger postboxes, you know? But I remember that we didn't have one free at the time so I asked him to come in."

"And how do you let a customer know they have a package?" Kay asked.

"We put a notice card in their box."

"And if they ignore the notice?"

Finn had an idea where Kay was going.

"We call them."

"You have the guy's number?"

The girl hesitated. "Yeah, but I don't know if I can—"

"You can," Kay assured her, and waited as the girl typed at the computer terminal behind the main counter.

Finn wasn't surprised when she gave them Graves's cell.

"I need your phone." Kay gestured for the handset, and Finn knew she was considering the likelihood of Graves having caller ID.

He waited as she punched in the number, listened to the rings.

Then: "Yeah, Mr. Graves? Hi, this is Linda from Mail Boxes." Kay sounded young. "How're you today? . . . Fine, thanks. I'm just calling cuz we got a package here for you and I thought you might wanna come in and pick it up, you know? . . . Really?

"Well, shoot"—Kay leaned across the front counter to read the girl's name-tag—"Debbie musta forgot to put the notice in your box. I'll talk to her about it. But this parcel's been here a few days already."

Kay's eyes went to the laminated placard on the front counter. "We open at eight. . . . You can't? . . . Sure, I can leave a key in your box. No problem, Mr. Graves. . . . You're welcome."

Kay replaced the receiver and slid the phone back to the girl. "Thanks, Debbie."

When Kay turned to leave, the girl called after her. "So should I put the key in his box then?"

"Do you have a package for him?" Kay asked.

"No."

"Then he doesn't need a key, does he?"

Finn followed Kay out into the cool evening air. Beyond the roof of the neighboring Chuck E. Cheese the sun was a red ball in the evening haze.

"So what now?" he asked her.

"Now? We wait for the son of a bitch."

65

HE'D LEFT HER ALL DAY.

Graves had half-hoped she'd died from her head injury. She'd clocked herself pretty good against the bed, lights out before she'd hit the floor. And only then had she finally let go of his ravaged balls.

At that moment, waiting for the searing pain to ease, Graves had wished her dead. Not just eliminated and gone, but dead and having suffered. For an hour after her attack he'd sat on the couch with a bag of frozen peas around his throbbing balls. He'd pissed blood once, but even after his urine had cleared, he still hated her. With every movement, every step, he cursed her.

Now as Graves's hand closed over the knob of her door, his heart quickened. Killing her wasn't going to be easy.

He heard her whimper as he eased the door open.

When he hit the light, she squinted. Her face was swollen, and almost immediately she started crying. She was still tied. He'd wondered about that, worried that—in his pain—he might not have secured her well enough.

"I'm sorry," she blubbered through her tears. "I'm sorry." She shook her head as he came to the side of the bed. "I'm sorry. I'm sorry."

Tears ran down her chapped cheeks, and she choked on her phlegm.

"I'm sorry. Really."

He hated her now, he realized, staring down at her. Hated everything she represented. She was his failure.

The girl that had been his Angel wasn't so pretty anymore, he noticed in the glow of the work lamp. Especially when she begged.

"Please. You gotta know I'm sorry. I didn't mean to hurt you. I'm so sorry."

He let his gaze take in all of her. Her pert breasts. The nipples hard, dark nubs from the chill. Her fine ribs expanding and contracting as her breathing quickened. The chiseled hip bones and the soft hollow of her belly. The pale mound of her pubic hair. Faint bruises had already settled on her legs and arms. He'd been anything but gentle when he'd thrown her back onto the bed last night.

"Please, Paul . . ."

When he looked at her face, he couldn't bring himself to meet her eyes. Just below her hairline he could see the dried blood. Her head probably hurt like hell. He almost felt sorry for her, and was about to check her injury when the movement triggered pain. His balls still felt as if they were trapped in a vise.

"Please, Paul. I'm so sorry."

He hated that she used his name. Trying to personalize the situation.

Well, fuck her.

"I was just scared. Don't . . . please don't . . . hurt me."

He knew she'd almost said *kill*.

"Do whatever you want with me. Just please . . . don't hurt me. Don't hurt me."

He shook his head and it seemed to quiet her for a moment.

"Don't worry," he said eventually. "It won't hurt."

Her cry came out in a sudden burst of spittle and snot. "Please! I'll do anything you want. Anything! I don't . . . I don't want to die. *Please!*"

But then Paul Graves had an unexpected response.

In spite of the pain in his balls, in spite of hating her, he got an erection. He knew it had nothing to do with the feelings he'd once had for her. This was something new. Something primal. Something he'd never felt before.

She begged more, her words lost in the sobs that wracked her body. And the more she begged, the harder he got.

She quieted somewhat, perhaps confused, as he began undressing, and her fear was palpable. He folded his clothes and laid them out at the end of the bed.

He watched her jaw clench as her eyes took him in. And when he reached for her, she cringed and he smiled. He felt the warmth of her face through the gnarled and puckered skin of the Hand. He touched her forehead, her eyes, her cheek and jaw. He traced the line of her mouth with the fused fingers, and she blurted out another cry, unable to contain her loathing.

"Please . . ."

There was the smell of hot urine, and when he looked down, her thighs were wet.

"I'm sorry! I didn't mean to do that! I'm sorry. Please, you have to believe me. I didn't mean to!"

And he did believe her. He guessed that this time it was pure fear that had caused her bladder to empty itself.

But Paul Graves no longer cared. He didn't care about the failures in his life. About the ridicule. About the Hand. His mother. There was only this moment. He felt such power. Such potency. Pure and absolute.

And as the image of his uncle's face stared down at him from the stain on the plastered ceiling, as Amber Estcott begged for her life, Paul Graves finally took her.

66

Tuesday, April 25

AT 5:40 A.M., as the sky over Baltimore turned from mauve to orange and the morning's heat brought banks of fog rolling in off the bay and the Patapsco, the Denny's in the strip mall in Goodnow started grilling up its Grand Slam breakfasts. The aroma of pancakes and bacon wafting through the open window of the Crown Vic made Kay's stomach turn.

She hadn't slept well. Dreams of Antwon. Dreams of Amber Estcott in the woods again. Dreams of Paul Graves with his disfigured hand. And in between, she'd thought of Amber in Graves's clutches, prayed the girl had made it through another night.

She'd been grateful when the numbers of her alarm clock had finally glowed 3 a.m. Up all the night before on the raid of Graves's former address, she and Finn had agreed to let Mo and Bobby take the first shift on the stakeout of the Mail Boxes Etc. Just after three thirty Finn had picked up Kay and they'd relieved Bobby and Mo by four.

They'd borrowed Laubach and Whitey's Crown Vic as their secondary vehicle and sat in it now, their own car parked next to it, keys in the ignition, ready should Graves make his appearance.

The Vic reeked of stale cigarette smoke. The ashtray was full and the air freshener hanging off the vent knobs was well past expiration.

Kay would have killed for a smoke. She'd quit after her near-death experience with Eales, but there were still days when the craving was strong, days when she wished Finn hadn't quit as well so she could bum one.

Finn must have sensed her longing. He flipped down both visors, checked the center console, then reached across Kay's lap to the glove box. "Cheap bastard," he said when he found no cigarettes. "Got any gum?"

Kay shook her head.

Finn yawned. "You should have told this prick he had to come during regular hours."

"He already knew the drill, about leaving the key in the box. I didn't want him getting suspicious."

"So what do you make of this freak?"

Kay shrugged. Twelve hours ago she'd talked to Paul Graves on the Mail Boxes' phone, and his voice still resonated in her head. Calm. Cool. A little sad sounding. "I think he probably had a shitty childhood. Raised by a mother who couldn't be bothered to get his hand fixed."

"Like that's any excuse. Besides, maybe she couldn't afford it," Finn suggested.

"The woman's been a shrink for thirty years. Don't tell me she couldn't afford the surgery." Kay thought of Antwon with his lazy eye, the lack of respect that came with the abnormality. "Something like that can really shape a kid."

"Yeah. And obviously make him into a fucking monster."

More silence.

"You don't look so good," Finn pointed out eventually. "Did you sleep at all last night?"

Kay nodded. "I'm fine."

She wished she didn't miss him. When he'd picked her up this morning, she knew he had come from Angie's. Even though he wore a fresh T-shirt and jeans, she'd just known. She imagined him moving back in with his ex-wife. And she imagined the day he'd come by her apartment to clear his things out of her dresser. The idea made Kay feel empty.

She shifted in her seat, arranging her Windbreaker over the nine at her hip. "I was just thinking," she said, "that maybe after this case, maybe I'd transfer. Gunderson's going to retire soon anyway. Could be a good time for a change." She watched the parking lot and Moravia Road behind it. Unable to meet Finn's eyes.

"Kenny Anderson's done in May," he said. "I was going to talk to Masorti about switching back to my old shift."

It shouldn't have surprised Kay that Finn had already considered the awkwardness of their working together. Or had it been Angie who'd suggested the transfer?

Kay nodded. Silent. She thought about working with Bobby, wondered if Gunderson would partner them. It wouldn't be the same. Not nearly.

She was about to ask about Maeve, how she was doing, but Kay didn't have the chance.

"There he is." She nodded to a white panel van slipping quietly through the entrance off Moravia and bouncing over the first speed bump. Instantly, Kay's heart rate notched up; she felt the blood rush through her and heat prickle along her skin.

"I don't believe it," Finn mumbled, and turned over the Crown Vic's engine.

"Wait for him at the exit," Kay said, her passenger-side door already open. She slid in behind the wheel of the Lumina, wedged her cell phone's earpiece into place, and nodded to Finn as he steered the Vic to the exit.

In seconds she had him on his phone.

"What's he doing?" Finn asked over the mobile line.

"Just getting out."

Paul Graves looked small. Smaller than Kay had imagined even though she'd read his height and weight on the

284 • Illona Haus

MVA database. He wore a white T-shirt tucked into a pair of tan cotton pants that hung low around his narrow waist.

"Is it him?" Finn asked.

Kay watched as he swung the van door shut. Caught a glimpse of the club hand.

"Yeah, it's him."

He circled the van then, without even a glance at the rest of the lot.

"And I don't think he suspects anything," she added.

Past the van and through the glass front of the MBE, Kay watched Graves in the vestibule. His movements were slow and deliberate. Unlocking his box, sliding out his mail, rifling through the envelopes for the key, then searching the slot. When he realized no key had been left, Graves shook his head, then slammed his box shut.

Outside he threw his mail on the dash and jammed the Chevy into gear.

"He's on the move," she told Finn through her hands-free. "Coming your way. Why don't you ride ahead of him awhile."

Kay started the Lumina and steered for the other exit.

"Got him going west," she heard Finn say.

Idling at the exit, she waited for Finn to pass, then the van. She lowered the sun visor as Graves drove by, and tucked in neatly behind him.

"How's the view from back there?" Finn said two blocks later.

"Never better." Kay eased off the gas and let a subcompact move in between her and the van, her knuckles white around the steering wheel. She needed to relax. Needed to maintain distance. If he figured them for cops, he might never lead them to Amber. Or worse, he'd run. And if the pursuit grew too dangerous and they had to abort, Kay didn't want to imagine what he'd do to Amber then.

Two more blocks. Three.

Graves's turn signal flared.

"Finn, left," she said, in case he hadn't caught the signal.

The Crown Vic slid into the left turn lane, two cars ahead of Graves now. It wasn't a clean merge. A car horn blasted. Kay heard Finn swear over his cell phone.

"You need to let him pass, Finn. I don't want him making you."

"Roger that."

Four blocks down Harford Road, Finn pulled to the curb. He didn't stay long before sliding back in, several cars behind Kay.

"Get ahead of him," Finn said into her earpiece.

Kay eased into the left-hand lane, casually overtaking the van. Several more blocks and Clifton Park spanned to her left, the golf greens and man-made ponds lying under a blanket of fog and stands of trees looking like ghostly sentinels in the distance. But Kay barely noticed; her eyes were on the white van in her rearview.

"Looks like he's gonna take Broadway," Finn said a minute later.

Kay watched the van tuck in behind her. Graves hadn't used his turn signal. There was no time for her to make the turn.

Kay sailed through the intersection. "Stay with him, Finn. I'm going to loop around."

She gunned the Lumina's engine then. In the rearview the van grew smaller, then turned left.

The lights worked to Kay's favor. She heard nothing from Finn as she raced west on North Avenue, then spotted the white van move through the intersection a half block ahead of her. When she hit Broadway again, Finn was only two car lengths ahead of her.

"Nice to have you back," Finn said, catching her in his rearview.

"Where the hell is he going?" she asked. "Why's he headed downtown?"

"I don't know what you're thinking, but this'd be the route I'd use to get to Patterson Park."

And Ramirez's apartment in Butchers Hill.

"He can't live down here," Kay said. "It doesn't make sense that he'd have his business mailbox so far out."

"Maybe he's going to where he's got her stashed."

"Or maybe he knows he's being tailed."

Traffic was too sparse, made it too hard to blend in.

"Finn, you need to get out of his rearview for a bit."

And like some choreographed maneuver, the Crown Vic took an easy right ahead of her and disappeared.

Only one car separated Kay from the white van. The temptation to ride closer was great. She had to relax. Keep back.

"What's he doing, Kay?" Finn asked from one block over.

She rattled off the names of the streets she passed, assured that Finn was running parallel to them now as all three headed south.

And then, at the lights at Biddle, there was only her and Graves's van. Kay stared at the van's windowless rear doors. The sick feeling in her gut grew.

Was Amber in the van? Her body stuffed in the back along with boxes of pool-cleaning supplies? Was he on his way to dump her body?

After all this, they couldn't be too late.

Through the lights and past the Glendale cemetery. The fog grew thicker the closer they got to the harbor, whole pockets of it enveloping the van ahead of her, then clearing again, swirling in its wake.

Another block.

The traffic light ahead turned yellow. But instead of slowing to a stop, the white van lurched into the left-turn lane at the last second. There was no option but to pull alongside him.

"Finn, I need you to pick him up on Eager."

"I'm on it." Over the earpiece she heard the brief squeal of tires, then the Vic's engine gun.

Kay inched her car forward. Aligned with the van now. Less than eight feet between her and Graves, sitting behind the wheel of his Chevy. Through the open window of the Lumina she could feel his eyes on her.

She fought the temptation to look at him. To look at the man who'd carved the heart out of Nina Gatsby.

Kay brought her left hand up, wedging her elbow against the window frame, blocking at least some of her face from his view.

"Finn, where are you?" she whispered.

"Almost there."

But the light was changing.

And as the traffic signal flipped from red to green, Kay could no longer resist. She looked up and over, through the passenger window of the van.

Heat prickled along her shoulders. Her hands went cold and her heart seemed to stop.

Graves's calm eyes met hers.

And in that one suspended moment, Kay felt his recognition.

"Fuck." She barely whispered the word.

The world seemed to slow around her. In disbelief, she watched Graves shake his head. An image she knew would stay with her for a long time.

"He just made me," she said to Finn.

And then the stillness erupted. Tires burned against the concrete, the rear wheels skidding as the van barreled left.

Kay came down hard on the Lumina's accelerator. She spun the wheel and the police car exploded through the intersection.

A quick glance in her rearview and she saw Finn run the red behind her.

"If we lose the son of a bitch, Finn," she said, "Amber's dead."

67

HE WAS TAKING THEM EAST.

Hurtling down narrow side streets, zigzagging through early-morning traffic. East Baltimore whipping past them in a blur of boarded-up row houses, marble stoops, and chain-link. Steadily bearing east. The van. Then Kay. And Finn bringing up the rear.

Finn had seen Kay slam the cherry onto the Lumina's dash within seconds of the chase starting. He'd grappled under the seat for Laubach's cherry, then gave up. He snatched the police radio from the seat beside him, opened the main channel, and requested radio units, reciting the streets as he passed them.

Ahead of him, the van took a skidding right, almost coming off two wheels. Graves was ignoring traffic signals now. Careening through intersections. Veering into oncoming traffic to pass slower vehicles. Horns blaring.

"Can't keep this up, Kay," Finn said into the hands-free.

"I'm not losing him!" her voice snapped over the static from downtown interference. "Where the hell's backup?"

"On their way."

"Son of a bitch!" Kay swore, then laid on her horn.

Past the flare of her brake lights Finn saw Graves's van sideswipe a small hatchback at the intersection at Collington. There was the gut-wrenching shriek of metal on metal. Graves didn't let up on the gas, even as the compact car spun into a 360 off the van's bumper, nearly hitting Kay.

"Kay! We can't—"

"I'm not fucking losing him, Finn!" she shouted, and the Lumina lurched on its frame as she swerved through opposing traffic after Graves.

As he passed, Finn saw the driver of the hatchback get out, weak in the knees, but apparently uninjured. Another car stopped to assist.

"Kay, we're gonna get someone killed."

Through the open window of the Crown Vic Finn finally heard the sirens. Another block, and he saw the first radio unit pull onto Eager. Then a second. Their light-bars strobing through the fog as they sped toward them.

With his options fading fast, Graves took the next right, bearing south again, Kay immediately on his rear, cornering tight, anticipating each move.

Then Finn heard Kay over the police radio, instructing the district units to stay up on Eager, shouting directions, trying to cordon Graves in. When the Lumina skidded at the next intersection, Kay left rubber on the street, the car's rear end fishtailing as she accelerated to catch up with Graves.

Kay was right. Graves swung the van north again, racing back up to Eager through a canyon of graffitied row houses. Finn knew then it couldn't end well.

Past Kay, past the van and the fog, Finn expected to see

the radio cars at the top of the street. Wondered if Graves would try to go through them. But there were no light-bars. Instead, the large turquoise hulk of a city trash truck gradually closed the opening of the brick canyon.

Finn heard the van's six cylinders scream.

"He's gonna go for it," Kay said over his earpiece a microsecond before she laid on the horn.

The sanitation truck continued lumbering forward.

And just when it looked as though there was no room left, the van surged. Like a round out of a gun's muzzle, the Chevy exploded through the shrinking gap. Kay's taillights were already blazing, and Finn floored the brakes as well just as Graves's van shot past the grille of the trash truck.

But there wasn't enough room. The van's passenger-side wheels caught the curb, the speed propelling the vehicle up and out, and then it was airborne. One moment careening into a slow-motion revolution, and the next it was on its side, metal grinding across the pavement, sparks flying up from underneath it. Horns blared out along Eager Street.

Kay threw open the Lumina's door and was running. Finn was behind her.

Graves's van had come to rest on the driver's side, the axle broken, the sway bar twisted, and fluids leaking out across the asphalt. The van listed slightly. Finn slowed, his hand going for his gun.

And when Graves emerged from the broken passenger window, Finn had the Glock out. Kay was only three steps ahead of him, her nine trained on Graves as he hauled himself out the window.

"Freeze! Police!" Kay shouted over the sirens of more district cars arriving on scene.

But Graves didn't acknowledge her. Scrabbling down the belly of the van, he hit the pavement running.

"Son of a bitch! Check the van," Kay yelled to the nearest uniform. "Check the van!" And she was after him.

Graves was fast. His movements lithe. Finn couldn't imagine Graves knew the territory, yet he never hesitated. He crossed Eager, narrowly missing the grille of a westbound delivery truck for the *Sun,* and raced headlong into a side alley.

Kay plunged in after him. Finn was vaguely aware of several uniforms joining the pursuit, but his focus was on Kay, and on Graves's back—the white T-shirt a blur through the shadows and fog. The alleyway was tight. Underfoot, trash and broken bottles, used syringes, and vials of spent crack stems. For a second Finn considered the irony of two white cops chasing a skinny white guy who cleaned rich people's pools through the back alleys of one of Baltimore's worst drug areas.

Graves's arms were pumping, maintaining the lead he had on them. At the end of the alley he didn't check for traffic, recklessly diving into the street and running.

At the next street Graves hung right. He angled across the deserted, potholed roadway, a glare of white in a bank of fog and Finn could tell Kay was gaining, but only slightly. At the mouth of another alley, Graves disappeared. Then Kay.

When Finn turned the corner, Graves was slowing, caught in a maze of backyards half-obscured by the dense fog. Broken concrete and fire escapes, rusted appliances, stained mattresses, and makeshift fencing corralled Graves even as he ran. The only way out, a six-foot chain-link.

Graves threw himself at the fence.

Finn wasn't sure which he heard first: Graves's "Holy fuck!" or the barking of the two rotties that seemed to materialize out of nowhere, hurling themselves at the other side of the fence.

Graves spun off the fence as if he'd just been jolted by a surge of electricity.

Finn had his nine out and braced in a two-handed grip, Graves clean in its sight.

Kay was closer.

"Paul, I need your hands in the air," she told him, her Glock solid in her grip, her voice steady even as she caught her breath. "Now, Paul."

But Graves's arms hung limp at his sides; the deformed hand seemed to glisten, the gnarled skin catching the dim light. His narrow chest heaved for breath, and his pale eyes, half-lidded, moved from Kay, to Finn, and back again.

The rotties behind him were frenzied, saliva flying from their wide jaws as they barked, their powerful, muscled bodies rocking the fence.

Graves seemed oblivious of the dogs now. His face calmed. A sort of surrender. Like a cornered animal, giving up. Or . . .

"Paul, hands in the air," Kay demanded again.

Over the commotion of the dogs, Finn heard the uniformed officers come up the alley.

Kay gestured for them to back off. A quick check over his shoulder and Finn saw them retreat . . . just far enough. Silhouettes in the fog.

"Paul, listen to me, we can talk about—"

He was quick. Finn barely saw Graves's good hand go to his pants pocket, barely enough time to apply a fraction of pressure on the Glock's trigger, before Graves had a box cutter clenched in his palm.

The dogs were going insane.

"Paul! Put the knife down," Kay shouted over the dogs. Standing ten feet from Graves, she shifted her stance, and Finn saw her index finger move to the curve of her gun's trigger.

"No one needs to get hurt. Just drop the knife and we can talk."

Finn took a step forward, Graves never coming out of his gun's sight.

"Where's Amber, Paul?" Kay asked. "Tell us where she is."

He shook his head, his hand with the knife starting to come up.

Finn's grip steadied as he watched Graves in its sight. Watched every line of the man's face, every twitch in his lean frame. Ready to put a slug through the bastard if he came at Kay.

"I know you don't want Amber hurt," Kay said. "I know you care about her. You love her, don't you?"

"No." Graves's voice sounded lifeless.

"We just need to talk to Amber, Paul. Do you understand?"

Graves's voice was lost under the wild barking of the dogs. "It's too late," Finn read the words off Graves's lips.

And then, something came over Paul Graves. Only later would Finn describe it as a kind of grief. A resignation.

Graves inhaled. Closed his eyes. Swallowed hard. His body slackened, serene almost, and in the same moment Kay yelled "No!" Graves struck with the box cutter.

The blade went deep. Not a quiver of hesitation. It sliced cleanly through muscle, tendons, the carotid artery, and the jugular. The blood coming a microsecond later. It washed across Graves's white T-shirt, spilling over the cracked concrete at his feet.

"Jesus," Finn managed to say, his stomach in his throat, as his gun came down.

Even the dogs quieted in that instant, perhaps confused at the sudden iron scent of so much blood.

Graves's hand came away, awash in his own blood, and

for a moment he seemed suspended in a whirl of fog and silence, teetering only briefly before his legs crumpled beneath him.

Finn was aware of Kay yelling for medics as she rushed forward. Graves's heart was still going strong when she reached his side, the blood pumping from the severed carotid in bright crimson waves.

Finn knew Kay was only thinking of Amber Estcott when she clamped her hands over Graves's mangled throat, frantically pressing the wound track together in the futile attempt to stanch the flow.

Finn knew it was bad. The blood pulsed thickly through Kay's fingers even as she yelled for medics a second time. Finn doubted the EMS team would even hit their sirens before Graves took his last breath.

"Paul." Kay bent over him.

Finn could see his pupils already dilating, his lips going cyanotic.

"Paul! Talk to me."

Graves's mouth gaped, but no words came.

"Dammit!" Finn stood over them. "Where do you have the girl?" he demanded.

There was a high-pitched wheezing sound and a low gurgle. Graves trying to suck in air. Asphyxiating on his own blood. Finn knew then that Graves couldn't have spoken even if he'd wanted to.

Kay: "Paul, where is she?"

Darker blood filled his mouth, bubbling up and out, his lips moving like a fish drowning on air. The flow of blood between Kay's hands was slowing now. The pressure diminishing, the veins collapsing, as almost half of Graves's blood washed across the filthy concrete.

"Where is she?"

Sweat beaded across Graves's face, his skin white. His

body twitching gently under Kay's continued pressure, then going into shock.

"Dammit, Paul, where is she?"

68

Journal Entry #50

You remember the eyes the most. Even behind the clear plastic of the bag over their head, you can see the eyes. If you push the plastic in, get rid of the steam on the inside from the breathing, you can watch the life fade from the eyes. It does something to you when you see that. It changes you.

You'd think it'd make you feel some kind of mortality. Looking into death's eyes like that. Realizing how easy it is to just snuff out a life.

But it isn't like that at all. It's power-ful. It's a rush. And it makes you feel even MORE immortal.

Each one is different though. Some struggle more than others. Some jerk and spasm for a long time. But the eyes . . . the eyes are always the same. There's that moment when they just seem to know. Just know that their time is up.

I wonder what I'd do. Would I keep fighting? Or just give in quietly? Take it as my fate?

And after the struggle, after all the fight-ing and the convulsions, and the life dims from their eyes, there's that silence. The stillness that stays with you for a long time afterwards. Until it, too, dims, and you need to refuel.

I'm feeling that need again. Can't put it off much longer.

I need more.

69

KAY WOULD NEVER FORGET Paul Graves's final look. How he'd focused on her long after his blood had stopped flowing, after his body had become still on the cold concrete. For the rest of her life, she knew she'd remember the feeling of his life leaking out between her fingers and his eyes going vacant.

Now, as she worked a towel over her hands, she looked at Graves's body. The white crime sheet that covered him billowed slightly in the meager breeze that found its way down the narrow alley. One edge of the sheet had flipped up, revealing Graves's deformed hand. Kay stared at it now. The fused fingers. The gnarled skin. A fleshy claw that could have easily been fixed when he was a child. In a way, she almost felt sorry for him.

But she had only to think of Amber for the pity to dissolve.

"This is the best I can do." One of the medics had returned from the ambulance with another towel and a bottle of saline.

"Thanks." Kay worked the wet towel over her hands, washing away Graves's blood.

She'd been covered. Her ruined jacket already lay in the alley, and when she got home, she'd throw her jeans and runners out as well.

"You're up on all your shots, huh?" the medic asked.

Kay nodded.

"You should go to Mercy," he said. "Get started on

antiretroviral meds, just in case." He nodded at Graves's body.

Kay shook her head. "I'll submit the report." The request would test Graves's blood, but Kay wasn't overly worried. Not enough to begin the four-week protocol of prophylaxis for HIV until the Department's Occupational Clinic got the results anyway.

When the medic left, the alley was quiet again. The owner of the rotties had called the dogs off shortly before the ambulance had arrived, and with police tape at the end of the alley, onlookers and uniforms were kept well away from the scene. Alone now with Paul Graves's body, Kay felt a strange uneasiness in the silence.

Staring at the unmoving form, she could still feel his throat in her hands, still feel her desperation as his life seeped away along with any hope of finding Amber alive.

Kay turned, picked up her jacket, and started back down the alley. Finn met her halfway.

"Nothing in the van," he said, leading her out. "They're just getting ready to move it."

The corners were almost deserted this time of morning, only the odd stragglers slinging their vials of crack, and a few rubberneckers. Police presence raised few eyebrows in "zombie land": a four-block area where the Eastern District conducted a good percentage of their drug raids, where most of the rental row houses were owned by felons, and those that weren't were abandoned and had become epicenters of crime.

The accident had forced traffic to reroute, and a tow truck had already righted Graves's van. It tilted awkwardly on its broken axle. And a flatbed had been brought in to haul it to the Police Impound on the Fallsway.

"It's a fucking mess in there," Finn said.

The doors had been opened, and several boxes and tubs

of pool chemicals had tumbled onto the pavement. Kay sidestepped the mess and peered inside. In the crash, the Chevy's contents had been flung about. Paperwork and receipts blanketed the interior of the panel van like snow. In the back, the equipment was a tangle of telescopic poles, nets, and hoses.

Kay tried to imagine Graves up in the county, shoving Amber through the back doors and onto the bare utility flooring. "Anything of Amber's?" she asked.

"Not that we can tell."

"What about an address?"

Finn shook his head. "Not yet. Any mail we're finding in there has the Mail Boxes address." He motioned for the tow crew to start moving the van.

Kay circled the van, then peered down the alley where the ME investigators were preparing to remove Graves's body.

"What is it, Kay?"

She shook her head. "This was too easy."

Finn came to stand beside her. "That he took the bait?"

"Not just that. We got the guy with the pit bull." She nodded down the alley. "Now we got the guy with the hand. Probably even take that box cutter and match it to the cuts on Gatsby's body, if Jonesy can do that."

"And?"

"And . . . we got all that, but there's still pieces missing, Finn. Someone put Leslie Richter's earring in my pocket, and it wasn't Graves. And then there was the other guy in Ramirez's car outside the strip club. That wasn't Graves either."

"We don't have time to speculate, Kay."

"I know."

"We've got a girl to find," Finn said as the tow truck's backup beeper went off. "And just because *that* scumbag's dead doesn't mean Amber's not still in danger."

70

BEYOND THE WINDOWS of the boardroom on the eighth floor of Headquarters, the city was a sea of lights. The JFX glowed gold, sweeping north out of the city, traffic thin but steady. And beyond it, Finn could make out the State Pen a half mile away. He wondered about Ruben Ramirez, if the kid was any closer to filling in the blanks for them.

"*Someone's* gotta know this guy," Kay said from behind him.

When Finn turned, she was putting another pin on the city map taped to the corkboard. They'd spent hours going through the paperwork from Graves's van. Using ATM printouts, fast-food receipts, addresses from invoices, and client lists taken from Graves's van, they were able to track his movements. Colored pins riddled the map, designating the places Graves had gone. The greatest concentration of pins lay in the Northeast District, north of Moravia Road and east of Herring Run Park, then gradually fanning west to where Graves obviously maintained a regular client base in the wealthier neighborhoods of Guilford, Roland Park, and Homeland.

They'd already sent as many patrol officers as possible to the areas Graves frequented, knocking at every address, showing his photo door-to-door. So far, Kay and Finn had heard nothing back. Graves's photo on the news hadn't garnered any leads either. Laubach and Whitey had spent the day fielding calls and on the phone with Graves's clients before finally calling it a day. No one could offer an address other than Graves's former south-Baltimore row house or the suite number at Mail Boxes Etc.

Kay stood back from the map. Finn knew she was frustrated. She'd gone home to wash up and change after they'd wrapped up the Graves scene. Finn contemplated suggesting she go home now, but knew she'd never agree.

She reached for the stack of photos of the wrecked panel van and its contents, some taken at the scene, others at the police impound.

"What the hell are we missing?" she asked.

He circled the table and joined her, both of them riffling through the five-by-sevens.

At the impound, with the Mobile Crime Lab at hand, they'd decided against luminoling the van's interior. The chemical that caused a luminescence when in contact with the hemoglobins in even trace amounts of blood would have given far too many false positives since it reacted in a similar way to bleach and other cleaning agents. Most likely the entire interior of Graves's van would have glowed blue.

Instead, they hit the van with the CrimeScope. Every inch. It had surprised both of them that the only blood in the entire vehicle was a trace amount on the floor at the passenger seat and on the handle of the driver's-side door. DNA results would take days, but there'd been enough to type and Kay had pushed the lab for results. They were still waiting.

As he watched Kay look through the photos yet again, Finn knew she wouldn't rest until the whole picture was clear in her head: the hows, the whys, the whos.

"What's this?" She slid one of the photos over, her finger planted on a burlap sack leaning against the wall of the panel van.

Finn took the stack of photos from her, riffled through them, and showed her the close-up. "Birdseed." The burlap sack with a red logo and some faded lettering had been opened at the impound and dumped out on the suspicion it might contain something other than the obvious. There'd been nothing.

"Finn. Kay." A detective from Masorti's shift called to them from the boardroom door. "You got Minneapolis PD on line two."

They'd called the Minneapolis authorities several hours ago, asking them to inform Dr. Elizabeth Graves of her son's death. Kay had filled MPD's Sergeant Karwoski in on the situation, stressing the urgency of finding out where the doctor's son was living.

As Finn punched line two, he could see Kay's hope rise.

"The woman's a fruitcake," Karwoski told Finn over the line. "Certifiable. We gave her the news at her office, and she went hysterical. They had to cart her off on a stretcher. Sedated her at the hospital."

"So you got nothing?"

"Sorry, Detective. We tried. I'm still at the hospital. I'll try again when she comes around."

Finn thanked Karwoski and hung up. "Nothing."

Kay tossed down the photos and turned to the map again. "Jesus. Where the hell is this girl?"

"We'll find her."

When Bobby came through the boardroom's door, he looked as frustrated as Kay did.

"How'd it go?" Finn asked him.

"Finally nailed down the little bastard," Bobby said, referring to Adrian Resnick, the student who'd almost mowed Kay down five days ago in Langley's halls. "The punk's got alibis coming out his ass with these murders. Working at a food bank doing some community time for vandalism. How are you guys making out here?"

Finn nodded to the boxes of paperwork from Graves's van. "Still sifting."

"Kay, listen." Bobby seemed uneasy. "You heard from Antwon at all?"

"No."

Bobby fidgeted with his tie, loosening the perfect knot. "It's just . . . I checked with Fugitive on his warrant. They've been asking around, trying to get a lead on him."

"And?"

But Bobby was struggling.

"And what, Bobby? Tell me."

"Word on the street is the kid's dead."

Finn saw the defeat take over Kay's posture, her shoulders sagging, her eyes closing.

"Of course, that word could be coming from his own boys, Kay," Bobby added. "They could just be saying that to keep Fugitive off him, you know?" Bobby didn't sound convinced though.

"You want to go look for him?" Finn asked her. "I can keep at this with Bobby. Call you if anything comes up."

"You sure?"

Finn nodded. Saw the appreciation and hope in her tired smile. Kay reached for her jacket and was out the door.

At the table, Bobby pulled over one of the boxes of paperwork. They'd already made the initial sweep through the contents, the half dozen of them sitting around the boardroom table discerning the relevance of each piece before Kay had decided that a geographical profile of Graves's movements would help narrow down the possible location of his residence. Like a raffle, Finn and Bobby drew one receipt after the next now, marking each new location with a pin on the map.

Fifteen minutes in Finn stopped at one sales receipt in particular. Like many others in the box it was for pool supplies, but on the back, scrawled in ballpoint, was what appeared to be a Web address. He moved to the computer terminal they'd set up in the boardroom and logged on.

"What've you got?" Bobby asked, wheeling up a chair next to him.

"I'm not sure." The screen filled with a list of a half dozen file names and dates, the entries appearing almost daily. Finn recognized numerous names: Jeffrey Dahmer, Gary Ridgway, Ted Bundy, Albert De Salvo, Eddie Gein.

"A fucking who's who of serial killers, huh?" Bobby said, scanning the list as well. "Looks like these are all text files. See the suffixes?"

"Text files. Like documents?"

Bobby nodded. "Looks like he's been writing about serial killers, then saving his writing onto this server." Bobby pointed to the text and numbers in the address window. "These were probably uploaded through a file-transfer program."

"Why?"

"Safekeeping. Or maybe file-sharing."

And then Finn spotted an entry dated mid-February, "Richter," and another at the end of March, "Crypt Girl." It shouldn't have surprised him that Graves hadn't even known Julia Harris's name. He shuddered now as he imagined the content of the diary entries.

Still, Finn dragged the cursor to an entry titled "The Reservoir." His finger hovered over the mouse's button, uncertain he was ready to read Paul Graves's firsthand account of the mutilation of Nina Gatsby's body.

Bobby seemed to share his tension. "Go ahead," he encouraged Finn. "Like it or not, we gotta read these."

And Finn double-clicked on the entry.

71

KAY FELT LIKE A FIGHT.

For thirty minutes now she'd driven around Harlem Park, steering up and down Edmondson, searching for Antwon and his boys. Cruising with the window down, Kay tried to clear her head of the images of her day. But with the dimebaggers and the hand-to-hand men working the corners, whistling code to one another across the streets while kids on their BMX bikes acted as lookouts, Kay realized she was only trading one hell for another.

She needed a break. Needed to find Antwon. Or Amber. Better yet, both.

"Yellow tops. Got yellow tops here," one of the corner boys shouted out like some vendor at a produce market.

In her 4Runner she didn't stand out as police, got more eye contact from the corner dealers ready to serve her. She tried her luck up on Mount Street, slowing to a stop when a runner caught her nod. The kid checked the street, then crossed to her open window. Couldn't have been more than sixteen in his baggy jeans and oversize hoodie, a Nike sweatband around his shaved head. He had a pretty face, Kay thought.

He didn't speak, only thrust his chin in the air in a half nod, inviting her to initiate the deal. When he leaned in, one arm braced against the SUV's roof, Kay flipped her shield wallet open in her lap.

"What da fuck?" The kid started to back away.

"Relax. I'm looking for Wattage. You seen him?"

He scanned the street. Nervous.

"You know who I mean?" she prompted.

"Yeah. Yeah, I know the little motherfucker."

"When did you see him last?"

He debated for a moment. "Him and his boys went off an hour ago."

Kay tried not to get her hopes up. "Are you sure?"

"Yeah. Yeah."

"Where'd they go to?"

"Dunno."

She could see the lie in his eyes. "Where?" she asked again.

"Shee-it. Far's I know they be hangin' wit' them Harlem boys over on Calhoun. But you didn't hear it from me."

She didn't bother to thank the kid, and as she drove off, she heard his whistle follow her down the street. It was a new one to her, but she was sure it signaled police.

As she backtracked the two blocks past Harlem Park Middle School to Calhoun, she thought of Amber. They had nothing to give them Graves's exact address. Of course, there was no saying that even once they found Graves's house, they'd find Amber. As Kay passed abandoned and boarded-up row houses, she contemplated the real possibility that Amber Estcott could be held captive anywhere.

If she was still alive.

Kay had counted on Amber being Graves's primary goal all along, on him wanting to keep her alive. But if she *was* still alive, she was heading into her fifth night of being captive. The odds weren't in her favor.

And then there were Graves's final words: *"It's too late."* Kay hadn't decided if he'd meant Amber was already dead, or if their time was limited in finding her. Had Graves been working with someone else? And would *that* person dispose of Amber when Graves didn't return?

Possibilities ran through Kay's head. She didn't like any of them.

For now, though, she couldn't think of Amber already

dead. She had to believe there was still a chance. Just like she had to believe there was still a chance for Antwon.

Then hope flared. Past the lights at Calhoun, Kay slowed the SUV when she spotted one of Antwon's boys. Midge was the smallest of his crew, and Kay hadn't figured out if he was the youngest or the kid was just small for his age. He dragged the frayed cuffs of his jeans along the sidewalk, hands buried deep in his pockets, and glanced over his shoulder as if he knew he was being followed.

Kay flashed her headlights. Midge stopped, tried to peer past the glare to make her out.

"Get in," she said, when she pulled alongside him.

He checked the street, wary of anyone seeing him.

"Now," Kay prompted.

He did. But he wasn't happy. Like Antwon, he slumped in the passenger seat, his head forced forward by the bill of his backward cap.

Backing the SUV into the alley, Kay killed the lights. "Talk to me, Midge."

"'Bout what?"

"Where's Antwon?"

"Dead."

But Kay could tell. "Don't fucking lie to me, Midge. Where is he?"

"Dunno."

In the glow of the dashlights, the kid looked ten. But his sneer looked twenty-five.

"He's got a warrant out on him, Midge, but you knew that, didn't you? That's why you and your boys are telling Fugitive he's dead, right? Is he going after Dante tonight?"

An apathetic shrug.

"Dante's going to kill him, you know that. That's why you're not with him right now, isn't it?"

"Wadda ya mean?"

"He didn't take you along because he doesn't want you to get hurt." But Kay knew it was far more likely Antwon didn't take his homeys along for the ride because he didn't want witnesses. "Did he take the others?"

"Nah. He went alone."

"Where?"

The kid let out a breath, realizing he'd slipped. One hand on the door handle, his eyes on the street past the hood of the 4Runner.

"Come on, Midge. I know you don't wanna see him dead like his brother."

Silence.

"You know Antwon's using himself as bait, don't you? If you don't let me help him, he's as good as dead."

Kay could see the inner struggle in Midge's eyes. Thought he might bolt.

And then: "Out past Tubman," he said, referring to the Harriet Tubman Elementary School. "All's I know is Antwon says Dante's got hisself a crib out there"

But Kay suspected Antwon had lied to his boys. Dante wasn't flopping in some boarded-up house. Antwon was setting himself up as a sitting duck, to draw out his brother's killer.

"What house?" she asked.

Midge hesitated. Reluctant.

"Come on, Midge. I know you know."

Finally: "House them Lafayette boys used ta run outta. It's boarded up now, since the cops shot it all up last month."

Kay knew the house. Less than a half dozen blocks from the Western District station.

"When did he head over there?"

"Dunno. Said he had to take care o' stuff first."

Like buy a gun. "What time d'you see him last?"

Midge pulled up his sleeve. Antwon's gold watch circled the kid's small wrist. The watch Antwon had told her his brother had given him.

And then Key knew: Antwon wasn't counting on coming back.

"'Bout an hour ago," Midge told her.

Kay wondered how long it would take Antwon to buy a gun and get to the Lafayette house.

"All right, Midge. Get out of here."

And as the kid scrambled out of the SUV, Kay dialed HQ. She needed Finn. Needed backup.

If they weren't already too late.

72

FINN MET KAY down on Franklin five minutes after she'd called, and they bore west, the lights shooting past them in a blur. With the radio open to the Western District, they listened to the codes and static blurt out, expecting to hear a Harlem address crackle across the channel. But so far, the night was quiet.

Finn had suggested stopping in at the district offices for backup, but Kay refused, worried that if Antwon saw the radio cars, he would run again.

"I'm not going to lose this kid again," she'd told Finn.

And he hoped they weren't already too late.

He'd left Bobby at the offices, trying to rouse Albert Arbor, the department's computer whiz, on the phone. The files on the server space had been restricted with pass codes. All of them.

Bobby had seemed psyched as he'd hammered away at the keyboard, trying to break the encryption on the individual files, checking properties, looking for a back door into the server. But by the time Kay had called, Bobby had made little progress and agreed they'd have to let Arbor handle the decoding.

Kay had been excited by the news of the website Finn had found, even though he knew her mind was with Antwon.

"We might actually get answers from those files," she said. "Are you sure Bobby can't damage them somehow?"

Finn shook his head as he maneuvered the Lumina through the deserted streets of the Harlem Park area. "He seems to know what he's doing. He figured out that the site, if you can call it that, actually belongs to Ramirez. Not Graves. A bit of Web space on the server or whatever where he was transferring and saving his files."

"So he's actually documented his murders?"

"That's what it looks like." Finn knew Kay was hoping for the same thing he was; more than him, she needed answers, needed to see the whole picture. She wanted to know what had gone on in Ramirez's apartment and how Graves was linked.

"Not that it's necessarily going to help us find Amber," Finn added.

But he suspected Kay hadn't heard his last comment as they passed Tubman school and neared the address Antwon's friend had given her. Kay's priority tonight was saving Antwon.

They drove past burned-out row houses, abandoned cars, the streets almost deserted in these few blocks of desolation. Finn slowed when Kay pointed to a two-story Formstone with newly boarded-up windows and front door. It appeared that a rival gang of the old Lafayette crew's had already started work on graffitiing the place.

"That's it," Kay said.

Driving around back, Finn killed the lights and nudged the Lumina through the tight side alley. He could feel the tension coming off Kay and guessed a part of her already imagined Antwon dead inside the house.

Her eyes were fixed on the busted-out back door five houses down.

"Let's go in," she said as soon as he stopped the car at the top of the alley and turned off the engine.

But Finn grabbed her arm before she could open the door.

"Wait." He nodded down the row of houses. He'd spotted movement.

And just when he thought he'd been seeing things, Finn saw the figure again. Dressed in black, a bandanna tied around his head. Slinking up the back alley, checking over his shoulder several times.

"That your boy?" Finn asked, wondering if Kay could make out the kid any better than he could in the darkness.

She was shaking her head. "I don't think so."

Finn watched with her as the figure moved closer, another glance down the alley, and then he turned into the shallow, junk-filled backyard. Five strides and he was up the back steps.

It wasn't until he ducked in through the busted door that Kay finally recognized him.

"Son of a bitch. That's Dante," she said as he disappeared into the house. "And Antwon's probably inside."

Kay had the door open and was scrambling out before Finn could stop her.

73

THE HOUSE WAS DEAD QUIET. Picking their way over trash and refuse, Kay and Finn crouched through the broken plywood over the back door.

Under the compression of her vest, Kay felt her heart race. Finn had stopped her at the car, demanding they put on their Kevlar. It had cost them time. Given Dante a good minute lead.

Now there was no telling where in the house Dante could be.

Kay didn't want to use the Mag-Lite. The beam of the flashlight would give them away. At the same time, she couldn't afford to waste precious moments for her eyes to adjust.

Behind her, Finn had come to the same conclusion. There was the faint click, and the bright shaft of light from his Mag cut through the dark. The house had been gutted, neighborhood scavengers ripping out whatever they could, including the copper pipes from the walls to hawk at the salvage yards.

Nothing moved on the lower level except dust motes in the beam of her Mag. And then Kay heard a muted footstep from the second floor. She started for the stairs to her left.

Finn behind her. Both of them moving cautiously, one step at a time, working their way up, backs pressed to the wall.

Kay kept her breathing shallow, listening for any sound. Her nine tight in her grip as she imagined Dante Toomey scouring the house for Antwon. Or waiting to ambush them as they came upstairs.

The police radio, clipped to her belt, was turned off. Out at the car, she'd argued that they didn't have time to call and wait for backup.

"We need to get Antwon," she'd said.

If Dante didn't get him first.

Another sound from the second floor. Scuffling. And a voice. Muted. ". . . da fuck?"

Then Finn behind her. "Dante Toomey! Baltimore police!"

Finn's words were answered by the crack of a gunshot. Kay felt the shock wave of the bullet passing within inches of her face and heard the crack as the slug—traveling at twice the speed of sound—burned the air around her. In almost the same instant, she saw the flare from the gun's muzzle just past the top step.

She and Finn killed their Mags. They went down. No cover.

Two more shots ripped through the house.

Kay's ears rang in the sudden silence. And then there was only a dull clicking. Metal on metal. And Kay registered what she was hearing. If it had been Dante firing, he was out of rounds or, more likely, his street gun had jammed.

She heard more swearing.

Kay dared to raise herself partly off the stairs, aiming the flashlight and switching it on. In the bright beam, Dante Toomey looked in her direction, squinted, then turned back to the semi in his hands, his fingers working furiously at the jammed slide.

"Dante! Put the gun down!" Kay yelled, squaring Dante Toomey's center mass in her nine's sight as she stood.

But Dante continued to work at the blocked slide, desperate to clear the shell.

"I mean it, Dante. Put the gun down." She moved up the stairs.

"Fuck you!"

"Drop it!"

"Hafta shoot me first, bitch."

And Kay knew it wasn't the three murder warrants on Dante's head that made him prefer to die by cop than be taken in. It was the gangster code, life on the streets, go out in a blaze of glory rather than rot in some jail cell. Death before dishonor.

"Put the fucking gun down, Dante!" She hit the top of the stairs now. From what little she could see in the beam of her flashlight, the second floor had been gutted too, exposed two-by-fours, crumbling Sheetrock, and dangling electrical wires.

Kay felt Finn at her side. Her gun trained on Dante, she snatched a quick scan of the shadows for any trace of Antwon. Nothing.

"Drop it!" Finn this time.

Dante sneered.

And then the world seemed to tilt. Kay saw Antwon. First, just a dark movement, then he edged into the circle of light. Two silent steps. She watched his arm come up, a semiautomatic solid in his hand, its black muzzle leveling at the back of Dante's head.

"Antwon, wait!"

"Eye for an eye, Dante," he said, his voice eerily calm.

What Kay would remember most was not the flash at the muzzle of Antwon's gun or the smell of burned gunpowder, it wasn't the snap of Dante's head as the slug drilled through his skull and spewed blood and brain matter out his forehead, his face covered in blood, suspended in the light of Kay's Mag, before his knees gave out and he crumpled to the floor at Antwon's feet. What Kay would remember most was the rock-steadiness of the twelve-year-old's hand when he drew back on the trigger.

"Jesus Christ!" Finn was moving first, clearing the last of the stairs and navigating the debris across the second floor. His gun was still out. "Antwon, drop the gun. Do you hear me, son? Set it down."

When Kay moved past Finn, Antwon was still staring at Dante's lifeless body. "Antwon, give me the gun."

His gaze slid over to her, the lazy eye not quite meeting its mark. Kay thought he looked a little shocky.

She reached for the semi, her fingers closing around his, feeling his grip gradually loosen.

The beat-up .380 Llama had clearly paid its dues on the streets, its matte finish scuffed and scarred, the serial number burned off with acid, and the grip worn. A semiautomatic whose spent rounds had probably long since made it into the Drug-Fire system—the weapons tracing program developed to track and compare slugs and casings in order to connect crimes nationwide, and ultimately match them to the weapon used . . . *if* that weapon was ever found.

Kay wondered how many other murders could be pinned on the gun she held in her hand now. The gun with Antwon's prints all over it.

"He's dead," Finn said, squatting next to Dante's body, a thick pool of blood seeping across the dusty floor. He stood, panned his flashlight onto her, and gestured for the radio. "I'll call it in."

Kay shook her head, left the radio clipped to her belt, and nodded to the stairs. "Outside," she said, and tried to ignore the confusion on Finn's face.

The night air was a relief from the cloying mustiness of the row house and the dense, miasmic odor of death. In the alley, Kay opened the back of the Lumina and motioned Antwon into the backseat. The kid said nothing as she closed the door.

At the trunk, Kay took off the Kevlar and stuffed it into her duty bag.

"Kay, call it in," Finn said.

But Kay refused to look at him. She stared at the semiautomatic that had killed Dante. Once again, she held Antwon's future in her hands.

There was only one thing to do. For Antwon.

Kay pulled a towel from her bag and wiped down the gun.

"Kay, what the fuck are you doing?"

She didn't answer. Kept polishing the Llama, the grip, the slide, even the magazine.

"Kay!"

"You know what I'm doing." Comprehension darkened Finn's face when she wrapped the gun in the old towel and shoved it into her bag.

"No. No way. Not like this."

"I'm not having this kid's life ruined." She nodded back to the house. "Not over a piece of shit like that."

"Kay, come on."

"I'm not losing this kid, Finn." She zipped up her bag, closed the trunk. "No way we're explaining that away as self-defense. The guy's got a close-range bullet hole in the back of his head."

"Juvie, Kay. The kid's gonna do some time in Juvie and be out. A cakewalk."

She shook her head. "Not for *this* kid, Finn."

When she snatched the car keys from him, she was glad he didn't put up a fight.

Kay circled to the driver's side and nodded again to the house where Dante's body lay cooling in his own blood and soiled pants. "Now, you can either stay here with that piece of dirt, or you can get in."

THEY CROSSED THE CITY in silence. Even Antwon was mute, watching the lights zip past as he slumped in the backseat.

Kay's hands were clenched around the wheel, her jaw set

and her eyes fixed out the windshield. Finn knew she was shaken. Knew that what he saw in her stark profile now was the culmination of Joe Spencer, Valley Regester, Julia Harris. Even Amber Estcott. All the people she hadn't been able to save.

She was right: no jury could ever be convinced that Antwon Washington's shooting of Dante Toomey was self-defense. The kid would be charged, processed, put into the system.

And for what? Dante Toomey? Finn thought of the dealer lying facedown in his own blood back in the Lafayette row house. Wanted for three cold-blooded executions, Dante would easily have walked on at least two of those charges because of the limited evidence they had. Maybe all three, depending on how Antwon would have handled himself on the stand, being the only eyewitness to his brother's murder.

Truth be told, Antwon had done the world a favor.

Even so, Finn questioned what kind of evidence they might have left, what witnesses might come forward. But in a neighborhood of dealers and junkie squatters, it was more likely there'd *be* no witnesses or reports of gunfire.

Still, it was Kay's career on the line for the life of a kid. And his *own,* Finn thought.

Kay pulled over at the top of Hamburg Street outside her apartment and got out. She said nothing.

Finn met her at the trunk.

In the distance, somewhere over the water, a siren cut the night.

When she hauled out her duty bag, Finn put his hand over hers, felt the fierceness with which she gripped the handles of the bag.

"You're sure about this, Kay?"

"Aren't you?" She studied his face for a moment, then

unclipped the police radio from her belt. "If you're not, then call it in, Finn. Go back there and call it in."

He guessed it was disappointment he saw in her face. He took the radio anyway.

"I've made *my* decision," she said, closing the trunk. "I'm not losing this boy to the system."

Finn turned off the radio and looked out across the harbor. The glowing red sign of the Domino Sugar plant over on Locust Point reflected off the still water.

He felt Kay's hand on his arm then. "He's a good kid, Finn."

He looked to where Antwon was a shadow in the backseat of the Lumina. "I hope he's worth it."

"He is." Kay opened the back door of the car. "Come on, Antwon. You're staying with me tonight."

Finn watched the kid drag his lanky frame from the car, caught the mistrust in his quick side glance.

"I'll see you in the morning," Kay said to Finn before she turned to her front door, Antwon at her heels.

"Hey, kid," Finn called out to him. "Come here."

Antwon hesitated before crossing back to Finn. There was still some attitude resonating in the kid's loping gait, the hands buried deep in the pockets of his hoodie, his chin jutting out when he approached Finn.

Finn grabbed the kid's shoulder and roughly turned him so his back was up against the car. It didn't seem to faze him. Finn could still see the glimmer of the street in his eyes.

And then, as Antwon met Finn's stare, Finn tried to look deeper, tried to see what Kay saw in Antwon Washington. There were a couple specks of blood on the kid's forehead that Finn guessed he didn't know were there. Blowback from the shot he'd put through Dante's head.

Twelve years old.

And Finn was surprised that Toby came to mind. His son would have been close to Antwon's age.

Finn leaned into the kid. "You realize what she's done for you tonight, don't you?" he asked under his breath.

"Yeah, man."

"It's 'yes, sir.' " His hand tightened around the kid's shoulder.

"Yes, sir."

Finn nodded over his shoulder to where he knew Kay couldn't hear him. "You owe her. For the rest of your life, you owe her, you got that?"

"Yes, sir."

"You fucking let her down, and I'm coming after you, do you understand? I'll be your fucking shadow. Make your life so miserable, you'll be wishing it was *you* lying back there in that house instead of Dante, you got that?"

Antwon's eyes narrowed, and finally he nodded. "Yes, sir."

Finn let him go then, and as he watched the kid cross the street and disappear with Kay into her building, he prayed Antwon wasn't playing her. And him.

Both of their careers.

He hoped Kay was right about the kid.

75

HE'D KNOWN she might get loose: out of the bedroom, into the rest of the house. It was almost as if he'd counted on it, Amber decided as she wiped her tears and felt the last of her hope threaten to seep out of her.

It was an hour ago, maybe six, maybe an entire day—there was no way to know—that Amber had first crept out of the bedroom . . . stepping into the inky darkness of the house, uncertain what might lie beyond the safety of her room, terrified by the possibilities her imagination had laid out for her. Groping in the dark she'd found a wall switch, and in the tilted glow of two overturned lamps, she lunged across the cluttered living room. It wasn't surprise that she'd felt when she'd discovered the front door bolted. It was defeat.

And as she moved on shaky legs from the front door to the back, from one window to the next, the true level of the freak's planning became frighteningly clear.

Everything had been either boarded up or double- and triple-locked. Heavy plywood covered every window, just like in the bathroom and her bedroom. The back door had been padlocked from the inside, as well as two interior doors. One of them no doubt led to the garage, while the other, Amber guessed, was to his bedroom.

She tried the front door again. Pulling on it, wrenching at the handle, and screaming until she collapsed in an exhausted heap, crying hysterically as she imagined the heavy bolts on the other side.

Wearing her Langley sweats from the box under the bed, Amber hugged her knees to her chest and cradled her damaged wrist. A halter shirt that he'd stolen from her room served as a makeshift dressing. The fabric bit into the wound, but at least it had stopped the air from stinging the oozing abrasions.

It was the wound that had given her freedom. The wound and luck. If she hadn't attacked Paul, if he hadn't retied her while he'd been in such pain, he might have secured the ropes tighter. If he hadn't raped her, she might not have pulled so hard on the bonds and torn her skin to the point of bleeding.

The rope had become slippery with her blood. And she'd known then what she needed to do.

She'd waited till she heard him leave, heard the garage door rumble shut. She had no idea how long it had taken her to rub the fresh scabs raw against the braided surface of the rope until the blood flowed. She'd stopped several times, crying herself to sleep, then waking again, her determination renewed, only to start all over again.

As the rope became soaked, it had stretched. Not much, but enough that, coupled with the slickness of her blood, she'd managed to slip her hand free. In the pitch black, she'd fumbled for what felt like hours at the knots around her other wrist, and her ankles.

Amber woke with a start on the floor by the front door. A moment of disorientation. A flash of panic. She gained her bearings with a sob, wondered how long she'd been out. Minutes? Hours? Her legs were asleep, the pins-and-needles making it difficult to stand.

How long had he been gone?

Think, Amber. Use your head.

There had to be a way out.

And if not, then she needed to figure out a way to reach the outside. She'd already searched for a phone, then decided the freak must have stashed it in his bedroom. And she'd already tried throwing her weight against that locked door. Her shoulder felt bruised from the attempt.

At the very least she needed to be ready for the freak when he did come home.

Standing in the middle of the living room, Amber surveyed the aftermath of his tantrum.

No, not a tantrum. A blind rage.

The coffee table was toppled and the TV had been smashed in. Even his computer had been demolished in his fury: bits of plastic and tangled cables strewn clear across the dingy room.

Amber picked her way through the litter now.

A weapon. She needed something, for when he came back. She'd have the advantage of surprise, but only once. She could *not* afford to fuck up again. Because when he *did* come back, Amber knew he was going to kill her. She'd seen the hatred in his eyes as he'd raped her.

In fact, she'd almost expected him to kill her right after and guessed that he'd decided not to because he hadn't been able to finish. To come. Not as far as she could tell anyway.

She'd stared at the ceiling, at Ruben's face in the stain in the plaster, and endured the freak's hammering, until, finally, he'd collapsed on top of her. He'd said nothing, and after a minute he'd pulled himself out of her and, wordlessly, left the room. She'd heard him crash through the house after that, heard the smashing of glass and other breakables. And Amber had cried.

Now she wondered if he had let her live simply so he could try again. Remembering the rape, Amber wanted to shower, to wash every last trace of him from her skin.

But there wasn't time.

There was no telling when he might return.

Sifting through the wreckage of the living room, Amber worked her way to the sagging sofa. She kicked magazines aside, shoved the coffee table away, even dared to look under the sofa. Nothing. She cursed the freak as she lifted the stained and threadbare seat cushions, hurling each one across the room. Her screaming didn't stop until she saw it.

There, tucked behind the sagging armrest, the dull glint of metal silenced her. The seat cushion still dangling from one hand and her heart racing, Amber reached for the stashed weapon.

Her hand shook as she extracted the shotgun from its

hiding spot with the same wariness she might use to handle a live snake. Keeping the short double-barrel pointed away, she turned the heavy piece in her hands.

The shotgun felt foreign. Heavy and cold. With trembling fingers she caressed the oiled steel and the age-darkened wood. Her thumb fluttered over the lever at the top of the stock, prodding it cautiously, as though the weapon might somehow go off on its own.

It took a couple tries, but with a little force the body of the gun broke at the stock. Amber's breath caught at the sight of the single cartridge with its brass top nestled in one of the two barrels. Hope rekindled.

She drew the large cartridge out and turned it over in one hand. It was good. Live. At least, as far as she could tell. And for a fleeting moment Amber imagined blasting her way out the front door.

No. She couldn't afford that. Not with only one round. She might need more than that to get through the door. And she couldn't count on a neighbor hearing the shot and calling police. For all she knew, she was in the middle of nowhere. The freak had already told her that she could scream all she wanted, that no one would hear her. And he was right. Her throat was raw, and no one had come.

Still, with the weight of the gun in her hands, Amber felt the odds shift then. Dramatically.

One round. It was all she really needed.

And as her gaze flitted back to the shadows that lay beyond the open door of her bedroom, as she felt the memory of his body on top of her, inside of her, the repulsion moved through her then, Amber knew she could do it. Violation. Humiliation. They fueled her dark rage, and Amber knew she could kill him the second he walked through the door.

No, she *would* kill him.

Sliding the cartridge back into one of the short barrels, she balanced the shotgun in the crook of her arm and turned from the room. Weapon in hand, it was her stomach that called her now.

In the kitchen the wallpaper was yellowed and peeling. The counter was old and chipped; it reminded her of the retro diner her dad took her to for breakfasts on weekends up in Lutherville.

The linoleum was cool under her bare feet as she propped the gun on the counter and turned her attention to the cupboards. A couple plates, a half dozen bowls, plastic glasses from fast-food restaurants. She filled one under the tap and drank greedily as she searched the empty utensil drawers.

In the corner, the fridge hummed. An old one with a small, ice-encrusted, tin freezer compartment. Amber welcomed the cool air that washed over her as she stood in front of the open door.

The interior light was busted. Still, she could tell the shelves were almost bare. Condiments, a couple shriveled apples, a take-out food container. Starving, she tore off the lid. Rice spilled across the floor, dried and hard. And whatever else had been in the container was growing mold. Amber tossed it onto the counter.

A can of Pepsi had rolled to the back of the top shelf of the fridge. Amber cracked it open, the carbonation making her eyes water as she gulped the sugary drink. Also at the back of the fridge, in the dark, lay a large blue-tinted Ziploc.

Amber eyed the bag warily, the contents indiscernible. Setting down the Pepsi, she reached for the corner of the bag. Drew it across the shelf toward her.

The contents were heavy and dense. And gray in color. Her first thought was bad meat.

She lifted the bag, almost dropping it, then catching it against her belly. The contents cold against her palm, slippery within the plastic. Amber turned from the fridge, angled the bag to the light.

Her stomach lurched at that first moment of recognition, and the Ziploc tumbled to the floor, the closure giving way under the pressure of the impact.

Something slid from the mouth of the bag, settled coldly on the linoleum. Wobbled a bit. Amber retched, trying to keep the soda down. Disbelieving, yet knowing.

She retched again.

And as she stared at one of the two excised, rotting breasts, a nipple ring still attached to the gray, flattened nipple, Amber threw up.

76

Wednesday, April 26

THE MORNING HAZE over the Northwest Harbor was tinged mauve. For the past half hour, Kay had been watching the sky lighten, cradling her coffee to her chest as she sat in the Adirondack chair on her apartment rooftop. Next door, Mr. Drummond's pigeons rustled in their white-washed lofts, cocking their heads as though to greet the sun.

Balanced on the low, brick roof-crest that overlooked Federal Hill, Antwon nursed a can of Coke he'd found in her fridge. He looked like any other twelve-year-old boy this morning, wearing his black jeans and a white BPD T-shirt she'd given him. He looked serene, his shoulders slack, his profile calm.

She wondered if he was thinking of Midge and his

homeboys. Or if he was thinking of his brother and remembering the kick of the .380 as the slug left its muzzle and dropped Dante Toomey.

Eye for an eye.

In the growing light of day, Kay had gone over last night's events countless times, worrying—as she suspected Finn did—about the Dante crime scene and the possibility of witnesses. It wasn't just her own career she was jeopardizing, and countless times since they'd left the abandoned house last night, Kay had wished she'd been able to leave Finn out of it.

And as she watched Antwon sip his Coke, she prayed she was right: that he *was* worth it, that he'd go to school, make something of his life now that he'd accomplished what he'd been so hell-bent on doing.

For the first time in weeks Kay had slept last night, knowing Dante was dead, and having Antwon safe, sleeping on her couch.

It was thoughts of Amber Estcott that had woken her before dawn, leading her to the stillness of the roof. Looking out over the city, she'd wondered where the girl was, if she was still alive. And as Kay watched the sun rise, she willed Amber to be strong.

Now, as the pigeons cooed softly and Antwon sat in his own silence, Kay couldn't escape the feeling that if they didn't find Amber today, they might never find her alive.

"You want more coffee?" Antwon pointed at her mug.

"No. I'm fine. Thanks."

He nodded and let his gaze take in the hill and the harbor beyond.

"You can't say anything, Antwon," she told him then.

"I know."

"I mean, ever."

"Yeah. Don't worry, Ms. Kay. You can trust me." He finished his Coke and crushed the can in one hand. "So, you gonna drive me to Dundalk or what?"

"You'll let me?" She tried to conceal her surprise. Figured she would have had more of a fight.

"I promised, didn't I? I always keep my promises. Why'd you think I killt Dante?"

"You promised your brother, is that it?"

"Uh-huh." Antwon dropped off the wall and paced the peastone surface of the rooftop, poking at some of the planters Kay had started for the season.

"You know, we could have convicted Dante. On your testimony, we would've had him."

"Maybe." He turned away from her stare, but not before she saw a shift in his eyes that made her wonder.

Vicki wanted Antwon in for a second statement. *". . . something's not jibing between the two stories,"* she'd told Kay after she'd interviewed Tyrel Squirl. *"One of them isn't telling the whole truth."*

Kay had wondered what aspect of Antwon's story wasn't gelling with Squirl's, and now she started to suspect, started to realize how conniving Antwon really was.

She set her coffee down. "Antwon, look at me."

She waited till he did.

"You didn't see it, did you?" she asked.

He bit at his bottom lip, and shrugged. "Don't know what you mean."

"You didn't see Dante shoot your brother."

Another shrug.

"Antwon. Tell me the truth." She tried to calm her voice. "Not exactly."

"Not exactly? Christ, Antwon! Were you even there?"

"I was there. Just . . . not right *there*. I heard the shot. By the time I got there, Dante had took off."

"So how did you even know it was him?" she asked, her anger rising.

"My brother."

"He was still alive?"

Antwon nodded.

Given the gross damage done by the rounds Dante had fired into Texaco's face at close range, Kay hadn't thought Texaco had even been breathing when he hit the concrete in that filthy back alley where she and Bobby had found him.

"He told me it was Dante shot him," Antwon said, and even from ten feet away, she could see the kid's eyes tear up as he, no doubt, remembered his brother's last moments.

"Why the hell didn't you tell me?"

"Cuz I knew it'd be . . . whadda ya call it? Hearsay? In a trial, it'd probably get kicked out by the defense, right? I knew if I said I actually *seen* Dante do it, it'd be better. And if I *didn't* lie, he'd walk, like on all them other charges."

"You're not lying to me now, are you?"

Antwon shook his head. Not that it truly mattered. With Dante dead, Texaco's murder, as well as the two other homicides with warrants out for Dante, would be cleared by exception, although Kay was certain Vicki would still go after Tyrel Squirl for his involvement.

"Ever, Antwon," she said again. "You can't *ever* say anything about what happened last night."

"I know."

And Kay trusted the kid then. *Had* to. There were no other options.

She watched as he tugged at one of the three gold chains around his neck, drawing it out from under the T-shirt and untangling it from the others before pulling it over his head. From the necklace dangled what looked like a dog tag, only it wasn't military. It was gold-plated, and as he turned it in his fingers, Kay saw it had been engraved on one side.

Antwon handed it to her. "Want you to have this. My brother gave it to me a long time ago."

"No. You should keep that."

"Nuh-uh. It's for you." He pressed the gold tag into her hand.

"It was your brother's, Antwon."

"Yeah, and then it was mine. And now it's yours. I want you to keep it, Ms. Kay. So you'll know."

The gold was warm in her palm. "Know what?"

"That everything's aaiight." He reached over and turned the tag over, wanting her to read the engraving.

In valor there is hope.

Kay stared at the words. Antwon, agreeing to go to Dundalk, to leave the streets, the only life he'd ever known . . . that took more valor, more courage, than shooting Dante. Kay wondered if Antwon knew that. Wondered if his decision to leave gave him hope.

"We gonna be aaiight. Both of us," he said.

Kay liked the smile he gave her when she nodded. "Come on. We'd better get you to Dundalk." And when she put her arm around his shoulders, Kay felt an ease in them, a looseness that hadn't been there before. It gave her peace.

As she guided Antwon to the stairwell door, Mr. Drummond stepped onto his rooftop, a bag of feed balanced on one shoulder. Almost four decades working ore at the Bethlehem Steel plant out on Sparrows Point had hardened the retiree's features. Kay couldn't recall if she'd ever seen Malvin Drummond smile, but in spite of his crustiness, he'd always maintained an admirable serenity about him whenever Kay had watched him with his pigeons, moving calmly in and out of the hutches, speaking softly to the individual birds as he held each one in turn.

"Morning, Mr. Drummond."

The old man nodded, his expression unchanged. His eyes narrowed only slightly as he regarded Antwon.

"This is Antwon," she introduced. "Mr. Drummond."

"Morning, sir."

Another nod, and he let the bag of feed slide off his shoulder to settle onto the rooftop as he extended his hand over the low divider-wall and shook Antwon's hand.

"You want help with that, sir?" Antwon asked, pointing to the full feed sack.

"I got it, thank you."

And when Malvin Drummond reached for the sack, Kay noted the inked logo stamped on its plastic front.

Paul Graves's van. The one item that had seemed misplaced amongst the pool chemicals and equipment. Birdseed.

Kay was certain it was the same logo. Her heart tripped.

"Mr. Drummond, that feed, where do you get it?"

"This here?" He kicked the fifty-pound sack. "This's from Warren Smith out on Falls Road. Why you asking?"

"So that's his own stamp on the bag then?"

"Far's I know. It's his own mix. Made special for racing pigeons."

"Mr. Drummond, do you know a Paul Graves? Maybe he keeps birds as well?"

"Graves? Don't know 'im, but I recognize the name. You'll be wanting to talk to Warren. He'll know him."

Kay turned to Antwon, the adrenaline flushing through her now. "I have to go. Will you be okay on your own here?"

"Yeah, sure. I'll just chill."

And when Kay stole a glance over to the old man, he seemed to understand her dilemma.

"I could use a hand cleaning out these cages," Drummond said, shoving an arthritic thumb to where the birds scrambled over one another in anticipation of their morning feeding. "You got nothing to do, kid?"

"Nope. Wadda you need?"

"Just those muscles on ya."

As Antwon cleared the roof ridge that divided the two houses, Kay thanked Drummond and started down to the apartment. She'd barely crossed the living room when Finn knocked at her door, and Kay tried not to be saddened by the realization that he would no longer let himself in.

"Laubach caught the case," he said even before he crossed the threshold.

"What?"

"Dante's murder. Reggie's squad was on last night, and he was up. He's primary."

"How did the call come in?"

"Anonymous. And don't think it was me, Kay. Must have been one of Dante's crew called it in."

In Finn's tight expression Kay could tell he harbored the same unsettling feeling that moved through her now.

He came into the apartment and closed the door. "Where's the kid?" he asked, glancing around as if he suspected Antwon might have taken off in the middle of the night.

Kay indicated the roof.

"I got the car. You wanna run him down to Dundalk?"

"Not right now." She turned to her bedroom. "We gotta go see a guy about some pigeons."

"Pigeons?"

She explained as she got dressed, Finn waiting respectfully out at the head of the hallway. Kay wondered if he felt as awkward as she did, or if Finn had simply shifted gears, moved back to Angie, heart and soul. Cut the ties. Clean and simple.

Kay fought back nausea as she fed her belt through her gun's holster and slid into her suit jacket. It was the tension of the case, she tried to convince herself. But over the past several days, Kay had begun to suspect a different reason.

"Give me a second," she told Finn.

Straightening her jacket's collar, she slipped into the bathroom.

With the door shut behind her, Kay drew in a steeling breath. The room seemed to narrow then, the walls closing in, as she looked to the small plastic stick balanced on the sink's ledge.

And another wave of nausea rippled through her as she stared at the pale blue lines in the stick's window.

77

KAY HAD SEEMED WOUND from the moment they'd left her apartment, and Finn guessed it was the notion of the anonymous caller who'd reported Dante Toomey's murder. At the office, Kay had paused by the board where the names of victims were listed under each primary detective in red or black—depending on the case's status. Dante Toomey's was in red under Laubach's name. Finn knew that Kay too counted on its being in red forever. Counted on the case never being cleared. Dante's killer never found.

They'd avoided Laubach's cubicle, where the slob hunkered over his keyboard, hunting and pecking out his twenty-four-hour report on Dante's homicide. At their own desks, Kay double-checked the photo of the feed sack taken from Graves's van, while Finn looked up Warren Smith's pigeon supply store.

They briefed Bobby, Mo, and Gunderson and were on the road by eight forty. Kay drove, steering them north along the old Falls Road, which ran parallel to the JFX and through the Jones Falls Valley, past historic cotton mills and Druid Hill Park, and then on up to the south end of Hampden.

Warren Smith's store, simply called The Loft, was run out of the corner unit of a converted feed mill tucked almost impossibly between a steep granite ridge and the roadway.

Kay drank her coffee in silence as they sat in the police car and waited for Smith to arrive for opening. She checked her watch several times.

"Listen," she said to Finn finally. "I'm sorry about the position I put you in last night. With Antwon and all."

"It was my choice."

"Not like I gave you much of one."

"What are you going to do with the gun?"

"I'll deal with it. I don't want you to worry, Finn. This thing, it's not gonna bite us in the ass. I promise."

He'd considered that possibility long and hard after he'd crawled into Angie's bed at 2 a.m. Thought about Kay's decision, about Antwon, about Dante Toomey's body. She'd crossed that thin blue line last night. Taken him with her. And as he'd lain awake next to his ex-wife, Finn had questioned how deeply that crossing might affect Kay in the long run.

Still, eventually, he'd managed to sleep, finding comfort in knowing Maeve was safe in the room across the hall. He wondered what comfort Kay took to bed with her last night.

"Masorti got back to me," he said, uncertain if Kay had seen the memo on his desk this morning. "Anderson's leaving in two weeks. I can transfer squads by the end of the month."

Kay was silent.

"You okay with that?" he asked.

"Of course."

But he could see the sadness in her eyes when she glanced over.

"I don't *have* to take the transfer," he said.

"No. Take it." She looked back out the windshield. "It'll be better. For everyone."

And he guessed she was thinking of Angie more than herself.

"That's probably him." Kay sat straighter and nodded toward a white van. Memories of Paul Graves. Only twenty-eight hours ago Finn had watched half the man's blood spill into a back alley. It seemed a lot longer than that.

Warren Smith was a tall, ropy man with quick eyes. He led them through his cramped shop with brisk movements, and his words came fast.

"Yes. Yes. I know Paul. I haven't seen him in a while, though. He's not into birds anymore," he said, pulling out a well-used Rolodex from under the back counter, the cards dog-eared and yellowed. "Quiet guy. But if you get him onto birds, he knows what he's talking about."

Smith flipped through the stained cards, until he found the one he was searching for. He slid it across the counter to Finn.

"Never had much call for the address, though. He always paid up front."

"Damn," Finn muttered. In block letters, the Mail Boxes Etc. address had been printed under Graves's crossed out south-Baltimore address. "You don't have a street address?"

"That's all I got."

"Ever make any deliveries?" Finn handed back the card.

"Not to Paul."

"You said he's not into birds anymore?" Kay asked.

"That's right. He dispersed his flock."

"When was that?"

"Few months ago. Would've been early December. I think he had three or four dozen birds in his loft."

"And do you know who might have bought some of his birds?"

Smith shook his head. "Not really. When you disperse a flock, it's mostly for breeding, so there could have been a half dozen people buying from him. I bought a few myself."

"*You* did?" Kay asked.

Smith nodded.

"So you *do* know where he lives then," Finn said. "You went to see the birds?"

"No. He brought 'em here. I didn't need to see them. I know his stock, his times and speed. He started some nice lines of racers. Janssens. Meulemans. Blues and grays, mostly. A few whites and—"

"Wait a second"—Kay stopped him—"you said a dispersed flock is used only for breeding?"

"That's right. Once the bird is homed, once its internal compass is set, it can't be rehomed. Not usually. Why?"

"Mr. Smith, we're going to need those birds," Kay said.

78

THEY'D FOLLOWED WARREN SMITH to his home in Hampden and walked with him through the tight maze of cages behind his house. The birds had seemed spooked by Kay and Finn's presence, taking to the air, beating their wings against the chicken wire as pinfeathers snowed down around them.

Already sensing Kay's impatience, Smith didn't waste time calming the birds. He disappeared into one of the lofts and came back with an aluminum carrier. They waited as

Smith loaded it into the back of the van, and while Finn led him east, Kay had taken out the map in the passenger seat and reviewed the general location where they suspected Paul Graves lived.

In the Hamilton Hills area, Finn had already circled them around once and was starting his second run up Old Harford when he slowed the police car.

"How about there?" he asked, pointing to a school set back off the road, six stories of glass and concrete. Morning recess had flooded the grounds with kids.

Kay shook her head. Running on an adrenaline rush of hope. They were so close.

She continued scanning the buildings, gauging the lay of the land. Out here in the northeast corner of the city, where the foothills started and the land flattened out to the east marking the beginning of the continental shelf, a high point would offer them a good survey of the area. But Kay hoped for something taller than the six-story school.

"No," she said, then gestured for Finn to hang a right.

He drove another couple minutes, pointing out other possible vantage points, until Kay saw the church.

"There."

The old stone church had been built probably over a century ago on a low hill. Its rough-hewn granite walls and slate-shingled roof shadowed the neighboring buildings, and its square bell tower rose a couple hundred feet.

Finn pulled into St. Christopher's lot, Smith's white van behind them.

"This it?" Smith asked, hopping out of his van.

Kay nodded and spread the map across the hood of the Lumina, battling the wind as it tore at the edges.

"According to our geographic profiling," she explained while Finn radioed Gunderson with their location, "we're placing Graves's house somewhere in here." She traced her finger around the one-square-mile area, then pointed to its approximate center: St. Christopher's Church.

Smith did a quick visual scan of the neighborhood, ending with the bell tower. "Looks good. Let's do this," he said, and opened the back of the van to retrieve the bird carrier.

Kay took the set of binoculars from the glove box and started for the church.

Hang on, Amber. We're almost there.

With Finn and Smith behind her, Kay mounted the wide marble steps. They found the heavy middle door unlocked.

As Kay stood in the dim narthex—the lingering odor of incense, burning votive candles, and linseed oil from the polished cypress pews—the memories flooded back. Her mother's funeral. Spence's funeral. She couldn't remember the last time she'd been to an actual Sunday service. Probably before she was fifteen, before she'd told her father she no longer believed in God.

Past the intricately carved pulpit, the vaulted ceiling was fully illuminated, but the church was empty. Morning sun angled through the double-lancet, stained-glass windows flanking the nave, and in the shafts of light, dust motes swirled, stirred by their entrance.

"I'll go to the rectory," Finn said. "See if I can find the pastor."

In its carrier, Kay heard the bird's soft coo, then the rustle of wings as it rearranged itself, perhaps sensing its impending significance.

Kay felt distinctly out of place in this holiness, this peace. Felt as if she somehow defiled its sanctity with her presence, with her gun and with the memory of Dante's execution last night.

Smith set down the carrier and wiped his calloused

palms against his trousers. "Sure hope this works for you. You say that girl they're looking for might be locked in Paul's house?"

Kay nodded. After everything they'd been through, she *had* to be alive.

"You think this bird will still home?" Kay asked.

Smith nodded. "She's young, but Paul told me he'd flown her. Some impressive times too."

When the door opened behind them, Gunderson was just a silhouette against the glare of the morning until he closed the door.

"Saw your car," he said. "Bobby and Mo are sittin' out on Beechland. Kid's got money riding on the house being up there."

"And the district units?" Kay asked.

"They're all in position. Where's Finn?"

"Gone to get the pastor so we can go up."

"Good thinking with the tower," Gunderson said, and turned as the door swung open again.

Reverend Mitty was a tall, rawboned man with a sober expression. He wore all black except for the clerical collar. "I'm not sure I understand," he said as he led the four of them to the base of the bell tower. "I saw the news coverage of the missing girl. And you intend to use a bird to—"

"It's all we've got right now, Reverend," Finn said as they started up the steep spiral stairs.

At the top of the tower, the wind whistled at the belfry door, echoing down the hollow stairwell like a long, mournful cry. It ceased the instant Mitty opened the door and ushered them outside.

The wind buffeted them. It sucked at Kay's clothes, whipping her jacket back and tearing at her hair as she traversed the perimeter of the belfry. Almost two hundred feet below, the city sprawled out around them. She could see the sun on the bay, the flatness of downtown, and even make out Towson five miles northwest.

Kay scanned Hamilton Hills, searching for landmarks, orienting herself as Smith opened the aluminum carrier behind her. When he joined her at one of the openings in the solid granite walls, he held Paul Graves's bird. It looked lost in Smith's big hands, its pearl-white plumage a stark contrast against his tanned, work-roughened skin.

"It's a dove?" Kay asked, raising her voice against the battering wind.

"No, she's a white homer. A pigeon. Same as they use for wedding releases and stuff like that. People only think they're doves."

The bird didn't struggle, but Kay still sensed anxiousness in its large red-black eyes. A wildness. It cocked its small head a couple times, one round, inky eye angling at the sun in the clear sky.

"Is the wind going to be too much for it?" Kay asked.

"She'll be fine."

"Are we ready?" she asked Gunderson, then listened to him check in with each unit via the police radio, confirming positions and alerting them of the release.

Kay turned to Smith. "Do you have to do anything?"

"Just let her fly."

"All right then." She shared a nod with Finn and Gunderson. "We're ready."

With a tenderness Kay hadn't expected from the man, Smith pressed a quick kiss to the top of the bird's small, domed head and stepped to the closest arched opening.

The bird released in a flurry of wings.

Kay held her breath.

Squinting against the sun, she watched the bird rise, then disappear over the steeple. "Where is it?"

"I got it over here," Finn said from the south side of the belfry. "Wait, it's gone. Around to your side, Kay."

She saw it. Wings a pure white against the blue sky.

The bird circled again. And a third time.

"Is it lost?" Kay asked Smith.

"No. She's gaining her bearing. Finding north."

The bird's circle widened and now it flew at eye level. Kay could watch its course through each arched window, a stuttering visual like a movie in frames. Around one more time, and finally Smith pointed.

"Now, she's got it," he said, pride in his voice. "There she goes."

Kay and Finn joined Smith as he raised his own binoculars. Kay tracked the pigeon's flight with her naked eyes, afraid to so much as blink in case she lost the bird, its small, white body disappearing fast across the rooftops of northeast Baltimore.

Kay called out several street names, areas she recognized, as Gunderson reported them into the radio. The white speck in the sky was barely noticeable now, and when Kay brought her binoculars up, she panicked as the visual field was nothing but clear blue.

"You still got it, Mr. Smith?" she asked.

"Yup. She's staying true to her course."

Kay lowered the glasses for one second, checked her position, then brought them up again. She could just make out the white speck.

They couldn't afford to lose the bird. Not when they were this close.

"It's too late." Graves's dying words.

No. Kay refused to believe it. After everything they'd

gone through to save her, after losing Julia Harris, they couldn't be too late. Amber Estcott *had* to be alive.

And then the speck in the binocular frames vanished at last.

"Anyone see it from the street?" she asked.

Gunderson kept the channel open. Nothing.

"Dammit! We're going to lose it." Kay grabbed the radio from Gunderson. "Nobody sees that bird?"

She waited. One heartbeat. Another.

Then the police channel came alive. Crackling as the first unit responded with a sighting. ". . . heading east across the cemetery."

"We got it on Sefton . . . making a beeline to the Eastern Parkway. There a unit there?"

Fifteen long seconds later. "Got visual. She's wingin' straight down Bellevale."

Kay brought the radio closer to her ear, her hand freezing from the wind as she turned up the volume. Across the channel she could hear the revving of a car, a horn blast, then another.

". . . that winged rat's really motoring," she heard the patrolman say. "Hang on. I think we got her. I think . . . Wait a second."

More crackling.

And finally the patrol's voice: "Base, the eagle has landed."

79

AS THEY SPED ACROSS Hamilton Hills, Kay's anxiousness was palpable. From the moment the address had sputtered over the police radio and they'd raced down the steps of St. Christopher's bell tower, Kay had said little. And even now as Finn blasted through another red light with Gunderson on their tail, he knew he wasn't driving fast enough for her.

Bobby's voice had filled the airwaves shortly after they'd been mobile, reporting that the bird had landed and seemed in no hurry to go anywhere.

It had to be the right house, Finn thought. They needed it to be. They needed the work they'd put into the case to result in at least one girl being saved. Not to mention the promise he knew Kay had made Mark Estcott: that they would find his daughter.

When Finn turned off Bellevale and onto Blucher, he counted four patrol cars already parked on the potholed, dead-end street along with Mo's gray unmarked. There was no sign of the bird.

Kay was out the door before Finn had even stopped the Lumina. She jogged to the closest patrol car, where Mo and Bobby spoke with the uniforms. Finn was right behind her.

"Where's the bird at?" Kay asked them.

Bobby pointed across the street.

The single-story bungalow sat lower than its neighbors, obscured by a tangle of overgrown shrubs and hedges. Only the uppermost portion of the aluminum-sided house was visible from the street, and even then he and Kay had to move around the visual barrier of a half-dead sycamore to spot the white pigeon. It strutted along the house's main peak.

"Anyone go around back yet?" Kay asked. "See if he's got lofts?"

Bobby nodded. "They're all empty."

"This is it," Finn heard Kay mutter, as she studied the squat house from the end of the walkway.

"How do you want to handle this?" Bobby asked.

"Quietly," Finn said. "We don't know there isn't someone besides the girl in that house."

Back at the cars, Kay briefed the men, instructing two uniforms to cover the back, while she and Finn, along with Bobby, Mo, and two more officers, took the front.

"We don't know what shape the girl is in," Kay said, taking off her jacket and checking her gun. "Where's EMS?"

"They're en route."

"Good. Everyone know their position?" Kay waited for their nods, then led the way up the cracked cement walk to the front of the house.

Finn could feel Kay's senses jacked up as much as his own. His heart raced as the six of them took the steps and crowded the narrow prefab concrete porch. Kay stood as far to the right as the railing would allow, while Finn took the left. He caught Kay's look as she pointed out the two industrial, sliding-bolt locks mounted above and below the doorknob.

There was hope. If Graves had locked her inside, it could only mean that Amber Estcott must have been alive when he'd left her last.

They all held a collective breath. Listening for any sound from within the house.

Nothing.

Kay made eye contact with Finn, then quietly slid each bolt free.

"Who's got a ram?" Kay whispered.

"Don't need one," Bobby said, and he held out a set of keys. "From Graves's van."

Kay gave him a smile when he dropped them into her palm.

"All right then. We ready?" She waited for everyone's nod. Then slid the key home.

80

AMBER WOKE with a gasp. Her heart instantly tripping over itself.

Something had woken her.

Sitting in the doorway of the kitchen, she'd fallen asleep, the double-barrel shotgun resting in the crook of her arm.

Had it been the garage door she'd heard? Had the freak finally come back?

She felt nauseous. Hot. Her sweatshirt was damp.

Behind her, the breasts still lay in the middle of the kitchen floor. Two puddles of fat with her vomit spilled over them, and the silver nipple ring glinting in the over-head light.

What kind of sicko cut the tits off a dead body?

She hated the freak now more than ever. He probably thought he could do the same to her. Cut her up when he was done with her.

Well, the joke was on him. Amber stood, her legs shaky but her determination solid.

The image of him and his twisted, fucked-up hand, the memory of his body all over hers, only added fuel to that determination.

And when Amber heard the freak's key in the door, she almost found herself smiling.

81

THE FRONT PORCH was tight. Kay wished for more room.

Her senses were alive. She could feel the air on her skin,

hear the sparrows fluttering in the hedges, smell the sun on the grass. Every nerve quivered, tuned and alert.

Be alive, Amber.

Kay handed off the key ring. A silent nod to Finn. He knew better than to argue with her decision to be first into the house. She brought her nine up and turned the knob.

The door swung freely on its hinges. Slowly. A maw into a stifling blackness.

Hot, stale air poured out around them as Kay's eyes adjusted to the pitch darkness. She led with her gun, hugging the doorframe. Bobby right behind her. Finn and Mo to her left.

One step inside. Two.

Too dark. The only light was the daylight flooding through the open door behind her.

The house smelled rank, of old carpeting and mold. A slight odor of decay. And it felt too still. Too quiet.

They couldn't be too late. Not after everything.

Kay opened her mouth, the girl's name almost on her lips. But it was Finn's voice that shattered the black silence.

"Down!"

Kay's mind had barely grasped the implication of Finn's words, the world moving too slowly for her to react, when the gun blast nearly floored her.

One shot.

Close.

Kay felt something pepper into her shoulder, her neck. Hot and stinging. Like wasp bites, only far worse. She spun, even as her brain struggled to register that she'd been shot.

The whites of Amber Estcott's eyes flashed in the darkness. Wild eyes. And her grip was fierce on the short body of what appeared to be a sawed-off. Finn held the upper stock in one hand, the double barrels raised to the ceiling.

The acrid smell of burned gunsmoke filled Kay's senses even as the first thin stream of blood slid along her skin.

And then the wailing started.

"Oh God! Oh God!" Amber. Her hands trembling. "Oh God!" Her entire body convulsing as she relinquished the shotgun to Finn.

"I'm sorry! I thought you were him. I thought he'd come back. That you were *him*. I didn't—"

"Kay, you're hit." Finn's voice was calm but Kay heard his fear.

"Oh my God. I didn't mean to! I thought you were him!"

Kay was aware of Finn handing the shotgun to Mo. There was panic in his eyes. "Are you all right? Kay?"

She nodded. She felt weak in the knees, but knew it was more her body's physical reaction to being shot than any kind of real damage. She lifted a hand and wiped at the hot blood along her neck and shoulder. It was minimal. Surface. Grazes from the outermost pellets of the cartridge's spread.

"I'm fine," she said, her concern more for the girl.

"I'm sorry. I'm sorry. I didn't know." Amber Estcott was chanting. Hugging herself, standing there in her bare feet and sweats, squinting against the wash of light. And when she took a staggering step forward, Kay caught her.

"I thought you were him. I thought—" She was crying now, her words blubbering out in a flood of tears.

Finn then: "Is there anyone else in the house, Amber?"

She shook her head. "No. No. No one. He left and—" But the tears were coming too fast, her relief too great.

"It's all right." Kay holstered her Glock, arm around the girl's shoulders as she guided her into the light. She smelled of vomit, and her hair hung in heavy, greasy locks around her sallow face. Her lips were cracked and she sported a makeshift bandage on her wrist.

Dried blood had crusted along her temple and Kay took Amber's chin and angled the girl's face to the light. Under the matt of blood and hair, there was no discerning the extent of the injury she'd sustained.

"Are you okay?" Kay asked.

"No! I thought I was going to die here. I—"

"Amber"—Kay lowered her voice—"did he hurt you?"

Amber nodded, the memory clearly washing over her as she realized Kay wasn't referring to the head injury. "He . . . he had me tied up. And he . . ."

But she didn't need to finish. "It's okay, Amber. You're all right now. EMS is here. We'll get you out of here. Get you looked at, okay?"

Her nod was shaky, and as Kay guided her out and down the steps, she was aware of Bobby and Mo and two officers moving past her to secure the rest of the house. Within seconds there was the sound of a door splintering. Then Bobby's voice: "All clear."

Out in the street, EMS's beeper droned as it backed into the drive. A small group of onlookers had already gathered along the dead-end street, craning to see past the hedges and the uniformed officers.

All of it was a blur for Kay. For her there was only Amber, accepting Kay's guidance, trembling as she dried her tears.

When she spoke again, her voice was broken. A whisper. "He raped me," she confided to Kay.

"I'm so sorry, Amber. I'm sorry we didn't find you sooner."

"He was going to kill me. I know it. When he comes back, he . . . You have to be here and get him when he comes back."

"He's not coming back, Amber. Paul Graves, the man who took you . . . he's dead."

The girl stopped, and in her eyes Kay saw relief. "Really?"

Kay nodded. "He killed himself yesterday morning while evading arrest."

Amber appeared to process the information for a moment, then her chin came up as though she found strength in the news. "Good. I'm glad."

Down the walkway, to the back of the EMS van, Amber accepted Kay's support.

Kay wouldn't tell her about Ramirez. Not yet. She didn't have the heart. On top of everything else, Amber didn't need to know that her boyfriend was a serial murderer and was up on three counts of first-degree murder.

"Have 'em look at you too," Finn said, behind Kay now, waving over one of the EMS technicians.

"I'm sorry I shot you," Amber said. "I didn't know it was—"

"It's all right, Amber. Don't worry about it. Just let these guys look you over," Kay said as she felt the sharp bite of alcohol in the graze wound along her neck and shoulder.

". . . should go in to Hopkins and have these looked at," the EMS tech was saying to her. Kay nodded, only partly aware of the gauze and tape being applied to her injuries. Her eyes were on the girl. She thought of Leslie Richter. Of Julia Harris. Nina Gatsby. Lost lives.

But Amber was alive. The residue of terror still lingered behind her blue eyes, and Kay couldn't even begin to imagine the long-term affects the ordeal with Paul Graves would have on the girl.

There was the squeal of tires out in the street, and Kay looked up just as a black Lincoln careened off of Bellevale onto the dead-end street.

Mark Estcott. She recognized him even before he threw open the driver's-side door and sprinted up the short drive.

"Gunderson called," he said. "Where is she?" And the instant he rounded the corner of the ambulance, his eyes went from Kay to his daughter.

Amber was in her father's arms then, and when Kay looked over to Finn, she knew he was thinking of Maeve.

"Kay." Mark extended his hand, took hers, and held it tight. He'd have hugged her too, Kay guessed, if not for his daughter in his arms. "I can never thank you enough."

"You don't have to, Mark. Just let them get her to Hopkins. We'll have some questions for her, but she needs medical attention first." Kay reached for Amber's hand, squeezed it. "We'll see you later."

Kay waited for the girl's nod before turning from the ambulance and starting back up the walkway.

"You should probably go too." Finn was behind her.

Kay shook her head. Closed her eyes. The adrenaline slowed as she exhaled. The sun warmed her face. When she opened her eyes again, she looked to the pigeon on the roof. Its head tilted, round eyes blinking as it surveyed the commotion below before finally taking to wing again. It circled twice, then disappeared behind the house to the empty lofts.

"I want to be here," she told Finn, nodding to the house. "Too many unanswered questions." And given Graves's connection to Ruben Ramirez's victims, Kay hoped they'd finally find the answers they needed to close the case.

82

THE HOUSE WAS HOT.

Even with his jacket off and the front door propped wide, Finn felt the sweat crawl along his skin under his damp shirt.

For two hours now they'd directed the Mobile Crime Lab technicians through Paul Graves's bungalow, indicating what they needed photographed, dusted, and taken as evidence. Still, besides Amber Estcott's abduction, they'd found no other indicators of foul play, and unlike in Ramirez's apartment, there was nothing to indicate that any of the victims had ever been in the house.

Unless, of course, you counted the breasts on the kitchen floor in front of the open fridge.

They had to be Nina Gatsby's. The rate of decay looked to be in keeping with the disposal of her body up by the reservoir, even if Graves had kept them refrigerated.

Finn turned from the kitchen just as a lab technician scraped the breasts off the floor. In the foyer, Finn glanced back to the open doorway of the master bedroom—where Graves had kept Amber.

The halogen work lamp had been switched on so the techs could process the scene. The room had disgusted Finn. The stench of the urine-soaked bed, the hot, musty air, and the blood-soaked bonds. Finn had stood over the big four-poster bed a long time, needing little help to imagine Amber Estcott's terror. Being strapped to the bed for four days, subject to whatever depraved fantasies drove Graves, and finally bleeding herself in order to slip out of the knots. The ordeal was sure to scar the girl, deeply.

When Finn had involuntarily imagined Maeve on that bed, he'd felt sick and finally left the room.

To his right, three officers worked on the living-room window. Someone had brought in a cordless drill, and as the last screw was removed, two uniforms peeled back the heavy plywood. Dust swirled in the sudden flood of light, and Finn wondered how long Graves had had the place boarded up.

Had it all been just for Amber? Or had there been others? *Would* there have been others if they hadn't caught him?

Kay was right. There were still unanswered questions. Why had he kept Amber captive? Why not the others? And besides his obsession with Amber, what was Graves's affiliation to Ruben Ramirez?

Finn turned to the door Bobby had kicked in earlier. Graves's bedroom. The only room in the house with a functioning window.

The bed was unmade; the blue-and-teal, floral-print comforter with matching shams and bed-skirt had been pushed to the foot of the bed. The techs had finished processing the room an hour ago, tackling it first while the windows of the other rooms were being opened.

Unlike the rest of the place, the back bedroom smelled clean, of fresh laundry. Kay had spent most of her time in this room, no doubt keen on understanding Graves's mind, his motivation, and his madness, through his most intimate surroundings. In a shaft of afternoon sun, she sat on the edge of Graves's bed. Finn's eyes went to the blood staining her shirt and the gauze dressing taped to her neck.

Coming through that front door into the dark, the four of them crowding the entranceway, then seeing the glint of light against the black barrel of the shotgun-pistol from behind the door . . . Finn still felt sick when he considered just how close Amber Estcott had come to accidentally taking Kay's life this morning.

Kay didn't seem aware of his presence. She was reading. There were papers in her lap, more in the drawer of the old maple nightstand and spread across the unmade bed around her.

Watching her, the reality hit home for Finn that this was likely the last case they would ever work together. The idea left him with a feeling more profound than sadness. He'd learned so much from Kay, as a cop and as a person. He'd never had a better partner. Truth be told, he'd never had a better lover.

Finn cleared his throat. "What have you got?"

Without looking up, Kay handed him a fistful of computer-generated pages. "Looks like Graves broke the passwords on Ramirez's journal entries. These are printed off the kid's server," she said, indicating the header that appeared at the top of each page.

Finn dropped his gaze to the first page.

Journal Entry #52
I hadn't thought Ellie would get into it too. That girl from the strip club . . . waking up and smashing through the apartment the way she did, then having to whack her just to shut her up. And the blood everywhere. And the screaming. It must have been the screaming that got Ellie worked up, even more than the blood. The way she bit into the girl's leg and started tearing at her, started shaking her when she tried to beat her off.

I think it's cool the way a dog sorta knows what has to be done. It senses an injured animal and just takes care of it. Even cooler, though, was the way Ellie seemed to get off on it. Like me.

Finn didn't have the stomach to read more. Not now.

He set the pages down on the corner of Graves's bed. "Well, let's hope that between these entries and talking to Amber, we can finally get some answers."

He couldn't tell if Kay was listening. The full intensity of her focus was directed at the entry in her lap.

"I hope Amber's well enough to talk to us soon," he added.

But Kay was already shaking her head, and a muscle along her jaw twitched madly. When she spoke at last, her voice sounded thin. "Let's just hope Amber's well enough to arrest."

83

Journal Entry #60
I wonder if Karla Homolka ever got jealous when Paul Bernardo had sex with those unconscious girls, with her little sister especially. Being right there, watching it all. She'd probably say it turned her on, or like she told the cops, that she HAD to do it otherwise Bernardo would beat her. But I bet it was all her behind the killings, and I bet she DID get jealous.

Or Lawrence Bittaker and Ray Norris. Those two guys shared teenagers in the back of their van before taking turns strangling them to death and tossing them over the cliffs of the San Gabriel Mountains. I bet they got jealous of each other.

Not me though.

I WISH you'd had sex with Leslie. That would have been the ultimate insult to that prissy little drama-queen. The ultimate turn-on too. I saw the hard-on you got when I played with her. You should have done her. Then the one from The Crypt. You could barely get it up, never mind finish. Staring at me the whole time you were banging her, telling me you only loved me. Like love has anything to do with this?

At least I know we won't get caught like those idiots Bittaker and Norris. Bragging about what they'd done, like they didn't think someone would go to the cops. And Bernardo and Homolka. Videotaping themselves doing those girls. That's even stupider than Bittaker and Norris's Polaroids and the audiotapes they made of their victims screaming and screaming and screaming.

But we won't get caught.

And so what if we do? We'll be famous. They'll write books about us. Websites. Maybe even make a movie. You and me. And we can write the music. That would be the coolest. A modern-day Bonnie and Clyde.

The first time Kay had read the diary entry back at Paul Graves's house, she'd felt winded, as if she'd taken a blow to the gut.

Now, she felt numb.

As Finn steered the Lumina down the ramp of the parking garage and careened onto Frederick Street, Kay shifted in the passenger seat. The cuffs she'd tucked in her belt as they'd left Headquarters dug into the small of her back. She liked the discomfort of the cuffs and everything they promised: tightening, then locking them around Amber Estcott's privileged wrists.

They'd called Vicki even before they'd left Graves's house in east Baltimore, Kay's cell connection hissing as she broke the news. Vicki had sounded stunned . . . as stunned as Kay had felt when she'd first read the journal entries that made Amber's culpability clear. Going over the probable cause needed for the warrant, Kay knew they had the girl. And by the time they'd gotten downtown, written up the warrant, and raced over to the courthouse, Vicki was already waiting with Judge Niedermeyer in his chambers.

Niedermeyer's signature graced the bottom of the arrest warrant that now sat on the dash of the Lumina as Finn drove east. Kay looked from the warrant to the pages in her lap.

More entries from the electronic journal Amber had kept. Careful documentation of the murders: the fantasizing, the planning, the research, the execution, and, finally, the celebration of her victories. Even Amber's last entry, written the morning of the day Graves abducted her, brimmed with pride as she gloated about putting Richter's earring in Kay's pocket. All of it uploaded to Ramirez's server, then printed out by a jealous Paul Graves.

As Kay read through more, her mind staggered, desperate to grasp the revelations within the chilling content of each entry, trying to find a measure of reason, of explanation.

But there was no reason. Only an obscene contradiction.

What Kay held in her hands was pure, undiluted insanity.

She remembered Amber Estcott in the counselor's office at Langley the first time she'd met the young girl: her bright smile, her pretty blue eyes. To think that *her* twisted brain was the impetus behind the ruthless and calculated murders of Richter, Harris, and Gatsby.

Thrill kills, really. Getting off on the violence. Empowered by the pain and suffering she could cause.

And the more Kay read, the sicker she felt. She wanted to throw the pages away, to rid herself of the depraved documentation of such a twisted and heinous mind.

Still, Kay welcomed the calm that arrived with the clarity of answers. At last the puzzle was complete.

Paul Graves's obsession with Amber had likely started a long time ago, maybe even before she'd ever met Ruben Ramirez. Graves had stalked her, his obsession coming to a head when he'd discovered her romance with the college kid.

Graves had, no doubt, been the first to know of the connection of violence that bound the two together. *Bonnie and Clyde.*

He had watched them. Kay imagined Graves sitting in his van, observing Amber and Ramirez as they disposed of Leslie Richter's body, then—after they'd driven off—going to see the remains for himself.

The bludgeoning of Richter's body had been Graves's handiwork; the handprint on her throat was the proof. Kay suspected it was Graves's anger and rage at Amber's relationship with Ramirez that had fueled the postmortem violence.

Kay could see it all now.

Graves would probably have done the same to Julia Harris if he hadn't discovered her low vital signs as she lay in the drainage ditch off the I-95. Kay imagined him scrabbling back up the slope and driving off in his van to make the 911 call.

After all, Harris was a victim. And Graves wasn't a murderer.

And Nina Gatsby. It was Graves who'd cut out the

dancer's heart, taken her breasts. That's why he'd covered her face with dead leaves. Because he wasn't the merciless killer who'd taken her life and therefore couldn't stand seeing her face while he cut into her.

No wonder Ramirez had known nothing of the post-mortem savagery on Gatsby.

Graves had taken the heart for Amber, to win her, to prove to her he was worthy. That *he* could be everything Ramirez was to her. And more.

"We should have seen this," Kay said to Finn.

His expression was severe as he steered the car east toward Johns Hopkins. Kay knew that he too struggled to grasp the reality of Amber Estcott.

"Ramirez's love for her," Kay went on, "his covering for her. He took the fall because he knew that if we found out Amber's involvement, we might not have tried so hard to find her. And all along, *she's* the one behind the murders. How could we not have seen this?"

"Look at the girl, Kay. How *would* we have?"

Kay shook her head. "It's the number one rule of investigating, Finn. Above all you have to keep your mind open to any possibility, to *any* suspect. And there we were, all along, stuck on these murders being the worked of a man, not some seventeen-year-old girl. Blinded by our assumptions. Face it, Finn, we failed."

"Don't beat yourself up, Kay. It was a solid investigation. But that girl was good. Right down to the detail about her neighbor Eddie Bahn in his black Mustang. Giving us his description as the guy who'd picked up Leslie at the school, sending us out on a wild-goose chase. She was playing us from the start. Playing Ramirez. Playing everyone."

Kay looked to the excerpts in her lap again and felt the numbness slip away now. In its place: a raw anger. Anger at the idea that they'd spent so many days, so many resources, not to mention their own invested emotions, to save a cold-blooded killer.

Three girls had lost their lives. And—ironically—if not for Paul Graves, there might have been more.

"You want to know the truth?" she asked Finn then.

"What?"

"I almost wish Graves *had* killed her."

When he looked across the interior of the car, she saw his surprise.

"You don't feel that way?" she asked.

"No."

"How can you not? After what she did to those girls? Julia Harris, Finn . . . that could have been Maeve they picked up at the club for Christ's sake. You can't forget that."

"You're just pissed off, Kay."

"Damn right I am."

"You got taken. Scammed. Face it, we all did. Conned by a teenage girl."

In the silence Kay tried to make sense of it, tried to understand how a young girl like Amber Estcott—with all the privilege in the world—became what she had. And then there was her polar opposite, Antwon Washington—brought up on the streets, witnessing death firsthand. Even *then,* Antwon didn't possess half the arrogance Amber Estcott obviously did in order to plan and execute her murders.

And then another thought galvanized Kay suddenly. For Amber to believe she'd get away with it, for her to possess such absolute assuredness . . .

Leslie Richter could *not* have been Amber's first.

The absence of remorse wasn't something that emerged overnight. It was far more likely that Amber Estcott never *had* a conscience.

What indicators had her parents missed? Teachers?
And when had the killing truly started?

Kay thought of Amber's bedroom back in Guilford. The framed photograph next to the girl's computer. The infant boy in his sister's arm. Nathaniel Estcott.

A crib death? Or, could six-year-old Amber have been responsible? Could she have proven her abilities to herself even back then, with that first act of infanticide? Would Kay find reference to it in the girl's journals?

"You should probably call the hospital," Finn said, slowing for construction on Broadway. "Make sure she's still there. Ask them to hold her."

"They wouldn't have released her already, do you think?" But Kay reached for her cell phone.

The switchboard put her through to the nurses' station by the time one of the construction crew waved them through the mess of Jersey walls and traffic cones.

"Yes, Detective," Kay was told, "Miss Estcott was here."

"Was?"

"She was discharged just a few minutes ago. Her father didn't want her staying the night. And who could blame him after what that poor girl's been through—"

Kay snapped her cell phone shut. "They let her go," she said, and Finn's foot came down harder on the accelerator.

"We can still catch them," she added.

The Lumina flew through the yellow light at Fayette, speeding north toward Johns Hopkins.

"I'll call Mark," Kay started to say, but Finn reached over and closed his hand over her cell.

"And what, Kay? What are you going to tell him? That his daughter's a serial killer and could he please pull over so we can arrest her?"

There was a gravity in the look he gave her. "I'm not about to give him any warning. I want this girl."

"What are you suggesting, Finn? That Mark Estcott's going to whisk his daughter away? Take her out of the country? You think he even *knows?*"

"Anything's a possibility at this point."

"Mark would never let her run. Even if he *does* somehow know about her involvement. Flight is the strongest indicator of guilt."

But as the Lumina surged through another yellow light, Finn's hands were tight around the wheel.

"One thing you should never underestimate," he said then, "is what a father will do to save his only remaining child."

84

THE FREAK WAS DEAD. Killed himself.

Amber wondered how he'd done it. She hated him even more for not giving *her* the pleasure of ending his miserable life for him. When the cops had come through the door of the freak's house, she'd *so* badly wanted it to be him, wanted to blow a hole right through him with the shotgun, watch him fall to the ground and bleed. The whole time she'd waited for him, she imagined standing over him as he writhed on the floor at her feet, watching his life drain out of him.

And she would have smiled. No, she would have laughed.

Maybe it was better this way though. A dead freak couldn't talk. The cops would pin the murders on him, especially with the two gray lumps of decomposing flesh sitting in the middle of the freak's kitchen floor.

Amber had recognized the breasts the instant they'd slid from the baggie, the nipple ring gleaming in the overhead light. She'd known it belonged to the dancer Ruben had picked up from The Condor Club, who'd come into the back lot, hanging off his arm, giggling as if she were already high on something.

Ruben did have a way with the girls.

He said he'd chosen the dancer because she looked like Amber. Amber hadn't thought they looked *anything* alike, but she knew Ruben had fantasized he was making love to *her* when he had his dick inside the unconscious stripper.

Still, he hadn't been able to finish, and Amber had gotten out a fresh condom and begged him to come inside her instead. He'd made love to her then, while the girl lay on the living-room floor, and Amber had watched her supine body as Ruben finally came. And again later . . . the next night, after the dancer was already dead, Amber had demanded sex from Ruben while she stared at the bag over the girl's head.

The thrill had been indescribable. She'd tried to write about it the day after, but words hadn't been able to capture the high she'd been on after that one. The best so far.

They'd come a long way since Leslie.

Leslie had been easy, convincing her to come to Ruben's apartment under the guise of using his equipment to record their music assignment. Even Ruben hadn't known of the plan until it unfolded before him. Amber thought she'd lost him that night when she'd finally turned on Leslie. But when Ruben had seen how much the killing turned her on, Amber had been able to ease his horror with their love-making.

"I can be your Clyde," he'd told her the morning after. And she'd known then just how true his love was. More important, she'd learned how powerful *she* was.

She'd felt immortal.

And she was. Walking out of that house, right under the

cops' noses. They didn't know a thing. Probably figured they had their case wrapped up with the freak dead now.

The freak . . . the Bahns' pool guy.

It was all clear to her now . . . how he figured into everything, how he'd gotten the dancer's breasts, how he knew where she'd be the day he took her. She'd sometimes suspected she'd been followed. But she'd always written it off to paranoia, especially during that long drive up to the reservoir with the body in the backseat of Ruben's mother's shitbox car.

But now Amber knew. The sick son of a bitch had been following her and Ruben all along. He'd gone into the woods after they'd left the dancer's body and hacked her up.

Amber hadn't believed him when he'd told her he had cut the heart out. But the breasts were proof. Had he counted on her finding them? Or had he hoped to show them off to her?

It didn't matter.

The freak was dead. And she wasn't.

Immortal, she thought as she stared out the passenger-side window of the Lincoln, watching the city slip past them.

Nothing could touch her. It was a reality she'd come to embrace from the time she was six years old, standing over her brother's crib. The crying finally over.

She was untouchable then.

Untouchable now.

And everything else Daddy would take care of.

WITH THE CHERRY on the dash, Finn floored the accelerator and the Lumina surged through the intersection at Orleans.

". . . *discharged a few minutes ago,*" the nurse at Johns Hopkins had said.

Kay prayed that in those few minutes Mark Estcott had had to wait for elevators, retrieve the car from the Broadway garage, and that he was still in the vicinity of the hospital with Amber.

Finn seemed to be counting on that too. He slowed at the entrance of the parking garage, then shot up to Jefferson and cut across the hospital grounds before heading back down to Orleans.

Traffic was already congesting along Route 40, one of the main arteries east out of the city, and Kay felt Finn's tension.

"Where is the son of a bitch?" he mumbled, overtaking several vehicles that gave way to the strobing cherry.

And before Kay could voice her skepticism in Finn's choice of direction, suggesting that Mark could have headed to the JFX and home to Guilford, Finn pointed out the windshield.

"There he is. Black Lincoln," he said, and Kay spotted the vanity plate in the right-hand lane: INTRIAL.

Through the rear window of the big car Kay's eyes locked onto the back of Amber's head where she sat in the passenger seat. Kay knew, even if she served another seven years in Homicide, she would never fully comprehend the evil that boiled beneath the girl's skull and in her heart.

It was only once Finn brought the Lumina up alongside the Estcott car that Amber turned. And in that moment— the girl's eyes meeting hers—Kay imagined Amber knew.

Then there was Mark. Kay looked across to him behind the wheel. Less than three feet separating them. Confusion bloomed across Mark's face. Kay hoped it was genuine.

She waved him over.

The Lincoln's brake lights flared as Finn steered in behind it, and when Mark took the next right, Finn pulled to the curb ahead of him. Kay was aware of Finn radioing for district units.

"What's going on, Kay?" Mark was out of the car, circling to meet her as she got out. "What is this about?"

Kay held up one hand. "This isn't about you, Mark. Just stay back. Please."

"Not until you tell me what—"

But Kay ignored him. She moved to the passenger side of the Lincoln, her eyes on Amber unmoving in the passenger seat. Even as Kay stood next to her, only the closed car window separating them, the girl stared blankly out the windshield.

She knows.

There was no surprise in Amber's face when Kay swung open the door.

"Get out," Kay told her, one hand going for the cuffs in her belt.

The girl hesitated, but only briefly, perhaps sensing the edge Kay was riding now.

"Out," Kay said again, no longer fooled by the wide-eyed gaze.

She waited for the girl to pull herself from the car, her hair still greasy, her face gaunt, and a bandage covering her temple. But what Kay saw before her was not Amber Estcott's suffering, nor her youth. Kay no longer cared what the girl had endured at the hands of Paul Graves. All Kay saw were the lost faces and extinguished lives of three young women.

Snatching Amber's thin wrist, she spun her. Perhaps too severely; the girl had to catch herself on the car's roof. "Amber Estcott, you're under arrest for—"

"Kay! What the *hell* is going on?" Mark was at her side.

"Mark, stay back. Please. Amber Estcott, you're under

arrest for the murders of Leslie Richter, Julia Harris, and Nina Gatsby."

Kay had thought she'd feel more when she snapped the cuffs around Amber's wrists. Victory. Satisfaction. Something.

But she felt nothing.

"You have the right to remain silent. Do you understand?"

"Kay, listen to me." Mark shrugged off Finn's hand when he tried to pull the attorney back from Kay. "You've got it wrong. You can't—"

Kay felt the girl flinch only slightly as she snugged the cuffs tight.

"Anything you say can and will be used against you in a court of law. Do you understand?" Kay heard dispassion in her own voice.

Still, Amber said nothing.

Kay yanked her away from the car. "Amber, do you understand?" She gave the cuffs a sharp jerk to emphasize her question this time.

"Fuck! Yes, okay? Yes."

"Good. You have the right to an attorney," Kay went on, unable to meet Mark's eyes. "If you cannot afford an attorney one will be appointed for you. Do you understand?"

"Whatever."

"Don't do this, Kay." Mark tried to block her path as one radio car pulled to the curb. Then a second. "I'll bring her in, Kay. We'll talk. You'll see you've got this all wrong."

"Do you understand?" Kay asked Amber again, pushing her past her father.

"Yes," she said at last.

Then Finn was there, one hand on Kay's shoulder, the other grasping Amber's cuffs. "I'll take her," he said softly.

And Kay was only too glad to hand her over.

Standing on the sidewalk as afternoon traffic flowed past them, cars slowing, drivers rubbernecking, Kay felt hollow. There was none of the satisfaction she'd hoped for. No real sense of retribution for Julia Harris, Leslie Richter, Gatsby. All she felt now was disgust, as if she couldn't be far enough away from Amber Estcott at that moment.

She watched Finn guide the girl to the nearest district unit.

"Kay, listen to me, you——"

When Kay looked at Mark at last, she could see the fear in his eyes. "I'm sorry, Mark. I truly am."

"You don't know what you're doing."

"You can ride downtown with one of the district cars, if you like. Talk to Amber there."

"Kay, you've got——"

"She's going to need counsel, Mark. And I don't think it should be you."

"Kay."

"I'm not saying any more. I'm very sorry." And she was.

With a shake of his head, Mark left her and followed Finn and his daughter. But after a few words, even Finn turned the defense attorney away. At the rear of the second radio car Mark snapped open his cell phone. Used the speed dial. No doubt a colleague.

Kay could only imagine the high-powered lawyer Mark Estcott would hire, and no doubt he would sit second chair himself throughout his daughter's trial.

It wasn't going to be clean.

It wasn't going to be simple.

And Kay wondered what kind of deal Mark would try to negotiate with Vicki for Amber's testimony against Ramirez, because Kay knew the boy would never turn on his "Bonnie" and Finn was right: Mark Estcott *would* do anything to save his daughter. His actions proved that.

He'd been driving east, away from the Estcott home. Route 40 became Pulaski, which led to the Harbor Tunnel Thruway, and then it was a quick jaunt south to the airport. Kay didn't want to look, but she had to. Stepping toward the rear of Mark's Lincoln, she looked through the back window.

Suitcases. Two of them on the rear seats. And a couple overnight bags stuffed in the footwells. All for Amber? Or had Mark intended to go with her?

Kay had hoped, had *prayed,* that Finn had been wrong. The idea that Mark Estcott—a man whom Kay respected as an honored mainstay in the city's judicial system—could have been cognizant of his daughter's brutal crimes was almost more than Kay could take in.

And how long had he known? If Amber had just told him, how would he have had their bags packed so quickly?

When Kay glanced up this time, Mark Estcott's gaze met hers. She saw a dark comprehension in his look. Awareness. He knew she knew.

"Don't underestimate what a father will do to save his only remaining child." Finn had said.

Kay wasn't a parent, couldn't understand the way Finn did, but in a small way, she did. She had Antwon. Last night she'd done what Mark had tried to do for his daughter today. For Antwon, Kay had crossed that blue line in a way she'd never thought herself capable . . . to save the life of a child.

And as Mark looked away from her now, Kay guessed he knew there would likely be an arrest warrant issued for him as well.

At the district unit Finn finished patting down Amber and checked the handcuffs again before easing the girl into the patrol car. He was gentle in his handling of the girl, and even though Kay couldn't make out the words, she knew his voice was calm.

She admired him for that and guessed that—in the end—for Finn, Amber Estcott was still a child, like his own daughter.

It was a somber realization, in that moment, that this was, in all likelihood, the last arrest she'd ever make with Finn. Their partnership was over.

You don't realize what you've got until it's gone, her father had once told her, after her mother's death. She'd been thirteen the only time she'd ever seen her father cry.

But Kay *did* realize what she'd lost. Far more than just a partner.

When Finn's eyes met hers, Kay thought of the plastic stick back in her apartment. The positive pregnancy test. Kay wondered how she was going to tell him. What it would end up meaning. How it would change things.

And past Finn, in the backseat of the patrol car, Amber Estcott . . . sullen and defiant.

After everything Kay had seen today, the idea of bringing a child into a world that was so appallingly unpredictable, so violent and unjust, seemed so wrong.

Still, a life was growing inside her. Another life. It was little more than an undefined presence right now, but certainly not one she'd ever expected to face in her life. And that presence that gave Kay a new and strange kind of determination, a sense of preservation that didn't quite fit yet. It represented a future, a path with new challenges.

Challenges that Kay couldn't even begin to predict.

Not sure what to read next?

Visit Pocket Books online at
www.simonsays.com

Reading suggestions for
you and your reading group
New release news
Author appearances
Online chats with your favorite writers
Special offers
Order books online
And much, much more!